The O'Connor Family Series

KATIE REUS

Cover Art by Sweet 'N Spicy Designs
Editors: JRT Editing & Julia Ganis, JuliaEdits.com
Digital Formatting by Author E.M.S.

The O'Connor Family Series/Katie Reus. — 1st ed.

ISBN-10: 1635560454
ISBN-13: 978-1635560459

For my wonderful, wonderful readers.

Praise for the novels of Katie Reus

"Sexy military romantic suspense!" —USA Today

"...a wild hot ride for readers. The story grabs you and doesn't let go." —*New York Times* bestselling author, Cynthia Eden

"Has all the right ingredients: a hot couple, evil villains, and a killer action-filled plot. . . . [The] Moon Shifter series is what I call Grade-A entertainment!" —Joyfully Reviewed

"I could not put this book down. . . . Let me be clear that I am not saying that this was a good book *for* a paranormal genre; it was an excellent romance read, *period.*" —All About Romance

"Reus strikes just the right balance of steamy sexual tension and nail-biting action....This romantic thriller reliably hits every note that fans of the genre will expect." —*Publishers Weekly*

"Prepare yourself for the start of a great new series! . . . I'm excited about reading more about this great group of characters."
—Fresh Fiction

"Wow! This powerful, passionate hero sizzles with sheer deliciousness. I loved every sexy twist of this fun & exhilarating tale. Katie Reus delivers!" —Carolyn Crane, RITA award winning author

"You'll fall in love with Katie's heroes."
—*New York Times* bestselling author, Kaylea Cross

CONTENTS

Merry Christmas, Baby

CHAPTER ONE

The bell above the front door to Nora's Books and Brew jingled, but Nora didn't bother to glance away from the customer she was helping. Since renovating this place seven months ago it was no longer just a bookstore, but a combination bookstore and coffee shop and they sold more coffee than books.

Which wasn't exactly surprising since Holly, North Carolina saw a lot of tourists, especially during December. Located in the Blue Ridge Mountains, it was a popular tourist getaway that boasted cobblestone streets, Victorian gingerbread architecture and an old-world feel that made her never want to leave. And it was Christmas twenty-four-seven, year round. Nora's friend Ella, the town scrooge, hated it, but after growing up with a mom who got depressed every damn holiday and refused to do anything special for either of her daughters, Nora loved everything about Holly.

"Trust me, your daughter, no matter what age, will love the elf, even if she doesn't read the book. My sister's seventeen and goes crazy with this thing. Every morning I find him in a different place around the house."

The woman with pale blonde hair and a bright smile nodded. "I'll take two sets and a pound of the White Christmas coffee. Whole beans."

"I'll meet you at the cash register." Even though the town was Christmas-themed year round, the month of December was still always their busiest. In addition to her regular employees, she'd hired three seasonal ones, all high-school students, to help out in the afternoons. They were all busy so she headed to the back to grab the Elf on the Shelf book sets and the coffee.

As she passed Macy and Eleanor Baker, sisters in their sixties barely a year apart, sitting at one of the high-top tables in the café, she paused at the odd way they were watching her. "What? Do I have something on my face?" She'd been working since eight o'clock this morning and had barely taken a bathroom break.

Macy, the brunette, gave her a Cheshire cat smile. "Nope. Though it wouldn't hurt you to put some lipstick on."

Nora blinked in surprise.

Eleanor nudged her sister. "Don't be rude. She looks fine. He won't care about lipstick anyway."

He? Since she had no idea what they were talking about, Nora gave them a polite smile, murmured something about grabbing stock from the back, and kept going. She adored the sisters, but they could be eccentric on their best days. And today, she didn't have time for their dose of crazy. She slipped behind the counter, the rich aroma of coffee, coconut, vanilla, caramel and nuts all filling the air. The scents were soothing and familiar, as were the little beeps from the cash register as Kelsey rang up another customer. Music to Nora's ears.

"I'll grab what you need. I overheard you and the snow bunny. Two elf sets and coffee, right?" Marjorie, one of her full-time employees asked as she pushed open the swinging door to the back.

"Yeah, but you don't have to—"

"Go see your man. I got this." Marjorie tilted her chin in the direction of the café before disappearing through the door.

What the heck? Nora turned around and froze for just a second. Jackson O'Connor, Mr. Too-sexy-for-his-own-good stood at the high-top table talking to the Baker sisters. He held a bouquet of white snapdragons, her favorite. Her immediate instinct was to duck in the back and just avoid seeing him, but screw him. He was in her territory and she certainly didn't want his flowers. So she pasted on her "shopkeeper smile" and skirted around the counter.

As she rounded it, he looked over, those striking blue eyes landing on her. And damn it, she felt the effect of that stare all the way to her toes. She tried to pretend she didn't, but her body didn't lie. Everything around her funneled out, the rich scents and chattering customers all seemed to fade away as she maneuvered her way through the tables. She wished she was in something sexier than jeans, a red and green striped top and her apron, but there was nothing she could do about it. Now she understood the lipstick comment, but not the 'your man' one. Jackson certainly wasn't hers.

He'd made that perfectly clear with his radio silence over the last three weeks. One date and he'd completely ghosted on her; no calls, nothing. Considering they'd been friends before their date, it cut deep that he'd simply decided to ignore her for no reason she could decipher.

"O'Connor," she said politely as she reached the table. Oh yeah, it was back to O'Connor, what pretty much everyone in town called him. Calling him Jackson was way too intimate and she wanted to set up clear boundaries between them.

She saw the slight way his eyes narrowed when she did. "You have a few seconds, Nora?" His voice was deep and delicious, the baritone making all her nerve endings flare to life.

"Ah…" She glanced behind her. The line at the register wasn't too bad, but the truth was, she didn't want to talk to him, much less see him. "I'm pretty busy."

"Oh go on, honey." Macy winked at her. "No one will blame you for taking a few minutes to yourself."

"And if she's not interested, we are," Eleanor continued.

To Nora's surprise, Jackson's cheeks flushed red. Clearing his throat, he motioned toward the front door. "I shouldn't have come at such a busy time."

Though she wanted to tell him that he was right—and give him a piece of her mind—she simply smiled and headed for the front door with him. "Don't worry about it." She had to keep her "shopkeeper smile" in place until they were alone. Otherwise everyone in town would gossip and though she might hate it, she had to uphold a certain appearance. When she was Nora Cassidy, business owner, she had to keep a smile on her face and be professional at all times.

Which normally wasn't hard at all. She loved her job and she loved the people of Holly.

"That's the fakest smile I've ever seen," Jackson murmured as he held the door open for her.

The bell jingled overhead as a blast of wintry air rolled over her. She shivered, wrapped her arms around herself as her boots crunched over the icy sidewalk. And she kept the smile in place even as she gritted out, "No joke. What are you doing here?"

"I..." He practically shoved the flowers at her, the awkward move out of character for the former SEAL. "These are for you."

"They're lovely." Her voice was wry as she reluctantly took them. They really were pretty, but she didn't care. Flowers didn't make up for anything.

"You look a little like you want to throw them in my face." He rubbed a hand over his inky black buzz cut.

She lifted a shoulder. "That would imply I care enough. Look, I've got work to do. We went out and you've made it clear it was a one-time thing. I'm okay with that." Which was a big fat lie. They'd been friends for months, dancing around their attraction until he'd finally asked her out. It wasn't as if they'd been strangers going on a date. No, they'd been way more and he'd just pulled the rug out from under her as if she didn't matter.

"I want to take you out again."

Unable to stop herself, she snorted. "Not interested."

"Nora—"

"No. You can't show up in the middle of one of my busiest days and expect to talk to me about this."

"You're right. I'm sorry. The timing is crappy, I just...I needed to see you. I've missed you."

She blinked, surprised by the sincerity in his voice. But she refused to be swayed by it, not when she was still so hurt.

"Can I call you later?" he continued.

"You can call," she murmured. Didn't mean she'd actually answer. And yeah, she knew she sounded like a complete bitch but she was beyond caring. After one of the hottest nights of her life she'd thought...hell, she hadn't known what she'd thought. That there was a connection between them past just friendship. Something real.

She'd barely dated in the last four years, hadn't been able to. But she'd let Jackson past her defenses, opened up to him, and had almost slept with him. He'd promised to call and for three weeks afterward, *nothing*. She was just glad they hadn't had sex. Well, not technically, because they'd certainly gotten intimate. Holding on to the flowers only because she didn't want any prying eyes to see her give them back to him, she headed back into her shop.

Time to put her game face on and pretend everything was okay, even when it wasn't. A healthy dose of embarrassment and hurt skittered through her and it was all because of him. She was being stupid anyway. It wasn't as if they'd made any commitments to each other or anything.

Still, when she'd heard that he'd taken Angelia out days after Nora, it had hit her hard. Not only had Nora and Jackson been friends for months, he'd turned things in another direction and pursued her for weeks as if she was the only thing that mattered to him. Even though she'd been hesitant to cross from friends to more, she'd said yes.

Well she wasn't going to get charmed by him again. No way in hell.

Jackson scrubbed a hand over his face as he strode down Main Street. He'd screwed up good this time.

Sweet and adorable Nora had barely been able to look at him, much less talk to him. She'd put on a smile, but he knew it hadn't been for him. She just didn't want the locals gossiping. And he couldn't blame her. After their date he'd said things, made promises he meant to keep. Hell, he still planned to keep them. They'd been friends for months and then he'd finally worked up the courage to ask her out. Something he'd never had a problem with before.

Nora was different though; she'd been skittish and he'd wanted everything to go right with her. After their date though, he'd realized that she was it for him—and it had freaked him out. So he'd done the complete cowardly thing and just not called her. Which was, yeah, beyond messed up.

Now that he knew what she looked like when she orgasmed, it was all he'd been able to think about when he'd been talking to her. Or *trying* to talk to her. Around her he got tongue-tied like some teenager. Except he'd never been shy as a teenager. But everything about Nora got him all sorts of twisted up.

Her long, dark wavy hair had been pulled up into a ponytail, but he'd run his fingers through the thick tresses as he claimed her mouth, had sucked on her perfect pink nipples as he stroked her to orgasm with his fingers.

Nope, not continuing that line of thought right now.

Rolling his shoulders once to ease the tension there, he continued down the street, needing to burn off energy before he headed back to his truck a few blocks away.

Garlands and pine wreaths were wrapped around the cast iron street lamps lining Main Street, the scent and sight of Christmas permeated everything in Holly. He'd grown up here, had been dying to move away as soon as he was old enough. Now he couldn't imagine living anywhere else. Especially not since Nora Cassidy had moved to town nine months ago.

She always had a smile on her face for everyone. Until today. She'd covered it up with coldness, but he'd seen the hurt in her gaze and it clawed at him. He would make it up to her, prove that he was sorry. He *had* to.

Flowers had been a lame attempt, but he hadn't been sure how else to break the ice. And what had he been thinking, going to see her when she was busy? He hadn't been thinking, that was the problem. For three weeks he'd managed to avoid her, but today he'd just snapped.

The need to see her, to hear her voice, had been overwhelming. As he passed Silver Bells, the combination salon/flower shop—where he'd gotten the snapdragons for Nora, he saw her younger sister Sasha heading his way.

When the seventeen year old spotted him, she immediately broke eye contact and stared straight ahead. Guilt suffused him. He'd gotten to know Sasha over the last few months too. She was Nora's sister and always around. He'd known they were a package deal, especially since Nora had been Sasha's guardian the last four years and he genuinely liked her.

"Sasha," he said quietly, sidestepping a mother pushing a double stroller down the sidewalk.

She gave him the same cold look Nora had, but with the disinterest only a teenager could pull off. "Hey."

"How are you?"

She hiked her backpack against her shoulders, still avoiding his gaze. "Good."

"I fucked up."

Her eyes widened as she met his gaze full-on now. "Dude, you can't say that."

Wincing, he rubbed a hand over his buzz cut. "Sorry, you're right." He was all sorts of twisted up today. What was the matter with him? He'd been a SEAL for a decade and had grown up with two brothers and a sister—who was more a tomboy than anything—so his language was usually rough but she was right. "Maybe don't tell Nora?"

"Whatever. But for the record, you're right. You did screw up. You and her flirted for like, freaking *months*, you pursued her like crazy, then after one date you just fall off the face of the earth. And you've been hooking up with someone else since then? Don't worry, I won't be mentioning your name to my sister. You're not worth her time." She gave a snort of derision before stalking off.

Jackson frowned. He hadn't hooked up with anyone else. Hell, he couldn't think about anyone other than Nora. Hadn't since the day he'd met her. But that wasn't the conversation to have with a seventeen year old kid. Shit, if Sasha thought he was with someone else, then Nora must too.

He had to apologize to her, needed her to listen to him. And he knew if he called her she'd just ignore him. He needed to play this right. He'd already screwed up, maybe too much for her to forgive him.

No, he refused to believe that. He'd been a SEAL. He'd never failed a mission yet and he wasn't going to start now.

CHAPTER TWO

Nora inhaled the fresh scent of hazelnut coffee as she started the economy size coffeemaker. This was her favorite part of the morning; before everyone else showed up it was just her and her shop. The fact that she owned something like this was still hard to wrap her head around.

As she pulled her 'World's Best Sister' mug out of one of the lower cabinets, she realized there were two dirty mugs in one of the industrial sinks. She was the one who'd locked up last night and everything had been clean. A low grade tingling started at the base of her skull. It was probably nothing, but...no, this couldn't be nothing. She was a complete neat freak; she hadn't left this.

Frowning, she did a walk through the coffee shop then moved onto the other half of her place. The bookshelves were divided into genre with romance dominating the majority of her books. It would be impossible to tell if a couple books had been taken on sight, but after she did a walk through all her stock looked fine as did the books. There was a little nook with big throw pillows that looked as if it had been disturbed. She usually tucked the pillows up against the corner wall when she was straightening things at the end of the evening but they'd been pulled out and left on the floor.

Had someone been in here? Only Sasha and a few other employees had keys. She couldn't imagine any of them coming in here without asking. Before she could ponder it a knock at the front door made her nearly jump out of her skin.

When she looked up she saw Jackson standing at the entrance to the bookshop door. Just like that her heart rate kicked up about a thousand notches. She should not be happy to see him, but yeah, her body didn't listen to reason. It was screaming that he must be sincere if he was here again, that she should give him another chance.

Stupid hormones.

A skull cap covered his dark buzz cut. The sharp lines of his face seemed more prominent this morning. He gave her a half-smile that melted her insides as he lifted a small tin of something in one hand. Well, she certainly couldn't leave him standing out in the cold. It had snowed earlier this morning so there was a light dusting over everything.

Hurrying to the door, she opened it and was nearly knocked over by a harsh gust of wind. Her little bell jingled wildly as Jackson stepped inside. "Thanks for letting me in."

"Is everything okay?" she asked, shutting the door behind him. She hated how much his nearness affected her. All her senses just seemed to go into overdrive. She wanted to reach out and cup his cheek, to stroke his soft skin, and feel the way his jaw clenched when she did. But they weren't together, they weren't anything.

"Yeah, I, uh, have a peace offering. And I was hoping you'd have a few minutes to talk before your rush." He held up a small tin with snowmen decorating it.

Her eyes narrowed ever so slightly. "Is that snickerdoodles?"

"Maybe."

Despite her simmering anger at him, she felt herself softening. It was those clear blue eyes that weakened her resolve. The same intense gaze that had sucked her in to begin with. Who was she kidding? It was everything about him. He had a deadly edge to him that made him ridiculously sexy, but he was so sweet. Or he had been the last six months. He'd been coming into her shop pretty much every day until their date. At least the days she'd been working. And he'd made a few custom pieces of furniture for her shop, something that had deeply touched her. She'd paid him, but she knew enough that he'd given her a hefty discount.

Jackson had made her feel special, different. So his total silence after she'd gotten mostly naked with him had yanked that proverbial rug out from under her and she hadn't found her balance since.

"You fight dirty," she murmured, taking the tin from him.

"I play to win." There was something in his tone that made heat flood between her thighs.

She ignored the reaction. "Did Fallon make these?"

"Yep. She said to say hey too."

Nora adored his sister Fallon but for the last few weeks she'd been avoiding Fallon. Which was a totally crappy thing to do but Nora had felt too weird and hadn't wanted to talk about Jackson. And she'd known the subject would come up. "Come on. I've got coffee brewing next door. Let's grab some and you can tell me why you're here." Because no matter what, she wasn't going to bullshit with him like nothing had happened between them. She simply wasn't wired that way. Yesterday she'd probably been too bitchy but he'd taken her off guard and they'd had somewhat of an audience. Today they were alone so she could be civil and grownup, but she still wanted answers from him.

He tugged his cap off as he fell in step with her. She was average in height but being next to him she always felt smaller. It was his shoulders more than anything. They were broad and muscular and she'd clutched onto them as he'd kissed a path down her jaw, neck and...nope. No, no, no. Not going there this morning. Too bad her nipples didn't get the memo. They tightened into hard buds as she remembered how he'd sucked and teased them while he brought her to climax with his very talented fingers.

"I screwed up," he blurted as they reached the front counter.

Not caring at all about the coffee, she stopped and turned to him. "Yes, you did." She crossed her arms over her chest, knowing it was a defensive gesture but unable to stop herself. The man put her on edge in more ways than one. Since moving to Holly she hadn't thought about dating or the opposite sex. Or for the last four years really. At least not in more than an abstract way. She could appreciate a sexy guy as much as the next woman but when she'd taken guardianship of her sister she'd been twenty-one. Dating or men hadn't even been on her radar—until Jackson.

He looked her right in the eye as he spoke. "I should have called and I'm sorry I didn't."

Jaw tight, she nodded. "Okay." As apologies went it was pretty lame, but she would accept it. And move on from him.

"I got...okay, this will sound like bullshit, but I got scared."

She dropped her arms, snorting in disbelief. "That does sound like garbage. You got *scared*?"

He scrubbed a hand over his head in a gesture she'd come to learn meant he was nervous. The action was rare from him. "Yeah."

Bullshit. "So you got scared...but still managed to take Angelia out a couple days after me." After he'd told her that he didn't want to be with anyone else. It wasn't as if they'd made promises to each other, not exactly. But she deserved more than a man who'd pursued her hard, hooked up with her, then just stopped calling. Damn it, she hadn't wanted to bring up Angelia, hadn't wanted him to know it had hurt her so badly.

Which just made the confusion on his face piss her off even more. "I didn't take her out."

Nora's lips pulled into a thin line. "Gossip in Holly spreads fast, Jackson. You know that more than most." He'd grown up here, unlike her, so he should definitely be aware.

"I don't care what you heard, I didn't take Angelia out." His expression darkened for a moment before understanding seemed to dawn in his gaze. "I took her home a few weeks ago when she got a flat and didn't have a spare, but that's it. Nothing's ever happened between us and never will."

She bit her bottom lip. He sounded as if he was telling the truth. He might have hurt her, but Nora had never taken him for a liar. "Okay, I believe you. It still doesn't explain what happened. Damn it, Jackson, we were friends."

"Were?"

She shrugged, the action jerky. "You know what I mean." When they'd become intimate they'd taken a step from friends to lovers. Or so she'd thought. Which was why it had cut so deep. They'd talked and texted every day for months. Then nothing. Like she didn't matter.

"I'm sorry, Nora. When we crossed that line it was, I don't know. I could see more happening with you."

"More?"

"More than just…" He cursed again. "I saw a future with you and it scared me."

She wasn't sure how to take that at all, but she knew she didn't like the knot in the pit of her stomach. "Why?"

"I've been single a long time. You knocked me on my ass when we met. Then when we got together, it was intense. I pussied out. There's no other excuse for it. But I want another chance, to start over with you."

"No." She held up a hand when he started to protest. "I like you Jackson, but no. We can be friends." She wasn't going to give him more than that. Because what happened when she let him back in and he got 'scared' again? No way. Her last real boyfriend had bailed when she'd gotten guardianship of Sasha.

His jaw tightened, the gleam in his eyes something she couldn't quite define. "Friends?"

She nodded. "We were friends before. We'll just pretend that little…date never happened." Even as she said it, her cheeks warmed up. Pretending she'd never felt his hands and mouth on her body was going to be very hard. She'd missed him so much; more than she would admit to anyone. She'd missed the way he made her feel just by being in the same room, the way he always made her smile, the way—

He took a small step forward, slightly crowding her against the glass counter. He didn't touch her, but placed his hands on either side of her, caging her in. A subtle, spicy masculine scent teased her nose, wrapping around her and making it difficult to think straight. That and the way he was looking down at her with unrestrained lust in his gaze. "You want me to pretend I've never kissed you, never seen those pretty pink nipples shiny from my kisses?"

His words sent a rush of heat through her, flooding between her legs with no warning. Her nipples tightened as well as she remembered him doing exactly that. She resisted the urge to squirm. "Yes." The word came out as a scratchy whisper.

He leaned a fraction closer. "Pretend I've never felt your slickness on my fingers and watched you come apart in my arms?"

Oh, God. His words set her on fire. She ached for him everywhere, the pulse between her legs wild and out of control. It was almost too much. Somehow she managed to nod, which was good, because she couldn't find her voice.

He watched her for a long moment, those intense eyes searching hers. For a second she thought he might kiss her. The weakest part of her considered letting him, but he just nodded and stepped back a few inches.

She immediately missed the warmth of him—and cursed herself for it. But at least she could breathe now that he'd given her space. It was as if all her surroundings came back in a rush; Jackson O'Connor was no longer her sole focus. It was like she'd completely forgotten where she was. This man was dangerous in so many ways. Even being friends with him was going to wreak havoc on her senses.

"Are you free tonight? To get together—as friends." The last word held a note of distaste.

A small part of her was disappointed that he was accepting just friendship so easily, but she knew it was for the best. "I can't. Sasha and I are going Christmas tree shopping."

He blinked, all lust fading to be replaced by shock. "You don't have a tree yet? Christmas is in—"

"Four days, I know." She threw up her hands in mock self-defense. "Sasha was crazy with school and I've been the same with work since she got out for winter break. It just got away from us. And in my defense, it's Christmas here year round. It's easy to lose track of time."

"I can meet you guys here, help you lug it home." The offer sounded innocent enough, but there as a glint of well, hunger, in his gaze as he said it.

"Look, Jackson—"

"As friends. Seriously. You're never going to be able to get a proper sized tree tied down on your car roof."

She hated that he was right. She'd been dreading trying to figure out how they'd even get a tree home. Since she lived downtown she'd thought about just dragging it. "If Sasha's fine with it, then okay."

"I, uh, saw her yesterday."

"She told me."

"She also tell you I dropped an F bomb?"

Nora's lips twitched. "Yeah but I wouldn't worry about it. I'm sure she's heard worse at school." The fact that he looked guilty about it, however, just served to melt her heart even more. Which only annoyed her. There would be no melting for Jackson O'Connor.

"Want me to meet you here after work?"

She nodded. "Yeah, I'm going to let one of the girls close up so five is good if it works for you." And if Sasha was fine with him coming.

"I'll be here at five unless you tell me otherwise."

"Okay."

When he left she ordered herself not to stare at him as he walked away but it was hard not to drink in the sight of him. Thick, muscular legs, a tight...gah. They were just going to be friends from now on.

Unfortunately she figured that was something she'd have to remind herself of more than once. And that pretty much sucked. She'd allowed herself to see a future with him, especially after he'd opened up to her, had told her that he wanted to be with her and no one else. Now...she shook her head. She wouldn't allow herself to go there. Not again.

CHAPTER THREE

Jackson cursed under his breath when he saw his mom stepping out of Silver Bells. Her auburn hair fell right below her shoulders and had clearly just been styled. He loved his mother, but she was going to ask what he was doing and if he told her the truth she'd offer advice about courting Nora, as she put it.

Her blue eyes lit up when she saw him. "My favorite son." Smiling, she pulled him into a tight hug.

"You say that to all of us," he murmured, laughing against the top of her head. For such a petite woman she had a firm grip. "Hair looks good."

Stepping back, she patted it lightly. "It does, doesn't it? I heard you were in here yesterday buying flowers."

His lips quirked up. "Is there a question in there?"

"Don't be smart with me. And no, because I also heard from Macy Baker that you gave them to Nora. Why haven't you invited that girl to our Christmas Eve dinner?"

"We're just friends." Unfortunately. His fault. "Besides I think she's going to the Winter Wonderland Festival."

"So? Invite her as your friend. She can come after the festival. Half the town's going to be there. Oh, invite Sasha too. I just love those girls. Best thing that ever happened to that shop was Nora taking over." She snorted and flicked a glance down the semi-crowded sidewalk. "Doesn't even look like the same place anymore."

He nodded in agreement. An aunt, some distant relative of Nora's on her father's side, had left the place to her because she was the only family left. Before Nora had whipped it into shape the place had been a used bookstore in serious need of help. It had been the only eyesore on Main Street. "It's not."

"Oh, I heard through the grapevine that there are a few young men interested in Nora. Some have asked her out—and she's said yes. Thought you might want to know." Her tone was so mild she might as well have been talking about the weather. Before he could respond she'd turned on her heel, her long green coat billowing at the ends as she swiveled.

Jackson frowned as he continued down the sidewalk. Since his mom was just coming from the beauty shop there was no doubt she'd heard all the latest gossip of the week. And *young men* to his mom were guys his age. He couldn't blame anyone for being interested in Nora. She was beautiful, smart and sweet. Didn't mean he had to like it. He wanted to know who had asked her out, but knew that would be a bad idea to actually ask Nora. He had to play things right with her. He wouldn't win her affection by grilling her about potential dates.

"Jackson."

Blinking, he realized he'd reached Nora's shop and she was standing outside, bundled up in a thick black pea coat, crimson scarf and a red and white, knitted cap with candy canes on it. She half-smiled. "You okay?"

"Yeah." He'd just been lost in his thoughts—something that *never* happened to him. He had situational awareness at all times. It had been drilled into him in the Navy, specifically when he was with the SEALs. He could traverse any terrain on the planet, kill someone countless ways with his bare hands and can and had survived behind enemy lines with his team on more than one occasion. But the thought of Nora going out with someone else twisted him up. He could try to chalk it up to simple jealousy but it was more than that. "I like your cap."

"Sasha told me it was geeky."

He lifted his shoulders. "I like geeky." Or her brand of it. God, he adored everything about her. He'd never had a problem with women. Not talking to them and certainly not bedding them. With

Nora, he seemed to lose most of his charm because it was too damn hard to think and breathe around her. Mainly because he knew that she was *it* for him. He'd known on one level that once they crossed the line from friends to lovers things would change, but after their date he'd realized that it was more than a simple change. He'd seen his bachelorhood completely wiped out. He was fine with that, wanted a future with Nora, but it had knocked his legs out from under him. Which was a lame excuse for why he'd stopped calling her, but there it was.

Her cheeks flushed pink; a delicious shade he'd seen her turn when he'd made her come. Something he shouldn't be thinking about right now. Too late to forget about it though. "Where's Sasha?"

"I was just about to call you. She cancelled because she wanted to hang out with friends instead." Nora smiled but it didn't reach her eyes.

Though she'd never say it, he knew that it likely hurt her. "She's seventeen."

"I know. God, am I that transparent? I'm glad she's made so many friends since we moved here. I was just looking forward to getting a tree today."

"I'm still game." Anything to hang out with Nora. He just loved being with her, and being alone with her was even better because it allowed him more time to show her that he was still the same guy he'd always been — and to win her over for good.

"You sure? Don't feel obligated — "

"I'll pretend you didn't say that. Come on." He slung an arm around her shoulders in a completely friendly manner. At least that was what he told himself. He just wanted to touch her, to hold her close — to claim her mouth so intently she never wanted to walk away from him. When she was pressed up against him, he always felt content in a way he'd never imagined. She simply fit with him; this was where she was supposed to be.

Thankfully she leaned into him. "You smell good."

"Yeah?" He'd just come from his woodworking shop.

"Like pine and some kind of oils."

"I finished up on my dad's new rocking chair." He'd been working on it for weeks.

"Is it a Christmas present?" she asked as they maneuvered around a woman walking three poodles — all of them wearing little Santa hats. Poor pooches.

"Yeah, been working on it the past few weeks." The instant the words were out of his mouth he felt her stiffen just the slightest fraction. If they'd been talking the last three weeks it was something he would have shared with her. God, he was such a freaking idiot. "I'm right here," he tacked on as they reached his truck. He'd managed to snag a spot right on Main Street.

She stepped out of his embrace and he felt the loss immediately. "This will be so much easier to get the tree back to my place. Thanks again."

He didn't audibly respond, just opened the passenger door for her. He didn't want her thanks, he just wanted her — in his bed and in his life with a ring on her finger. Yeah, it was too soon for the ring, but he knew himself well enough that she was it for him and the ring would come soon enough. When he made a decision, he rarely changed his mind. Nora was his. Now he just needed to convince her.

"Jackson O'Connor. You're not paying for that." Nora went to snatch the cash out of his hand but he did some sort of smooth sidestep thing — unapologetically blocking her — as he passed the cash over to Mr. Collins, the man who ran the local Christmas tree lot.

"You want me to help you load it up on the truck?" Mr. Collins asked, both the men completely ignoring her.

"Yeah, thanks," Jackson said.

She followed after them, not holding onto her steam very well. She couldn't exactly get mad that he'd paid for her tree, but it felt like too much for just a friend to do. Who was she kidding? She wanted more than friendship and knew he did too. And she only got whiplash thinking about that. She wanted to give him another chance, but...the hurt of the past few weeks was too fresh. She'd forgiven him, but she still felt raw.

Refusing to think about that right now, she watched his graceful movements as he hoisted up one end of the tree as if it weighed absolutely nothing. He was wearing his favorite beat-up leather jacket that looked as if it had been custom made for him. A bomber jacket, dark jeans and work boots apparently equaled the sexiest thing she'd ever seen on a man. Or at least on Jackson. She loved the way it smelled too. Like leather, wood, oils and something masculine that was all him.

Part of her hated that she'd felt his hands on her bare skin, stroking across her breasts, down her stomach and... Yeah, they were just friends all right. She nearly snorted at the thought. She missed his touch way too much for that to be true. And there had been nothing friendly about his teasing and kisses.

Once the men had tied the tree down to the bed of the truck she slid into the passenger seat. "Jackson, you didn't—"

"I wanted to," he said as he started the engine.

"Okay, then thank you. And I'll make you hot chocolate when we get back to my place. If you can stay?" She chose her words carefully because he'd just offered to help with the tree, nothing more.

"Yeah, I'd love to."

That shouldn't make her so happy, but knowing they'd get to spend more time together turned her inside out. She'd missed him so much these past few weeks. Settling into Holly had changed something inside her for the better. The people here were real and she finally felt like she'd come home. "I think Sasha is interested in a boy," she said as he turned down a side street. Her townhome was only about five blocks away.

He shot her a quick glance. "Who?"

"I don't know, that's the problem. She's been a little secretive lately and she's always been nuts about texting but in the past few weeks it's been out of control. And, it's a girl thing, but I can tell from her expressions when she's texting that it's someone she's into."

"She hasn't said anything?"

"No. And we've always shared everything with each other." Nora had had to tow the mother-sister line pretty carefully since becoming Sasha's official guardian. Though the truth was, she'd always been more of a mother than their own had been so slipping into the role hadn't been much of a stretch.

"You think that's who she's with today?"

"Maybe. I mean, I don't think she'd lie to me though." Nora hoped not. They'd always been honest with each other and she'd made it clear that her sister could come to her about anything.

"Fallon never said anything when she was interested in someone. It's probably just a teenage girl thing."

Nora snorted. "Fallon probably didn't say anything because of her three older brothers."

Jackson's lips pulled up in a smile that melted Nora from the inside out. "Yeah, there's that too." He cleared his throat. "By the way, my mom wanted to know if you and Sasha were available on Christmas Eve. My parents do this big dinner party thing. No pressure though." The words came out in a rush, which was unlike him.

"Ah, I'll let you know." Christmas Eve dinner seemed like a big deal. She didn't know from personal experience considering her own mother had rarely done anything special for the holidays, but she'd always tried to do something fun for Sasha the last few years. Even if it was just the two of them. A big thing with Jackson's family sounded fun, if a little intimidating. Though she didn't know his brothers well, she adored his sister and mother. She'd planned on going to the local festival but she could do that first.

"I'd like you to come as well. In case that wasn't clear." The deep tone of his voice wrapped around her, making her lightheaded as it often did.

She simply nodded, unable to find her voice. What was she doing, thinking they could just be friends? The longer she was around him, the clearer it was that was pretty much an impossible feat. Thankfully they'd reached her place and apparently it was a

Christmas miracle because there was parking in front of the townhome next to hers.

"If you get the door I'll get the tree."

"You're sure?" It was over six feet and pretty thick.

Jackson just gave her a look that said he couldn't believe she'd asked that question. And yeah, okay, it was clear he could get it by himself. That didn't mean she wanted him to have to. Anticipation hummed inside her as she headed for the door. She might have said they were just going to be friends, but soon they'd be hanging out alone. She wasn't sure she had the willpower to resist him, even to protect her heart.

Jackson lugged the tree into Nora's place, ready to move 'Operation Win Nora Over' into full effect. If Sasha was out with friends, now was the perfect opportunity. "It smells like Christmas in here already," he said, moving past the entryway into the foyer.

She let out a light laugh and motioned to a glass bowl on the small table by the front door. "I sprayed the decorative pinecones with cinnamon oil."

"Where to?"

"Living room. I've already got a place ready." She held out a hand, motioning to the room right off the foyer.

Careful with the blue spruce tree, he maneuvered it inside. Two gold and red throws were draped over her couches, stockings were up on the faux fireplace mantel and a stack of shiny presents were next to the window nook. She already had a gold tree skirt and stand laid out.

"I'll take this end while you maneuver the bottom in," she said, moving up beside him. Her sweet vanilla scent teased him. Even with the Christmas scents permeating the air, he could pick out her scent anywhere. It was subtle and all Nora—and made him crazy.

"Sounds good." It only took a few minutes until they had the tree in place and screwed in tight. He'd sensed her softening at the tree lot and on the way back to her place. He wasn't sure how much yet, but the attraction between them was still there full force. It was one hurdle he didn't have to worry about.

When he pushed up from his crouching position Nora was tugging her scarf and cap off. Her dark hair was slightly mussed and her cheeks were a perfect shade of pink to give him wicked, wicked thoughts about taking her mouth in a demanding, hungry kiss. At that thought his jeans started to get too tight so he cleared his throat. "I think I remember something about hot chocolate."

Laughing, she tilted her head toward the kitchen. Yeah, this was the Nora he'd fallen for. "Come on."

"How is it you never visited Holly before taking over your aunt's shop?" She'd been evasive when he'd asked her that months ago but he was still curious. Hell, he wanted to know everything about Nora.

She shrugged slightly, the action jerky as she pulled down a couple mugs from one of the cabinets. He sat at the center island, watching her movements, drinking in every line and curve of her tight body. She'd taken her coat off too and her dark jeans were snug and showed off her perfect ass. Yeah, staring at her like that wasn't helping the fit of his jeans either.

"She was my father's aunt and after he split, my mom didn't want anything to do with his side of the family. I didn't find out until after she died, but I guess Aunt Tammy had reached out to her multiple times over the years, but my mom..." She let out a sigh, shook her head. "She was an unhappy woman."

It was hard to picture that when Nora was the opposite. "Because your dad left?"

"I honestly don't know. He left right after Sasha was born and I remember them fighting a lot before then but I don't...I was eight, I just don't know. I only ever remember my mom being sad." There was a touch of the same emotion in her voice as she spoke. "She was never officially diagnosed but I think she was depressed most of her life."

"I'm sorry," he murmured.

"Thanks. The cancer was hard to deal with." She pulled a bar of chocolate from another cabinet. "And I've never said this out loud to anyone…" She glanced over her shoulder, gave him an assessing look.

"What?"

"I feel bad saying this, but…when she died, it was like a huge weight had been lifted. I'm still sad she's gone, but the emotional burden of taking care of her and Sasha had been draining. And she wasn't the best mother." The words came out in a rush, as if she didn't want to say them at all.

Jackson was glad she was opening up. They'd been flirty and friendly over the last six months but this was more real and what he wanted from her. If she was telling him this, she at least trusted him. "I can imagine."

"God, I hope not. Your mom is like Mary Poppins, I swear. I…" Trailing off, she cleared her throat and set a pot on the stove. "So tell me about this big Christmas shindig."

He wanted to dig more into her past, but didn't want to push too hard, too fast. "My mom's obsessed with Christmas—like most of the town. So she invites half the town."

Nora adjusted the pot on the stove and turned to face him. "Really?"

"Nah, it just feels like it. That first Christmas back was hard." The words were out of his mouth before he could think about censoring himself. But if she was going to open up to him, he wanted to be more honest with her.

"You mean after you got out of the Navy?"

He nodded, glad she understood him. "Yeah. I didn't think I'd have trouble adjusting to civilian life, but…" He shrugged. It had been a hell of a lot more difficult than he'd imagined. Adjusting to the crowds and more than that, dealing with civilians. It had been hard to care about seemingly trivial things when Americans were losing their lives overseas. That battle had been the hardest to get over and some days he still struggled with it. Not as much anymore since the whole reason he'd volunteered was to protect his country.

In a move that was completely Nora's style, she crossed the small kitchen and laid her hand over his. "I'm sorry. I can't even imagine how hard it would be to come back from…all that. And then settle in with any sense of normalcy."

Somehow he thought Nora could imagine it just fine. She was a fighter in her own right. It sounded as if she'd been raising her sister since she was eight years old. He slid his other hand over hers, the need to touch her overwhelming. Even before they'd kissed, before that first date, he'd made excuses to touch her all the damn time. Over the summer it had been even worse because she loved flirty summer dresses. And she wore the type reminiscent of the fifties; retro, she'd told him they were called. Whatever they were, they showed off sleek toned legs he'd fantasized about for far too long.

When his hand settled in place, he saw her eyes dilate. The pulse point in her neck beat wild and out of control and her breathing increased just a fraction. He wanted to lean in, to capture her mouth with his. She'd let him too, he could see it in her eyes. But he wasn't sure if she was just having a weak moment and he didn't want to take advantage—and give her a reason to regret kissing him later.

Being just friends was never going to work for them. Not since they'd gotten a taste of each other. That first taste wasn't nearly enough though. Something told him it would never be enough. That was fine though, he was going to take things slowly, do things right with her.

A soft buzzing sound filled the air and it took a second for it to register it was her phone vibrating across the counter. She blinked and withdrew her hand from his, breaking the spell. Immediately he missed the warmth, her softness.

When she looked at the screen her expression paled. "It's my security company for the store. The alarm must have gone off."

Which meant someone had likely broken into her store.

CHAPTER FOUR

"Jackson, you don't need to go with me." Nora looped her scarf around her neck and tucked her gloves into her jacket pocket. She wasn't exactly scared, but she wasn't looking forward to dealing with the aftermath of a break-in—if there even was one.

He snorted, as if she'd lost her mind. "Your car's still down by your shop."

"Yeah, and I can walk." She lived downtown so it wasn't too far. Plus the cops would be there.

"It's after dark."

"Holly is one of the safest towns in probably the world."

"And your shop was just broken into."

"We don't know that." She'd just gotten a call from her security company that the alarm had been triggered, but didn't know anything beyond that. "And the sheriff's department has already been alerted so I'll be fine."

"The longer you argue with me, the longer you waste time. We could be there by now." When she started to respond, he cut her off. "And if you try to walk on your own, I'll just follow in my truck."

Nora saw the determined set to his jaw and the tight line of his shoulders. "I never knew you were this stubborn." It shouldn't be so sexy. But apparently everything about him was, at least to her—and any woman with a pulse.

He nodded once. "I am when it comes to someone I care about."

Okay then. She cared about him too, but...she wasn't going there right now. She was still rattled from their almost-kiss in the kitchen. Maybe he hadn't intended to kiss her, but the sparks had been there, at least for her. And she'd felt herself falling, falling, falling. She'd been ready to lean into that kiss, into him, and lose control in a way she'd sworn to herself she wouldn't again. "Well I can't exactly argue with that," she murmured, grabbing her keys from the hook by the door.

He gave her a look of pure satisfaction that reminded her a lot of the way he'd looked after he'd made her climax. Nope, not going there either.

As she slid into the front seat of his truck she pulled her cell out. "I'm going to call Sasha just to check on her." The call from the alarm company probably shouldn't rattle her so much, but it was instinct to check on her sister. Didn't matter that they lived in a safe town, bad things happened every day, everywhere. And okay, she was being totally paranoid. But she wouldn't apologize for it.

Jackson turned down the radio as she called, the thoughtful action not lost on her.

"Hey," Sasha answered after the third right, slightly out of breath.

"Hey yourself. You doing okay?"

"Uh, yeah." She let out a short laugh. "Why, what's up?"

"Nothing, just checking on you. Got the tree set up."

"We can decorate in the morning if you want," Sasha said, excitement in her voice.

The excitement meant way too much to Nora. She wanted her sister to have the best Christmas this year. Things felt somehow different since settling in Holly. More permanent. Now that she'd heard Sasha's voice most of her worry dissipated. If her store had been broken into, yes, it would be a pain in the butt to deal with, but her sister was okay. That was what really mattered. Nora had just needed to hear her voice.

"Sounds good to me. I want to grab a few things from Carol's place tomorrow." Her friend Carol ran Christmas Carol's Shop & Crafts and had wreath making kits. Nora was going to try her hand at making one. The good thing about living in Holly was, she could use the wreath year round.

"Okay. Listen…I wanted to stay over at Liz's house tonight if that's okay?"

She was out for winter break and Liz was a good kid. "Okay, put her mom on the phone, I want to talk to her first."

"Ah, hold on..." There was a slight rustling in the background, then Sasha came over the line. "She's at a Christmas thing with Liz's dad."

"Unless I talk to her mom, you're not staying over there."

"They won't be back 'til after midnight." Sasha's voice bordered on whiny, which was unlike her.

"Then you should have thought about it sooner. Listen, I'm pulling up to the shop so unless I hear from her mom directly I expect to see you home by your curfew."

"Why are you at the shop?"

"Ah, it's no big deal, but I just got a call from the security company." She decided to downplay it until she knew more. No need to make her sister worry. "I see the sheriff. I've gotta go but I'll see you later tonight." The flashing blue lights of his car reflected off the big glass windows of her shop and the neighboring ones. The sight of a police car against the backdrop of Main Street with its vintage light poles and pretty sparkling twinkle lights lining the street seemed out of place.

"The sheriff?" There was a note of panic in Sasha's voice.

"Oh, it's nothing to worry about. Just a glitch." She hoped — and she certainly wasn't going to worry her sister. This wasn't something Sasha needed to think about. "I'll call you later."

"That was some nice parenting," Jackson murmured as she ended the call.

She laughed. "I try. There's Brad." Nora was glad it was the sheriff and not one of his officers. Not that she had anything against them, but she was comfortable with him. He came into her coffee shop at least twice a week.

"Brad?" There was a strange note to Jackson's voice as he parked his truck along the curb behind a four-door sedan.

"Yeah, Sheriff Fulton. He grew up here, I thought you'd know him." Jackson couldn't be more than a year or two older than him.

"I do." Everything about Jackson's posture was stiff.

She wanted to ask him about it, but couldn't dwell on it. Not when she had to deal with whatever had happened at her shop. An icy blast of air rolled over her as she stepped out onto the curb. She'd barely taken a step before Jackson was at her side, his arm around her shoulders. She leaned into his warmth as they headed for the sheriff's car. Even though she'd protested his coming with her, she was grateful he'd pushed. It was nice to have someone to depend on.

Brad nodded at both of them, his expression polite and professional as usual. Broad and muscular, he was probably about six feet even if she had to guess. She'd heard that he had a bunch of medals from his time in the Marine Corps and had literally saved a drowning puppy once. He was an All-American hero and he certainly looked the part in his pressed uniform.

"The alarm's gone off and two of my guys are inside already."

Worry punched through her as she glanced at the front doors. She'd been trying to keep it at bay but couldn't now that she was here. Neither the entrance to the coffee shop nor the bookstore should have been open. And she didn't see any broken glass from the doors or windows. "How did they get in?"

"Back door was unlocked."

"Unlocked or open?" Jackson asked before she could speak.

"Just unlocked." He turned his focus back to her. "We're going to need you to do an inventory, see if anything was taken or broken before you make a report."

She nodded, fighting the tension racing up her spine. "I can make some coffee for you and your guys before I start."

"I'll do it," Jackson murmured, kissing the top of her head in a way she could only define as completely, and utterly possessive. Especially considering the pointed look he shot Brad after he did it.

It was so blatantly, well, possessive was pretty much the only way to describe it. And she liked it a little bit too much.

"So far nothing seems to be missing," Brad said as Jackson slid him a mug of coffee across the counter.

Nora had already gone through the coffee shop and was now in the bookstore, meticulously going through everything. Jackson wanted to be with her, but knew she needed to focus and he'd just be a distraction. "Yeah. It's a little weird." He didn't like it. "Have there been any break-ins around here lately?"

The sheriff shook his head. "No. Few residential things but we know who did it."

"Teenagers?"

"Yep." He shot Jackson an assessing look. "When are you going to man up and make things official with Nora?"

Jackson's fingers froze around his own mug. "What the hell are you talking about?"

Lips twitching, Brad just lifted a shoulder. "There's a bet going at Silver Bells. Just curious is all, especially considering the 'stay away from my woman or die' look you gave me outside."

"What the fu—"

"Hey, your mom started the bet." He gave another shrug.

"My mother started a bet on *what* exactly?"

"Not sure what the actual term that she used was, but as soon as Nora's officially your girlfriend, the winner gets a pretty big pot."

His gaze narrowed. "How big?"

"I think it's up to six hundred bucks. Plus they win a gift certificate to the spa and a free salon day at Silver Bells. The works."

"My mother's insane."

"I think that's up for debate."

"You're just saying that because she brings you cookies all the time." His mom was absolutely shameless.

"There might be some truth in that." His lips quirked again before he took a sip of the coffee. "Man, Nora's got the best brew in town, I swear."

Something about the way Brad said Nora's name rankled Jackson. It was too familiar. He hadn't even realized they were friends. "You ever ask her out?"

Now the sheriff full-on smiled. "God, you are so done. And no, not that I didn't think about it." When Jackson just scowled Brad's smile grew even wider. "But she never gave me the vibe and you put a claim on her pretty early on. Not that you've ever done anything about it." He cleared his throat. "Never thought SEALs were cowards."

"Shut it, jarhead." Fulton had been a year behind Jackson in school, had gone on to join the Marine Corps and after doing four years — almost the entire time overseas — got out and earned a degree in criminal justice before settling back in Holly. And Jackson knew the guy had some notable medals that he never talked about.

Shaking his head slightly, he slid his mug back to Jackson. "Top it off?"

Nodding, he did. As he grabbed the pot, Fulton continued. "You know of any issues Nora's had lately? Any enemies, anything like that?"

"No and she would have told me." Or he assumed she would have. He couldn't imagine anyone having anything against Nora anyway. There'd been no destruction of property either. So far it looked as if her back door had been opened after the alarm had been set, which set it off.

"I figured as much. Gonna head down to talk to the employee who closed up after this, but this doesn't feel like a break-in."

It didn't, but Jackson still didn't like it. When another thought occurred, he frowned. "What date did my mom pick?"

"Christmas Eve."

He sighed. Yeah, that sounded about right.

"I'm glad that's over." Nora wrapped her arms around herself, fighting off a shiver as they watched Brad and his officers drive off. They'd gotten a few curious onlookers headed to Yuletide Spirits earlier, but luckily not too many people had stopped to talk.

Wouldn't really matter though. By tomorrow it would be all over town that she'd had the cops at her store tonight. Which was actually a good thing. She'd get even more foot traffic during the day from curious people and she'd do even more business. A win-win as far as she was concerned.

"Me too." Jackson's deep voice rolled over her.

It was like her body was attuned to him. Whenever he spoke in that dark, delicious way, everything inside her seemed to wake up and take notice without fail. Well that and being around him in general. After the way he'd helped with her tree, then stayed at the shop while she dealt with the tedious job of checking out everything, she couldn't help but question the decision she'd made to keep things platonic between them. The fact was, they had chemistry and he was such a sweet man. There was no getting around it. But...gah, she was such a coward. She'd had enough loss in her life, she didn't want to lose Jackson too.

"You feel like heading home or you want to grab a drink? I'm not sure if there's a live band at Yuletide's tonight, but they'll have good music regardless."

She started to glance at her phone but then nodded. Screw it. Sasha was on holiday break and Nora didn't need to be home for a while yet. And she really wanted to spend time with Jackson, even if she was unsure if she wanted to give things a shot with him. She hooked her arm through his. "Yuletide's."

Right off Main Street and Mistletoe Avenue, it was the perfect place to relax.

"What's your curfew tonight?" Jackson murmured as they reached the main door. The glint in his eyes was pure wicked hunger.

Somehow she found her voice. "I don't have one." She trusted her sister to get home in time so if she was a little late, well, she was freaking twenty-five years old. She'd just be late.

"Good."

When he opened the door, an energetic song filtered out. No live band tonight but the place was packed with customers three-deep at the long, mahogany bar. Bottles upon bottles were stacked behind it.

"I don't know if we'll even be able to find—" She stopped when she saw Carol Cardini waving at them from a high-top table. And there were two empty chairs there. Even if she was waiting for someone, Nora and Jackson could join her for a few minutes. At least long enough to grab a drink. When Carol pointed to the empty seats, Nora smiled and nodded.

"That woman is always happy, I swear," Jackson said, barely loud enough for her to hear.

He wasn't wrong. Tall, blonde and on a scale of one to ten, she was fifteen on the gorgeous meter. No surprise she had on a red, formfitting dress—her favorite color. With killer curves, it would be easy to dislike the bombshell on principle, especially since she would have given Marilyn Monroe a run for her money, but Carol was so damn sweet. And she always had a bright smile on her face. Lately though, Nora thought she looked a little sad and distracted, no matter the put-together picture she portrayed. She knew Carol's mom had been mayor, but then had gotten sick. That was before Nora had moved to town though so she didn't know all the details.

"Jackson!" A familiar and slightly annoying female voice drew both their attention as they made their way through the throng of high-top tables.

Nora turned to find Angelia sliding up to him in a skintight, shimmery silver dress, even though he had his arm around Nora.

Completely ignoring Nora, the pretty blonde gave him a hug and kissed him on the cheek noisily. If he hadn't turned his head at the last minute she'd have gotten his mouth.

The thought of another woman's lips on Jackson's made imaginary claws flare up inside Nora. She hadn't realized she could actually feel that jealous of another person, but damn.

"I've gotta run, but thanks for the ride home the other night." The way she said 'ride', there was no mistaking the innuendo of what she really meant.

The words were a slam to Nora's senses. She'd believed Jackson when he told her that nothing had happened between him and Angelia. Still, there was a tiny, lingering doubt in the back of her mind. She'd never taken Jackson for a liar, but she'd been fooled before. Her last serious boyfriend had dumped her when she got guardianship of her sister. He hadn't wanted a readymade family. Given how young they'd been she hadn't exactly blamed him. It had cut deeply though since she'd never pegged him for being so cold and callous. Then he'd pulled the rug out from under her.

It was hard not to wonder if she was wrong about Jackson too.

CHAPTER FIVE

"Are you freaking kidding me?" Nora muttered to herself as she glanced around the bookstore. After closing up and heading out with Jackson and the police last night she'd been extra conscious of where everything was. She'd even snapped some pictures with her phone. After she double checked the photos on her phone with the actual window nook in her shop, sure enough the pillows had been moved around.

Nora had taken the pictures once everyone was out of the shop, so there was no chance one of the officers had moved the pillows by accident. She didn't like knowing someone had been in here, someone who must have the security code. Well, they would have to because she'd reset it after she'd left. At least it narrowed down her suspect pool to three people. Frowning, she bent to adjust the pillows when a bright red scrap of material caught her eye. Tugging it out from under one of the pillows, her eyes widened when she saw it was a bra.

Oh, Lord. Was one of her employees in here doing…whatever with someone? She rubbed the bridge of her nose. At least someone was getting some action. Tucking the bra under her arm, she headed back to the coffee shop side and pulled out her phone to text Jackson. They hadn't stayed at Yuletide's long last night and she was still feeling weird about that run-in with Angelia. Jackson had assured her that nothing had ever happened between them, but doubt edged its way in.

Think I solved the break-in mystery. Found a bra tucked in the pillows at work. Someone was in here after we left. They must have the code. Gonna talk to everyone after Christmas, figure out what's going on. She could call an employee meeting today with the ones who had the code but tomorrow was Christmas Eve and she closed up early. And they weren't open at all on Christmas so, yeah, calling a meeting like this could wait.

You need better security.

My security's fine.

There was a pause and she could practically hear his snort of derision. *What time do you close today?*

Six. She was closing a little early today too.

I'll be there at six sharp. We're going to set up a sting operation.

She laughed out loud as she turned her **open** sign over and unlocked the door. *I can't tell if you're kidding.*

Not joking. We'll set up a camera and can watch the feed on your laptop. You owe me hot chocolate anyway. We can do it tonight if you're free.

She wanted to say no, but Sasha had already begged her to stay over at Liz's house tonight since she hadn't been able to last night. Nora thought they'd get to decorate the tree tonight at least—since Sasha had slept in this morning they hadn't gotten to yet. But Sasha was such a good kid and if she wanted to hang out with her friend, Nora wasn't going to stop her. Her sister had lost a good portion of her childhood because of their mother.

Her fingers flew across the screen's keyboard. *This feels over the top but I'm curious so okay. You want to help me decorate my tree?*

Yes. I have an extra present for your tree too. See you at six.

He'd gotten her a present? Her heart started doing that crazy pitter patter again, kicking up a billion notches. She'd actually gotten him something too, weeks ago before their first and last date. She wasn't sure how to respond and was luckily saved by the little jingle of her front door.

Or so she thought until she looked up to see petite, pretty Angelia striding into her shop. She wore dark pants, boots and a thick jacket and scarf. What was up with this woman? And why did she have to show up before anyone else? Nora didn't know much about her other than she worked for one of the local real estate companies, and that she apparently had a thing for Jackson.

"Hey, Nora." She slid her sunglasses back on her head. "You're here bright and early. Smells good."

"Thanks. Do you know what you want or do you need a few minutes?"

"Yeah. Latte with non-fat milk, sugar free syrup and no whip. Sixteen ounce."

"One skinny latte coming up." Thankful to be busy with her hands, she turned back to her work station.

"So, you and Jackson huh?"

As she readied the espresso machine, Nora just smiled over her shoulder and made a noncommittal sound.

"Look, the reason I stopped by is because I feel bad. I didn't know you guys were together. If I had I never would have hooked up with him a couple weeks ago."

At the woman's words, everything inside Nora went still. She knew Jackson, not this woman. And deep down, it was too hard to believe he'd flat-out lied to her. But she suspected Angelia was. She gave a casual shrug as she turned back with the drink. "Okay. I put this in a to-go cup but I should have asked. Did you want to sit?"

"Uh, to-go is fine. Do you want to talk?" The words came out stilted, the previously confident woman looking completely unsure.

Not even a little bit. "We're good, no worries." She gave her best "shopkeeper smile" and rattled off the amount. She wanted the woman out of her shop.

Angelia blinked in surprise but pulled out a bill from her purse.

After making change she slid it across the counter. "Hope you have a great Christmas." Nora couldn't hide the fakeness from her voice no matter how hard she tried. Which wasn't very much.

Once the woman was gone, she let out a sigh of relief. She knew herself well enough that she'd ask Jackson about this, but she wasn't going to let jealousy eat her up inside. Heck, they weren't even together. They were just friends.

Keep telling yourself that, maybe you'll start to believe it, she thought.

"You don't think four cameras are overkill?" Hands on her hips, Nora looked up at Jackson who was on a ladder, hiding the last camera on the top of one of her bookshelves. They all had a wireless connection and some other specs he'd outlined—and sounded impressed with.

"Nope." He'd been completely focused since he arrived. They'd had to wait an extra fifteen minutes for some straggler customers, but as soon as they'd been alone he'd gone into what she considered his work mode.

It was a little intense. She'd shown up at his workshop early months ago and had seen him show the same sort of intensity when working on a project. He'd acknowledged her, but hadn't done much other than that. It was the same now. She wasn't sure why, but that sort of intensity on him was sexy, especially since she kept imagining him showing it in a very different setting.

"I can see why you were a good SEAL," she murmured.

That caught his attention. He looked down at her, gave her that trademark wicked grin. "I've never left a mission unfinished."

"This is a mission?"

"Yep." He was back to ignoring her as he finished situating the camera into place. When he was clearly satisfied his 'mission' was complete, he let out a grunt that could have meant anything before descending the steps.

"Oh, my God, you look like a kid on Christmas morning. You're seriously excited about this?"

"Hell yeah. We're going to bust whoever this is."

"This is an interesting side to you." She didn't bother fighting her grin. It had to be one of her employees with the code but she still wanted to know who it was. Right now she just couldn't imagine any of them coming in here for some sort of liaison.

"Come on, let me check the laptop, see if all the feeds are coming through." As he moved to the counter in the bookshop, she decided to just ask what had been on her mind all day.

It didn't matter that she'd tried to ignore that little conversation with Angelia from earlier, it had kept replaying in her mind all freaking day. "Angelia stopped by my shop today."

He barely glanced at her, nodded as he typed commands into the keyboard. "Oh."

"She said she was sorry she hooked up with you a few weeks ago and that she wouldn't have if she'd know you and I were together." Which they weren't, but that wasn't the point.

"Oh…wait, what the hell?" He straightened, all his focus on her now. Raw indignation played across his features. "She said that?"

Nora nodded, a frisson of relief sliding through her veins at his reaction. "Yeah. I don't know her at all and I didn't really believe her but I wanted to tell you." And okay, ask him if it was true. She didn't need to ask him though, not now. The truth was written all over his face.

"I haven't touched another woman since we met."

She blinked. "Since our date or since we met?"

"Met."

Oh. Hell. She did *not* know how to respond to that. At all. Jackson was a gorgeous man, that being an understatement. Everything about him screamed raw sex appeal. And the way he was looking at her now, as if he was a predator about to pounce, had her completely melting. She wanted to step closer, wrap her arms around him and—

Gah, not right now. Clearing her throat, she glanced at the computer, breaking his gaze. "We, uh, should probably check the laptop then get out of here."

She could feel his gaze on her, scorching hot. But she was apparently feeling extra cowardly because she refused to look at him. Too many emotions slammed through her at that revelation. And she just couldn't deal with how it made her feel. It was hard to believe that he hadn't been with anyone since meeting her, but that knowledge warmed her from the inside out. She just needed to figure out what she wanted to do about it. Well, the truth was, she wanted to see where things went with them. She'd been fantasizing about the sexy man for way too long.

After what felt like an eternity he turned back to the computer. "Feeds are working," he murmured after a few minutes, pinning her with his gaze again. "Let's get out of here. I've been thinking about that hot chocolate all day."

The look in his eyes told her he'd been thinking about more than hot chocolate. Way more. So had she. She was pretty sure she was done just thinking about it. Every time she looked at him, she remembered the way he'd stroked her to orgasm, the way his expert fingers had slid inside her, teasing and gentle... Just like that her body heated up and she felt her cheeks warm. Yep, it was definitely time to move on from the "just friends" category.

"I can't believe you've never seen A Christmas Story." Jackson had his arm stretched out across the back of the couch as she set their two mugs on the side table next to him.

"Then I'm glad I'm about to remedy that." Ignoring that little voice in the back of her head that told her she was asking for heartbreak, she sat next to him and curled into his side. She wasn't going to flat out jump him, but she'd come to realize that they would likely never be *just* friends. Not with the sizzling chemistry between them.

Jackson's only reaction was the slightest jolt so imperceptible she wouldn't have felt it if she hadn't been tucked up against him. His arm dropped from the top of the couch and curled around her shoulders, holding her in a loose enough embrace. That subtle, spicy scent that always drove her crazy teased her as the previews started. They had the laptop set up on the loveseat and so far, nothing exciting had happened at her shop. Which was just as well. Every second that passed she was finding it harder to care about anything but what it would feel like to have Jackson in her bed.

"You want me to pick you up tomorrow?" he murmured, his deep voice sending little shock waves across her senses.

His voice shouldn't affect her so much. "No, but thanks. I was going to bring her a bottle of wine or some dark chocolate truffles from Holly Jolly Chocolatier, but should I bring something else?"

"Just yourself." His voice had taken on a different tone, his grip tightening ever so slightly. They'd decorated her tree with lights and two boxes of ornaments when they'd first arrived and the sparkly white lights reflected off the television.

Not that she was really focused on anything else other than Jackson. Being held by him like this, all she could focus on was his strong embrace and the crazy way he made her feel. Her skin felt too tight for her body. She wanted to strip off his shirt and jeans and do the same with her own clothing so she could feel him skin to skin.

After a few minutes the arousal was so intense she couldn't ignore it. "Jackson..." She looked up to find his gaze hot, intense and completely on her. He didn't seem to care about the movie either.

Before she could think about the consequences of their actions — other than blinding pleasure — he grabbed her hips and tugged her so that she straddled him.

She braced herself against his shoulders and sank down completely over him, savoring the feel of having him between her legs like this. She was done fighting these feelings. It would suck if she got hurt, but if she never gave into this temptation, she'd never know what they might have. The truth was, the thought of him with someone else while they just remained friends shredded her up in ways she'd never imagined.

Jackson let out a groan as he grabbed her by the back of the head in a completely dominating grip. He met her half way and pulled her down to him, his mouth hungry and insistent. When his tongue demanded entrance into her mouth, she moaned into him, meeting him stroke for stroke. It was like her body had a mind of its own as she rolled her hips against him.

His erection was thick and insistent even through his jeans. She wanted to feel it inside her, wanted to be completely taken by him. Her nipples pebbled tightly against her bra cups as his hips jerked once, his arousal something she couldn't ignore.

Jackson tore his mouth from hers, his blue eyes bright with hunger as he stared up at her. "Want to see more of you," he rasped out, his breathing as erratic as her heartbeat.

She nodded, her heart rate out of control. She wanted to see more of him too—all of him. When she started to reach for the hem of his shirt, he froze.

"Damn it." The sudden curse made her fingers freeze on his shirt.

"You don't want—"

He tilted his head at the laptop. "Someone's in your shop."

The most insane part of her brain wanted to just keep doing what they were doing. To strip off the rest of their clothes and— "We've gotta go, huh?" Because if he said no—

He groaned and pressed his forehead to hers. "I think I might kill whoever's in there."

Forcing her muscles to work, she slid off him. The pulsing ache between her legs was even more insistent now. Now that her body knew she wasn't getting any more from Jackson, it wanted him even more badly. "I think I might help."

Suddenly he gripped the back of her neck again in that purely dominating way that made her melt. "We're finishing this when we get back." His voice was a low, raspy growl.

Unable to find her voice, she simply nodded. Oh yeah, they were definitely finishing this.

Chapter Six

Jackson kept his weapon tucked in the back of his pants with his leather jacket covering it. He had a license to carry and used it more often than not. Just because he'd gotten out of the Navy didn't mean he'd lost all his survival instincts. Tonight, however, he wasn't going to need it. Not after who they'd just seen on Nora's laptop.

"She's so freaking dead," Nora muttered as they entered the storeroom of her shop. It was dimly lit but there was more than enough room to see everything.

The storeroom was split into two sections. This half was filled with open boxes of books and neatly stacked books ready to be stocked when necessary. It was all very organized, just like Nora.

"How do you want to do this?" he asked as he shut and locked the door behind him.

"Just...ugh, I don't know. I'll go in and figure out what she's doing here. Do you mind waiting in the storeroom?"

He shook his head and brushed his lips over hers. Nora's eyes widened slightly, but then just as quickly her cheeks flushed pink. They weren't going back to friends. Ever. Nora was it for him and after tonight, it was pretty clear that she wanted to be more than friends too. Hell, he'd known that for a while.

Sighing, she opened the door from the storeroom to the shop. When she heard a male voice, Jackson grabbed her upper arm out of instinct and tugged her back. She let out a soft gasp, but he ignored it and moved into the shop. A ten foot high bookshelf was to his left and a display of Christmas books and other Christmas items to his right. The soft murmur of a male voice filled the air. It carried enough that he guessed it was coming from the front of the store. The counter and too many displays blocked him from seeing for certain.

All of Jackson's instincts went on alert. They'd seen Sasha on the screen, but she'd been alone. If someone else was here, no way in hell was he letting Nora go in by herself. He started to reach for his weapon but then he recognized the voice.

Turning to look at Nora, he motioned to the line of light switches on the wall, then pointed to the shop. She knew how the light system worked better than him. "The front area," he whispered.

She nodded and flipped them. As soon as she did, he heard a female yelp of surprise. Without pausing, he strode forward with Nora right behind him. Sidestepping the counter and moving around the displays, he stopped at the front nook to find Sasha buttoning up her sweater and his own freaking cousin moving to step in front of her.

"What the heck is going on?" Nora demanded before anyone could speak.

Sasha's face was as crimson as her sweater as she stepped out from behind Donovan, who'd just turned eighteen. "Hey, Nora, I uh…" She cleared her throat and Donovan held out a hand for Nora after giving Jackson a wary look. "I'm Donovan O'Connor. I'm your sister's boyfriend. And Jackson's cousin."

"Boyfriend?" Sasha blurted.

Donovan turned before Nora could respond or attempt to shake his hand. "Are you seeing someone else?" he demanded.

"No, I just thought…"

"I'm not hiding us anymore, Sasha. I'm barely one year older than you. It's not illegal for us to be together. I care about you and I don't want to be with anyone else."

Jackson scrubbed a hand over his face. He so did not need to hear any of this.

Nora cleared her throat. "So, Sasha's boyfriend? Is there a reason you two have been sneaking around here? And why aren't you at Liz's house?"

Sasha looked mortified as she wrapped her arms around herself.

"Her parents are heavy sleepers. I was planning on staying there, I swear, I just wanted some time alone with Donovan." She looked at the kid then, her expression softening to one of complete adoration.

Donovan looked just as smitten. Freaking puppy love.

"And you thought using my store was okay for that? You thought lying to me was okay? I'm assuming it was you who set off the alarm the other night?" Nora sounded more hurt than angry, her voice cracking on the last word. Jackson wanted to reach out and put his arm around her, but he could tell she needed to hash this out with her sister.

Sasha nodded. "Yeah," she whispered. "I'm really sorry. When you told me the cops showed up I should have said something but I thought you'd be pissed. We didn't touch anything and I punched the wrong code in when trying to enter, that's all. I was just distracted and..." Her cheeks flushed even deeper and Donovan actually looked embarrassed then.

Wasn't hard to guess why she'd put the wrong code in if Donovan had been distracting her. Oh, sweet Lord. By the panicked look on Nora's face she'd come to the same conclusion. Yeah, this was not the type of conversation the sisters needed to have in front of Jackson or Donovan.

"You drive here?" he asked his cousin.

"Yeah."

"I'm going to follow you home."

"Dude, that's not—"

"Yeah, it's freaking necessary and it's happening. We're leaving *now*." He turned to Nora and not caring about their audience, he cupped her cheek. "See you tomorrow night?"

"Yeah." Her voice was soft, breathy and all he could envision was the way she'd straddled him on her couch barely twenty minutes before.

He should wring his cousin's neck for the interruption. He pressed his lips to Nora's, just a brief brush to reinforce his claim on her. Because she was his, no doubt about it. It took willpower he didn't know he had to pull back. But he wasn't starting something he couldn't finish. Nodding tightly, since he couldn't find his voice, he looked at his cousin and jerked his chin toward the back door.

"I'll call you later," Donovan murmured to Sasha before falling in step with Jackson.

Nora watched as Jackson left, thankful he'd taken the boy with him. Well, more like a man than a boy. God, when had her sister grown up so much? This was definitely new parenting territory and she wasn't sure she was ready for it. Not that she really had a choice.

"You want some chocolate cake?" she asked quietly. Chocolate pretty much fixed everything.

Sasha blinked and to Nora's surprise nodded as tears filled her eyes. "I'm sorry for lying."

She held out her arms and tugged her sister close. "I'm not mad."

"Yeah but you're disappointed, which is way worse," she sniffled against Nora's neck.

"Well, yeah, I am. Come on." She slung an arm around her sister's shoulders and pulled her to the connected shop. "Sit and I'll grab us food."

"Okay." The word came out watery as Sasha slid onto a chair at the closest high-top table.

"Let's start with why you lied to me," she said as she rounded the display counter. Her mouth watered as she pulled out the chilled triple layer chocolate cake with chocolate buttercream frosting.

"I don't know."

"That's not an answer."

"Gah, fine. Donovan is really hot and well, popular. I guess I thought if things didn't work out it would be easier if no one knew about it."

Nora slid the dessert plate and fork in front of her sister, struck by how young and vulnerable she looked at the moment. "So you figured it would hurt less if you hid your relationship?"

"I guess when you say it, it sounds dumb."

She bit back a smile. "Not dumb. It's just that you should never hide any relationship. You're one of the brightest, most beautiful girls at that school—"

Sasha snorted before stabbing her fork into her cake. "You have to say that because you're my sister."

"I don't have to say anything. And it's true, regardless. Not that your looks matter anyway. Does Donovan make you feel..." She struggled to find the right words. "Grateful he's dating you?"

"No! I mean, like, I'm glad we're together, but no. If you mean does he make me feel like he's doing me a favor or something, *no*. I'm not stupid. I'd never be with a guy like that." She snorted the last part as if it was ridiculous.

It eased some of Nora's fears. Not all of them because it was pretty clear her sister was getting physical with a boy. Something she hadn't really prepared herself for. They'd had the sex talk on multiple occasions but it had been more abstract than anything else because Sasha had never been interested in guys. Until now apparently. "Have you two had sex?" Might as well just ask the question. Nora had been older when she'd first had sex, well into college, so she'd just assumed she wouldn't have to worry about this until later.

Sasha shook her head, embarrassment clear on her face. "No. I've thought about it but I'm not ready. I don't know that I'll be ready anytime soon either."

"If you do start thinking about it, will you come to me first?" She needed to make absolutely certain that Sasha protected herself.

Sasha nodded. "I promise."

"And no more lying?

"No, I swear."

"Good. I'd like to invite your boyfriend over for dinner, get to know him better. I promise not to embarrass you — too much."

Sasha snickered. "His mom embarrasses him all the time so don't worry, there's nothing you can do worse."

"You've met his parents?"

"No. He's asked me over but I was too nervous. I've just seen her at games before. She's really loud and makes these homemade signs that all the guys hassle him about." A grin lit Sasha's face. "I think he secretly likes it though."

"You know we've been invited to Jackson's mom's house tomorrow for a Christmas Eve party. Will Donovan be there?"

"Yeah. He says he has a present for me but I didn't get him anything."

"I'm sure we can figure something out tomorrow." How hard could a teenage boy be to shop for? Apart from sex, something Nora was definitely not going to think about, they liked food, right? "Maybe you can bake him something? Or you can just get him something from Gemma's shop." The Holly Jolly Chocolatier had melt-in-your-mouth goodness on every shelf. There was no way to go wrong.

"He does eat a *lot*… So, am I, like, grounded?"

"This might be a parenting fail, but no. Tomorrow's Christmas Eve, I'm not a monster." And the truth was, Sasha was such a great kid. This whole mess aside, she'd always been so great and honest about everything.

"I think maybe you should ground me anyway," she muttered, picking at her cake now. "I've been feeling really bad. I know you were looking forward to decorating the tree and…" She trailed off, setting her fork down. "I'd feel better if you grounded me."

"You're getting a free pass for this one but only because your guilt is real. And I remember what it was like with my first boyfriend."

"Your first boyfriend was a d-bag."

Nora lifted a shoulder, not bothering to deny it as she cut off a chunk of chocolately goodness.

"Not like Jackson. What's up with you two anyway? And how did you know we were here?"

"Jackson set up video cameras and planned this whole 'sting' as he called it—"

"Ohmygodyousawus?" She shouted the question, all the words running together.

"No! I didn't even realize you were here with someone." Well, she'd suspected it considering the bra she'd found earlier. "We were watching a movie and saw you—just you—on the feed, then came over here." Thank God she hadn't seen more than that.

"Oh, good. I mean, it wasn't like we were—"

"I so don't want to hear about it. If you decide to have sex then we need to talk, but until then, I'm good." And she never wanted any details anyway. Maybe when Sasha was older and their relationship shifted they could talk about more personal things, but as of now Nora needed to keep her parental figure in place. She cleared her throat. "Listen, I think Jackson and I are going to start dating." Hopefully a lot more than just dating. There was no way to keep him at arm's length. And she didn't really want to.

"Cool. Even though he was dumb before, I like him."

"Really?"

"Yeah, he's cool. And the way he looks at you it's clear he's all about you."

Okay then. "So if he came by for Christmas breakfast, would that be okay?" She hadn't actually asked him yet, but really hoped he could.

"Totally. Can I ask Donovan too?"

"If it's okay with his parents."

The grin Sasha gave her was blinding.

Suddenly Nora couldn't wait until the party tomorrow. She was going to tell Jackson that she wanted to be with him and only him. She owed it to both of them. So he'd gotten scared before? She could deal with that as long as it didn't happen again. If she was being honest, the intensity with him had scared her too. Still did, a little. She'd never imagined feeling such an intense attraction to someone. Not only that, she adored Jackson as a person. He'd always been respectful and he made her feel good about herself in a way no one ever had before. He was worth holding on to.

Plus he was sexy, protective and…he was hers.

CHAPTER SEVEN

"Stop fidgeting," Sasha muttered. "You look great."

With her free hand, Nora used the old fashioned knocker on the O'Connor's front door. "I'm not fidgeting." But she was nervous. She'd decided on a bottle of wine for Jackson's mom. It seemed like a safe enough hostess gift.

"Remind me how many times you changed tonight?"

"Ha, ha. Keep pushing it and maybe I really will ground you." Nora felt a little silly being so nervous to be at Jackson's parents' place. Their long, winding driveway was filled with vehicles and the stately two-story home was lit up with an impressive display of white and multi-colored lights as well as a Santa and reindeer on their roof.

"I don't care. Donovan's grounded." She gave Nora a sly grin.

"Really? I thought he was eighteen."

"He still lives at home and apparently Jackson narced him out to his mom —"

The door opened and to Nora's surprise, Donovan opened the door. Music and laughter trickled out with him, the noise level seeming to grow with every second that ticked by. He really was a good looking kid. Tall, boyishly handsome with dark brown hair and blue eyes that seemed to run in the O'Connor family, he definitely had heartbreaker written all over him. She just hoped he didn't break her sister's heart.

He stepped forward, pulling the door shut behind him. "Miss Cassidy —"

"Call me Nora. Seriously." She was twenty-five, thank you very much.

"Yeah, sorry." He shoved his hands into the pockets of his dark slacks. His attire made her glad she'd worn a party dress. "Listen, I really wanted to apologize to you in person for sneaking around like that."

"It wasn't even his idea—" Sasha began but he cut her off with a shake of his head.

"Doesn't matter. We, *I*, shouldn't have been using your place like that. I like your sister a lot and I want to keep seeing her. I hope you don't base your opinion of me solely on this."

Nora half-smiled. He was so earnest and brave to stand there and take responsibility like this, it was hard not to. "Apology accepted. I don't know if Sasha's asked you yet, but if you'd like to join us for Christmas breakfast you're welcome to come over." She was going to ask Jackson tonight if he could make it as well and was a little nervous about it. She knew his family didn't do anything big until dinner so she hoped he'd be able to.

"Yeah, she asked and I'm in. Thanks." He looked at Sasha then, his expression softening. "You look beautiful."

"Thanks." Sasha shot Nora a look that pretty much said 'get lost' so she murmured something nonsensical and sidestepped him, opening the front door.

Nora knew Sasha wanted to give Donovan his present and she didn't need her big sister hanging around for it. And Nora didn't need to witness anything between the two of them. The foyer was festively decorated with garland and lights lining the staircase. Next to it was a white bench with a stuffed, life-sized Santa Claus holding red and silver presents in his lap. And next to that a tree that had to be at least eight feet tall was covered in fake snow and red and silver decorations.

Before she'd taken two steps, Fallon appeared out of nowhere in a slinky green dress. Her auburn hair was piled on her head in some sort of complicated twist. As usual she looked stunning, and a little flustered—which wasn't normal for her. "I'm so glad you're here." She grabbed Nora's hand and pulled her inside what turned out to be a small guest bathroom that smelled like cinnamon and vanilla. Little candles lined one of the windows, the sight of them flickering in the mirror creepy until Fallon flipped on a light.

"You okay?" Nora asked. "You seem high strung—even for you."

"Yeah, I just...might have kissed someone I definitely shouldn't have."

"Who?"

Fallon's lips pressed into a tight line. "I can't say."

"I need a drink if we're going to play this game. And I really need to find your sexy brother." Okay, maybe she didn't need a drink. She was wired and feeling practically desperate to see Jackson. They'd texted each other all day. She'd been crazy busy but had made the time for him. The anticipation of seeing him had her feeling almost buzzed.

Fallon's mouth dropped open for a fraction of a second. "Are you two finally..." She made an obscene thrusting motion with her hips.

Feeling her cheeks heat up, Nora nodded. "You are such a guy, I swear. And yeah, I think so. I just need to talk to him." And kiss him because it was all she'd been thinking about today. Straddling him on her couch last night, then having to stop, had been the last straw. She needed Jackson's mouth on hers as soon as possible, and his body on top of hers as soon as possible after that.

"Well come on. Get that coat off and give me that bottle of wine."

"That's for your mom and she better get it," Nora said, laughing.

"No promises. Now come on, give me the coat." Fallon held out a hand as Nora slid her black coat off to reveal a red dress that would have been way too expensive if she hadn't gotten it on sale at eighty percent off.

Formfitting, it had a lace overlay and fit all her curves to perfection. It was like the thing had been made for her. With her four-inch heels and their thin straps wrapping around her ankles, she knew she looked good. It gave her the confidence she needed to put herself out there completely for Jackson.

Fallon let out a low whistle. "My brother's totally a goner. If you guys get married I better be one of your bridesmaids—and the dress better not suck."

Nora probably should have been taken back by that statement but the truth was, she could see a future with Jackson. And she wanted it more than she'd wanted anything. "Deal. And I want to know who you kissed."

Fallon mimed zipping her lips and throwing away the key.

"I'll find you later after you've had a few glasses of champagne and we'll see how quiet you are then," she said as she opened the door.

"Ha, ha. I'm going to put your coat in the front closet, okay? I saw Jackson in the living room earlier." She pointed to the nearest open entryway, also decorated with garland and lights. Man, the O'Connors didn't mess around with Christmas.

"Yeah. Oh, wait." She reached into the pocket and pulled out the sprig of fake mistletoe she'd brought with her. If she lost her nerve she just planned to hold this over his head.

Fallon just laughed and headed for the foyer. Now Nora was on a mission.

"You've got to be kidding me," she muttered the second she stepped into the packed room. Nolan and Maguire, Jackson's two brothers, were in a lively debate about something to do with beer, the elderly Baker sisters were definitely on the way from tipsy to having to be carried out and Angelia had her manicured nails brushing up against Jackson's forearm as they stood next to the fireplace.

For the briefest moment, stupid insecurities flared wild and hot inside Nora…

Until she read Jackson's body language.

His jaw was clenched and his shoulders were stiff as he took a small step back from the petite blonde. It was almost imperceptible but she could practically see him making his getaway.

Well, she could help with that. Someone called her name but she ignored them and made her way across the plush, festive room, smiling at the Baker sisters, who were perched on the edge of a couch, talking animatedly to each other.

Jackson looked up and saw her when she was about three feet from him and the mixture of relief and hunger in his eyes was almost enough to make her stop in her tracks. Yeah, she had nothing to worry about. Never with Jackson.

She didn't even bother to look at Angelia, just held up the mistletoe and grinned at Jackson.

He murmured something that sounded a lot like "hell yeah" before he crushed his mouth to hers. She felt the claiming—and that's exactly what it was—all the way to her toes. His tongue flicked against hers with a heated urgency, probably a little too long in a setting like this before he pulled back, his breathing erratic.

"You're mine," he murmured, his expression hard, as if he was daring her to argue.

"I know."

He blinked those beautiful blue eyes as if he'd been expecting an argument or something. "Officially."

"I know," she murmured, sliding her hands around his waist. She was vaguely aware of the people, music and pretty lights, but all she could focus on was Jackson. She couldn't wait to be alone with him later.

He narrowed his eyes. "As in you're my girlfriend now."

A laugh bubbled up inside her and it felt so damn good. "Do you think I need convincing? I'm agreeing with you."

"Good." His expression was as fierce and possessive as his grip around her. "I don't even care if my mom wins the bet—"

"Bet?"

He snorted. "Apparently there was a bet—that I just found out about—that started at Silver Bells on when we'd make things official. The pot's over six hundred bucks, I think. Plus some other stuff."

"We should have gotten in on that action!"

He blinked once before that wicked grin that had completely stolen her heart—and breath—widened. "God, I love you."

Before she could respond his mouth was on hers again, teasing and delicious, until one of his brothers told them to get a room.

"That's not a bad idea," she murmured, pulling back from him. Angelia was thankfully long gone now and Nora didn't care where she was. "But first, champagne."

"Sounds good to me." He slid his arm around her shoulders in that familiar, possessive way and it felt like the most natural action in the world.

Being with Jackson felt like coming home.

CHAPTER EIGHT

Nora rolled over in bed at the incessant ringing. What the heck? It took her a moment to realize it was her phone. She grabbed it from her nightstand after two tries and barely made out Jackson's name and picture on the screen. Gah, the screen was way too bright in her dark room. She held her arm over her eyes.

"Hello? What's wrong?" Because there was no reason he was calling for anything other than an emergency at four in the morning.

"I'm downstairs. Let me in." His deep voice had the usual effect even if she was half asleep.

"What?"

"I'm freezing out here. Come on, I've got a present for you."

"Is that like a euphemism?"

His laughter warmed her straight to her toes. "No. Come on, it's cold."

"Hold on," she mock grumbled.

Forcing herself out of bed, she snagged her robe from the back of her bathroom door and cinched it around her waist — then quickly brushed her teeth for good measure. If he was here, there was a good chance kissing would be involved. They'd spent most of the party last night together, then a little after midnight he'd had to head back to his place to get the rocking chair he'd made for his dad. She'd taken Sasha home and had finished wrapping up the last few presents for her sister. Nora knew she'd gone a little overboard this year for Sasha but she didn't care. Next year she'd be eighteen and likely off to college so Nora wanted to spoil her just a little more. Besides, it made up for all the years of their mom doing nothing.

Downstairs she turned off the alarm. Jackson barreled inside on a gust of icy wind with a cloth bag in his hand. As soon as he'd shut and locked the door his mouth was on hers, his cold, gloved hands cupping her cheeks.

Even that couldn't chill her, not with his tongue invading her mouth, teasing and taking. She clutched on to his shoulders to steady herself until he pulled back. Though she still didn't let go.

"I missed you," he murmured, his eyes raking over her face as if he could devour her.

She'd missed him too. "It's only been a couple hours."

He winced slightly. "Sorry for waking you up."

"No you're not. And I'm not either." She slid her arms around him, the chill of his body against hers and just his presence making her nipples tighten. She'd wanted some private time with him earlier, but between the party, and then getting Sasha home it just hadn't been in the cards.

The grin slid right into place, making her heart melt. "I'm really not," he murmured. "You want your present?"

If it involved him naked in her bed, yes.

She nodded and after he tugged his boots off, she pulled him into the living room. She'd left the Christmas tree lights on, but turned on one of the lamps. She was finally going to get to experience all of Jackson—and she didn't plan to let him go. "Did you get the rocking chair to your parents' house?"

"Yeah, my mom helped me sneak it into the garage."

"I'm sure your dad will love it."

"I hope so." Without warning, he tugged her into his lap as he sat on the couch. The cloth bag he'd brought was next to him. "I like being able to touch and kiss you any time I want."

"Me too." She brushed her lips over his, savoring his taste. She liked that he could touch her and kiss her anytime too. No more denying her feelings. If things didn't work out between them it would shred her up, but she couldn't go into this relationship expecting the worst to happen. That was a complete recipe for disaster and the truth was, she saw something real with Jackson.

He was the first to pull back, much to her surprise. "I didn't have time to wrap this one," he said as he reached into the bag, "And I probably should have just waited until nine to bring this but I needed to see you." The raw hunger in his voice mirrored her own feelings.

"I'm glad you didn't wait." She let out a little gasp as he placed the hand-carved jewelry box in her hands. "This is beautiful. What kind of wood is this?" She ran her fingers over the intricate ivy and vine carvings along the top.

"Walnut."

There were so many details it was unbelievable. The 'N' in the middle with butterflies somehow intricately carved as if they were flying through the letter made her smile. It was even more special because he'd made this with his own hands. "Thank you feels inadequate. This is amazing," she said, looking at him now. "Thank you for something so thoughtful and beautiful."

His cheeks flushed slightly and he gave a half-shrug. She'd noticed he didn't take praise well. "Open it."

It opened up to two compartments, both lined with a soft, pale blue velvet.

"If you slide this panel out…" He moved the front lower panel to the left, and another panel inside slid open to reveal a small secret compartment. "You should put expensive stuff in a safe anyway, but I thought you'd like this."

"You're amazing, Jackson." Cupping his cheeks, she intended to just brush her lips over his and pull back so she could give him his present, but the moment they made contact she swore she could feel something shift inside him.

He let out a sort of growling sound and crushed his mouth to hers. All her nerve endings flared to life as his tongue teased against her.

She was vaguely aware of him moving the jewelry box off her lap before he suddenly stood, scooping her up in his arms. She let out a soft gasp, realizing what he intended—and what she wanted. "My sister's here."

"She's asleep upstairs, right?"

Nora nodded. And her sister was a heavy sleeper too. She wouldn't be up for at least a few more hours. "I've got a present for you too though."

"Give me another present first," he murmured, a question in his eyes. Did she want this?

That was an easy answer. "Upstairs, now." The words were barely out before he'd moved into action. "Second door on the right." Luckily the bedrooms were across the hall, not next door to each other.

His mouth was on hers again by the time they reached it. She didn't have time to think or care that her room was a little messy before she heard the snick then lock of her bedroom door.

Jackson moved with an incredible efficiency, carrying her as if she weighed nothing, until he had her splayed out on the bed. "Tell me if you want to stop." His voice was surprisingly unsteady as he stood back.

Her heart was pounding. She was glad to know she wasn't the only one so affected. "No way." Moonlight and streetlights streamed in from her two windows to give them more than enough illumination. "Now strip." Because he'd already seen her naked once and she desperately wanted to see all of him.

As he started stripping off his jacket, then his long-sleeved sweater, she sat up and slid out of her robe—but pretty much froze when he tugged the sweater completely over his head. Washboard abs that should be illegal tightened under her scrutiny. He was like a work of art, all those stark lines and striations absolute perfection.

She wasn't sure how long she stared until he cupped her cheek, then slid his fingers back into her hair. The way he swept his gaze over her face was so full of lust and hunger, her breath caught in her throat. He tugged her hair slightly as he tilted her head to his. The tiny bite made her suck in a breath. His expression was intense as he looked at her, his blue eyes seemingly darker in the dimness of her room. It was so quiet right now, the only sounds permeating the room their harsh breathing. The intimacy of it made her feel as if they were the only two people in the world.

"I wasn't kidding what I said earlier. I love you, Nora."

She'd been wondering if it had been just one of those slips at his parents' place earlier. To hear him say the words now with a look of such love on his face, made her throat tighten with emotion.

"I love you too." Saying the words out loud was a little terrifying. Meeting and falling for someone like Jackson had never been in her plans. Heck, she'd never imagined there was someone as wonderful as him out there.

His mouth was on hers again, demanding and taking everything she had to give. She fell back against the sheets as he climbed on top of her, his body covering her with all that warmth.

She slid her fingers down his chest and abs, tracing her fingers along the ridges of his abdomen, moving lower and lower until he grasped her by the wrists. Before she could ask why he was stopping her, he held her hands above her head, his mouth hovering right over hers.

On instinct she arched into him, wanting more skin to skin contact.

"No touching me until you've come against my mouth." His words were a soft order she felt all the way to her toes.

If it had been possible to physically melt, she would have done so on the spot. That was probably the hottest thing anyone had ever said to her. Combined with the expression on his face that said he meant every word, and yeah, she was a goner.

Moving with that sexy predatory grace, he released her wrists and shifted down the bed. When he tugged her pajama pants and panties off in a quick move, she couldn't stop the thrill of hunger that shot through her.

"I've fantasized about this," she murmured.

He froze, his big palms stilling on her inner knees as he crouched between her legs. But for only an instant. "My mouth on you?"

She nodded and shimmied out of her top, completely baring herself to him. When their gazes connected she felt insanely powerful at the lust practically vibrating off him. All that hunger was for her and her alone. He'd seen her before when she'd been on his lap straddling him after that first date. He'd licked and teased her nipples with his mouth and made her come with his oh-so-talented fingers.

But then he'd put the brakes on, not wanting to rush. Now to be stretched out for him, completely bare like this, was exhilarating. She hadn't been naked in front of a man in years other than him, and she didn't feel an ounce of anxiety with Jackson. Because he would never hurt her. She could see that promise in his eyes.

"I've also thought about my mouth on *you*. A lot," she continued, her voice dropping a few octaves.

His fingers tightened around her knees. Cool air rushed over her exposed body. She loved the way he stilled, loved seeing that she affected him as much as he did her. Her nipples hardened even more and heat flooded between her legs as she watched him. He was still crouched between her legs but those words seemed to light him on fire.

Groaning, he took her by surprise when he buried his face between her legs with no warning. She arched into him, her hips rolling instinctively. "Jackson," she rasped out his name as he tongued her clit with enough pressure to drive her crazy.

He moaned against her, the vibration increasing her sensitivity to his teasing.

She slid her fingers through his inky black hair, holding onto the dark strands as he flicked his tongue up the length of her folds. She was already so wet for him she knew it wouldn't take long for her to come. But she felt almost empty inside, desperate with the need for him to fill her.

He'd yet to take off his pants so she still hadn't gotten a look at him — and she had definitely fantasized. Just the thought of seeing him completely exposed to her as well, of getting to stroke him with her hand, then mouth —

"You're so wet," he murmured as he slipped a finger inside her.

"Because of you." He groaned again at that. She couldn't respond when he slid another thick digit inside her. Her inner walls tightened around him as he pushed deep, his tongue working magic against her clit. The sensitive bundle of nerves ached and throbbed, her release just out of reach.

When he began moving his fingers inside her faster, she pushed right over that edge. "Jackson." His name came out like a prayer as her body bowed tight under the onslaught of that first cresting wave.

Streams of pleasure spiraled out to all her nerve endings as he curved his fingers at just the right angle, dragging them against her inner wall as he wreaked havoc on her clit. Her climax punched through her, completely taking over until the only thing she was aware of was Jackson's face between her legs and his wicked, wicked tongue.

She wasn't sure if she cried out too loudly or what she said, she was too lost in her pleasure. By the time she collapsed back against the sheet, panting and sated, she looked down to find him watching her intently.

Wordlessly he withdrew his fingers from her and she immediately felt the loss. The empty ache between her legs was even worse now. She needed to feel him inside her like she needed her next breath. When he slid his wet fingers between his lips she sucked in a sharp breath.

If what he'd said earlier was the hottest thing she'd heard, then this was the hottest thing she'd ever *seen*.

"Love your taste." He closed his eyes for a long moment, seemed to savor her.

Oh yeah, she'd completely fallen for Jackson O'Connor, no doubt about it. Now it was her turn. Her body buzzing with the aftereffects of her orgasm, she sat up and reached for the button of his jeans, but he moved fast, sliding off the bed.

"Not coming in your hands." His jaw was tight, his expression warrior-fierce as he shucked his jeans.

When his erection was freed, her eyes widened. Long and thick, he was definitely big all over. She wanted to trace every inch of it with her tongue. Even the thought of that had her nipples tightening even more.

"You on the pill?" he rasped out as he grabbed a condom from his discarded pants.

"Yeah, for years." For health reasons, none of which she wanted to talk about right now. She just wanted to feel him inside her.

At her words, his hands stilled. "I'm clean. I was tested over six months ago and I haven't been with anyone since then."

"Me too." And it had been a lot longer than six months. "We don't need to use the condom," she said, answering his unspoken question.

"You sure?"

"If you are."

He dropped it like it was on fire. "I can't go slow this time."

"Good." She didn't want that, not now, not when she felt like a giant mass of trembling energy.

Then he was on her, his mouth covering hers as he reached between their bodies. Despite the fact that he'd just felt her climax against him, he cupped her mound and tested her slickness—and shuddered. She loved the feel of his callused hands on the most sensitive part of her.

She spread her legs wider for him, wrapping them around his waist. The feel of his bare chest against hers was the most erotic sensation. She wanted to rub up against him like a cat in heat. She knew she should be sated, but as he shifted slightly, nudging his thick erection between her folds, she wanted more.

"Nora," he groaned out her name as he looked down at her, his gaze full of too many emotions for her to filter. His muscular arms caged her in on either side.

She lifted her hips, not wanting to wait a second longer, impaling herself on him.

He hissed in a breath as he filled her. All his features seemed sharper as he kept his eyes pinned on hers. To have him watching her so intently felt incredibly intimate. Even if she wanted to, she couldn't look away. Then he started thrusting inside her, slowly at first until his movements were unsteady and wild.

She met him stroke for stroke, savoring the way he completely filled her with each thrust. His jaw clenched tight and though she'd never seen him come before, she guessed he was close. She ran her fingers up his abdomen, over his chest then his strong arms. It was as if the man had been carved from stone, everything about him utter perfection. The scars and nicks covering his body only added to his ridiculous sex appeal.

And he was all hers.

That knowledge pushed her over the edge again. She simply let go of any semblance of control and let the orgasm rip through her. Just like that, he came too, with a shout that sounded a lot like triumph as he buried his face against her neck.

She wrapped her arms around him, clutched him to her as he emptied himself inside her. She wasn't sure how long it took before they both came back to themselves, but eventually her breathing evened out. And Jackson hadn't made any attempt to move off her.

He just nuzzled her neck as he stroked those big hands over her breasts and hips. It was as if he couldn't get enough of touching her. And it didn't seem to matter that he was half-hard in her now, he just wanted to touch her. Definitely fine with her. She couldn't wait to explore more of him. She wanted everything from him, to move in with him, maybe…even more one day.

"Merry Christmas, baby," he murmured, sounding surprisingly drowsy.

She grinned, stroking her fingers down his muscular back. "Best Christmas present ever." And she was never letting him go.

EPILOGUE

Jackson wiped his palms on his jeans as he sat at one of the high-top tables waiting for Nora to lock up her shop. Tonight was it. He was proposing because there was no way he could go another day without claiming her forever for everyone to see. Dating wasn't enough for him. He wanted everything and he wanted his ring on her finger so the entire world knew she was his.

Caveman attitude? Yep. He didn't care.

He'd gone on countless missions where he'd been sure he would die and he'd never felt an ounce of the fear he experienced now. What if she said no? Things between them were incredible, and the sex… He couldn't think about that now. Otherwise he'd start kissing her the moment she joined him and they'd end up naked in her storeroom.

Again.

The past two months had been the best of his life and he couldn't imagine not having Nora in his life forever. He wanted to move in with her but she'd told him not until Sasha was out of the house. Which he respected. He liked that she was setting a good example for her sister, but if they were married, they didn't have to wait. And he wasn't waiting any longer.

"You okay?" Nora asked, her expression worried as she walked up to him, her boots clicking softly on the tile of the café floor as she reached him. In just a couple months it would be spring and she'd be wearing those sexy dresses again. He couldn't wait.

Clearing his throat, he nodded. "Yeah, just want to make those reservations." He'd booked a table for them at her favorite place and planned to propose afterward once they had privacy. It was almost

Valentine's Day so she didn't seem suspicious about the reservations. He was going to suggest they take a walk down Main Street since it was a perfect moonlit night and it wasn't far from her favorite park. Tonight needed to be perfect.

She let out a light laugh. "We've got plenty of time." She gave him a quick kiss on the lips before moving through the throng of high-top tables. "You want some tea or something? I've just got to run the end of the night reports. It won't take long."

"I'm okay but I'll make you something." He slid off the stool and trailed after her, rounding the counter as she did.

Nora gave him another curious look as he practically ran into her. Turning, she placed her hands on her hips. "All right, what's going on?"

He kept his expression blank. "Nothing."

"Are you breaking up with me?"

"No!"

She snickered and he realized she hadn't been serious. "I didn't actually think that, but jeez, what's going on?" Gently, she ran her hands down his upper arms and forearms. "You're all tight... Is something wrong at work? Or with your family?" She sounded horrified at the last question.

"No, nothing like that." He tried to force himself to relax but he simply couldn't. God, he'd never felt like this in his life, as if he could crawl out of his own skin from raw fear that she would say no.

Jackson hadn't even realized he was moving until he'd pulled the small jewelry box from his jacket pocket and was on one knee before her. But hell, he couldn't wait another second. The desire to see his ring on her finger, to officially start their life together, was overwhelming to the point he could barely think straight.

She blinked down at him, her green eyes filled with confusion until he held open the box.

With trembling fingers, he flipped it open. "Marry me?"

When tears filled her eyes, panic set in, but only for a moment. Her smile was blinding as she nodded. "Yes!" She practically tackled him as she threw her arms around his neck.

They would have both tumbled to the floor if he hadn't steadied them. Relief like he'd never known flowed through him, hot and fierce. He had the ring out and on her left hand ring finger as she wiped tears from her eyes with her other hand.

"It's beautiful," she said, not even looking at it as she cupped his cheeks. "I love you so much, Jackson."

"I wanted to do it right, take you to dinner and —"

She shook her head. "This is right, it's perfect."

"You're perfect." They argued like any other couple but she was everything he'd been looking for when he hadn't even known he was looking.

Laughing, she shook her head. "I don't know what I did to deserve you."

"Right back at you." He was never letting her go. "I love you, Nora. And I don't want to wait to get married, I want to do it this year." Living apart the past two months had been sheer torture. He'd stayed over at her place, sure, but it wasn't the same thing as waking up to her beautiful face every morning.

"It's only February, that leaves a lot of months to plan —"

He shook his head. "A spring wedding."

Her eyes widened so he crushed his mouth to hers, taking away any argument she might have had. He wanted to go to bed with her every night and wake up with her every morning. When she tightened her grip around him and groaned into his mouth, he figured they were probably going to be late for their reservation after all.

He didn't mind one bit. Not when the woman he loved had just agreed to become his wife.

Tease Me, Baby

CHAPTER ONE

Fallon O'Connor shoved her hands in her jacket pockets as she stepped out of Yuletide Spirits, one of the local bars in Holly, North Carolina, a picturesque mountain town where it was Christmas year-round. Something she adored.

Normally.

Right about now, however, she wanted to go home, get out of the icy weather and feel sorry for herself. Which was freaking pathetic. She'd been offered a coveted spot in a culinary school across the country. Something she should be thrilled about.

But the thought of leaving her family, the unique town she loved, her friends... It just wasn't as appealing as it should be. No matter how hard she tried to convince herself it was what she wanted.

A flash of blue lights reflected against the bank of windows along Main Street. The sight made her jump, and even before she'd turned around, instinct told her exactly who she'd see. Not one of the many deputies of Holly, but the sheriff himself.

Sexy Brad Fulton, who she'd been avoiding for a month and a half—ever since the Christmas Eve party when she'd made a fool of herself and kissed him. Okay, maybe not exactly a fool, since he'd been into it at the time. But what had she been thinking dragging him into the privacy of the pantry at her parents' house and attacking his mouth with hers?

Mr. Boy Scout was not for her. He was exactly the type of man her family would expect her to settle down with. Freaking perfect.

She didn't want perfect. She already didn't live up to her mother's standards; she didn't want to end up with a man who was so perfect that she'd always be compared to him. The kind of man where people would tell her that she was "lucky" someone so perfect was with her.

Ugh.

"Fallon." That deep, sexy voice rolled over her like the sweetest aphrodisiac.

She felt it all the way to her core, even if she wanted to deny the effect he had on her. Kind of impossible when heat rushed between her legs just looking at him. It didn't matter that there was a light layer of snow dusting everything—that voice warmed her up from the inside out. Swallowing hard, she half-turned to see his window rolled down, but kept walking. Her vehicle wasn't that much farther. Just another block. "Hey, Boy Scout."

His jaw tightened at her use of the nickname. "You been drinking?" he asked through the open window as he slowly cruised down the street alongside her.

She stopped in her heeled ankle boots and turned fully to him as she placed her hands on her hips. "Seriously? That's what you want to ask me?" It was after eleven and she had been leaving a bar, but still. The question annoyed her.

"No." He put the patrol car in park and turned off the engine.

Before she could blink he was out and in front of her in full uniform. The uniform was what gave him that sexy, strong vibe. *Yeah, right.* She couldn't even lie to herself. Yes, the uniform on him made her think bad, bad things, but Brad was like a pillar of strength and hotness even without it.

"I want to ask why you've been ignoring me since Christmas."

"Christmas Eve." The two words popped out.

"Technically Christmas, since we kissed again after midnight." Lights from the garland-wrapped cast-iron Victorian poles reflected in his dark eyes as he stared at her as if she was the only person in the world who existed. Who mattered.

And that was the crux of the problem. She could fall for him if she wasn't careful, and that so wasn't happening. Not when she was leaving in two weeks and she was nowhere near the kind of woman he should be with. Someone who had their life together. She cleared her throat. "Who says I'm ignoring you?"

"You want to play that game?" he murmured, his gaze dropping to her mouth as he took another step closer so that only inches separated them.

And oh, she felt that look between her legs. "No, but I could think of another game to play." Her voice sounded all seductive and sultry. Gah, what was she doing? She should be turning away from him. Walking to her car. Driving home. Going to sleep. *Alone.*

His gaze narrowed again, this time for a different reason. "*Have you been drinking?*"

Okay, the question was fair. She'd been ignoring him since that insane kiss and now she was flirting. But come on, it was impossible not to when he was in front of her looking like Captain America. "I had a glass of champagne almost two hours ago. But..." Placing her finger on her nose, she turned slightly away from him and started doing the "DUI walk," putting one foot in front of the other as she walked a perfect straight line. After taking ten steps down the sidewalk she swiveled, her little skirt flaring out—and she didn't miss the way Brad's eyes landed on her legs, and stayed there a moment too long. Apparently it didn't matter that she had on leggings under her skirt—he was watching her as if he could imagine her naked. Something she liked very much. Because she imagined him naked every time she saw him.

Striding back to him—with just a bit more of a sway of her hips—she only stopped when she was inches in front of him. His wide chest was rising and falling a little faster than normal, his eyes dilated as he stared down at her. Even in her heels he still towered over her, since she was only five feet two inches.

The man was huge, and absolutely gorgeous. Of course, he'd probably hate the term gorgeous. But he was a spectacular specimen of a male. Wide shoulders, close-cropped dark hair, a hard, angular jaw, ripped muscles that even his boring black polyester uniform couldn't hide. She'd been wrong—Captain America had nothing on him. His badge glinted under the streetlights, making her think bad,

bad things. Like how sexy would it be to feel him inside her while he had on his uniform? Or part of it, at least.

She wanted this man with an intensity that defied logic. Which was part of the reason she'd been ignoring him. A girl only had so much self-control when faced with all this deliciousness. Even as she knew she would regret what she planned, she said, "I don't feel safe walking to my car. Would you mind being my escort?" She knew he had to say yes since he was an officer of the law, but she also knew that he was fully aware she wasn't scared to walk to her car.

Not in Holly, where the town looked like something out of a Thomas Kinkade painting and they hadn't had a murder in who knew how many years. In the heart of the Blue Ridge mountains, the town's shops were decorated three hundred and sixty-five days a year with Christmas trees, snow globes, garland, twinkly lights and anything else someone could imagine. The Victorian gingerbread architecture just added to the appeal, and the tourists and locals alike loved it. Right now, she wasn't thinking about any of that.

No, she was thinking about how she could get another taste of the sexy Boy Scout.

What was the matter with her? This was beyond stupid. She was leaving soon and he was not the type of man she wanted. Nope. Nope. Nope.

He cleared his throat, looked up and down the street, then back at her. And there was only heat and hunger in his gaze this time. "You like playing with fire," he murmured, that hot gaze landing on her mouth once again.

Shoving her hands in her pockets, she turned away from him and headed down the street, her heels clicking on the sidewalk with each step. He'd either follow her or he wouldn't.

Seconds later, he fell in step with her, the radio on his belt squawking occasionally as they walked in silence. And it wasn't her imagination either—the air between them crackled with an intensity she'd never experienced before.

He turned the radio down as they walked so that it was on a low setting, the words all background noise.

Just being around him, and she turned into this puddle of need. It made no sense. She'd dated in college, had a couple boyfriends, though things always fizzled out because the chemistry wasn't there. Since moving home a year ago, she hadn't dated at all. She lived on her own while doing contract work as a pastry chef, but she had three protective older brothers and people in town gossiped, simple as that. Besides, she hadn't been interested in anyone enough to say yes to requests for dates.

Brad was the first man she'd wanted to say yes to—but he checked every single box of what her mother would want for her. Mr. Perfect. He'd literally been in the papers for saving a drowning puppy years ago. Not only that, he had a box full of medals from his time in the Marine Corps, which okay, was incredible. He really was a good man.

Deep down she figured that he'd realize she wasn't the right kind of woman for him. At a crossroads in her life right now, she felt almost adrift. And she was never going to be that perfect woman like her mom. Who made everything look so easy. Raising four kids, had the perfect marriage after decades, and all sorts of expectations for Fallon. And all her brothers had stacks of medals from their time in the military too. Just like her father. Everyone was so accomplished. What did she have? A business degree she wasn't using, and contract work because she couldn't figure her life out.

"How've you been?" Brad's deep, delicious voice cut through the cold night air and her depressing thoughts.

"Good." She inwardly cringed, trying to think of something better to say when all she wanted to do was shove him up against the nearest wall and climb his hard body. Maybe that would get him out of her system. She nearly snorted at the thought. More likely it would just make her want him even more.

"I hear you've been delivering baked goods to Nora's. Had a couple of your mini cakes."

Nora owned Nora's Books and Brew, a combination coffee shop and bookstore—she was also the fiancée of one of Fallon's brothers as of tonight. "Yeah, Nora wanted to experiment with selling more baked goods, see how they went over with everyone."

"Well they're a hit as far as I'm concerned." He patted a hand over his flat stomach. He shot her another heated look as they reached the alleyway she planned to cut through.

Motioning in which direction they should go, she said, "I... I've been thinking what it would be like to run my own food truck. One purely with baked goods." She wasn't sure why she was telling him. She hadn't told a soul about her silly dream.

"That's a great idea."

"Really?"

He nodded. "Yeah. Holly is the perfect place for it, too."

"That's what I was thinking too. I even have a name—Sugar Rush." She'd also saved the social media links and domain name for a website. Just in case.

His lips kicked up, making him so handsome she could hardly stand it. "I like it." There he went again with that voice. And that look. And...everything about him made her want to jump him, right freaking now.

"That's me," she said as they approached her brother's truck. "My car's in the shop."

He frowned a little but didn't respond as she pressed the key fob. When he opened the driver's side door for her, her heart did a little flip-flop. The man had manners, sexiness, and could kiss like no one's business.

Something she'd been trying not to think about since Christmas. Trying and failing. She moved a little closer to the running board, planning to step up into it.

She wasn't sure how that first kiss on Christmas Eve had happened, exactly. One moment they'd been politely talking, Brad watching her with those dark eyes she could drown in. Then she'd asked him to help her get something out of the pantry at her parents' house in the middle of the holiday party—and once they'd been alone inside they'd basically attacked each other. She'd been toying with the idea of maybe kissing him, but he'd made the first move. Which had been incredibly hot. She didn't like chasing after a man, and for him to take that initiative? It had just spurred her into action.

Before she was able to step up into the truck, Brad was on her. Maybe he'd been remembering the same thing she had.

Everything was just like before — his taste, his masculine scent, the feel of his muscular shoulders under her fingertips as she clutched at him like her life depended on it. His gun belt dug into her hips as she found herself hoisted up into the truck. Seconds later, the hum of the seat moving back filled the cabin and Brad was on top of her as the door closed behind them. Everything happened so fast, she could barely catch her breath. And she wasn't sure she wanted to.

This was all sorts of wrong. In fact, she couldn't believe the Boy Scout was doing this at all, especially when he was supposed to be working. When he was actually in his *uniform*. She managed to tear her head back for a moment. "What are we —"

He cut off whatever she'd been about to say with another savage kiss. And savage was the only way to describe it. He ate at her mouth as if he was starving and only she could fill him. Something she understood well because she felt exactly the same.

This man could be an addiction, one she'd never seen coming. He was older than her by about six years, so they'd never had the same friends and never run in the same circles, but she knew his reputation. He wasn't a ladies' man. If anything, he'd *earned* his nickname. He'd been an All-American type of guy before heading off to college. Then he'd moved back home two years ago, been elected sheriff and had taken to the job like a fish to water. Everyone in town loved him.

His reputation was stellar, untarnished. And if anyone saw him doing *this*, it could seriously damage his career. Because that was how small towns were.

She shoved at his shoulder once. When he pulled back he was breathing hard and staring down at her with an expression that said *Why are we stopping?*

"Brad —"

He groaned softly, leaning down to nibble at her bottom lip. "I love it when you say my name."

For a moment, she arched into him, dug her fingers into his

shoulders—then shook her head once. "Don't distract me. What the heck are we doing? This could get you in a lot of trouble." And she found that she cared very much. She might tease him about being a Boy Scout but she sure didn't want to see him hurt professionally. She didn't want to see him hurt at all, which was why she needed to keep her distance from him.

"Don't care." And his mouth was on hers again.

She wanted to push the subject, tell him to stop, but no one was around and he was a grown man who made his own decisions. This little strip of parking was reserved for Nora's bookshop during the day, but it was well past closing hours. No one should be back here, and even if they were, the truck windows were tinted. So yeah, that was how she convinced herself that this was okay.

And when Brad's hand slid under her skirt and started tugging at her leggings, she didn't stop him. No, she shoved the leggings and her panties down until they were around her ankles. She should feel ridiculous but instead when his big hand cupped her mound she shuddered. She was mostly clothed but felt more exposed, more vulnerable than she ever had.

She'd never done anything like this before. Had only ever had sex with a boyfriend, and usually after a whole lot of dates. Never in a vehicle, and not with a man who she'd shared only a couple kisses with.

This was new, and she decided right then and there she wasn't going to overthink this. She was leaving in two weeks. This would just be fun. She could freak out later.

When Brad slid a finger inside her, she pretty much forgot to think altogether.

"So tight," he murmured against her mouth, sliding another finger inside her as he pulled back to look down at her. "I'm going to make you come." His words sounded a lot like an order.

Fallon found herself simply nodding as her inner walls tightened around his thick fingers.

Continuing to watch her, he slowly drew his fingers out of her slickness, then just as slowly pushed back in. With her leggings tangled around her ankles and the way she was plastered against the seat, it was impossible to move much, but she rolled her hips into his hold as much as she could.

"You know how many nights I've thought about you, about this?" His voice was dark, seductive as he stared at her mouth again.

She wasn't sure if the question was rhetorical or not and it didn't matter, because she couldn't answer. Her nipples were painful pebbles against her bra and all she wanted to do was shed the rest of her clothing—and his—and feel him skin to skin.

To hell with any consequences.

"Way too many, Fallon." The way he said her name was like a prayer.

She automatically tightened around him, and he crushed his mouth to hers again, even as he continued those slow, steady strokes inside her.

The man was determined to drive her crazy. And had been for a while. In the year since she'd moved home, every time she saw him it was like a switch flipped inside her.

She moaned into his mouth when he started teasing her clit with his thumb, rubbing the sensitive bundle of nerves with just enough pressure to make her insane.

"You like that?" he murmured before biting her bottom lip.

She jerked against him and let out another moan of approval. *Like it?* She freaking loved it. "More," she managed to rasp out as he kissed a little path along her jaw that seemed to spark to life nerve endings she hadn't known she even had.

He increased the pressure on her clit just as he began thrusting his fingers faster and faster inside her.

Just like that, she was coming apart in his arms, her inner walls clenching convulsively as a sharp orgasm tore through her. She jerked against the seat and wrapped her arms around him, digging her fingers against his back as he made the sexiest rumbling, growly sound against her neck.

Her climax seemed to go on forever, the only thing interrupting it the little squawk of his radio. Blinking, she stared up at Brad as he let out a curse, grabbing for his radio with one hand.

Though he kept his other hand cupped around her mound, his fingers still buried in her slickness. She tightened her inner walls around them as he answered his radio—which earned her a soft groan from him.

"I'm on my way," he said after a brief conversation with one of his deputies. Apparently there was an issue at one of the local bars with a tourist getting too rowdy.

Groaning again, he withdrew his fingers from her—and licked them. Aaaand another rush of heat flooded her core. Talk about hot. No way could she find her voice after that.

He pinned her with a hard stare as he then slid his radio onto his belt and not so subtly adjusted himself. "This isn't over."

Oh, he was right about that. This was definitely not over. Taking herself by surprise, Fallon reached between their bodies and cupped his erection through his pants. She rubbed her hand over his hard length once, twice—

"I don't want to leave you." He grabbed her wrist, pulled her hand away as he kissed her again. "Not over," he murmured as he somehow managed to extricate himself from the truck. "Lock the door when I close it." The slight command in his voice sent another rush of heat between her legs. And she did as he said.

Once she was alone in the front seat, she righted her clothes and started the heater. Because she suddenly realized how very cold it was without Brad's big body covering her.

As she steered out of the parking lot, warmth spread through her and she shifted slightly against the seat. She was slick from her orgasm and still turned on. All she could think about was the next time she and Brad did this. Without any interruptions.

Even as a teeny bit of mortification slid through her veins and she wondered what he must think about her after tonight, she still knew there would be a next time. It was inevitable.

CHAPTER TWO

Brad steeled himself to see Fallon as he entered Nora's Books and Brew. It was a little after ten, and Fallon had texted him that she'd meet him here. He'd called her, wanting to lock down a time and place for a date.

He always had to mentally prepare to see her, because every time he did it was an assault to his senses. She was petite, with thick auburn hair she usually wore up, and was the sexiest woman he'd ever met. Her bright blue eyes and genuine smile had drawn him in initially, and her spitfire personality had nearly knocked him on his ass. She was all attitude.

The little bell jingled again as the door shut behind him. A steady hum of voices, mostly female, and laughter filled the shop. He frowned as he glanced around at the full high-top tables, surprised he didn't see her. Her brother's truck was parked a block back on the curb of Main Street and he assumed she was still driving it. When he'd passed the truck, he'd had to fight a hard on. Every time he saw that truck he was going to think of her and the way she'd looked as she'd climaxed against his fingers, her sweet body writhing underneath him.

He rolled his shoulders once. He couldn't be thinking about that right now. If he let his mind head down that path he was going to get kicked out for public indecency.

She'd ignored his call, instead texting him back telling him she'd be here, keeping her text vague. The woman was hot and cold and making him crazy. And okay, he liked the chase. A lot. He liked everything about Fallon O'Connor. Had since the moment she'd moved back into town a year ago.

He'd remembered her as the kid sister of the O'Connor brothers. Seeing Fallon all grown up, and literally walking, talking sex appeal had moved her from the category of the O'Connors' sister to the woman he wanted to date. More than date. But he was taking things as slow as possible because she was skittish.

He'd thought that after Christmas things would finally move forward with them, but Fallon had practically fallen off the planet the last month and a half. Last night in her brother's truck had definitely shocked him. In a very good way. When he'd seen her walking alone—on Valentine's Day, no less—he'd had to stop her. To talk to her. And do more, as it turned out.

"Hey, sheriff," Nora Cassidy, the owner, said as she wiped off one of the high-top tables. "I don't think I've ever seen you out of uniform."

He nodded politely, not wanting to get into small talk. Not when the woman who consumed his every waking thought was somewhere nearby. "I'm meeting Fallon here."

"Oh, she's in the bookstore. It's crazy about her leaving, huh?" Nora said almost absently. "If we have a going-away party I'll make sure to let you know." She tucked the white cloth into her apron and had moved on to talk to a group of customers before he'd processed her words.

Leaving?

A low buzz built along his spine as he made his way through the throng of tables, nodding politely at people instead of stopping to talk. Where was Fallon going?

And why hadn't she told him?

As he entered the quieter, empty bookstore, his heart rate kicked up a hundred notches when Fallon stepped out of the storeroom. She had on dark leggings, knee-high boots, and a leopard print tunic that stretched across her full breasts. She didn't notice him at first so he took the uninterrupted moment to drink her in. Normally when he saw her he was working and in professional mode. He'd been hiding his attraction to her for the better part of a year because she'd never shown any interest—until the Christmas Eve party.

One minute they'd been making idle talk in her parents' kitchen and the next she'd asked him to help her get something out of the pantry. That had been the first time he'd ever seen a true spark of interest from her. And it had been more than a spark once they'd been alone in the pantry. Then it had been full-on lust as they'd gone at each other like starving wolves. He was still starving for another taste of her. Last night in the truck hadn't been nearly enough.

"Hey, Red." She finally glanced over as he covered the distance between them.

Her cheeks heated up as she met his gaze. "Boy Scout."

And for the first time since he'd met her, he realized that the nickname was a way to keep a wall up between them. But he didn't care what she called him.

Unable to stop himself, he reached out and cupped her cheek, stroked her soft skin with his thumb. He wasn't sure he had the right to touch her like this yet, but after last night, he was taking a calculated risk. "Nora said you're leaving?" God he hoped he'd misunderstood her.

She cleared her throat, but didn't break his gaze or his hold. If anything she leaned into it. "Yeah. I got accepted into culinary school. In California. I leave in two weeks."

The news was a punch to the solar plexus even as he noted that she didn't seem excited about it. "Why do you make that sound like a bad thing?" Which to him, it was. *Damn it.* He'd barely had a chance to see where this thing with them could go.

"It's not. Look, Brad—"

That sounded a lot like she planned to give him the "last night was fun, but nothing else is happening between us" type of speech, so he did the only sane thing. He backed her against the storeroom door and kissed her. There was no one in the bookstore, and even if there was, he didn't care at the moment.

There was no pause, no push from her. Instead she moaned into his mouth, grinding up against him as if they'd been made for each other.

For how he felt now, they absolutely had. He'd known attractive women, had been with some, but he'd never believed in this type of heart-stopping, "everything funneling out until no one else existed" lust at first sight. Until Fallon. He wanted more than just a couple hookups, however. He wanted something real with this woman. If only she'd give him the chance.

He reached behind her, twisted the door handle to the storeroom and guided them inside. Still kissing her, he locked the door behind them. This way lay insanity, but he didn't care. His cock pressed up against his zipper, demanding to be inside her right now.

Which again, was insane.

He was respected in the community, and it was a huge part of the reason he'd gotten his job. What they were doing wasn't smart.

He *still* didn't care. He didn't care about anything other than Fallon as he shoved his hands through her thick hair. She tasted like coffee and mint. And his. All his.

He groaned into her mouth as she consumed him, arching her body against his in a way that felt as if their bodies fit together like puzzle pieces.

Breathing hard, Fallon pulled back and stared up at him. "Is this smart?" she whispered. Her eyes were wide, but filled with undeniable hunger. For him.

He'd been locking down his attraction to her for a year. Now that he'd gotten a full-on taste, he didn't want to stop. Because he was afraid if they did, she'd walk away. He wasn't above locking her down with pleasure. "You want to stop?" He sure didn't.

She shook her head, her red hair swishing around her face. There was a hint of indecision in her gaze, however.

He might want her, but he wanted her completely into this. No regrets or second-guessing. "Let's just leave—"

Fallon went up on tiptoe, brushing her lips against his. "You bring out this wild side of me," she murmured, nipping at his bottom lip.

The feeling was mutual. He'd always been a rule follower. Her nickname for him wasn't far off the mark and didn't bother him—but she made him feel out of control.

And he liked it.

He wanted to hold on to her and not let go because some intrinsic part of him knew he'd regret it if he didn't.

"Maybe I'm not the Boy Scout you think I am," he said, pinning her to the nearest wall. He sure wasn't acting like one right now. There wasn't much space because of all the shelving so he'd take what he could get.

She just snorted as she grappled with his belt. He couldn't believe they were doing this. In the storeroom of a store neither of them owned. He didn't do things like this. Until Fallon, apparently.

He'd planned to take her on a date—multiple dates—then give her a lot of foreplay, to tease her until she was coming against his mouth before they finally got completely naked. This definitely hadn't been in his plans for the day. His fantasies? *Oh, yeah.* When he went to push her top up, she batted his hands away and shoved his pants and boxers down his hips.

"This is about both of us," he managed to rasp out as she grasped his cock. Holy hell, she felt good.

"Not right now it's not." Her voice was a whisper as she pinned her gaze to his, stroking him once, long and hard. "And this is about me, anyway. I want to watch you come. I want to *make* you come."

His brain short-circuited and he got lost in her electric blue eyes and the feel of her hand on him. The base of his spine tingled with pent-up need as she stroked him again.

He'd had stuff he planned to say to her, make clear to her—like, this wasn't casual for him—but he couldn't string a sentence together as he savored the feel of her soft hand around his hard length. So he cupped her cheek and brought his lips to hers as she continued stroking him to orgasm.

Over and over, she pumped him until they were both moaning, their breathing overly loud in the storeroom, and all he wanted to do was drown in her.

"Gonna come," he growled out after what felt like an eternity. While he'd rather come inside her, rather feel her tight body wrapped around him, this was the second-best thing. Her hand was so smooth and silky, his own hand would never do again after this.

She bit his bottom lip, the action setting him off, and he let go. Tightening his jaw, he forced himself not to cry out as loudly as he wanted to. Instead, he buried his face against her neck as he held the back of her head in a dominating, possessive grip.

There was no denying he felt possessive of her. Didn't matter that it made no sense — he wanted this woman all day, every day. And he wouldn't share her.

When he finally came back to his senses and pulled back to look at her, she appeared as dazed as he felt. "That was incredible." Okay, it was the single hottest thing he'd ever done, and all she'd done was stroke him off. Maybe it was the setting, or more likely the fact that it was Fallon who'd just brought him to climax in a storeroom in the middle of the damn day that made this all the more intense.

She gave him a sweet, almost shy smile as she blinked a couple times. "I can't believe we just did that," she whispered.

"No kidding." And he wasn't done just yet. He'd started to reach for the top of her pants when there was a knock on the storeroom door. They both froze for a fraction of a second before he grabbed some wipes from a nearby shelf.

"Uh, hold on!" Fallon called out, her voice shaky.

They quickly cleaned up, and even though it pained him to do so, he zipped up and straightened his clothes. Though he was pretty sure that whoever was behind that door was going to know what they'd been doing. Or at least guess.

He stayed glued to Fallon's side as she opened the door to find, no surprise, Nora on the other side. The other woman's eyes widened as she looked between the two of them, but she didn't say anything — just snickered as she hurried past them, murmuring something about grabbing stock.

"I could die of embarrassment right now," Fallon whispered as she took his hand in hers and pulled him back into the bookstore. She kept going until they exited out onto the sidewalk.

An icy wind whipped around them and he instinctively wrapped his arm around her shoulders. To his surprise, she didn't push him away, just buried her face against his chest.

"What the heck is wrong with us?" Her voice was garbled, but all his focus was on her sweet vanilla scent and the way she felt in his arms.

"Not a damn thing." Brad didn't care who on the street saw them. If anything, he wanted every man in town to know she was off-limits. That she belonged to him and they'd better keep their distance. "How long do we have before you leave?"

She looked up at him then, still in his embrace, which did something foreign to his insides. He liked this closeness, craved more of it.

"I leave in two weeks, which is why starting anything now is crazy. Right?" She tentatively placed her hands on his chest.

"I just want to take you on a date." *Liar, liar.* "Let's start there and see where things go before ending anything."

She pushed out a hard sigh and tension built in his chest until she spoke again. "Okay. But I can't do anything today. Or tomorrow. My friend called me last minute in a panic. She needs help prepping for a wedding. There's a lot to do and she's in a bind. I got the call right before..." Her cheeks flushed the sexiest shade of pink. "Ah, right before you showed up. Oh, and I can't Monday either. Family dinner thing."

He wanted to claim her mouth again, but resisted the urge. Barely. "What about Tuesday, then? I work until six. I can pick you up a little before seven." It was only two days away. He could deal with that.

When she nodded and gave him one of those sweet, genuine smiles, he felt it bone deep. He wanted to wrap her up in his arms, take her back to his place and not leave for weeks. And he wasn't even going to think about the fact that she was leaving in two weeks and heading across the country.

Though he knew it would invite town gossip, he leaned down and brushed his lips over hers, the barest hint of a kiss. "I'll see you Tuesday night."

She nodded and stepped away from him. He started to offer to walk her to her vehicle, then she gave him a wry smile. "And now I have to go back in there to grab my purse—and explain to my friend what we were doing in her storeroom."

He barely stifled a laugh. "Pretty sure you won't need to explain."

Fallon covered her face with her hands for a moment. "I still can't believe we did that."

He couldn't either, but he didn't regret it. He couldn't regret anything to do with her.

CHAPTER THREE

Fallon stood back with her friend Halley and surveyed the surroundings of the impending wedding reception. Halley had just started a catering business and was quickly learning to deal with the bumps and obstacles that came with it. Usually in the form of family members who couldn't seem to remember that weddings were about the bride and groom. So far it didn't seem Halley was having that problem with this particular wedding. She was just engaging in standard fretting.

The reception was medium-sized and right on the lake of a local country club. Fallon had actually been invited to the wedding because the bride's mom was friends with her mom, so she'd been planning to attend. She didn't mind that she'd missed the actual nuptials. The reception would be where the fun was.

Now that she'd helped prep the food and set up, she was going to be enjoying the reception at least, since the waitstaff on Halley's payroll would be taking over from here.

"Everything looks great," she murmured, squeezing Halley's forearm.

Her friend bit her bottom lip, her dark eyes slightly panicked as she scanned the indoor seating. "Yeah?"

Everything was done in soft cream and lavender with big centerpieces of white roses. Instead of the standard lighting, they'd strung up strands of lights over swathes of tulle that had been hung just for the event, giving it a fairyland feel. Outside, the same style twinkle lights crisscrossed over a huge dance floor ringed by lamp heaters to ward off the cold. Apparently the bride had wanted an outdoor reception but hadn't wanted to wait longer to get married, so this was their compromise by getting married in February. With the heat lamps, people could move indoors *and* outdoors as they pleased.

"Yes. It's perfect. The food is perfect. And you're perfect."

Halley snorted at that, but the tension in her shoulders immediately drained away as she put her hands on her hips. "You're right. I've got this." She spoke into her headset, communicating with someone on her crew before turning to Fallon again. "Thank you for all you've done. I'm going to add payment for all the extra hours you helped with."

Fallon had already been hired by Halley to do the cake and other desserts, but helping prep everything else was beyond her scope of duties. She'd done it because they were friends. "You don't have to—"

"I do. Your time is valuable. And…I know you're leaving soon, but if for some reason you decide not to, I'd like to work with you again. Or heck, whenever you move back home—if you do. The cake is gorgeous, Fallon. I'd be open to something exclusive with you."

She found her face heating up at the compliment, but she nodded as she digested her friend's words. "Thanks. If I stay, we'll talk."

The four-layer cake was one of her best creations and she'd be adding it to her portfolio. Each layer looked like a bundle of roses, the layers moving from a dark purple, fading to lavender, then cream. And she'd added little edible butterflies throughout the layers. It matched the color scheme perfectly but it was almost a shame to cut into it. Almost—because it was buttercream and delicious. A lot of pastry chefs used fondant for cakes, but the downside was they didn't taste good. With her designs, people got edible art, flavor *and* decadence.

"Just got a call from the bride's mother that the guests will be arriving soon, so I'll see you later." Halley hurried away, her kitten heels clicking against the indoor dance floor as she crossed it.

Fallon made her way toward one of the bars since the bartender had already set up. So had the DJ, and an upbeat Pharrell Williams song was playing.

"Hey, sweetheart." Her mom's voice made her turn around just as she'd taken a seat at one of the wooden, high-backed stools.

Fallon smiled at the sight of her mother. While they had a complicated relationship, she loved her mom. At five foot two, with auburn hair and the same blue eyes—and sometimes the same temper—it would be impossible to hide that they were related. Not that she wanted to. "You're here early."

"We parked along the curb across the street from the church instead of in the parking lot. You know how your father hates traffic. Ah, two white wines," her mom said to the bartender before turning back to Fallon.

She glanced over her mom's shoulder toward the entryway. "Where is Dad, anyway?"

"Parking. He dropped me off so I wouldn't get these dirty." She stretched out a foot, showing off sparkly black-heeled platform pumps.

Fallon's eyes narrowed slightly. "Those look familiar."

Her mom gave her a smug, oh-so-familiar smile. "You must have left them when you moved out."

"Or more likely you snagged them when you were at my house last week."

"Dropping off food, I might add." Her mom gave a little sniff that she'd perfected over the years, indicating the conversation was done. "Let's not talk about my shoes," she said as a few couples and families strolled in, all talking animatedly about how beautiful the ceremony had been. Some made their way directly to the dance floor, courtesy of the DJ who had a great playlist going, while others beelined for the appetizer table. "I want to talk about you," her mother continued.

Fallon blinked once. "Ah, okay. What's up?"

"Oh, nothing. I just heard from one of the girls at the salon that she saw you with the sheriff."

Fallon kept her expression blank before pasting on an equally neutral smile. "Oh yeah, I saw him at Nora's shop. We were both grabbing coffee."

"And?"

"And what?" Her mom's eyes narrowed and Fallon realized she was just fishing. She didn't know anything. If she did, her mom would be asking more personal questions. And oh thank God, she wasn't.

"He's such a nice man. And he's done such a great job running Holly."

Fallon nearly snorted. He *was* a nice man. A nice man who'd given her the best orgasm of her life in the front seat of a truck. "Agreed. He's a great sheriff."

Her mom had started to say more when Terry Mathers, a man Fallon had gone to high school with, strolled up to them and slung an arm around her mom's shoulders. He still looked like he could be in high school with that baby face and dimples that appeared in his cheeks as he smiled broadly. "Hey, Mrs. O'Connor. Can I steal Fallon for a dance?"

She glanced over and saw through the open doors that the outdoor dance floor was already filling up with people. They weren't wasting any time enjoying themselves. Fallon knew from Halley that the newly married couple were doing pictures at the church and had instructed everyone to head to the reception for appetizers and drinks. It was a smart way to do things—they'd get a lot of their pictures out of the way and people wouldn't be standing around waiting. They'd get to enjoy themselves before the couple made their big entrance.

Her mom patted Terry's cheek once. "Look at you, all handsome and dressed up. And you'll have to ask Fallon, not me."

Since she was ready to escape the current conversation with her mom, she slid off the stool and kissed her mom's cheek before linking her arm through Terry's. "How've you been? I haven't seen you in months." While Holly was small, it wasn't *that* small. She loved running into people she'd gone to school with, especially since so many of her classmates had gone away for college or trade schools, and in some cases, the military.

"Good, started my own business."

"Yeah?"

"Yep. Personal trainer. I have a job at the local gym but I also freelance. So if you're ever looking for a personal trainer let me know."

She arched an eyebrow. "Are you saying you think I need one?"

"Ah…"

She nudged him in the side. "I'm messing with you."

Letting out a breath, he grinned again. "Hope you can keep up with me on the dance floor."

"Get ready to find out." She really wished she was here with Brad, and wondered what kind of dancer he was. Or if he even liked dancing.

When they reached the outside dance floor she was glad that another fast song was playing so she wouldn't have to spend more time making small talk. She liked Terry, but he had a look in his eyes that told her he was interested in more than just a dance. While he was nice and definitely handsome, only one man occupied all her thoughts. And she shouldn't even be thinking about Brad.

Of course, that was *all* she'd been doing. Obsessing over the sexy man and counting down until their date Tuesday—and what would come afterward.

She had no doubt what would come after.

Plenty of fun, naked times. She barely knew the man but that didn't seem to matter. Their chemistry was off the charts and she genuinely liked him, could see something real developing between them.

As the dance with Terry came to an end, a slow song started to play. She inwardly winced, not wanting to slow dance with him or anyone *not* Brad. Before she had to make a decision, Brad stepped into her line of sight right behind Terry.

She blinked once, her gaze traveling over him in a suit. The man certainly cleaned up nicely. He always looked sexy in his uniform but this was a different side to him—and he looked a bit like he was ready to punch sweet, harmless Terry in the face. She blinked again, wondering if she was imagining things.

"Hey, sheriff," Terry said as he realized that Brad was moving in behind him.

"Terry. Hope you don't mind if I cut in." Brad nodded once at the other man but didn't take his eyes off Fallon as he smoothly sidestepped so that he was in front of her. The move was so slick she wondered if Terry even realized Brad had flat-out cut him off to get to her.

"No, of course not."

Without pause Brad pulled her into his arms for the upcoming dance, and she was under the impression that no matter what Terry had said, Brad would've cut in. Which seemed very un-Boy Scout.

"You look beautiful," he murmured, his dark eyes locked on hers.

The song was slow, seductive, and with the twinkling lights above them she felt as if they were the only two people in the world. "You look pretty handsome yourself. I like your tie," she murmured. His suit was dark and clearly he'd had it tailored to fit his large frame, and the tie was a pretty, light blue.

"I bought it because it reminded me of your eyes."

She sucked in a sharp breath at his admission. He really held nothing back. She cleared her throat even as she pressed closer to his muscular body. She could really lose herself with this man, get wrapped up with him in more ways than one. "I didn't know you were coming."

His grip around her waist tightened and the subtle scent of his woodsy cologne teased her senses, making her a teeny bit lightheaded. "Yeah, I'm friends with the groom's side of the family. Served with one of his brothers."

Darius, the groom, had a big family. "Darius and Dawn are so young." They almost seemed too young to get married at twenty and twenty-one, but Fallon's own parents had been married even younger.

He nodded once. "You come with a date?"

She laughed lightly at his bluntness, shook her head. "No. Did you?"

"No—and I would have asked you but I returned my invitation

with just me attending checked long before this thing between us started."

She raised an eyebrow. "Thing?"

His gaze darkened slightly as it landed on her lips. The way he watched her mouth was like a physical caress she felt all the way to her toes. "I don't know what to call this."

No kidding. And she didn't feel like trying to figure that out, either. Not when she was leaving in two weeks.

"So what's the plan after culinary school?" His deep voice wrapped around her as sure as his firm grip did. She wanted to sink into it, bury her face against his neck and inhale.

"I'm not actually sure. I worked in various bakeries and restaurants while in college and I honestly can't see myself working for anyone else. At least not long term. It's why I've been doing contract work since I moved home." Which brought her back to the food truck idea. Once it had lodged itself in her mind, she couldn't let it go. She'd even started making a business plan for what she'd do her first year.

"Do you need culinary school to run a food truck?"

"No, but…" Yeah, she wasn't going to go there. She almost felt like she'd be a fraud opening up her own business without the education to back it up. Except she did have a degree in business and she'd worked in enough bakeries to know what would and wouldn't work. For her, at least. "So what are you doing after the reception?" she asked, wanting to get to more important things. The reception wasn't supposed to go super late, and as far as she was concerned, the night would still be young. And she wanted to spend more time with Brad. No reason to wait a couple days until their date.

"I'm leaving a little early to stop by my dad's. I haven't been able to see him all week." That made her melt just a little.

His dad lived in the local Holly retirement community, which was more like a village unto itself. "I saw him a few days ago when I was visiting my aunt. He challenged me to a chess match."

At that, Brad grinned. "Sounds about right. Want to come with me tonight?"

"I'd like that." The answer was out before she could overthink it. And she really did like his dad. "Ah, I caught a ride here with Halley though. If it's not too far out of your way—"

"I'll take you home afterward." His voice deepened as much as his gaze darkened.

A shiver rolled through her at the heat in his words. As the song came to an end, she spotted two of her brothers eyeing her and Brad suspiciously from the edge of the dance floor.

"Fair warning, my brothers are watching you. You might want to steer clear of them. They probably want to grill you about us or something." Nosy older brothers that they were, it would be so typical of Maguire and Nolan to try and corner him later.

Brad just snorted, clearly unconcerned. "I'm planning to head out in an hour. Is that okay?"

She nodded, and found herself oddly disappointed when he stepped slightly back from her. His warmth and the feel of his arms around her were heaven. She didn't want distance. She wanted to burrow into the man and not let go.

"I think Halley needs you," he murmured, his voice slightly frustrated as he tilted his chin toward the other side of the dance floor.

Sure enough, her friend had a panicked look on her face and was waving a hand at her. "I'm guessing it's a dessert emergency. I'll meet you by the bar in an hour if I don't see you before then?"

"Deal." Moving with the stealth of a predator, he leaned down and brushed his lips over hers as if it was the most natural thing in the world.

She blinked. Then blinked again. The man might as well have hung up a neon sign right on Main Street announcing that she was his. That was such a bold, guy move, telling all other men to stay away. She couldn't believe he'd done it right in front of her brothers.

But...she liked it.

Ignoring some raised eyebrows as she made her way through the growing crowd of people on the dance floor, she hurried to Halley, who now just looked a bit shocked.

"You and the sexy sheriff?" her friend asked.

"Didn't you need help with something?" Because if Halley had pulled her away from Brad for nothing, they were going to have words.

"Oh, right. The bride and groom are set to arrive in the next ten minutes and I want to get the cake out of the cooler. I don't trust anyone but you to help me move it. I'm terrified I'll drop it. Come on." She turned and was off in a flurry of movement in typical Halley style.

Following after her, all Fallon could do was count down the minutes until she was alone with Brad.

CHAPTER FOUR

Brad tried not to stare at Fallon and the jackass dancing with her. After she'd helped Halley, someone had asked her to dance. Then another guy, before he'd had a chance to move in. He didn't want to be annoyed, didn't want to be that guy. It wasn't like he had a claim on her. But that didn't mean he had to like it when another man was dancing with her, had his hands on her hips.

Those hands better not go any lower.

Tightening his jaw, he turned away, needing to be *anywhere* but here, but he ran right into Fallon's mother. The woman was a force of nature, just like her daughter.

"Hello, sheriff. You're looking handsome tonight." She gave him a warm smile.

"You look lovely." That seemed like a safe enough word. And she did. In fact, if she was an older version of Fallon, he had no doubt Fallon was going to be a stunner for the rest of her life.

"It's so nice seeing you out of uniform. So you and my daughter are seeing each other now?" She took a sip of her white wine, watching him carefully over the rim of the glass in the way a predator watches prey.

He nearly jerked back at her bluntness but caught himself. He'd survived his Marine Corps drill instructor. He could deal with a little information gathering from Fallon's mom. "We're friends, ma'am." He wanted more, but didn't think Fallon would appreciate him saying anything else—especially not to her mother. A woman who Brad knew liked to run betting pools on various would-be couples around town. She'd started a pool on her own son Jackson and how long it would take him to get together with Nora. Brad still wasn't sure who'd won that one.

"Well that's good. Because she *is* leaving soon, as I'm sure you know." She continued to watch him with eagle-eyed precision.

"I do." And he wasn't happy about it at all.

"And she's a busy woman. But I guess all you young people are." Fluffing her dark auburn hair, she made a little tsking sound.

He was thirty, not exactly young in the way she made it sound, and he wasn't sure where she was going with this.

"When I was younger I couldn't imagine dating more than one person at a time, but I guess that's just normal now."

"Ah..." How did he even respond to that? He wasn't dating anyone else. Wait...was Fallon? He frowned, his gaze straying to the dance floor again. Fallon was stepping away from her dance partner, looking beautiful in a blue dress the same color as her eyes. It hugged her petite body in all the right places.

When she caught his gaze, she made a subtle motion for him to follow her. She didn't have to tell him twice. And this conversation was headed into uncomfortable territory. He'd graduated college with honors, had served in the Marine Corps—and been to Afghanistan more than once, but Mrs. O'Connor had a way of making him feel like he was in elementary school when she talked to him.

"Sweetheart, I see my husband and he's going to push me around the dance floor. But I'll see you later." She smiled and squeezed his forearm once before disappearing into the crowd.

He was sure he responded, but wasn't sure what he'd said as he headed in the other direction. Because all his focus was on Fallon and that beacon of a blue dress. The bride had nothing on her as far as he was concerned. No one did.

When he covertly slid out a side door into one of the hallways, he saw her opening another door about twenty feet away. He'd been to the country club before but wasn't familiar with the layout. Her face lit up when she saw him.

"In here," she said before ducking out of sight behind the door.

It turned out to be a sitting room of sorts with cushioned chairs, two couches, a minibar—and the windows that should be facing one of the pools were hidden behind floor-to-ceiling striped drapes. The only thing he cared about was the privacy factor, because he planned to get another taste of Fallon. He wanted her coming against his mouth this time. He didn't plan to wait until later either.

"What was my mom talking to you about?" Fallon shut the door behind him and locked it before she turned and planted her hands on her hips.

He drank her in from head to toe, hoping she'd brought him in here for a very specific reason. She was petite and slender, and the dress she had on accentuated her curves. He wasn't sure how she walked in those high heels but he liked what they did to her calves.

"Brad?" She stepped closer, looking up at him expectantly. The subtle scent of her perfume wrapped around him.

What had she asked him? "Oh, she was telling me what a busy woman you are and I'm pretty sure she insinuated that you're dating other people." The thought of that rankled him.

Fallon just rolled her eyes. "Typical. I love that woman but she makes me crazy."

"Well, are you?" He took a step closer so that only inches separated them, inhaled her sweet vanilla scent.

"Am I what?"

"Dating people?"

Her lips quirked up at the corners. "Are you?"

"Nope."

"Neither am I."

"Good. You're mine until you leave." *Smooth, man. What happened to subtle?*

Her eyes narrowed the slightest bit. "Is that right?"

Yeah it was.

Going on instinct, he leaned down to kiss her again. As if drawn by that same invisible force, she moved in at the same time. Once again he was desperate to taste her. They had to leave the reception soon, should probably be out there talking to people, but he didn't much give a fuck as he backed her against some sort of bookshelf.

Not when Fallon arched into him and linked her fingers behind his neck. As her tongue danced against his, he rolled his hips against hers. He wanted her to feel how much she affected him because this woman owned him.

When he was in uniform—which was almost all the time—and saw her out in public he was always careful not to stare too long or linger in her presence. It wasn't like he needed to see her to fantasize about her. But when she was right in front of him it was impossible to keep his body under control. Something that had never been a problem until her.

Feeling her body against his, her tongue teasing his, was sensory overload. Especially when he'd already had a small taste of her.

She dug her fingers into his shoulders and rolled her hips against his in the sexiest writhing motion that had all his muscles pulling taut. "I think we have a problem," she murmured against his mouth, even as she slid her hands over his arms, squeezing and making appreciative moaning sounds.

"Problem?" He nibbled along her jaw, drowning in her scent, in holding her like this.

"This. *Us*. In pseudo-public places."

He laughed lightly as he reached her earlobe. He'd never been one for public anything, but if he had a chance to touch Fallon, taste her, the location didn't much seem to matter. "Not a problem for me," he murmured before biting her earlobe gently. "Besides, you locked the door." Which meant he was going to do exactly what he'd been fantasizing about right now.

Well, one of the things.

His erection pushed against his zipper as he went down on his knees in front of her.

She let out a breathy little sound as she looked down at him, confusion filling her blue eyes. Until he pushed her dress up to her hips to reveal a nude-colored thong. This was what fantasies were made of.

"What are you doing?" she whispered, even though it was just the two of them.

Obviously she knew what he was doing, but he must have taken her off guard. Good. Her Boy Scout didn't mind being bad with her. Without responding, he slid his fingers under the edges of the material and slowly began pulling it down her legs.

"This is crazy." He barely heard her this time—and she didn't make a move to stop him. No, she stepped out of the thong when he got it to her ankles.

Now she was free of the only thing stopping him from doing exactly what he wanted. Keeping his gaze pinned to hers, watching her eyes dilate, her chest rising and falling as she gazed back at him, had him on the wire's edge of control.

"Spread your legs." Impatience he couldn't hide laced his voice. He wanted to see all of her. Taste all of her.

She immediately did as he said, her breathing growing even more erratic. Not taking his gaze off hers, he reached between her legs, slid a finger along her folds. Her incredibly slick folds. Her dress was shoved up to her hips, and with her in her heels standing like this in front of him, so exposed, his dick was never going to go down.

"This for me?" He knew it was but he needed to hear the confirmation.

She nodded, her auburn hair swishing around her face, highlighting her flushed cheeks. He loved that she wore her emotions out in the open.

"Aloud."

"Yes. You know it is," she rasped out.

He slid a finger inside her, shuddered when she tightened around him. He'd felt her the other night in the darkness of the truck, but seeing her displayed like this—all for him—was something else altogether.

"I'm going to taste you." He wasn't sure why he was telling her. It was pretty obvious. When she tightened around his finger again, heat punched through him. She liked his dirty talk.

He could have stretched this out all day, but his patience was gone. He'd been building to this for a year.

"I've wanted to do this from practically the moment I saw you a year ago." Leaning forward, he buried his face between her legs.

Yeah, he could have worked up to it, but he wanted a reaction, wanted to shock her senses—wanted her to come against his mouth.

"Brad." She moaned it as she slid her fingers through his hair. Not pushing him away, but clutching onto him and holding him close.

He loved the sound of his name on her lips as much as her taste. She was sweet perfection. Flicking his tongue against her clit, he savored her moans as he began moving his finger in and out of her. He'd learned exactly how much pressure she liked the other night, and he planned to use that knowledge to bring her even more pleasure.

She rolled her hips with each thrust of his finger, each teasing tongue stroke. When she tried to clench her thighs together, he pressed on her inner thigh with his free hand. He wanted enough room to finish this.

"Oh…this won't take long." Her fingers tightened in his hair again, the movements of her hips growing more erratic, unsteady.

"Throw your leg over my shoulder," he murmured against her.

Again, without pause she did it, digging her heel into his back. Oh, hell yeah. This gave him the best position to taste her. He added another finger, increased the tempo of his thrusts.

"Oh!" She jolted once before her inner walls gripped him tight.

He started to add another finger, then she began convulsing around him faster and faster, her climax hitting hard and sharp.

He increased the pressure of his tongue on her clit, massaging that little bundle of nerves harder and harder until she shouted out his name.

"Brad! Enough."

No, it wasn't enough. He was going to wring every ounce of pleasure out of her. That invisible force was driving him, her pleasure the only thing that mattered. He wanted to imprint himself on her mind and body. To make sure she fantasized about this, about *them*, about the pleasure he could give her.

Only when the feel of her contractions around his fingers started to subside and she gently squeezed his head did he stop and look up at her.

She stared down at him in a daze, blinking a couple times before she gave him the sweetest smile. "That was incredible."

No, *she* was incredible. And he was addicted to making her orgasm. Seeing that expression on her face when she came, that blissful aftermath when she was sated was... There was no word for it. But he wanted to see it again and again.

He pushed to his feet and cupped her cheek with one hand. Her skin was soft against his palm. Leaning close, he whispered, "Soon you're going to do that while you're underneath me and I'm fully—"

She put a hand over his mouth. "You've got to stop. I'm already about to die from pleasure."

He just grinned against her palm before nipping at her fingers. "You're sexy when you come."

Her cheeks flushed crimson as she slid her arms around his waist, pulling him close. Going up on tiptoe, she made a move to kiss him. He didn't need any encouragement. Meeting her mouth with his, he flicked his tongue against the seam of her lips, demanding entrance. He loved that she was tasting herself, wanted to ask her if she liked it, but they needed to slow down for now.

She arched into him as he pushed her back against the shelving again and it took all his restraint to start pulling her dress back down her hips to cover her.

With a protest, she leaned slightly back, but didn't put any distance between them. "What are you doing?"

"We don't have the time or space for what I plan to do to you next."

Her cheeks flushed again and he got even harder, something he hadn't thought possible. She rubbed the front of his pants once and he gritted his teeth.

"You sure we don't?" Her voice was seductive, breathy.

On a razor's edge, he nodded and slowly eased back using control he was surprised he still had. "I'm sure. But I'm going to need a few minutes."

Her gaze dipped down to the front of his pants and she took her bottom lip between her teeth. The hunger he saw on her face almost pushed him over the edge.

"Go now, before I change my mind. I'll meet you by the valet in ten minutes."

After a pause, she nodded and hurried out the door—without her thong. He pocketed the scrap of material and decided he wasn't giving it back.

Now he just had to get his body under control so he could leave the room and face the people outside without giving himself away.

CHAPTER FIVE

"Thanks for letting me join you guys," Fallon said as she sat across from Brad's father, John, who was in his recliner.

The retirement community wasn't an actual care facility, but a neighborhood where only people over a certain age were allowed to live.

"Of course. The more the merrier. And one day I'm going to get you to play chess with me. I hear from your aunt that you're quite the master." In his sixties, John Fulton was adorable, though she knew he wouldn't like that description.

He was fit, since he still jogged a couple miles a day, the same height as Brad, and had a head full of salt-and-pepper hair—and had most of the single ladies in the community bringing him baked goods or casseroles every day of the week. At least that's what her aunt said.

Fallon grinned. Almost every time she came to visit her aunt she saw John. And every time he asked her for a chess match. "I'm okay."

"More than okay, I hear." Brad stepped into the room with three mugs of decaf coffee, set them on the rectangular table before handing his dad, then her, a mug. "And I also hear you have a victory dance."

"I might have a victory dance." And it was a little embarrassing that he knew about that. She took a sip of her coffee, and sighed in appreciation. Normally she didn't care for decaf but it was too late to drink regular. "Hey, how'd you know how I like my coffee?" Because it was prepared exactly the way she drank it—lots of cream and a bit of sugar.

"I pay attention." He shot her a brief, heated look that set off butterflies in her stomach before he turned back to his dad. "I don't think you'd like to play with her. She's not a good loser, from what I hear."

The older man nodded solemnly. "Ah, must be for the best, then."

She blinked, then narrowed her eyes at him. "I know what you're doing."

"Not sure what you mean." Brad lifted his mug to his mouth and she had a memory flash of him pressing his lips to something much more intimate. Heat flooded her body and she was suddenly very aware that she wasn't wearing anything under her dress. The bra was built-in and Brad had taken her thong and refused to give it back. Which was, okay, crazy hot.

"You're trying to goad me into playing him." Which she normally wouldn't mind, but she really liked Brad's father and she was pretty sure she would beat him. That wasn't arrogance either. She just hadn't lost to anyone since she was ten.

"Is it working?"

"Maybe, but…fair warning, I won't go easy on you," she said as she turned to face his dad. She might feel bad beating him, but it wasn't in her nature to toss a game.

John's eyes twinkled mischievously. "I wouldn't expect you to. Good, we can set up a date and then you can tell me about this food truck idea."

She shot Brad a surprised look. "You told him?" Which meant he'd been talking about her to his dad. That was…interesting. Warmth settled in her belly.

He lifted a broad shoulder. "It's a good idea."

"No, it's a great idea," John said. "And the retirement community would love something like that. All my friends watch those cooking shows. You'd probably make a bundle right here."

She'd actually thought about that as part of her business plan. Marketing to different areas for different days of the week. Being mobile would give her the ability to be flexible, see what worked and… Damn it, why was she even thinking of that? She'd just signed a six-month lease for a fully furnished place in San Francisco. It was close to the culinary school and surprisingly affordable. But *only* because they had a deal going with the school. She'd looked up the actual prices in the immediate area and they were three times what she'd be paying in Holly.

And sadly, at the moment she couldn't care less about it.

Fallon cleared her throat, really not wanting to talk about herself. "It's definitely something to think about. Though what I really want to know is how you scam all those single ladies into bringing you so many meals every week when you're not even dating anyone."

Brad nearly choked on his coffee but his dad just grinned. "You know about that?"

"My aunt says you have a racket going and that you're absolutely shameless."

Brad looked between the two of them, frowning. "What's she talking about?"

Now she laughed, hiding behind her mug of coffee.

John just shrugged, doing a good impression of looking helpless as he said, "Some days, the ladies in the community like to bring me meals. I can't very well say no."

Brad's eyes narrowed. "Some days?"

"Most days. Come on, son, do you really think I make all those casseroles for our weekly dinners?" Grinning, he turned back to Fallon. "Your aunt is the only one who doesn't bring me anything." She'd started to respond when he continued. "And the only woman I wish who would."

"I..." She cleared her throat. Yeah, not touching that one. Her aunt and Brad's father always flirted, but she'd just assumed it was harmless. Maybe there was more to it, though. That would be...weird.

"You can tell her I said that, too." He gave her a pointed look.

"All right, we're not turning Fallon into your matchmaker." Brad shook his head slightly, but was clearly fighting a grin.

And he looked just as adorable as his father. He was such a big, intimidating guy, but he was sweet, honorable, and visited his dad at least once a week. He went out of his way to help people and not just when he was in sheriff mode. She'd heard enough stories from her mother and others around town.

In that moment she realized how hard she could fall for him. If she was smart, she'd end things tonight. Walk away, make it clear that nothing else could happen between them. Not with her going all the way across the country for at least a year and a half. They could be friends, but that was it.

She must not be smart, however, because she couldn't do that. Not when she wanted another taste of him as much as she wanted her next breath. Losing him once she left would burn, but it would be worth it.

They stayed at his dad's another hour and a half before it was clear John was getting tired.

"I didn't realize you'd spent time with my dad before," Brad said as he reversed out of the driveway.

"He always pops over when I'm visiting my aunt. Speaking of, was he serious about her? Because I'm pretty sure she has a thing for him too."

He nodded. "Yeah, he's mentioned her more than... Actually, she's the only woman he's ever mentioned since moving here. Fulton men must have a thing for O'Connor women."

Smiling, she unstrapped her seatbelt and moved to the middle of the bench seat. "Well, this O'Connor woman definitely has a thing for you."

"Do you care that I told my dad about the food truck idea?"

"No. I don't think he'll spread it around. So, this is probably a dumb question, but is it weird for you if your dad starts dating?" Because as far as she knew, John hadn't dated since Brad's mom died of cancer ten years ago. At least according to her aunt.

"I wish he would. I've mentioned it a few times to him, but my dad has always done things his own way."

"Can I ask you some personal questions?" She figured if they were going to be intimate — and it was very clear that neither of them were going to stop this crazy train ride until she left a couple weeks from now — she wanted to know everything about him.

"You can ask anything." He slid his fingers through hers as they pulled up to a stoplight, and squeezed.

"Why did you get out of the Marine Corps?" All of her brothers had been in different branches of the military, and each of them had gotten out for different reasons. She was curious about Brad's but didn't want to be too pushy. Especially on a topic she knew from experience he might not want to talk about.

"I'd never planned to be in for life. Being deployed overseas is tough, and it's a young man's game. Though game is a shitty word for it. Basically I'd seen enough death, and friends die, and I knew if I didn't get out when I did, it would change me too much. There's so much good in the world but it's hard to see it when you're stuck in the sandbox. Six years was enough for me. I wanted to get my degree and settle down, move back here and put down roots. What about you? Why didn't you go to culinary school instead of college?"

"I wasn't sure what I wanted to do back then. I love baking and cooking but I guess I never thought I could have a career out of it. It just didn't occur to me that was possible. And I'm really good with numbers, so getting a business degree seemed like a smart decision. I'm glad I have it because I learned a lot, but I keep going back to food."

"This is only partially selfish reasoning, but you already have the culinary skills, plus the business background... Aren't you tempted to stay here and try to get a future business off the ground?"

"Yes, I'm very tempted." More than she wanted to think about. Because she was afraid that this thing blossoming between her and Brad was clouding her judgment. "But I've committed to this and I need to follow through. And—" She shut down what she'd been about to say, not wanting to open up too much, to make herself that vulnerable.

Brad wasn't going to let it go, however. "And what?"

She let out a sigh. "This will sound stupid, but I feel like my mom expects it of me. Yes, I'm a grown woman and I live on my own, but I do care what my family thinks. And my brothers are all so accomplished. They've all been to war and my parents are so proud of them. I guess I want to feel the same acceptance from them as well. And the thought of starting a business without having more school under my belt scares me."

He didn't respond, just squeezed her hand and lifted it to his mouth, kissing the back of it as they neared the turnoff to her street. The drive had been much quicker than she anticipated. They hadn't hit many red lights and at this time of night there wasn't much traffic.

As he pulled into the driveway of her townhome, she realized she'd never told him where she lived, but she shouldn't exactly be surprised he knew. He was the sheriff and it was a small enough town. Heck, her mom had probably given him her address.

By the time she'd unstrapped and picked her purse up, he'd already moved around to the passenger side and had opened her door. A chilly wind rolled over her as she stepped out onto her driveway but the heated look in his eyes burned away some of it. She shoved her hands in her thick peacoat's pockets even as Brad wrapped his arm around her shoulders.

"Do you want to come in?" The question seemed like a moot point since she was pretty sure what was happening between them tonight.

At her front door, he turned and pulled her into his arms, held her close. Regret was in his dark eyes. "I do, but I'm not going to. Not tonight."

"You don't want to finish what we started earlier?" Going by the thick erection pressing against her stomach, she knew he did.

"I want that more than anything, but I want to do this right." There was a look in his eyes she couldn't quite read.

She wasn't sure what the heck he meant by that, but she wasn't going to push him—even if she was disappointed *and* turned on. "I think you just like teasing me, Brad Fulton."

The grin he gave her was wicked. "*That*, I definitely do. If I don't talk to you before Tuesday night, I'll pick you up at seven. I'm taking you on an official date before we cross the next line."

Ah, so that was his reasoning. A Boy Scout to the end…and she found she liked it a lot. "I think you need to text me a dirty picture in the meantime, since you're holding out on me tonight." Fallon had no idea where the words came from, but as soon as they were out she was glad. She liked flirting with Brad, liked everything about him.

This man was definitely going to break her heart, and she still didn't want to stop this.

Instead of responding, he gave her the most wicked grin before leaning down to kiss her. Nothing intense like the ones they'd shared before, just a brief meeting of lips. But she felt it all the way to her toes.

With a groan, he pulled back and pressed his forehead to hers. "Go inside before I second-guess myself."

She figured if she pushed him she could get him inside, but if he wanted to take her on a date first, she was going to let him. "All right, tease."

CHAPTER SIX

Brad paused as he stepped out of the shower, then he heard it again. His doorbell. He'd had a long day at work and was counting down until his date with Fallon tomorrow night. He wasn't in the mood to see anyone at the moment.

And it was rare for anyone to stop by his house unannounced. After quickly drying off, he tugged on a pair of gym shorts and hurried to the front of his house as it rang again.

A shot of adrenaline punched through him as it occurred to him that maybe it was Fallon surprising him a day early. That would be the best surprise ever. But that hope died as soon as he looked through the peephole. "Holy hell."

Since he wasn't a coward, he opened the door to face Fallon's three brothers. They all had on loose gym pants and pullover hoodies, looking like a grim-faced death squad. They were all former military like him. He knew all of them in passing and genuinely liked the O'Connor brothers, but he wasn't close with any of them.

"Hey, guys. Is everything okay?" Oh, shit. He'd been in the shower—what if he'd missed a call from the station… "Is *Fallon* okay?"

"Yeah, she's fine," Jackson said. "We just wanted to see if you were up for a round of hockey."

Bullshit. They wanted to ask what he was doing with their little sister and this was how they were going to do it. Since he planned to keep Fallon in his life and he was off work, he figured he needed to man up and do this. "Sure. Let me throw on some clothes."

Maguire and Nolan didn't say anything, just watched him with the same blue eyes as Fallon. Only theirs weren't warm or welcoming. Oh yeah, he was definitely going to get roughed up on the ice.

Mentally he shrugged. She was worth it.

He met them on the front porch and locked his door. "Where are we doing this?"

Jackson clapped him on the shoulder once, squeezed hard. "We reserved the rink at the community center. We can walk there."

"Your gear already there?" Because there wasn't a vehicle in his driveway so they must have walked.

"Yeah."

"All right. Let me grab mine from the garage."

"No need." Maguire gave him a tight grin. "We've got enough for you at the rink."

Okay, then. Talk about awkward. He didn't have brothers or sisters, but he was still a guy. He could appreciate what they were doing, even if playing hockey with them was the last thing he wanted to do right now. He'd had a long day at work and was ready to crash. "You sure you have enough pads?" Because if this was full-contact hockey, he wanted to get his own.

"We've got enough."

That would have to do. I wasn't like they were going to kill him. Though he hated the idea of using someone else's pads. He rolled his shoulders once.

"How's the furniture business?" he asked Jackson as they reached the sidewalk, looking for any sort of opening. Jackson was making custom pieces for people and had started selling them online, according to Fallon.

"Good."

Nolan and Maguire fell in step with each other, ahead of him and Jackson, practically stalking down the sidewalk toward their intended destination. Apparently they weren't into small talk, and clearly Jackson didn't give a shit either.

"This about Fallon?" he asked Jackson, already convinced it was.

Jackson gave him a sideways glance, his expression neutral. "This is about some guys playing hockey and blowing off steam."

He snorted, but let it go. "This going to be two on two, or are there other players there?"

"Just us."

Aaaand that still wasn't an answer. Ten minutes later they were at the community center, which was supposed to be closed, hence the almost empty parking lot.

They all geared up in silence in the men's locker room — and Maguire and Nolan looked a little too happy to be doing this.

"This won't be full contact," Jackson said, shooting his brothers a dark warning look.

They were geared up for full contact. For the most part. Brad was wearing a helmet but there was no face guard attached. And he had a feeling they wouldn't have an issue going for his face.

As they reached the door to the rink, he said, "Look, I've got work tomorrow and I don't need the little old ladies of Holly gossiping about me, so don't damage my face."

Maguire glanced over his shoulder and grinned. "I think I like you, Fulton."

Again, still not the response he was looking for.

"You'll be with me," Jackson said, giving him the same dark grin Maguire had given him moments before.

Just great.

"Where are the guys?" Fallon strolled into her parents' kitchen to find her mom pulling a delicious-smelling casserole out of the oven. Chicken parmesan, one of her favorites. She immediately went to the refrigerator and started pulling out the stuff to make a giant salad.

"What are you wearing?" Her mother frowned as she paused at the oven.

Fallon looked down at herself as she stepped back from the fridge, a bag of mixed lettuce and spinach in hand. "Uh, clothes?" She had on thick, black knit leggings and a fitted T-shirt that said "I bake because punching people is frowned upon." Her *mother* had been the one to give her the shirt, so it wasn't like she could be offended by it. And she'd left her boots at the front door, so she knew her mom wasn't mad about her tracking dirt and snow into the house. "Why?"

Her mom just pursed her lips and turned back to the stove.

Fallon took a deep breath and reached for the rest of the salad fixings. She adored her mother, but some days it was like all they did was butt heads. She was in way too good of a mood about seeing Brad tomorrow night to let anything bother her right now, however. She would have gone out with him tonight but family night was important to all of them. And she could freaking survive one night without seeing Brad.

"Why isn't Nora coming tonight?" She'd received a brief text from Jackson earlier and he'd mentioned that Nora and Sasha couldn't make it. When she'd asked why she'd gotten radio silence. Which was so typical of her brothers.

"She's helping Sasha with a school project. So, you ready for the move?" her mom asked, her back still to her as she started pulling plates down.

No. "Uh, yes. I found someone to take over my lease here, and next week I'm going to ask the guys to help me pack everything up and store it in the garage. If that's okay?" She'd never officially asked her parents but they wouldn't mind. Or she could just rent a storage pod, which would be just as easy.

"Of course, sweetheart." Her mom turned away from the stove and slid up next to Fallon as she added bacon bits to the bowl. "Listen, I hope you're going to this school for the right reasons."

She paused. "I thought you wanted me to go."

"Well, you've seemed so lost lately and I thought it was something you wanted. But don't go because you think it matters to me or your father. Obviously it matters if it's what you want, but...we just want you to be happy." She wrapped an arm around Fallon's shoulders and squeezed tight. Her familiar Chanel perfume teased the air as she laid her head against Fallon's. The scent always reminded her of her mom.

Putting the knife and cucumber on the cutting board, she turned and gave her mom a hug. She hadn't realized how much she'd needed to hear that. Not because she doubted that her parents wanted her to be happy, but they'd been so excited about her getting into the school. Maybe she was projecting a lot of her own baggage onto her relationship with her mom. Gah, who knew? "Thanks, Mom."

As she stepped back she heard the engine of her brother Maguire's muscle car. Which reminded her... "You never told me why the guys are running so late."

"I need to grab a bottle of wine, sweetheart. Be right back."

Wait, what? Less than ten seconds later she realized why her mom had ducked out, because the side door to the kitchen opened, and in strolled her brothers — with Brad. She stared in surprise to see him standing there — until she saw the beginnings of a black eye.

"What did you three do to him?" she demanded, looking at her brothers, none of whom would meet her gaze.

"Just played a little hockey," Jackson muttered, still not meeting her gaze. And he was normally the sane one of the bunch.

"I'm fine. This is nothing." Brad shrugged, then winced.

She didn't care what her siblings thought at that moment because she was close to whaling on all of them. Instead she took Brad's hand and towed him toward the kitchen doorway. "Come on, let me get a look at you." She glanced over her shoulder as she was about to step out into the hallway. "You're all freaking dead," she whispered at her brothers so her mom wouldn't hear.

Her mom clucked her tongue as she stepped back into the kitchen, a bottle of red wine in hand. "Language."

"I said freaking," she growled.

Her mom shook her head and sniffed haughtily. "It's just a substitute for the other word."

Oh, sweet Lord, she was not doing this right now. Quickly she ushered Brad to the downstairs guest bathroom, which wasn't very big, but at least they had a first aid kit in the cabinet.

The room always smelled like cinnamon and vanilla thanks to little tea lights her mom favored. Had since Fallon was a kid. And the scents always reminded her of home.

"Sit." She pointed to the toilet seat.

He did immediately, sitting on the closed lid. He looked huge and out of place in the dainty French-themed room. "It's fine, really."

She sniffed and knew she sounded exactly like her mother, but didn't care as she gently took his chin in her hand. She turned his head slightly and inspected his eye. She could stare into his espresso-colored eyes all day, but she didn't want to under these circumstances. "Man, they didn't hold back."

"This was actually my fault. I was too slow on the block. Should have defended myself better."

She wanted to ask more questions—like why he needed to even block his face, but she knew he wouldn't answer her. If he was anything like her brothers, he had a weird guy code about stuff like that. "You're completely insane," she muttered before kissing him oh so gently. She was afraid to touch him anywhere, but he had no such compunctions because he pulled her onto his lap so that she was sitting across his legs. The feel of all that strength under her sent a shiver down her spine.

"I don't want to hurt you." She pulled her head back from his, watching him worriedly.

"I just have a few bruises. Nothing's broken or even cracked. Trust me, I'd know."

"I'm going to make them pay later."

He laughed under his breath as if the thought was ridiculous.

"I shaved all their heads once. In Maguire's case, twice. And their beards. I've also put itching powder in their jockstraps and—"

Brad stared at her with a little shock, but also awe. "Seriously?"

"You obviously never had any siblings, and yes, seriously. They all deserved it, too. Hey, I'm just a girl. I had to hold my own." She put on her best innocent expression.

Which just made him laugh, then wince. "Just a girl," he snorted. "You could probably take over the world if you wanted."

She grinned. "I like the sound of that. So, you're staying for dinner?"

"Your brothers invited me… If that's okay with you?"

If they'd invited him, that meant they liked him. And approved of him. Dang. One more reason to like him. Not that she needed any more. "I'd like that. You know they probably think we're together, right?" She had no idea what they'd talked about, but if he was staying for dinner, her family would get ideas.

"Good. I'm not letting you go, Fallon."

Her throat seized at his words. "Brad—"

"You don't have to say anything. I'm just laying it out there. I like you. A lot."

"I like you a lot too," she muttered. And that was the crux of the problem. He was screwing up all her plans. She already didn't want to go to California. But if she made the decision not to go now, it would be like she was staying for a man. Which… Okay she didn't give a crap what people thought, but still.

"You look a little like you're trying to figure out the square root of pi."

"Eight slices," she said automatically.

He blinked once, then laughed out loud at her cheesy joke. The happy sound wrapped around her, infused her with warmth and a whole lot of feelings she wasn't sure she was ready for. Unable to resist, she leaned in and kissed him again.

Immediately he took over, his tongue teasing against hers in the most erotic strokes. Prickles of awareness danced along her spine and out to all her nerve endings as she leaned into him. Now was the most inappropriate time to do anything, but the feel of him under her, his taste, his spicy cologne, his damp hair… She realized he must have showered before heading over here and now all she could think about was sharing a shower with him later.

Groaning, he pulled back. "We've got to stop or I won't be able to face your family soon."

Even though stopping was the last thing she wanted to do, getting busy in her parents' guest bathroom with her family nearby? Not happening. Later, though. Things would definitely be happening later. As soon as they were alone and had privacy. Laughing, she stood and held out a hand. "You need any first aid?"

"Nah. Your kisses did the trick." He brushed his lips over hers again before taking one of her hands in his, linking their fingers. "Let's do this."

She filed out with him, ready to go face her family. She might have no idea what the future held for them, or where this thing would go, but she could enjoy tonight with the sweet, sexy man who'd gone to play hockey with her brothers even knowing he'd likely get a beating.

She'd never brought a guy home before, and while technically she hadn't brought him over, it was pretty much implied he was here for her. This was going to be very interesting.

Chapter Seven

"How badly do you want to ditch me and get out while you still can?" Fallon was only half-joking as she and Brad strolled around one of the local parks. The near full moon and splash of stars across the night sky illuminated everything. Snow tipped some of the pine trees and covered the plastic seats on the multicolored swing set. After dinner with her parents, they'd decided to go for a walk — and she needed to get space from her family even if she was chilled.

They'd all been perfectly nice to Brad, but it had been weird having him in her family home when she was casually dressed with no makeup, and her brothers were acting like he was their friend all of a sudden. Whatever had happened out on the ice must have been serious for them to be so welcoming. The way they'd treated him had been authentic, and she wasn't sure how she felt about it. She loved that they accepted him, not that it had ever been in doubt. There was just still this deep-seated fear that things between them would end badly — with her getting her heart broken.

"Are you kidding me? Your family is great. I always wished I had siblings." His fingers were linked through hers and he squeezed lightly.

Sometimes her brothers were a giant pain in the ass, but she wouldn't trade them for anything. No matter what, she always knew they loved her. "Okay, so what happened with my brothers? Because you couldn't have wanted something like *that* growing up."

He let out a low laugh. "I was in the Marines. Trust me, what they put me through was nothing. It was basically just roughhousing on ice. And I gave as good as I got."

She shot him a sideways glance. She had noticed that both Maguire and Nolan seemed to wince when they moved wrong so he'd probably nailed them in the ribs. Which they totally deserved. She couldn't believe they'd basically ambushed him. "You have a black eye. Speaking of, which brother did that to you?"

"I'm definitely not telling you that."

"It was Maguire, wasn't it?"

Brad just lifted a shoulder and she knew she had her answer. Oh, her brother was definitely going to pay.

"I knew it," she muttered.

The park was quiet since it was pushing nine o'clock. Something she was grateful for. She liked the peace and silence of the place. "I used to come here when I was a kid." It was within walking distance of her parents' house, so she and her brothers had spent many hours here playing.

"Yeah?"

"All the time. Over the summers, I think the only reason my mom brought us here was so we'd tire ourselves out and give her a break."

"She's something else."

"No kidding."

"I like her. And at the risk of you biting my head off, you're just like her."

"I know. Trust me, I *know*." Fallon wasn't sure she'd ever measure up to her mom. "God, she's incredible. Both my parents are. Raising four kids and keeping their sanity?" She shook her head. She wasn't even sure how they'd afforded everything, but she and her brothers had never wanted for necessities.

Brad wrapped his arm around her, the action coming to be way too familiar. She leaned into him, tightened her own grip around him as she buried her face in his chest and inhaled.

"You don't want that many kids?" he asked.

This seemed like heavier territory, but she found herself surprisingly okay with it as she looked up at him. "Ah…I'd like two. Maybe three, but spread out." She grinned, shaking her head. "But two seems more manageable. What about you?"

"Two, for sure. I was an only child, and even though I never felt cheated I always wanted a brother." His tone was slightly wistful.

She had the most insane thought that if things worked out with them, he'd gain three brothers. Just as suddenly as the thought entered her mind, she jolted, nearly tripping on her own feet.

He steadied her, moving his hand to the small of her back. "You okay?"

Clearing her throat, she straightened and leaned into him again. "Fine, just clumsy. And since you're clearly not going to tell me, did my brothers ask you anything? Grill you about me or us?"

"Oh, that's against the guy code. I can't tell you what we talked about."

Stopping on the sidewalk, she turned and pulled him close against her. "I bet I could make you tell me."

He groaned, his hips rolling against hers once as he fully embraced her. "You probably could."

"I'll let you keep your secrets for now. But," she said, shifting so that she fell in step with him and continued walking, "I do have another question. What's the deal with the story of you saving the puppy? Is that true?" She'd heard about it years ago, but he was six years older than her so it was only a vague memory in her mind since she'd been twelve at the time.

He groaned and rubbed a hand over his face. "I'm never going to outlive that, I swear." Frowning, he glanced down at her. "Is that why you call me Boy Scout?"

"Well, yeah. Part of it, anyway. So…details."

He let out an overexaggerated sigh. "I was eighteen and some jackass threw a bag of puppies—I'm talking newborns—over the Reindeer Bridge as he drove by. I wasn't sure what was in it, but me and some other guys were walking home from school when we saw it. I jumped in and was only able to save a couple of them. Most of the litter died, but the vet found the two of them good homes."

"So you saved puppies, as in multiple?" The man really was a hero.

His cheeks flushed crimson as he cleared his throat. "What was I supposed to do, not save them?"

She tugged him down to her and crushed her lips to his. This man was determined to melt her completely.

"Fallon?" Brad murmured against her mouth.

"Hmm?"

"Want to go back to my place?" He looked at her, his eyes dark pools she wanted to drown in.

Did she ever. And there would be no turning back after this. "Oh yeah."

Brad pushed Fallon up against his front door as he locked it behind them. "I'm clean," he murmured against her mouth. He hadn't been with a woman since moving back to Holly and he'd been tested before that.

"Me too. And I'm on the pill." Her voice was as unsteady as he felt.

And his hands were shaking. *His.* He'd been in more firefights than he wanted to think about. He'd faced down the barrel of a rifle with only his wits to keep him alive.

But this—being with Fallon, knowing what was coming—made him crazy. In the best way possible. As he crushed his mouth to hers, she hoisted herself up, wrapping her legs around him. He grabbed onto her ass, held her as close as possible.

There would be no interruptions. Unless he got called in—but he wasn't going to think about that. Not when she was with him and they were on the same wavelength. Using his body weight to hold her in place, he slid his hands into her thick hair and cupped the back of her head. She tasted sweet like the mint candy she'd popped in her mouth on the drive over. He didn't even remember the drive, not when he'd been so focused on getting home and getting her naked.

"Upstairs or the living room?" he managed to rasp out. Because he needed to get her out of her clothes and underneath him immediately.

"Living room." Her blue eyes were bright with longing.

That was all he needed to hear.

He couldn't wait to see her completely naked with her gorgeous red hair wild around her face. As he strode through his living room, he grabbed a big throw blanket off the couch. Once they reached the fireplace, he tossed it down, and though he hated to let her go, he did. "I just want to start the fire first."

Out of the corner of his eye he saw her straightening the blanket and grabbing pillows as he lit the gas fire. By the time he was done and turned to face Fallon, her jacket and top were already off.

He sucked in a breath at the sight of her. She had on a plain black bra that didn't do much to hide the perfect, full mounds spilling out. All that smooth skin was just begging for his touch, for his mouth.

Staying where he was, crouched down, he just stared for a long moment. "Take off everything." His voice was low, raspy.

Her eyes widened slightly, but then she grinned before doing what he ordered. Slowly.

She hooked her fingers against her leggings and shimmied out of them so that she was standing on the blanket in just a pair of simple black underwear that matched her bra.

When she went to take them off, he shook his head because he'd changed his mind. "I'll do it." His voice was as raspy and unsteady as he felt. He might have tasted her once before, but that wasn't nearly enough. Now he got to see all of her, undressed and his for the taking.

Skimming his fingers up the outside of her legs, he marveled at how smooth her skin was. She shivered as he reached her hips. He let his gaze trail up her body as he tugged the bit of material down her legs. Faint triangle tan lines marked her breasts and the light pink nipples he planned to tease with his tongue.

The firelight flickered around her, casting shadows and giving her hair and creamy skin a soft glow as she looked down at him. She was everything he'd ever hoped for but hadn't even known existed.

She'd gotten under his skin before the first time they'd ever spoken. He'd never believed in fate or bullshit like that until Fallon walked into his life.

"I'm never going to forget the way you look right now," he murmured.

Her expression softened as she reached for his face, cupping his cheeks with her soft hands. Moving lightning fast, he had her flat on her back in seconds.

He grinned at the little yelp she let out even as she arched against the blanket. "This soft enough?"

"I'm not made of glass…and you're still dressed." She cupped his cheeks again, watching him with an intensity that unnerved him.

He wished he could get in her head, figure out exactly what she was thinking. Because he wanted something real from her, real for them.

"You're going to climax before my clothes come off." And that was that. That primitive force driving him needed her to climax well before he did, before he slid inside her. He wanted to see that pleasure on her face, taste it on his tongue again.

Her lips parted — in pleasure or surprise, he wasn't sure — right before he dipped his head and did one thing he'd been fantasizing about. He sucked one of her tight, pink nipples into his mouth.

She dug her fingers into his back, calling out his name as he flicked his tongue over it, again and again. She squirmed under him, her breathing erratic as he kissed a path to her other breast. Couldn't have one feeling neglected.

"Love your mouth on me," she rasped out.

He smiled against her breast before oh so lightly pressing his teeth around her nipple. Not hard, but with enough pressure that she groaned and dug her fingers into his back.

"Biggest tease ever." Her voice trembled, her nails biting into him.

He loved the nip of pain.

"Next time, you're wearing your uniform."

He could get on board with that. His cock kicked against his pants as he moved lower, lower… As he reached the top of her mound he had to brace himself for a moment.

Splayed out like this, spread open for him — it took all his control not to strip and sink deep inside her. When he inhaled her scent, how turned on she was, he shuddered and shifted a little lower.

"You're perfect," he murmured before teasing a finger along her slick folds.

She lifted her hips in response, her harsh breathing music to his ears. She wanted this as much as he wanted to do it. If she was leaving—and he wasn't letting her go even if she did—he wanted to make sure she had a damn good reason to come home. Yeah, binding her to him with sex was just step one. But it was a start.

Because he was jumping feet first into a serious relationship with her.

Slowly, teasingly, he slid a finger into her tight wetness. A groan tore from his lips as her slickness coated his finger. The proof of her arousal had his erection straining even harder against his pants.

Well too bad for his dick.

Not able to wait another second, he flicked his tongue over her clit, smiling against her when her hips rolled up and she tightened around his finger.

He added another finger even as he increased the pressure against her clit. She was like a drug, and making her climax was the best addiction to have.

She slid her fingers through his hair as he continued stroking her, over and over. Time had no meaning as he thrust his fingers in and out of her, her hips rolling up with every stroke, and she let out these breathy little moans that seriously tested his control.

Fallon was better than his fantasy. The reality of her was something he couldn't have expected, even as she was everything he wanted. Needed. He just hoped she felt the same.

As her inner walls tightened around his fingers faster and faster and her movements grew jerkier, he knew she was about to fall over the edge.

He just had to get her there. Because he wanted her in a free fall of pleasure before he slid his cock deep inside her, before he made her come again.

Before he made her *his*.

"I'm—"

"I know." He tightly massaged her clit in a little pattern he'd learned she liked, making her arch off the blanket with a raspy cry. Her inner walls milked him as her climax hit hard and fast.

She tore her hands from his head, fisted the blanket beneath them as she rode through her orgasm. When she started making little whimpering sounds, he lifted his head and watched her. Her eyes were closed, head thrown back, and all that wild red hair around her face. Oh yeah, this would be captured in his memory forever.

Desperate with the need to be inside her, he withdrew his fingers and sat up, stripping off his clothes with no control.

Fallon was still coming down from her high as Brad started undressing. She wanted to be the one taking off his clothes, but she needed a minute as the effects of her orgasm subsided. Her entire body was oversensitive and fully sated.

And watching him frantically unwrap that delicious body of his? Forget television—this was the kind of show she wanted to watch 24/7.

When he was fully naked, his thick cock jutting out proudly, another rush of heat flooded between her legs. Seeing the outlines of his muscles under his uniform was nothing compared to all of this.

He was all cut lines, hard muscles, defined striations, and his cock… Her nipples beaded even tighter as he fell to his knees on the blanket.

For once, she wanted to take a little control. Not to get back any power or the upper hand, but because she wanted to bring him as much pleasure as he'd brought her. He was so giving and she wanted to give right back.

"On your back," she murmured, pushing lightly against his chest as she got to her knees.

A moment of indecision flashed in his gaze. She could see him fighting it, wanting to take over. Because that was the kind of man he was. Something she was more than okay with. But she needed to know he could give and take, especially in the bedroom—where he'd already proved to be a giving lover.

And she wanted to give right back.

Groaning in almost part frustration, part hunger, he did as she said, stretching out on the blanket before her.

He was definitely better than any dessert she'd ever made. And he'd already stolen her heart, whether he'd meant to or not. She had some serious decisions to make later, but for this moment, she just wanted to enjoy what was between them.

Looking up his sculpted body, his thick, muscular thighs, the erection that had her mouth watering... "I don't know where to start."

"Wherever you want."

Straddling him, she slid up his body, moaning as her slick folds slid right over his cock. Instead of pushing down on him, she teased the head of his erection with her opening, watching his expression change as she did.

Oh yeah, teasing him like this could become her hobby. Moving her hips, she couldn't help the little laugh that escaped as his jaw clenched as tightly as his fists around her hips.

"Who's the tease now, baby?" His voice was unsteady as he reached for her.

Leaning down, she crushed her mouth to his, needing to feel linked with him, to know this was more than just sex. Because it was for her. So much more. Their tongues teased each other as she held back from fully sliding onto him.

Even though she wanted to drag this out, she was on a razor's edge of control as much as he was. His fingers and mouth were incredible, but she wanted all of him. Wanted to experience everything he had to offer. She'd never wanted someone like this, with a desperate craving she felt bone deep.

Pushing down on him, she arched her back at the thick intrusion as he filled her to the hilt. His own groan of pleasure overshadowed hers as he thrust all the way inside her.

"Ah, hell, baby." All the muscles in his body seemed to be pulled taut as he stared up at her as if she was a goddess. And precious.

She'd never been on the receiving end of this kind of need and she could easily get addicted to it. To him.

As her hair fell down around her breasts, she started riding him in slow, even strokes. He cupped one of her breasts, gently teased a nipple even as he couldn't seem to let go of one of her hips. He held tight, as if he was afraid she'd change her mind.

No chance of that happening.

Not when she had the most perfect man she'd never expected. God, she'd never wanted this. Or she hadn't thought she had. But she didn't care what people thought, or if they thought she was lucky to have him. Because she was. His expression as he watched her was so intense she couldn't tear her gaze away. She liked being herself with him, without having to hold back, especially during sex.

Rolling her hips in erotic little thrusts that were pushing him toward the edge, she grasped onto that heady power, the dopamine rush she'd only ever experienced while being with him, and let go of any and all of her hang-ups.

At least for the moment.

Increasing her tempo, she watched in fascination as a flush crept up his body, as his jaw tightened more and more, as he pushed right toward that edge.

When he reached between their bodies and tweaked her clit, she felt the pleasure spark out to all her nerve endings. She hadn't thought she'd be able to come again, but this was too much.

And yet not enough.

She rode him faster and faster, savoring the way he completely filled her, hitting that elusive spot deep inside her. Each time he thrust all the way to her core, she was closer to coming again.

"Come inside me." The words were more plea than order. It was all she could squeeze out when she was barely hanging on to her control.

Her words seemed to unleash something inside him. A heartbeat later she found herself flat on her back, her wrists pinned above her head by one of his big hands as he thrust hard, over and over.

She arched up, meeting him stroke for stroke as he lost himself inside her. As she lost herself with him.

Oh, she was more than just falling for him. In that moment, she was pretty sure she'd already fallen. Heart first.

Her climax hit, sharp and intense. She tried to find some sort of purchase and just found him. She wrapped her legs around him, automatically fighting the hold he had on her wrists even as it turned her on more. She couldn't ever remember being so turned on, so slick with need.

His mouth crushed over hers with a wild hunger as he groaned out his release, coming inside her in long, hot thrusts, joining her in climax until they were both panting and sated against the blanket.

Breathing hard, he braced his forearms on either side of her head as he stared down at her. The firelight flickered off the sharp planes of his face, making him look savage.

She liked it.

Though she tried, she couldn't find her voice. Wasn't sure what to say, anyway. Luckily it didn't matter as he slowly pulled out of her.

"Let's get cleaned up. Then I'm putting you in my bed where you belong."

A shiver raced down her spine at his possessive words, at the rightness of them. She curled into his hold as he scooped her up, allowing herself to tune out the outside world and the decisions she needed to make.

Nothing else mattered except tonight with him.

CHAPTER EIGHT

"Something smells delicious," Fallon murmured without opening her eyes. The scent of rich coffee filled the air as she stretched her arms above her head. After spending the best night with Brad, she didn't want to move from his bed for at least a few hours.

The bed dipped slightly next to her so she opened her eyes to see Brad holding a mug of coffee, wearing only his boxers. "Morning," he murmured.

"Morning." She raked a gaze over him, remembering how much fun she'd had kissing and teasing all that exposed skin. "You about to get ready for work?" He'd told her that she could stay at his place until she was ready to go.

Instead of answering, he leaned forward to kiss her, but she covered her mouth with her hand. He blinked once, freezing midway to her face.

"Morning breath," she muttered against her hand, the words coming out garbled. "We're not kissing."

Laughing, he pulled her hand away. "I don't care." He brushed his lips over hers then pulled back and made a face. "Maybe you were—"

"Hey!"

"I'm kidding!" He kissed her again before handing her coffee. "And I'm bringing you the gift of caffeine."

She took the mug. "The coffee makes up for it. So, no work? I thought Holly couldn't survive without you."

Laughing, he nudged her leg to make room. She'd grabbed one of his T-shirts after their last bout of lovemaking but that was all she had on. Air rushed over her bare legs as she shifted the covers off and moved so he could get in with her. The navy blue curtains were pulled open, revealing a sunny day, but a light layer of white snow covered everything in his backyard.

He took her free hand with his, linking their fingers together as he laid his head against the headboard next to hers. "I talked to the guys. They're going to cover for me until around noon so we've got the morning together." His deep voice was an aphrodisiac, sending little pulses of pleasure down to her toes. He could talk about anything and she'd gladly listen.

"I don't want to get you in trouble."

"You won't. I never take time off. And you're leaving soon. I'm spending time with you." He said it so matter of fact.

Even as his words warmed her heart, they cast a slight pallor on the room. Some of the warmth blossoming inside her faded, but she shoved it aside and locked it up tight. She was going to focus on the positive. "Thank you for taking time off." She laid her head on his shoulder and closed her eyes, savoring his nearness. She was going to take advantage of every single moment they had together. "I can think of a few ways we can pass the time…after I finish my coffee, of course. Because a girl has to have priorities."

His warm laughter wrapped around her, soothed her, gave her this intense feeling of happiness. She couldn't ever remember feeling this…content. There was nowhere else she'd rather be right now than with him. She wondered if she could be brave, make the very real decision that was weighing on her mind nonstop.

"Listen…just because you're moving doesn't mean we have to end. I know this thing is new, but hell, Fallon. I've never felt like this."

She lifted her head so she could look at him, heart beating faster. "I haven't either. Never even imagined something like this," she whispered. "But I've seen what happens when people try long-distance relationships. Look at Halley." When her friend and her ex had tried the long-distance thing it had ended disastrously.

"We're not them. Are you looking for excuses to tell me that these two weeks are it?" His jaw flexed once.

"No. Maybe. I don't know. I'm afraid that this is so amazing now, but what happens when I leave and the new wears off?"

He cupped her face, stroked his thumb over her cheek. "Who says it will? Fallon, you're incredible. I can't imagine not wanting to wake up to your face."

Her heart clenched at his words. This man was going to destroy her. Or give her everything she'd ever wanted. "You're too good to be true." Her whispered words seemed over-pronounced in the quiet of his bedroom.

"Right back at you." He took her coffee from her, set it on the nightstand. "You don't have to make a decision now. I'm just telling you what I want. And that's you. We can fly out to see each other, alternate every other weekend or however. You're worth it."

Unexpected tears stung her eyes. "You're worth it too." It felt crazy to try to do long distance. Her school program was twenty-one months, which okay, wasn't that long. Still, starting a relationship long distance would be difficult. But he was worth it. Man, was he ever.

"Hey, why the tears?" He wiped a few away, the feel of his callused thumb against her cheek sending the best kind of shivers through her.

"Just can't believe we're finally at this place and I'm leaving." For a school she didn't even want to go to.

"Let's focus on the time we do have and how we'll make the future work."

"I agree." She was going to make the most of the time they had left together. And she planned to take advantage of the next few hours, since it was only seven o'clock. "If you have to be in by noon, I say we get a shower—together—then see what happens next. Unless you have plans?"

Grinning wickedly, he leaned in and bit her bottom lip. "A shower sounds like a plan. After that, we're going ice skating."

"Really?"

"Really."

That sounded…wonderful. Like something a couple did. Which she guessed they were, if they were talking about having a serious, long-distance relationship. "We'll be exclusive while I'm in California." A statement, not a question.

He let out the sexiest-sounding growl, as if her question had surprised him. "You're mine, Fallon. Yes, we're exclusive."

The relief that punched through her at his words was staggering. If they were doing this, she was all in. Moving quickly, she straddled him, heat already building between her thighs as she settled over his growing, unfortunately covered erection. Maybe they wouldn't make it to the shower after all.

"People are staring at us." Fallon whispered as they skated to the edge of the rink. Brad had to head in to work soon and she wanted to grab a sandwich with him before he left. She had to meet up with her brother in a bit so she could go pick up her car from the shop—then run an errand she didn't want to think about.

"It's because of my awesome skating skills. Happens every time I come down here." Brad's expression was deadpan, making her laugh.

He *was* an incredible skater, but that wasn't why people were watching them. The sheriff having a girlfriend was a big deal. "You're such a freak." She walked slowly on her skates, making her way to the nearby bench where they'd left their shoes.

He sat down beside her, started unlacing one skate. "Neither of us have dated for a while and I'm the sheriff—and you're the O'Connor brothers' sister. Of course people will talk. Do you care?"

"No. I like people knowing that you're off-limits." She grinned at his surprised expression.

"Same here," he murmured, leaning in to brush his lips over hers.

She fell into the kiss much like she'd fallen for him—only to be interrupted.

"Hey, slackers." Halley appeared out of nowhere holding beat-up ice skates by the laces, a huge smile on her face. A white knit cap was pulled low over her espresso-colored hair, the brightness a contrast against her dark skin. "I didn't believe it when I heard through the grapevine that you two were down here on a Tuesday morning skating and showing off your moves."

"People in town are already talking about this?" Fallon rolled her eyes, not that she was exactly surprised. Holly wasn't super small, but it was small enough that certain people didn't mind getting in everyone's business — and okay, she was going to miss it something fierce.

"Oh, girl. More than talking. I'm pretty sure your mom started another pool down at the salon."

She sighed, refusing to ask what kind of pool. Because there had been a big one last year for whoever guessed the right date that Fallon's brother Jackson and his now fiancée got together. "My mom is completely insane," she muttered.

"We should find out what the bet is for." Brad grinned as he slid a foot into a boot. "See if we can make some money off it."

"Fine. I'll ask Nora what the pool is for, see if we can get in on it."

He brushed his lips over hers again briefly, as if it was the most natural thing in the world. She was already used to it and loved that he was hers to kiss anytime she wanted. For now, anyway. In a couple weeks... Yeah, not going there.

"This is definitely going to take some getting used to," Halley said, shaking her head. "But I like it. I actually can't believe you two haven't gotten together before now. You're a perfect fit." She glanced over her shoulder, then back at them. "I've gotta go. Promised my cousin I'd teach her to skate. But remember what I said. If you end up staying in town, let's talk business."

"What was that about?" Brad asked once Halley was gone.

"Ah..." She stood, flexed her toes in her boots. It always took a few minutes for her to get her legs back after ice skating. "She wanted to talk about doing more business with me. Maybe something more than just commission work." There would be stipulations and a contract to iron out, but Fallon had no doubt they'd work well together. They already did.

Fallon hadn't taken on any new jobs in the last month, just focused on the ones she already had — which was why she didn't have steady income — because she'd been getting ready for her move. Now… "So, you mind dropping me off at Nora's before heading in to the station?" She could walk, but wanted to spend the time with Brad.

"Like you even have to ask." He took her skates from her and slung an arm around her shoulders as they made their way toward the parking lot. "What are your plans for the rest of the day?"

"I promised Nora I'd help out for an hour or so, then Jackson's going to take me to get my car. And then…I'm going to pick up some boxes. I want to start packing all my stuff so it's ready to move into my parents' garage next week."

He stiffened slightly, but didn't ease his grip. "I can help you with the packing."

"Okay, thanks." Or she might try to get most of it done without him because it was too depressing. Gah. She needed some down time to really think about this move, to pro/con it, and the best way to do that was over wine, or hot cocoa, with Nora.

"Our date still on for tonight?" Brad waved at a local as they reached his truck.

"You better believe it." Seeing him sounded like heaven. Leaving him, not so much.

CHAPTER NINE

"Another shot, please." Fallon held out her mug for Nora, who'd closed her shop fifteen minutes ago and was now running the reports.

"Um, no. You've had enough espresso."

She laid her head on the counter as Nora continued calculating numbers. "I'm a freaking mess right now." Earlier she'd picked up her car, then a ton of boxes from the local grocery store. They'd agreed to give them to her for free because the manager was friends with one of her brothers.

"No you're not. All right, I'm done here."

Fallon lifted her head to see Nora sliding her receipts to the side. She pulled out a yellow legal pad. "Give me the pros of staying."

"Brad."

Grinning, Nora scribbled on her pad.

"Incredible sex on a daily basis."

"You're such a guy." Nora shook her head, but wrote it down.

"Steady work. The ability to gain more work. Built-in contacts to grow my business—if I had one." Technically, she did. She freelanced, but she wanted to set up an actual business license and website. She'd already bought the domain and had talked to a local designer about the brand she envisioned. "If I decided to open my own food truck business here there's no competition right now, which means I'd be able to get a foothold in the market."

"What else?"

"My family's here. Though I'm okay moving away for a couple years knowing I'll come back. But I will miss them. Friends too.

But...don't put that on the list. I'm just thinking out loud." She looked at her empty mug, frowned. "Add Brad again." Because he was a big pro for staying.

"All right. What are the pros of leaving for school?"

"I get another degree."

"And?"

"And..."

"I already know the answer, and so do you, but do you need the culinary degree to do what you want?"

"No."

Nora lifted an eyebrow and dropped the pad on the counter. "All right, one more latte for you while you think, then I'm cutting you off."

"What if people think I'm staying in town for a man? And it doesn't work out? And by people, I mean my mom."

Nora didn't turn around as she started making Fallon another drink. "Who gives a crap what people think? If it doesn't work out, yeah, it'll suck. But take Brad out of the equation. What are you really afraid of?"

"Failing. Failing spectacularly and having my family see it."

"You're one of the most confident people I know. On the outside, anyway. Fake that shit until you make it." Nora slid a new mug across the counter to her. "It's what I did when I took over here."

"Fake that shit until you make it. I'm pretty sure that's going to be my new motto."

"Ha, ha. You know what you want to do. And you know what's right for you right now. Don't let fear help you make a decision you'll regret."

"Thank you." Knowing something was one thing. Having it confirmed by your best friend was another entirely. Especially when it was true. As Nora picked up the legal pad, Fallon's phone rang.

Tugging it out of her purse, she debated answering it, then saw it was her mom. They talked almost every day, but Fallon was mentally exhausted right now. Still... "Hey, Mom."

"Sweetheart, I don't want you to freak out. But I just heard that

Brad was in some sort of altercation. I...don't know if he was shot. I heard a gun went off and he's at the hospital now."

Fallon's heart skipped a beat as terror seized her chest. Shot? "I...I've got to go. I'll call you from the hospital." Not caring how rude it was, she hung up and grabbed her purse off the counter. "Something happened to Brad. My mom thinks he might have been shot. I'm going to the hospital now." Her words came out like machine gun fire to Nora as she hurried toward the front of the shop.

"Wait! Give me thirty seconds to set the alarm. I'm driving you."

Fallon wanted to say no, but she was shaking too badly. Brad had called her earlier and said he'd be late picking her up because there had been a last minute call-out.

She didn't remember getting into Nora's car, and the drive to the hospital was a blur.

It seemed to take forever as buildings and snow-covered trees and vehicles flew past them. Why weren't they going faster? Or there yet? The thought of Brad hurt, injured...worse. All the muscles in her body pulled tight and she couldn't seem to stop trembling.

"We're almost there. I'm going to pull up to the ER entrance and let you out." Nora's voice was soft, soothing, but it sounded like a firecracker going off in the quiet interior.

"Okay," she rasped out, glad she'd found her voice. Fallon wasn't sure why she'd always thought she'd be good in a crisis, because she sucked at it.

Once Nora pulled up to the entrance, Fallon had the door open before she'd even stopped. Jumping out, she raced through the main doors — and stopped short to see Brad talking to a doctor. Totally fine. Not shot. Though his uniform was ripped in places.

He smiled in confusion when he saw her, and the most overwhelming rush of emotions swamped her with the equivalent of a tidal wave. She burst into tears, unable to stop them from flowing.

He was alive, and unharmed.

A pair of strong, steady arms surrounded her and though she couldn't see through the blur of tears, she knew it was Brad holding her. She gripped him tight as he rubbed a steady hand up and down her spine. He murmured words she couldn't understand, but moments later she found they were in a private, quiet room.

Suddenly lights flooded the room as he flipped a switch and stood back. He led her to a bedside chair and crouched in front of her. "Are you okay?"

"Yes. I'm sorry." Her voice was scratchy as she cupped his cheeks in her hands. "My mom called, said something had happened. That you might have been shot. And my mind just went to DEFCON one. I raced right over here. I thought…" She swallowed hard, forcing back all those crazy tears and emotions she didn't want to let out again. Not yet, anyway. God, she was such a mess. She'd imagined the absolute worst, reacted like a total freak. But the thought of losing him now, when she'd just discovered him? Her heart twisted painfully and she tightened her grip just a bit on his face, reassuring herself he was alive.

He took her hands in his, held them between the two of them before softly kissing her knuckles. "I was in a brawl. A domestic thing. The husband's gun went off, but no one was injured. I'm so sorry you were worried."

"No, don't be sorry. I guess… I know what you do for a living. I guess I just never thought about the danger. The ins and outs of it." She'd always thought of it in an abstract sort of way. Like, he put on this uniform, looked all sexy, and went about his day. And that Holly wasn't a dangerous place. But the truth was, no place was completely safe. That was a simple fact.

His expression was serious as he watched her. "Is this something you'll be able to handle?"

"Yes. No doubt." She gave a wry smile, let out a watery laugh. "Clearly today isn't a good example of that, but I'm in this, Brad. And I don't care if it's too soon. I love you. I feel it in my bones. I've never felt like this before."

"I love you too. God, I love you so much." Moving slowly, watching her intently, he kissed her with an unexpected sweetness that made her want to cry all over again.

Not because she was sad, but because this man was it for her. And she wasn't letting him go.

CHAPTER TEN

Anticipation hummed through Fallon as she waited in the lobby of the small Holly sheriff station. Brad had gone in to work today, which she shouldn't have been surprised about since he hadn't been injured last night. After making a split-second decision to tackle a man holding a gun down by his side, he'd just gotten a little dirty.

She was the one who was shaken up, and maybe he was too, but he sure hadn't shown it last night. He'd been voracious in bed, to the point she'd finally had to admit she was too exhausted to continue. She had a feeling some of that had been his way of expending all his adrenaline.

Which was a fine way, as far as she was concerned.

While he'd been at work, she'd been taking back control of her life. Unfortunately, her townhome was leased out for the next year, and she'd lost her deposit for the first semester when she'd called to cancel her enrollment at the culinary school, but it was truly as if a weight had been lifted.

She had made the right decision. Of that she had no doubt. Especially after yesterday's scare. Now she was ready to tell Brad her news. She'd just wanted everything taken care of when she surprised him.

When she started to pace nervously, the administrative assistant, Mrs. Wiggins, glanced up at her. "You planning on sharing what's in that basket, Fallon O'Connor?"

She stopped midstride and looked at the older woman who'd been with the department forever. "Ma'am?"

"What's in the basket? It smells delicious."

"Oh...yes, this is for you. For everyone, actually." She lifted off the plaid-checked cover of her wicker basket. "Snickerdoodles, limoncello macarons, and berry muffins." She'd had a busy day getting things in order before coming to see Brad, but had decided to bake to expend more pent-up energy. Baking and cleaning up afterward always made her feel good. "I'll just leave the basket here and pick it up later this week if that's okay?"

The older woman gave her a sweet smile. "That is more than fine with me. And the guys are going to have a field day tomorrow." Pushing back from her desk, she headed over to their coffee station and picked up a small Styrofoam plate. "How's your mother doing, dear?"

"She's good. Staying busy—and harassing Nora over when she'll be popping out grandchildren." Her mom couldn't even wait until they were married to start with the nudging.

Mrs. Wiggins giggled as she returned to her desk. "Sounds about right."

Fallon set the basket on the desk, glanced at the closed door of Brad's office. Mrs. Wiggins had said he wouldn't be long. And okay, it had only been five minutes since she'd arrived. She was just nervous about what she had to tell him.

When the door opened, she nearly jumped.

Brad stepped out, looking as sexy as ever. She made a move in his direction but stopped when she saw the mayor coming out with him. Fallon smiled at the other man, exchanged a few polite words before they were alone again. Well, relatively alone.

"Is everything okay?" she murmured as the mayor stepped outside.

Brad nodded, then looked at the basket of goodies. "You make those?"

"Yes. I wanted to bring a treat for you guys." It had given her something to do when she'd had down time she definitely didn't want. Not today when she was bursting at the seams, ready to tell Brad her news.

"If this is a perk of you dating Fallon, then you can never break up with her." Mrs. Wiggins grinned before swiveling toward her computer.

"I don't plan to," Brad murmured, his gaze doing that super sexy heated thing as he turned back to her. Warmth spread through her at his words. "Thanks for stopping by."

They'd originally planned to get together later this evening, but she hadn't been able to wait. "I have something to show you."

"Is that a euphemism?" he murmured as they headed for the front door of the station.

Mrs. Wiggins cleared her throat. "I'm old, not hard of hearing."

Fallon watched in fascination as Brad's cheeks flushed a light shade of pink. "I've got something to tell you too." He grabbed his jacket off the rack by the door. "Make sure you have one of the guys walk you to your car, Martha," he said over his shoulder as he opened the door for Fallon.

"I always do."

Fallon knew that one of the deputies would be on call all night. It was the way it worked in small towns. "You can tell me your news while we walk to see my news."

His gave her a curious look, but wrapped an arm around her shoulders as they stepped out into the icy evening. "I know we haven't talked about long-term stuff yet, but I called a meeting with the mayor today to let him know that when the next election comes up, I might not be running again. I can't leave right now, but if you decide you want to stay in California or wherever, I can move too. I don't want you to feel like—"

In the middle of the sidewalk she pulled him to her, yanking him down by the lapels of his black, county-issued jacket. She pulled back almost immediately, unable to contain her grin. "I seriously love you, sheriff."

His lips curved up wickedly. "I'm seriously never going to get tired of hearing you say that. And please call me that later tonight."

"Definitely...now come on." Bursts of energy lit up inside her as she grabbed his hand. "This way." She motioned down the little side alley that led to the private strip of parking for the shop owners on Main Street.

When they rounded the corner, she held out her hand at her newly bought—and in serious need of work—food truck. Her brothers were going to help her fix it up. thankfully, because there was only so much she knew how to do on her own.

"This is going to be the food truck for Sugar Rush—eventually. It needs work, clearly." The red paint was peeling in patches, and revealed it had once been a white truck. All the tires were balding and the interior was rusted out in places. But according to Maguire, it was surface stuff and worth her investment. "I've still got a ton of stuff to do like set up a business address, a business bank account, file permits, figure out exactly what commercial kitchen I'll be using for food prep—but I'm doing this. I'm staying here. And I'm going to be jumping feet first into this business. Which means I'll probably be a busy mess for a while, but I want to live in the same city as you, wake up to you in the mornings. I didn't tell you last night because I didn't want you to think I'd made the decision because of what happened."

She rushed on before he could respond because she needed to get this all out at once.

"Okay, that sort of spurred me into action. But I was using going to school as a way to delay my real dream of starting my own business. I've just been so afraid of failing, but that's freaking stupid. Yesterday showed me, as cheesy as this sounds, that life is way too short. If I fail, then I'll try something else." She pushed out a long breath after her machine gun fire of a confession as he just watched her. Nerves danced along her spine as she waited for him to say something.

His expression softened, showing her the side of him she realized only she got to see. "I love you so much, Fallon. If you change your mind later, I'm still willing to move. I just want to be with you. I love Holly, but I love you more."

She threw her arms around him at the same time he reached for her. Burying her face against his neck, she inhaled the spicy scent of him as emotion clogged her throat. She had to take a deep breath as excitement for their future hummed through her. She felt lighter than she had in weeks. "Before the inspection, and after it's been fixed up, we're so christening that truck."

His deep laugh reverberated through her as he tightened his hold. "I would expect nothing less. How about we head back to my place and christen another one of the rooms?"

She leaned back to look at him, but kept her arms around him. "Maybe your kitchen this time?"

He just laughed again and crushed his mouth to hers. She had a lot of work in front of her to get where she wanted to be, but she was more than ready for it. Heck, she was excited about it. Especially now that she had someone like Brad in her life and by her side.

Fallon jumped up onto the kitchen counter next to the stove as Brad flipped an omelet. Even though it was well into the evening, he was cooking for them. And she was pretty sure this was one of the only things he knew how to make.

"Smells good," she murmured, shifting slightly against the counter, a little tender from their last round of lovemaking. In just one of his T-shirts, she felt perfectly at home here with him. She could be the real her, and she loved that he was the same.

He leaned over, kissed her once before he reached for a bag of shredded cheese. "So...I've been thinking. With you staying and being homeless, why not move in with me?" He didn't look at her as he spoke, as if the question was totally normal.

"Move in here?" She'd never lived with anyone before. Well, she'd had a roommate in college, but she'd never lived with a man.

He lifted a shoulder, his body language so casual when she was freaking out a little. "You're going to be over here every night anyway."

She laughed lightly because it was true. "That's a big step."

"I'm ready for it." Simple as that.

Her throat tightened for a moment at the seriousness of this. Moving in with him was a huge deal but it felt beyond right. "I'll pay for half the groceries and bills."

"Okay."

She pushed out a breath, surprised but glad he'd acquiesced so easily. He could be stubborn about some things, she'd learned.

"When do you want me to move in?"

He moved the pan off the hot stove as he turned it off then stepped over so that he was standing in between her open legs. "Immediately," he murmured. "Most of your stuff is in boxes already so it'll be easy. And you get half of the walk-in closet."

She grinned as she wrapped her legs around his waist. "Now you're talking. You won't mind my food truck being parked here?"

"No. We can work on it together in the back during our free time."

Swallowing hard, she brushed her lips over his. "You really are perfect."

"No, but if that's what you think, I'll take it." He kissed her again with a fierceness she embraced.

The spicy scents of the southwestern omelets filled the air as she pulled him tighter to her, and she had a feeling all that food was going to have to wait.

CHAPTER ELEVEN

Three months later

Brad grinned as Fallon jumped down from the back of her food truck. The actual truck was bright pink with white writing on it, and the awning that popped out over the order window was turquoise with thin white stripes. She'd agonized over the coloring longer than anything else but she'd picked right. No one would ever be able to miss her food truck.

The May Holly Smoke Food Festival was coming to an end and he knew she'd done well today, if the grin on her face was any indication.

"Hey, babe. We almost sold out today." The "we" referred to Sasha, Nora's younger sister, who Fallon had hired for the event in case it got busy.

"No surprise there." He pulled Fallon into his arms, not caring that he'd get powder or sugar or whatever was on her pink apron transferred to his shirt. "Got a long cleanup?"

"It won't be too bad. The only thing we have left are a few petits fours. But the mini cupcakes, pecan bites, macaroons, and even mini jam jars sold out quickly. And I'm glad we stocked up on extra coffee, because we almost ran out of that too." Her excitement was infectious as she bounced on her feet. Her auburn hair was pulled up into a ponytail and she had on a ball cap with Sugar Rush's logo.

"So the 'mini' idea was a hit?" At the last couple festivals he'd noticed that people, especially those with kids, didn't want plates to carry around. They wanted easy, and bite-sized desserts was as easy as it got.

"Oh yeah, and you'll get credit for that later," she murmured.

"And I'll take it." Especially after the day he'd had. Unlike her, people weren't always excited to see the sheriff at these events. He'd had to deal with teenagers trying to steal from vendors, and a couple guys who decided to get drunk and obnoxious. He would never understand how people could do that, especially around families and kids. Sometimes their own kids. "I've still got some paperwork to fill out, but I'll meet you at home?"

"Sounds perfect to me." She laid her head against his chest, and sighed contentedly. "I'm freaking exhausted, but man, this was a good day."

He rubbed a hand down her spine, closed his eyes for a long moment. Every day with her was a good day. Since Fallon had come into his life, everything had changed. In ways he hadn't seen coming. He'd never expected to ask a woman to move in with him as fast as he had Fallon. But he didn't regret asking her for one second.

He'd figured they were headed that way anyway and he really liked waking up to her every morning. The last few months she'd been incredibly busy getting her business off the ground, figuring out what worked and what didn't work. He'd even helped out some on his days off, and he loved spending the extra time with her. Not to mention it had put him in more contact with people in the community, which was always a plus. Eventually she'd have to hire someone but for now she was being smart about where her profits went.

"You too tired to head to my dad's later tonight?" On Sunday nights they had a standing dinner date with him, but tonight Brad had something else planned—he just wasn't telling Fallon.

She looked up at him. "Nah, but I'm not playing him in chess again."

Brad snorted. His dad had lost, but "barely" as he'd put it. "He's itching for a rematch."

"No way. I want to kick my feet up and relax tonight. When we get home, I'll even let you massage me." Her grin turned wicked.

The last time he'd given her a massage she'd lasted about two minutes before she'd jumped him. Not that he was complaining.

"Sounds like a plan to me. Listen…I was thinking we might look for a bigger place for us soon. Maybe someplace we can turn a mother-in-law suite into an commercial kitchen?" It would be good for tax purposes and it would cut down on how early she had to get up and over to Nora's kitchen to prep for the day. If she just had to walk out the back door to get to the kitchen, she'd get more rest, which he knew she needed. She couldn't go at this pace forever.

Her blue eyes lit up. "That's a great idea. Wait, are you talking buying?"

"Yes." And more, but he wanted to talk about that later.

"Wow, that's huge, but yes. Not gonna lie, I wouldn't mind getting to sleep in a little some mornings. You are a genius," she murmured before going up on her toes to kiss him. "I've got to help Sasha out so we can get out of here but I'll meet you at home after."

"See you soon."

All his muscles tightened as he watched her turn from him and head into the back of the truck. She completely owned him. And soon, he planned to lock her down forever.

"What is this?" Fallon glanced at him as he steered into the driveway of a home he'd been looking at for the two of them.

"A house I thought you might like."

Her eyes widened slightly. "Seriously? That's…fast."

He paused at her tone, wondering if that was a good or bad thing. "Come on. The Realtor gave me the code."

"I like this neighborhood," she said as she rounded the front of his truck. "And look how big the front porch is."

The band of tension loosened around his chest as they strode up the front steps. According to the Realtor, the style was rustic country cottage. All he knew was that Fallon would like it. A mix of brick and wood, it had a big wraparound porch with a large, lush backyard, and the interior had been completely modernized. Especially the kitchen. He punched in the code and the key from the holder fell out.

A layer of sweat formed down his spine as he opened the door. He hadn't expected to be so nervous. Suddenly, the little box in his back pocket seemed to weigh a ton. He wasn't afraid of what he was about to do, he just didn't want to screw this up.

"I bet this room is gorgeous in the morning with all that natural light streaming through." She linked her fingers through his as they stepped into what would be a living room. Brazilian wood floors gleamed under the soft light from the overhead fan. The fireplace would be perfect in the winter and he could think of exactly what he planned to do with her in front of it.

"And this place has a mother-in-law suite?"

"Yep. Out back. They never finished it, which is actually better if this is something we decide to put an offer on. It'll be a lot easier to turn it into a kitchen without having to rip out walls. Come on, let's go check it out before we explore the rest of the house."

"Why are they selling?" she asked as they headed down the hallway. "This place is gorgeous."

"Moving south to be closer to their kids. And the house was getting to be too big to keep up. They've actually already relocated so I think we could go in a little lower on the asking price."

"How many rooms is it?"

"Four bedrooms, three baths—two upstairs and one down here."

"Very nice. Buying is such a huge thing." As they stepped into the kitchen, her eyes widened. "Wow."

"I thought you'd like it." It had been one of the selling points. According to the Realtor it was any chef's dream kitchen with a "minimalist open concept, streamlined with flat-panel white cabinets and granite countertops." He just knew that it felt like Fallon. And the sparkly mirror backsplash behind the stove was something he knew she was going to adore.

She immediately went to the island countertop, running her fingers along the granite. "I love this color. And the pot rack." The oversized steel oval rack fit perfectly with the rest of the appliances and coloring. "I hope this can stay—you know, if we put in an offer. Hey, what's…" Her voice trailed off as she rounded the island, finally spotting the tray of cupcakes on the lone round table in the breakfast nook.

She let out a gasp as she reached it, and when she turned around to face him, he'd already dropped to one knee. He'd made the cupcakes himself so they weren't pretty, but there was a letter on each one spelling out *Will you marry me?*

"I've already talked to your family, but your answer is the only one that matters. Marry me, Fallon O'Connor?" He slowly opened the lid of the ring box.

"Yes!" Tears rolled down her cheeks as he slipped it on her left hand ring finger. "Yes, yes, yes," she whispered.

In a flash he had her in his arms, crushing his mouth to hers for a searing claiming. This was the woman he wanted to spend the rest of his life with, something he'd known for a long time.

"This is the sweetest proposal," Fallon whispered. "Though I don't think you have a future in baking."

"No kidding." He laughed as he cupped her cheek. "We don't have to put in an offer on this place. But I want to make you my wife."

"And I'm ready to lock you down and make you an honest man. Though I have to ask, how did you manage to keep this a secret?" She held out her hand, her eyes lighting up as she looked at the sparkly diamond.

He loved seeing it on her hand, loved that now there was a symbol that declared her off-limits. Caveman attitude? Yeah, it was. "I had to buy it a couple towns over so there was no chance of it getting back to you."

"This is perfect. I love you so much."

"I love you… You ready to go see the potential kitchen?"

An even bigger grin spread across her face. "Oh yeah. But when we get home tonight, we're going to celebrate properly."

"I already have a bottle of champagne in the fridge."

"Always prepared, my Boy Scout."

"Damn straight."

It's Me Again, Baby

CHAPTER ONE

"I'm here. Gotta go," Maguire said to his sister Fallon as he steered down the long driveway up to a two-story brick house he was interested in buying. There was an actual white picket fence lining the front of the five-acre property, an empty pen for chickens, and an industrial-sized steel work shed about fifty yards from the house. The work space was the main reason he was looking at the property. He needed enough room for his private vehicle restorations.

"Liar. You're just tired of talking about wedding stuff."

Yeah, no shit. But he wasn't going to say that to his sister. Because she could be mean when she wanted. When they'd been younger she'd shaved his head. Twice. And that was just the tip of the iceberg. Of course, he'd deserved the head shavings.

And he loved his only sister, so if she wanted his opinion on colors, he was going to give it. "I'm serious. I see the Realtor's car in the driveway." A black midsize BMW SUV. Nice, dependable vehicle.

"Fine. But if you get a chance will you call Mom and tell her if you're going to be at our Monday dinner next week? She keeps asking me, like I have any knowledge of your schedule."

He frowned at his sister's words, but committed to phoning their mom before ending the call. He'd actually been *trying* to call their mom the last twenty-four hours, but she'd only been texting him. Which wasn't like her. She said she'd found him a new Realtor — since his last one had been lazy — and told him where to be and at what time. The bossiness was vintage Mom, but the MIA act wasn't. She usually called him a few times a week. Minimum. She was like that with all four of her kids. And now that two of them were engaged, she called their significant others the same amount.

There were worse things in the world than a mom who called too much. After spending years overseas without much contact with his family, he could admit he liked how much she doted on all of them.

Rolling his shoulders once, he shoved his phone in his pocket and got out of his car, a 1969 Ford Mustang Boss 429—also known as the Boss 9—he'd restored himself. The color was called Aspen Red, and for a man who had no problem making split-second decisions in the heat of battle, it had taken him a full month to decide on a color. He ran his hand over the hood as he strode up the driveway, admiring her as he always did. This was his baby, and all the work he'd put into her had been the best therapy after his last tour in Afghanistan.

He hadn't been able to assimilate back into the civilian world easily. Having a task to work on in all his spare time had been the only thing keeping him focused. Now he had a "sexy muscle car," as his sister put it. He didn't know about the sexy part, but when he looked at it, he felt a sense of pride. He'd had so many offers on the car but he would never sell her.

As the front door opened, he started to smile on instinct, but it froze on his face as he came face to face with Samantha Murphy.

His mother had told him his Realtor's name was Sam and he'd been so busy with work he hadn't thought to ask for more details. *Aw, hell.* His mom had known exactly what she was doing and had set this up intentionally. Which explained the lack of communication. He shouldn't be surprised.

At least Samantha was as surprised as he was, if her deer-in-headlights expression was any indication. Her long, straight, dark hair was pulled back into some sort of twist thing, but he'd seen it down and around her face as she'd ridden him. He'd seen every inch of her sweet body, sucked on her pink nipples as she'd come apart in his arms. And had never been able to get the woman out of his head. It didn't matter that three years had passed.

"Maguire?" His name on her lips brought up too many naked memories.

Savagely he shut off all thoughts of the past. Especially after the way she'd cut him out of her life. That had blindsided him in a way he'd never expected. He couldn't even call what had happened a breakup. She'd simply ghosted on him, acted as if all the promises they'd made each other had never been.

He took a few steps forward, trying not to notice her long, toned legs and how incredible she looked in the formfitting blue and white dress. "I was supposed to meet my Realtor here. Sam?"

She cleared her throat, nodded once. "That's me. My mom asked me to meet a friend of... Oh, your mom's. She must have meant you, not a friend. I, ah..." Her cheeks flushed pink and it shouldn't be sexy, but everything about her was. Damn it. "I didn't realize it was you."

Yeah, he had no doubt of that. She'd have probably canceled had she known. He rubbed a hand over the back of his neck. "So, you're living back in Holly now?" As far as he knew she'd been in Oregon the last three years. He hadn't seen her since she was twenty-one and he'd been twenty-six. Even then he'd felt too old for her, had worried she wasn't ready for him—for a relationship. He'd been right.

"I moved back a month ago. Since my dad died. My mom's been handling everything well but I wanted to be here for her." Traces of pain etched her expression before a neutral mask fell into place.

Oh, right. "I'm really sorry about your dad." He'd been out of town and hadn't made it to the funeral. Hell, he hadn't realized she was back in Holly again. Obviously. No way was he going to be a dick to her now. Not that he would have been anyway. He was going to be so damn nice so she had no idea how badly she'd hurt him. He wouldn't give her the satisfaction.

"Thanks. Listen, if you want to find another Realtor, it's totally fine. In fact, I have some great recommendations."

He should say yes. It would be the sane thing to do. He didn't want to work with her when he wanted her—still. "Nah, it's okay. The past is water under the bridge. I never held anything against you." *Liar, liar.* He'd been pissed—and hurt—for a long time over the way she'd cut contact with him. As if what they'd shared hadn't mattered. It might have only been a week that they'd spent together, but they'd had a connection. Or he'd thought they had. Turned out she was just a pretty little liar.

She frowned, her eyebrows pulling together. And just as quickly her dark eyes popped with a fiery anger. "*You* never held anything against *me*?"

"We were young. You were only twenty-one. Me being overseas for so long? I get why you didn't want to deal with something like that." The lies rolled off his tongue and he even managed to sound believable. Like she hadn't cut him deep.

"You're unbelievable! I came to the airport the day you left to say goodbye, and ran into your other girlfriend. Don't try and feed me some bullshit. I talked to Amy Barret. I know you were screwing both of us! So when you called me, yeah I never returned your calls. And I blocked your email address. You deserved it." Her cheeks were crimson now and not because she was flustered. She looked a little like she was ready to throat punch him. Aaannnd that was way too hot. Even if her words were insane.

"Amy?" He vaguely remembered the woman. She didn't even live in Holly anymore, had moved not long after he'd gotten out of the Marines. He had no idea where she'd moved and didn't care. Hell, he'd met her at a party right around the time he'd hooked up with Samantha. He'd been home on leave, and after he'd met Sam he'd been obsessed, to put it mildly. He'd wanted to spend all his spare time with her, to eat, breathe and drink the woman. "I have no idea what she told you, but I wasn't sleeping with her. I wasn't sleeping with anyone but *you*."

Samantha rolled her dark eyes, one of her hands landing on a curvy hip as she stared him down. "I'm not having this stupid conversation. And I take back what I said about finding you another Realtor. Find someone on your own, jackass." She spun away from him, those luscious hips swaying as she stalked back toward the front door.

He moved lightning quick. Without thinking, he had his hand placed against the front door so she couldn't open it. That subtle apples-and-cinnamon scent he remembered clearly clung to her, dragging up even more memories he didn't want to be holding on to. Her smell shouldn't affect him so much and he hated that it did.

She turned and shoved at his chest, but he didn't move. He wanted to crowd her personal space even if he knew it was a dick move. He was beyond pissed. "I never slept with anyone when we were together—and I haven't been with anyone since!"

His shouted words hung in the air as she stared up at him. Yeah, he hadn't meant to admit that *last* little jewel, but what-the-fuck-ever. There were a multitude of reasons he hadn't been with anyone since returning to civilian life. Not because of her.

Birds chirping and the soft whistle of a cool wind rustling the leaves overhead were the only sounds as they stared at each other for what felt like an eternity.

"You're serious."

"Yeah." He stepped back, but only a foot, giving her a bit of space.

"I'm...sorry, Maguire. I thought, oh God." She rubbed a hand over her face, then closed her eyes. "I was so insecure back then. Especially where you were concerned. It was easier to believe what Amy said than believe you wanted to be with me. I'm sorry."

It pissed him off that she'd believed some flake over what they'd shared. But he still found himself saying, "I'm sorry too."

She let out a nervous little laugh. "You have nothing to be sorry for. And I'm seriously embarrassed right now. I, uh, probably shouldn't have called you a jackass."

He lifted a shoulder, his mouth curving up. "I like that show of temper."

She snorted, seeming more at ease as she shook her head. "You would. Can we start today over?"

Maguire wanted to start some other things over, but nodded. "Yeah. You still want to be my Realtor?"

That delicious shade of pink flushed her cheeks again. "Yes. And we can see how things work. I don't make my clients sign contracts requiring exclusivity. If you're not happy, I want you free to go to someone else. Everyone should be happy in this relationship."

"Can I take you to dinner tomorrow tonight?" Getting caught up with sexy Samantha Murphy sounded like a fine plan. It was just dinner anyway. Belatedly he realized he should have asked if she was single before asking her out. But around her his mouth seemed to get away from him.

She paused for a fraction of a moment, then nodded. "Okay."

"We can catch up." *Yeah, catch up. Liar.*

"Sounds good."

"All right, then." He'd find out later if she was dating anyone. Not that he was thinking of dating her. He nearly snorted at himself. Lying again. "Want to show me this place?"

She nodded and quickly morphed into professional mode, her body language and expression changing. "The owners are gone for the next hour so this is the perfect time. And based on the specs your mom gave me — she is very sneaky, by the way — I've got a few other places lined up today as well if you're able to see them?"

"I'm free." Even if he hadn't already taken off most of the day for this, he'd have done it now. And not to look at houses. He wanted to spend more time with Samantha. Tonight he planned to find out more about what she'd been up to the last few years. And why she'd been so quick to believe he would have cheated on her.

Soon he planned to claim what had been taken from him. It had sliced him up to lose Sam before. And to find out it was over a stupid misunderstanding — from someone he barely remembered — knocked his world on its axis.

CHAPTER TWO

Samantha crossed her legs, trying not to nervously tap her foot as she sat across from Maguire O'Connor. The sexiest man she'd ever known. After looking at houses with him most of the morning, she had a pretty good idea that he was going to place an offer on the very first property she'd showed him. He'd really liked that steel work shed. Or at least he was thinking really hard about it. She'd seen that familiar gleam in his pale blue eyes that she'd seen in so many clients over the years.

Normally the thought of a possible sale gave her a rush. Now, she didn't care so much about that as she did that the man she'd thought had been a complete and utter jackass was in fact not a liar, and was sitting across from her. Looking good enough to eat. Not only that, he'd asked her out and she was counting down the seconds until their dinner tomorrow. It didn't matter that it wasn't a date. She wanted to spend time with him in a non-work setting.

They'd stopped at Nora's Books and Brew—Nora was apparently his soon-to-be sister-in-law—to grab coffee and a snack. She was glad for the reprieve because her feet needed it. And she liked spending time with him. She was still a little horrified she'd jumped to conclusions years ago, but she hadn't been kidding. She'd been seriously lacking in the self-confidence department. Sometimes she still struggled with it.

Soon she had to head out to meet another client and he had to get back to one of his auto body shops.

"Can I get something off my chest?" she asked, keeping her voice low even though there weren't any patrons close enough to overhear them.

High-top tables were scattered around the dining area of the cute coffee shop. The bookstore was on the other side of the building, but the whole shop had a Christmas theme twenty-four hours a day, three hundred and sixty-five days a year. As did all the shops of Holly, North Carolina, with twinkle lights crossing over Main Street, garland-wrapped street lights, and snowmen and Santas in most store windows. Even the table they were sitting at was Christmas-themed. The legs had red and white striped stockings covering them and little elf booties at the bottom.

"Of course." There was a slight rasp to his voice and a hint of more than subtle lust in his gaze when he watched her. It was almost as if he was trying to temper it. And failing spectacularly.

Which...she didn't even know where to go with that. She cleared her throat, trying to quell the nerves in her belly. "I clearly reacted poorly years ago to Amy's revelation—"

"Lie."

"Yes, lie, not revelation. Poor word choice." Her lips curved up as she continued. "It's an excuse and probably not a good one now, but I was young, and you're, well, you. Maguire O'Connor. I was intimidated by you back then and couldn't believe you'd 'chosen' me, which I know is a silly word. But that was how it felt to my twenty-one-year-old self. I struggled with feeling confident in who I am for a lot of years. And this is probably too much information, but I wanted to put it out there and let you know why I reacted the way I did and why I cut off contact." Looking back, Sam realized how easily she'd let that liar Amy Barret feed off her insecurities. It was so clear now, but hindsight was a freaking bitch. Sam had lost a lot of weight in college and had just started to own who she was when she'd met Maguire.

Clearly not enough. She hadn't been used to guys paying attention to her. Then she'd come home for the summer after graduation and had met Maguire. A guy she'd crushed on hard when she'd been younger. He'd been years older than her, out of her league, and had no idea who she was back then. To be fair, she'd been in middle school and he hadn't paid attention to her or any of her friends.

Which was good, because that would have been gross if he had.

But that summer three years ago, when he'd shown an intense interest in her, she'd been surprised and flattered.

"Not too much info. I'm glad you told me," he said quietly. Relief slid through her that he wasn't holding the past against her. "Though I'm surprised you struggled with confidence. You're smart, funny, and even more stunning now than you were then."

His words warmed her from the inside out because there was only truth in his voice. She knew what she looked like, but that didn't change the fact that she hadn't always loved her body and herself. She could admit she enjoyed that he found her attractive. More than a little, if the hunger in his gaze was any indication. She felt the same for him.

"Are you seeing anyone right now?" he continued before she could respond.

"No." She'd just moved home, not that it really mattered. She hadn't dated much recently. Okay, in a looooong time.

She'd been consumed with work since longer than she wanted to admit. When she'd moved away on her own, her heart still broken by what she'd assumed was Maguire's betrayal, she'd been a workaholic, determined to carve out a name for herself where she'd lived. And she had. When her dad had died it had been a wake-up call though. In more ways than one. She hadn't been looking to settle down when she moved home, but she had wanted to slow down a little, to enjoy her life and spend time with her mom and friends.

"Are you?" she asked, continuing. She assumed he wasn't, after the surprising comment he'd made, but still wanted to ask. Not that he'd asked her out or anything, but still. She wanted to know.

"No." The way he watched her with such intense focus was unnerving—and incredibly arousing. She'd never been on the end of such single-minded attention from any man. Before she could respond, Nora Cassidy stepped up to their table, two mugs and two plated croissants on a tray. She set everything on the table, the overhead light glinting off her sparkly engagement ring.

It was as if that band around Samantha's chest loosened and she was suddenly able to breathe again. Just being around Maguire like this was seriously messing with her head.

"Sorry about the wait, you guys." Wisps of steam drifted off the latte Nora placed in front of Sam.

Maguire grinned when Nora set his hot cocoa down—complete with a candy cane in it.

For some reason, the fact that he'd ordered a hot cocoa made him that much more adorable to Sam. "No problem. Looks like your rush just cleared out."

"It did, but we'll see another one in an hour. Let me know if you guys need anything. Well, Sam, *you* let me know." She shot Maguire a semi-serious glare. "I'm only being nice to you because you're with a paying customer."

"What?" He placed a hand on his chest, mock insulted.

She shot her gaze to Sam. "Jackson got too roughed up on the rink on Saturday and I know it was him," she said, jerking a thumb at Maguire, "who bruised his ribs."

Maguire snorted, which wasn't a denial at all.

"Roughed up?" Sam asked once Nora was out of earshot.

He snorted again, shaking his head. "Brotherly sparring. We had a free weekend and hit the ice for a friendly game of hockey. Us, the sheriff and some guys from the fire department. Nora's only got a sister though. I think our type of roughhousing is a shock to her."

"So you're still playing hockey." He'd been sexy on the ice. And okay, off it, but when he skated it was a thing of beauty.

"Yeah...wait, you've seen me?"

Her cheeks flushed even as she nodded, realizing her inadvertent little confession. "Yeah. Many years ago. When I was in middle school and there was no way you would have noticed me." They were only a little over five years apart in age.

"Maybe I'll invite you out for our next game, then. You can tell me if I've improved."

"Or if you've gotten worse in your old age."

"Old?"

"I'm messing with you." Since she remembered when his birthday was, she knew that he'd just turned thirty and was well, delicious-looking.

His grin widened, taking him from good-looking to ridiculously handsome territory. Everything about him was sexy. With the sleeves of his long-sleeved T-shirt—advertising one of his auto repair shops—shoved up, he was showing off muscular forearms and a plethora of tattoos that made her mouth water.

Most of the tattoos he'd had when they'd been... Well, whatever they'd been. They'd had a lot of sex, shared a lot of promises to stay in touch and remain exclusive to each other, but calling him her ex-boyfriend felt too weird. Things between them had burned as bright as a shooting star—then suddenly been snuffed out. The death of what could have been between them had jarred her senses and she'd never dealt with it. No, she'd thrown herself into work. Part of her still hurt to think of what they could have had.

Shaking off thoughts of what might have been, she tried not to stare at his tattoos or to remember what the rest of them looked like. The ones that weren't showing right now. She could feel her cheeks heating up at that thought so she shelved it. For now. She'd return to it later.

"You've been very busy since settling back in Holly." Impressively so. He was a workaholic, something she understood well. He owned and ran two auto repair shops and recently had officially started a vehicle restoration company. Some of which she'd found out today from him, but she'd known about the auto repair shops even before moving back herself. She could admit she'd subtly, or not so subtly, asked her mom about the O'Connor family. Or one O'Connor in particular.

"Yeah. I haven't taken real time off in years. I've been spending all my weekends working on vehicle restorations."

"If that Mustang you're driving is any indication of your work, I'd say it's time well spent."

His smile went positively nuclear at her compliment, showing off dimples that made heat rush between her legs. "Thank you. She's the first car I ever restored."

Oh yeah, his smile should be illegal. "She?"

"Something that beautiful is definitely a woman."

Laughing lightly, she picked up her drink. "Maybe you'll take me for a ride sometime." As soon as the words were out she realized they could have a double meaning.

A flush of color tinged his cheeks as he kept her pinned with his ice-blue gaze that somehow burned. "Anytime."

Maguire didn't bother knocking as he unlocked the side door that led to his parents' kitchen. His childhood home. He and all his siblings had keys and his parents didn't care when they stopped by. If his mom and dad wanted privacy, they sent out a mass text and told all of them not to come by. Not very subtle, but neither of his parents had ever claimed to be. Since he hadn't received one from his mom, it was safe to come see her.

"I was just thinking of you," she said, glancing at him over her shoulder as she pulled a wine glass down from the rack under one of the cabinets.

"And I was just thinking about how sneaky you are." Sighing, he collapsed on one of the chairs at the kitchen table. After work he'd promised a friend he'd help install a surround sound system. In exchange, his friend had promised free beer and food. He'd gotten one out of two things, since his friend's idea of food was days-old takeout, and Maguire was now famished.

"So you met with Sam today?" She set the glass next to a bottle of red wine and moved to the refrigerator.

"*Samantha*? Yes. She showed me some nice places." And he'd enjoyed spending so much time with her. She was even more beautiful than he remembered. If he hadn't promised his friend to help with that installation he'd have asked her out tonight instead of waiting until tomorrow. Which seemed like an eternity away.

His mom heaped a big scoop of her homemade lasagna on a plate and covered it before putting it into the microwave. "She's a sharp girl. And it's good she moved back to be closer to her mom."

"So how'd you know about…" He wasn't even sure how to phrase the question. He and Sam had been hot and heavy but they'd been so wrapped up in each other. He'd barely seen his family when he'd been home on the leave he'd met her. No, he'd been with her every second he could get, but he hadn't told his family about their relationship. It had been too new and felt too special. He hadn't wanted his brothers giving him grief, and okay, he'd been selfish. He'd wanted her all to himself.

"Oh, sweetheart." His mom patted his cheek once before heading back to the counter for her wine. "When will you learn that I know everything?"

He snorted as the microwave dinged.

"I heated that up for you because I know you haven't eaten," she said as she opened the bottle.

Grinning, he stood. "Thanks. It smells amazing."

"Of course it does. I made it." She sat at the table as he grabbed utensils and his food.

He'd come over here because he was starving and because he'd wanted to ask how she'd known he had a thing for Sam. "Why didn't you just tell me she moved back into town?" Instead of setting up that meeting.

She arched an eyebrow. "I believe I did."

"You know what I mean."

Instead of answering, she shrugged. "Tell me about the places you saw today."

And that was that. He'd learned long ago that when his mom decided a topic was closed, there was no reopening it. Once he'd finished telling her about all the places, she smiled.

"I knew you'd like the Davidsons' property. It's perfect."

"Yeah. I'm going to bid lower than the asking price. It's overpriced." He could find a similar property and just have a work shed built. But it was the time waiting for it to be built he wasn't sure he wanted to deal with. Still, he was going to offer lower.

"I agree. I have a feeling they'll take it too. They're looking to downsize and have their eye on a condo downtown."

"How do you... Salon gossip?" She got most of her intel at Holly's salon/florist located in the middle of downtown. And she'd been known to start a betting pool or two on various things—including how long it would take Jackson to ask out the woman who was now his fiancée.

"Of course."

"Good to know." He savored the hearty lasagna and the comfort of his childhood home as he finished his meal.

"I think your Aunt Carly is dating Brad's father," his mom said after a few minutes.

He just raised his eyebrows, but didn't respond. Because he knew for a fact that those two were dating as of very recently. He'd been sworn to secrecy by Fallon.

His mom's blue eyes, the exact color of his own, narrowed. "You know something, don't you?"

Leaning back from the table, he linked his hands together behind his head. "I know this is the best meal I've had in ages. Thanks, Mom."

She sniffed once, but he saw the appreciation in her eyes. She loved cooking and it didn't seem to matter that none of her kids lived at home anymore. He was always over raiding the fridge. Which was probably sad, but he could live with the shame.

"Have you asked her out?" Her blunt question took him off guard.

Internally he cursed himself for not being prepared. *Should have known this was coming.* "She'll be showing me a few more places tomorrow."

Sniffing again, his mom stood, picking up her full glass as she slid the chair into place. "Just don't wait too long to make a move. I hear that nice young man Ethan Thaxter has his eye on her."

"I know what you're doing." Picking up his dirty plate, he headed toward the sink.

"Think whatever you want. It's the truth. Make sure you see your father before you head out. He has a car question for you." She was out of the room before he could blink, much less respond.

Frowning to himself, he washed the dirty dish and utensils and set them in the drying rack next to the sink. His mom was likely just messing with him, but if she wasn't... Well, it didn't matter if that rich asshole had his eye on Samantha.

Maguire wasn't letting her get away this time.

As soon as he had the thought his entire body jolted. What the hell was he thinking? She'd burned him before, even if it hadn't been intentional. Rolling his shoulders once, he tried to ease the sudden tension. He certainly didn't like the thought of her with someone else. Not one bit.

CHAPTER THREE

Maguire held his phone in his hand, staring at the dark screen for a long moment. God, it was like he was in high school again. Of course, when he'd been in high school he hadn't had a freaking cell phone and he hadn't been nervous about girls.

But he was nervous around Samantha. She brought out possessive feelings he'd never experienced with anyone else but her. He was protective by nature, but the possessive thing? He'd only ever had that for her. It seemed things hadn't changed.

Instead of texting he dialed her number and was pleased when she picked up on the second ring.

"Hey, Maguire."

The sound of her saying his name had all his muscles tightening. The memory of her saying it under very different circumstances was seared into his memory. "Hey. How's your day going?" He could hear a multitude of voices in the background, as if she was at a restaurant. Which made sense since it was almost noon.

"Good. Busy, which is always good." She let out a little laugh. "I found a few more places to show you this afternoon."

They'd already planned to see a couple but he wouldn't mind adding more if it meant spending additional time with her. "Sounds good. I found one I'd like to see as well. I'll text or email you the info?"

"Either works. I've got my phone attached to me."

"We still on for tonight?"

There was a slight pause. "Yes. If you still want?"

"I do." Very much so. He kept that last bit to himself, not wanting to come on too strong. He hadn't actually said it was a date, just that he wanted to catch up.

"Good. We can just go somewhere after the last showing if you want."

"How about I cook for you at my place?" Okay, *that* wasn't subtle.

She paused even longer. "I'd like that." Her voice was slightly raspier than before and he wished he could see her face. Wondered if her cheeks would be flushed.

"Want to meet and just ride around in one vehicle today?"

"Yeah, I've got a couple showings and an appointment but I can meet you close to one thirty."

"Perfect. Just text me where you want me to pick you up."

"Okay. See you soon."

He figured it was probably out of the ordinary for her to ride around with clients. She probably drove everywhere or just met people, more likely. But some intrinsic part of him wanted to see her sitting in his Mustang. Okay he wanted more than that, but the thought of her in his car was beyond sexy.

The next hour crept by as he worked on an older model Jaguar. Keeping his hands and mind busy helped hold the nightmares at bay. Which was why he worked so much, even over the weekends, adding vehicle restorations to his already slammed schedule.

"What's got you all twisted up?"

He turned at the sound of his sister's voice.

Blinking, he looked up from the engine he'd been working on and realized that most of the guys had gone to lunch. Hell. He'd been seriously zoning out, thinking about Samantha, which wasn't like him. Even when he was focused on a project, he kept his surroundings in check out of habit.

Always. It was ingrained in him. But he'd been consumed with thoughts of Samantha to the point of stupid distraction. He should have heard his sister arrive.

"When'd you get here?" he asked instead of answering.

Fallon lifted a shoulder. Petite and slender, she had the same build and coloring as their mom, with her auburn hair and blue eyes. "Two minutes ago. Harper said it was okay if I came back here."

Harper Pratt, his assistant/accounting guru, always let his family come back into the garage part of the shop. "What's up? Everything okay?" Fallon had on a bright pink T-shirt with the logo and name of her new food truck business, Sugar Rush, on it. He was surprised she wasn't working right now.

"Yeah. Already got a rush earlier for the breakfast crowd. I'm headed downtown to grab the after-lunch crowd who still want snacks. Then I'm headed to the retirement community. Thought I'd stop and see you on the way."

He crossed his arms over his chest, eyeing her warily. "Why?"

"A sister can't stop by to see her big brother?"

"What do you want?" he asked dryly.

"Dude, nothing!" She leaned against the front of a new Toyota Highlander whose windshield they were about to replace. "Okay, I wanted to know what's up with you and Sam Murphy. Mom said something about you two and I'm nosy."

"She's my new Realtor. And get off the vehicle." He nodded at the Highlander.

Fallon rolled her eyes and shoved up. "I'm not hurting anything. And don't try to change the subject. Come on, man. She's freaking gorgeous! And *so* sweet. You two a thing now?"

Oh yeah, he was not having this conversation with his younger sister. Or anyone, for that matter. His personal business was his alone. "You're turning into Mom."

She snorted. "I know you're just trying to get under my skin."

"Nope. Just telling the truth."

"You're really not going to tell me?"

He glanced at his watch, saw he only had about twenty minutes to clean up and head out to meet Samantha. "I've gotta run."

Her eyes narrowed slightly. "Kinda late for a lunch break."

He hadn't taken a break, but that was beside the point. "I'm the boss. I do what I want."

She stomped one of her feet. "You're infuriating."

"I'm not the one harassing my sibling in the hopes of winning some betting pool." He could be wrong, but he had a sneaking suspicion that was the only reason his sister was here. There was probably already some bet going on, if not at the salon, then among his family at least. They were shameless—and he included himself in that since he always joined in too.

When her cheeks went crimson, he knew he was right. "Damn it! Fine. I'm going to win this one. Oh, I left a tray of goodies at the front desk for you and the rest of the guys. Even if you are being stingy with information." She leaned up, gave him a quick kiss on the cheek. "Love you, dude."

"Love you, too." Grinning, he shook his head as his sister hurried out of the garage.

Using the private bathroom attached to his office, he hurriedly cleaned up, taking a quick shower to rinse off the grease and grime of the garage.

Anticipation hummed through him as he headed around to the back of his garage where his Mustang was parked. For years he'd been consumed with work, using it as an outlet to exorcise his demons, and for the first time in forever he didn't want to put in overtime tonight or this weekend.

He wanted to spend all his free time with the sweet and sexy Samantha.

Butterflies launched inside Sam at the sight of Maguire pulling up in front of the empty commercial property she'd been showing.

"You're meeting with Maguire O'Connor?" Ethan Thaxter asked, looking out one of the front windows.

"Yes. You know him?"

"Just by reputation. I was thinking of having my father's old Morgan restored. Enough people have recommended him that I've been leaning toward calling him."

Samantha nodded politely. "I hear he's the best. Did you want to do another walk-through?"

He shook his head, not one perfect blond hair out of place as he smiled at her. The man was classically handsome, but did absolutely nothing for her libido. Not that he was interested in her either. No, he was a dream client. Respectful of her time and not looking because he was bored or simply thinking of buying. He was a man on a mission right now and she hoped she was helping him find the right properties.

Her attention was snagged again when she glanced out at Maguire stepping out of his sexy muscle car. Her lower abdomen clenched as a wave of heat rushed through her.

He had on jeans and a simple T-shirt with the sleeves shoved up to his elbows—showing off ropes of muscles she'd kissed more than once, as well as that plethora of intricate tattoos that marked his time in the Marine Corps. She'd never thought of ink as particularly sexy, but on him? Oh yeah. It worked. His dark hair was still damp and a little mussed, as if he'd finger-combed it after taking a shower. Probably more her imagination than anything, but thinking about him naked and wet wasn't a bad thing. Of course, right now she didn't need to get hot and flustered in front of another client.

She cleared her throat. "Let's head out, then. Maybe you can talk to Maguire about car stuff." Her voice was calm and steady even as her heart was an erratic tattoo at the thought of spending more time with Maguire.

Outside in the sunshine, a cool spring breeze rolled over them, making the hem of her dress flutter slightly. May was one of her favorite times of the year. Not too hot, not too cold. Perfect. Everything was coming back to life; a time for new beginnings.

Maguire had sunglasses on so it was impossible to read his expression as he stepped up onto the sidewalk. "Sorry I'm a little early."

"It's okay," Ethan said before she could respond. He held out a hand for Maguire. "We're done here, but I was just telling Sam that I was looking for someone to restore an old Morgan. Your name keeps coming up."

Maguire gave a neutral smile as he nodded. "My team and I do a good job. If you're interested in a quote feel free to call the office. Harper will set you up with a consult and we'll see if we're a fit."

Ethan nodded and the two men didn't bother making small talk, just shook hands.

"I'll call you in the morning," Ethan said as he turned back to Sam. "I'm pretty sure I want to put in offers on a couple places. Need to run some numbers tonight."

"I'll talk to you tomorrow, then." She'd ended up gaining Ethan as a client because he'd been unhappy with his last Realtor. Called the guy lazy. And considering Sam's brief interactions with the man, she couldn't disagree.

"I got your text, and the address you sent me is closer than the places I found so we can start there if you'd like," she said to Maguire as Ethan slid into the driver's seat of his car.

Maguire pushed his sunglasses back on his head, and when she locked gazes with him she felt the full force of those beautiful blue eyes. They seemed electric out in the sunlight, pinning her in place. "You look beautiful today."

She blinked, taken by surprise at his words—both the bluntness and the sweetness of them. "Thank you. You look pretty good yourself." Oh, boy. This was not business talk, not even close. What the heck was she doing? She should keep this purely professional. For reasons that eluded her right now.

He gave her a slow, wicked grin, completely erasing the business professional mode of his expression when he'd been talking to Ethan. The transformation had another rush of heat surging through her. It didn't matter that it was spring and cool outside—her internal temperature skyrocketed to about a thousand degrees.

"Is that how you talk to all of your clients?"

"Only the ones who I've seen naked—and you're the only one, for the record." She tacked on the last part when she realized how it would have sounded. Apparently she'd decided to throw her professional mode out the window along with her sanity. Right now she was pretty certain she was playing with fire.

His grin widened even more, making those butterflies go crazy. This man had the most ridiculous effect on her. Chemistry? Whatever it was, she liked it a whole lot. And she'd never met anyone who made her feel the way he did. Years separated from him had done nothing to dim her attraction. If anything, it burned a little brighter now. She knew what they'd had together and desperately wanted another taste. Though one wouldn't be enough. Not even close. She could drown in this man.

When he didn't respond, she continued. "Are you ready to head out?"

He nodded, running a subtle gaze over her, though the heat simmering there was hard to miss. She'd worn a simple black cap-sleeve sheath dress that was professional but hugged her figure in the best way possible. It was clear he liked what he saw and she got a thrill from that. Because she certainly enjoyed what she saw when looking at him.

Moving to the passenger side door, he opened it for her. His thoughtfulness wasn't lost on her, nor did it surprise her, considering how sweet he'd been years ago. And she was glad that part of him hadn't changed. When she'd been living in Oregon she'd noticed that the door-opening thing wasn't as prevalent. And she didn't care what it said about her feminist sensibilities — she loved it when a man opened doors. Her father had always done it for her mother and some things were ingrained deep.

"Thank you," she murmured, sliding onto the soft leather. There was a fresh spring smell to the car, and the interior was as spotless as the exterior. Clearly he took care of it.

Taking her completely by surprise, he leaned down and strapped her in, his face only inches from hers as he took his time. He smelled fresh, crisp and oh so masculine. All she wanted to do was bury her face against his neck and breathe him in. Okay, she wanted to do more than that, but he smelled —

He brushed his lips over hers. Without hesitation she leaned into it, savoring the feel of his lips against hers and mourning how quickly that brief touch was over.

"Had to taste you again," he murmured before pulling back and shutting the door.

Slightly dazed, she mentally shook herself as he took a seat next to her and started the engine. So, *that* just happened. What. The. Heck.

Her lips still tingled from the all-too-brief touch as the car roared to life.

"Was that okay?" he asked as he strapped in. "Me kissing you?"

"Yes." She half-smiled and nodded, even as she ordered the logical part of her brain *off*. The man could kiss her anywhere, anytime. She wasn't going to tell him that just yet. She wasn't sure where this thing with them was headed and she wanted to be careful. The reason she'd walked away before might have been because of a misunderstanding, but it had sliced her open when their relationship had ended. It had been like she'd lost something intrinsic, *special*. Over the last three years she'd chalked it up to being young, and the relationship and sex so intense, but deep down she knew that wasn't true. Her age hadn't mattered. What they'd shared had been real.

Clearing her throat, she said, "Do you know how to get to the first place or should I pull it up on GPS?" He'd been the one to find it, but it had just been listed that morning.

"I know where it is. Heard about it from one of the guys at work. It's not too far from my place."

A little thrill shot up her spine at the thought of seeing where his place was in a few hours. When he'd offered to cook for her it had taken her by surprise, but she also really, really liked the idea of having privacy with him. Even if she was guarding her heart as much as she could, the anticipation of what might happen later had her endorphins out of control. He hadn't specifically asked her on a date, just to catch up. But it felt more like it might be an actual date now.

"I spoke to Valencia Curtis," she said. "There's a key in the lockbox and the owner is out of town for the next four days. He's selling the house, the work shed and the surrounding seven acres. Apparently he owns another ten acres neighboring the property but isn't sure he wants to part with it yet."

Maguire nodded. "Seven acres is more than enough for me, but if he's interested in selling and I like what I see I might put in an offer."

"Are you planning on expanding your businesses more? Is that why you want a place to work close to home?" He hadn't said yesterday and she hadn't wanted to push.

"Not exactly." He glanced at her as they came to a stoplight. "I've got the auto shops and the restoration business going but I still like to work on vehicles on my own. Separate from work. It'll be easier to do that close to home. Not having to head into work on the weekends, to just walk out my door and be able to get that kind of work done is something I've been wanting to do for a while."

"Will these be vehicles you restore and sell yourself?"

He nodded. "Yes. It's not as lucrative as restoring vehicles for others since it's more out of pocket and the process is longer, but I still make a profit. And it's something I enjoy."

"How long did it take you to restore the Mustang?" She ran a hand over the smooth black leather of the seat.

"Longer than it should have, but I took my time, wanted to get everything right."

Oh, she remembered well how the man took his time, as a sudden flash of him doing just that to her body entered her mind. She glanced out the window, willing herself not to blush. Jeez, what was wrong with her? She'd never been affected by anyone like she was by Maguire.

"What?" he murmured, his low, seductive voice wrapping around her like a silky caress. It was almost as if his fingers were skating over her skin.

"Just going over the list of places we'll be visiting today." Thankfully her voice sounded normal when she spoke.

When he turned onto a long, winding road with an explosion of mountain laurels on either side, she wished she was outside, savoring the scents as well as the visual. The pink and white burst of color dominating everything didn't even look real. It was like something out of a postcard.

"How'd you end up with Thaxter as a client?" Maguire suddenly asked, drawing her gaze back to him.

"What?" The question was so random.

"Ethan Thaxter."

"I *know* who you're talking about," she said, laughing lightly and definitely not answering his question. "Do you not like him?"

He lifted an unapologetic shoulder. "I don't like any good-looking, single jackass who spends time with you."

She blinked at his blunt words, watching the way his muscles flexed as he turned the steering wheel and they started down another side street. "That's…totally Neanderthal." And she couldn't believe he'd admitted it out loud. It wasn't like she was even dating Maguire.

"I know. Just being honest."

She couldn't bite back a laugh. "Ethan isn't a jackass." He was a surprisingly decent guy. Surprisingly, because he was all business. Which wasn't always the case with her male clients, married or not. When she'd been living in Oregon she'd dealt with more than her fair share of jerks who couldn't pass up the opportunity for sexual harassment. Sometimes it was as if they'd thought she was too stupid to understand their innuendos. But she'd held her own and had been successful—and refused to work with anyone who creeped her out.

Maguire let out an annoyed snort.

Which made her smile widen. She really shouldn't like this Neanderthal attitude, but she definitely did. "And I'm pretty sure he's interested in Mary Pierce." The owner of Pierce's Athletics. They sold sports equipment and clothing and did a lot of business with the tourists who came to snow ski. Normally she wouldn't talk about her clients, but she was fairly certain Maguire wouldn't be repeating any of this.

And after the way she'd bailed on him years ago, she had a need to ease whatever weird possessiveness he was feeling. The thought was almost laughable, considering how incredible the man was. But of all people she understood insecurity. It still felt a little surreal to be having this conversation with him, however. They hadn't even been on a date and he was basically admitting he didn't want anyone else to make a move on her. And the reason why was clear.

"We visited a commercial property today and he insisted we stop in to see her." And the man had stared at Mary as if she'd hung the moon. It had been ridiculously adorable.

"So?"

"So, just trust me. He's into her."

It had been so obvious to Sam, but clearly not to Mary. Either that or the woman had been just ignoring him.

"Huh," he said after a long moment. "Mary's my cousin, by the way."

"Really?"

"Yeah. Through marriage."

"I didn't realize that. Please don't say anything to her. I don't generally talk about my clients."

"I'm not my mother," he muttered, which drew another unexpected laugh.

According to Sam's mom, Maguire's mother seemed to know everything about everyone. "Man, she's something else."

He looked as if he might say something, but nodded instead. "This should be it," he said a few minutes later as they pulled down a quiet road on the outskirts of town.

She loved the city of Holly, but out here on the outskirts, everything was greener and brighter, especially this time of year. It was a feast for the senses. The other homes they were looking at today were on the outskirts of Holly as well. With the kind of acreage and a work shed with at least fifteen hundred square feet that Maguire was looking for, *all* the places were on the outskirts. It would be pretty much impossible to find a home and land in the city limits.

"After living in such a huge city the last few years, I can seriously appreciate the quiet out here," she murmured, soaking in the peacefulness of their surroundings. A three-foot-high white fence, more for show than anything, lined the front of the property. The style was similar to a lot of places in the country and fit with the oversized brick homes as well.

"Me too. When I first got back from Afghanistan it was hard to be around too many people at once. It's why I started working on my Mustang in all my spare time. I needed the space."

She was surprised at the unexpected admission, but liked that he was opening up to her. Everything about Maguire was so damn honest, something she should have realized years ago. If she could, she'd go back in time and knock some sense into her insecure twenty-one-year-old self.

"Even from your family?" she asked.

He put the car in park. "Yeah. Nolan went through the same thing so at least I knew it was normal. Jackson did too, but later, after I'd gotten out."

Samantha wanted to ask more, but didn't want to pry, especially since things were so new and fragile between them. It touched her that he was opening up to her though.

He looked as if he'd say more, but his phone rang, the jingle jarring and over-pronounced in the sudden quiet of the car.

Gritting his teeth, he glanced at the caller ID, frowned. "This is one of the shops. I've gotta take this. You want to unlock the house?"

She nodded, sliding out of the car as he answered his phone. Once she stepped out into the sunlight, the scent of blooming magnolias and freshly cut grass filled the air—and she could breathe steadily again. She hadn't even realized how fast her heart had been racing, how damp her palms were or how consumed she'd been in his presence until she got a little space.

If she wasn't careful, she was going to fall even harder for Maguire this time around. And she was pretty sure it would break her heart if things didn't work out.

CHAPTER FOUR

"What do you think so far?" Samantha asked as they stepped out of the kitchen and into the hallway.

"I like it." Maguire tried and failed to not stare at her toned calves—or higher—as she made her way up the wood stairs. She was in pure professional mode now, looking at notes she'd made on her cell phone earlier. Seeing her like this was sexy. Of course, everything she did was sexy. "But I keep going back to the first place," he continued. The first one he'd probably have to put time, money and energy into renovating the kitchen and updating the bathrooms, but he liked working with his hands.

And he'd like to get them on Samantha, as soon as possible. He still couldn't believe he'd kissed her earlier. He'd barely brushed his lips over hers, but it had been a kiss. Not something clients did with their Realtor. He'd felt possessed though. Just like he had years ago around her.

Sam glanced over her shoulder at him, gave him a knowing smile, as if she'd been expecting his answer, and it pulled him out of his thoughts of the past. So far they'd viewed the work shed—which was just as spacious as the one at the first property—and the bottom floor. Everything was nice, but overall he simply liked the layout of the first house. It was more open.

"You're not surprised?" he asked.

"No. You had a look I recognize well. You'd be surprised by how often people end up making an offer on the first or second place they look at. I think it's because they spend so much time researching what they want online that they've already mentally narrowed it down by the time they start visiting properties." She glanced around at the top of the stairs and motioned to an open doorway. "This should be the master bedroom. According to the overview, it has a nook with bay windows overlooking the pond and a custom master closet. The agent is supposed to be updating the listing with photos today."

When they stepped inside it was easy to see why the room had been one of the selling points. Natural light spilled into it, bathing the hardwood floors, Persian-style rug and furniture with an afternoon glow.

Maguire could easily imagine waking up in this room with Samantha next to him. Of course he could imagine waking up in *any* room with her. But... "This is really nice."

Nodding almost absently, she pulled open the closet doors and grinned. "Oh wow. If you were a woman, I'm pretty sure this would sell you on the place."

He let out a low whistle when he saw the space, which was more like a small room than what he thought of as a closet. Everything was clearly custom-made, the smooth white wood of the shelves a contrast to the dark wood floors, making it look bigger than it actually was. And it was already big. Two corners of the closet were lined with rows of dozens of shoes — who the hell needed that many? — and a small circular tufted ottoman sat next to one of the racks. The mini chandelier overhead sent a spray of glittering light over everything, illuminating the room like a showpiece. Maybe that was the intention. There was even a seating area with a marble-top built-in desk that matched the marble of the center island of storage.

"You look a little like you want to spend some time in here," he murmured when he glanced at Samantha.

The grin that split her face made his breath catch. "It has actual shelving specifically for *purses*, a built-in double hamper, padded jewelry drawers..." She pulled out a hidden drawer he hadn't noticed before moving to the small center island. She ran her fingers over the marble top, a soft expression on her face. "And this center piece is beautiful and functional. It clearly has a lot of storage. I could definitely show this room a good time." Her light, joking words made an unexpected laugh bubble up inside him.

He'd forgotten how funny she could be. Or maybe not forgotten, but forced himself to lock up memories of his time spent with her. Being around her now, it was all coming back with a vengeance. Even if he wanted to stay away from her, he knew he couldn't. "Well whoever owns this place likes having a good time," he said, motioning to the bondage wall mount rings above the bed—small, gold rings with a solid square backing anchoring them in place. They blended with the gold and cream of the comforter set.

She glanced past him and frowned—and he realized she didn't know what he was referring to.

Stepping fully out of the closet, he moved over to the king-sized bed and lifted one of the rings. "These are bondage wall mount rings for...bondage."

"I...didn't know what those were," she muttered, her cheeks going that sexy shade of pink he loved. "I'm so embarrassed right now. I've actually seen those at a couple houses before and I thought they were hooks for draperies or something...and I'm going to shut up now." She let out a soft groan, covering her cheeks, which just made him laugh as he stepped back into the closet with her.

He'd never been into stuff like that, but the thought of tying Samantha up? Hell, yeah. He could get on board with that. "You are sexy as fuck when you blush." The need to touch her was overwhelming and he wasn't going to deny himself now that they were alone.

Completely covering the distance between them, he loosely rested one hand on her hip, tugging her toward him. She didn't resist, just shifted against him, burying her face against his chest. "I feel so dumb not knowing that," she muttered again.

His body shook as he laughed again and a very caveman part of him was glad she hadn't known.

"No laughing at my naiveté." She leaned back and softly thumped his chest with her fist.

His gaze fell to her mouth and he couldn't have responded if he'd wanted to. The thought of having Samantha tied up, stretched out in front of him as he brought her to orgasm after orgasm? His cock decided to flare to life at that moment.

Her eyes widened as she felt his reaction to her, but she didn't pull back.

Hell. He'd never had a problem controlling his body. Not since he was a teenager, anyway. But being around Samantha again, a woman who could easily become an addiction if she let him in again... "I'm going to kiss y—"

She went up on tiptoe even before he'd finished.

Then his mouth was on hers, his tongue teasing against the seam of her lips, easing them open. Earlier in his car he'd gotten just a small taste. Too brief, and it had left him hungry for more.

All that need came roaring to the surface as he pulled her completely flush to him, rolling his hips against her so she fully felt what she did to him. Her sweet, subtle apples-and-cinnamon scent drove him as crazy as her fingers dug into his shoulders.

He loved that she was holding him as tightly as he was gripping her. He wanted to go skin to skin with her right now. Which was insane...maybe.

Nipping at her bottom lip, he pushed her back until she had to sit on the tufted ottoman. She let out a little yelp as her ass met it.

"What—"

He was on his knees in front of her before she could continue, cutting off her question with another searing kiss.

"The door downstairs is locked," he murmured against her lips. She'd locked it and taken the key inside instead of leaving it in the box. When he'd asked her why she said it was a safety precaution she always took. He was glad she looked out for herself and really glad the place was locked up tight because he didn't want anyone interrupting what he planned to do to her right now. He should wait until tonight, when they were alone in his house. But after three years of not touching her? He couldn't convince himself of any sane reason to wait when she was here and willing.

Looking slightly dazed, she nodded. "Yes."

He slid his hands up the outside of her smooth, lean legs, only stopping at the hem of her dress above her knees. "I want to bury my face between your legs," he murmured, not at all surprised when she let out a gasp. There was no holding back for him. Not now. Not when it came to her.

Her dark eyes flared with heat even as she seemed to struggle to find her voice. "Maguire," was all she could get out.

"I love hearing you say my name." Even after the way things had ended between them, he'd still fantasized about her. Hadn't been able to stop himself. "Say my name while you're coming against my mouth."

Her cheeks were bright pink as she bit her bottom lip. She wasn't saying no, so that was something. "We shouldn't," she whispered, her fingers straying to his shoulders. Definitely not pushing him away. Instead she dug in a little.

"Oh, we should." If she said no, they stopped right there, but all his muscles were pulled taut as he waited for her response.

"Maguire," she sighed and he knew he'd won.

This was happening. Anticipation hummed through him, a steady pulse in his ears as he leaned forward, taking her mouth with his again as he shoved her dress up her thighs.

She linked her fingers around the back of his neck as he slid a hand between her legs. The first time he'd gone down on her had been in the back seat of the truck he'd had at the time. It had been wild and intense, and right now he felt exactly the same way. He had to taste her right now. Even though he knew this might just be something physical for her, he still couldn't stop himself. If anything, maybe this would remind her of how things had been between them, how he'd been able to leave her boneless and completely satisfied.

He slipped a hand under the thin material covering her mound and groaned at her slickness. Oh yeah, she was wet and ready for this. Pulling back, he stared at her for a long moment, taking in her flushed cheeks, dilated eyes and erratic breathing.

"You want to stop?" A note of surprise slid through her words.

Not in a million years. In response he slid a finger inside her, keeping his gaze locked on hers.

Her dark eyes went heavy-lidded as he pushed deep, her slickness surrounding him. He remembered how tight she'd been, but feeling it again made a groan tear from his throat. The reality of her was so much better than the memory.

He would undress her completely — eventually, but not right now. This was about being a little wicked, about pushing her to the edge and reminding her how things had been between them.

Neither of them were the same exact person from three years ago, but the chemistry between them was brighter than before. And she was still that sweet, funny woman he'd fallen for. They'd both grown up more, and at her core she was still the woman he didn't want to lose. He'd tried to convince himself that he just wanted to catch up with her, make her dinner tonight, but he hadn't been able to believe his own lie. Now he wasn't even sure why he'd tried to lie to himself.

After withdrawing his hand, he groaned as he looked at her spread legs and the dampness on her lacy black panties. It took only seconds to get rid of those for her before she was bare to him, her wet folds glistening under the glitter of the chandelier, her clit peeking out, showing him just how turned on she was.

She shifted slightly against the ottoman. "Do something." The words were more plea than anything, making him grin. Yes, he was going to take great pleasure in this.

He lifted one of her legs and nibbled at her inner ankle. Her heels were black, strappy, and they were definitely staying on for this. He wanted to feel them digging into his back as he made her come.

She let out a throaty moan as he moved higher, kissing his way up her legs. He wanted to take his time, to kiss every inch of her, but that would be later. Now, he was hungry for her taste.

By the time he made it to her upper thigh, he could smell her arousal. His cock kicked against his zipper but it was going to have to wait until later.

"This reminds me of the first time I went down on you. You were squirming, begging me to get you off." It had been one of the hottest things he'd ever experienced.

"I didn't beg," she rasped out, sliding her fingers through his hair.

He lifted an eyebrow.

"Okay, maybe I did. You want me to beg again?"

Laughing lightly he shook his head before leaning down. He just wanted her to come. Instead of working her into it, he went right for her clit. He had to. The pink little bundle of nerves was peeking out, just begging for his mouth.

When he sucked on it, she cried out, her fingers digging into his head. Oh yeah, she liked that. He'd forgotten how reactive she was.

"Maguire." His name was a prayer on her lips, urging him on.

Sliding a finger inside her, he continued paying all his attention to her clit, teasing and stroking with his tongue with more and more pressure. The harder he stroked, the louder her cries grew. And the harder she gripped his head.

The bite of pain was heaven because it told him just how desperate she was for this. He added another finger, groaned against her as her inner walls clenched onto him, milking him.

It was impossible not to imagine his cock inside her instead. "Come for me." His words were a harsh demand. He needed her to—

She jerked against his face and fingers, her inner walls convulsing out of control as her climax hit faster than he'd imagined.

"Maguire!" Her back arched as she cried out his name again. Completely uninhibited, her orgasm was the hottest thing he'd ever seen or heard since…the last time they'd been together.

She let out a slight moan of protest as he lifted his head. Keeping his fingers buried inside her, he wiped his mouth before claiming hers again. She would still be able to taste herself on him, something that gave him immense pleasure.

When he finally pulled back, only because he wanted to see her expression, her dark eyes were heavy with a kind of sensual expression he felt all the way to his dick. He'd put that look there, given her all that pleasure.

Her normally stick-straight hair was mussed, so he thrust his hands into the thick tresses again and covered her mouth once again. She came off the ottoman, wrapping her legs around him as she basically tackled him to the hard floor.

With her dress up around her waist as she straddled him, he ran his hands up the back of her legs and over her smooth ass. He wanted to nibble on that too, to kiss every single inch of her, but especially that ass. Her breasts were a handful and her body incredible, but he would never forget the way she'd looked the first time he'd seen her at that random party all those years ago—in a halter top and little bitty shorts that had made his heart damn near stop. He squeezed once, groaned into her mouth.

"If we don't stop," he murmured, and only then did she pull back slightly, her hair creating a curtain around them, "we're doing this right here on the floor."

"I don't care."

But he did. He liked getting wild with her, loved that she'd let him do this, but some Neanderthal part of him wanted this new first time to be in *his* bed. Or at least at his house. He wanted her sweet scent all over his sheets, wanted to be able to take his time with her. Because once they started he wasn't stopping for a good, long while.

Groaning, he slid his hands down to her hips, squeezed once, savoring the feel of all her bare skin under his fingertips. "I want you in my bed the first time."

She reached between their bodies, started to rub her hand over his unfortunately covered erection, and he let out a hiss.

"You're going to kill all my good intentions."

"Screw your good intentions." Her grin was as wicked as the glint in her dark eyes.

He started to respond when a sharp knock from somewhere downstairs sounded. Oh hell.

Samantha's eyes widened before she jumped off him, shoving her dress down over her hips. "It's probably another agent," she whispered. "Shit, I don't know why I'm whispering." Quickly scanning, she stopped when she saw her panties, but he snatched them up and shoved them into his pocket as he stood next to her.

"Oh, these are mine. Go straighten your hair and see who's down there. I'll just check out the rest of the rooms until I get myself under control."

She looked as if she wanted to argue, but nodded and hurried out of the room. After a quick glance around he was certain everything looked to be in place, and he did exactly as he'd said he would. He stepped out of the room as he heard her heeled shoes clicking on the hardwood floor downstairs.

It was clear she knew whoever she'd opened the door to, if her warm reception was any indication, so he headed toward what turned out to be another bedroom and willed his dick under control.

It was difficult when he still tasted her and all he could think about was what tonight would bring. He wanted to completely possess her again, to sink deep inside her. If this was just about sex for her... *Yeah, not going there.*

CHAPTER FIVE

"Thank you for staying over last night." June, Samantha's mom, smiled as she poured coffee into Sam's travel mug.

"It was fun watching movies and vegging out with you." Sam had felt bad canceling her date with Maguire—especially after what they'd done in that house—but she'd moved home to be closer to her mom. And when she'd called her mom to check in with her yesterday afternoon, Sam had heard a heavy note of melancholy. Which was totally understandable since Sam's dad had recently died of a heart attack, despite being in great health. She was still coming to terms with that and knew it was obviously harder on her mother. Even if she'd wanted to see Maguire, she wanted to be there for her mom too.

"I just don't want to get in the way of your life." Her mom poured coffee in her own mug then added French vanilla cream.

"*Mom*. You are part of my life and I'm really happy to be back in Holly." She hadn't been positive how she'd truly feel until moving back, but it had been like slipping on a comfortable pair of shoes. She'd forgotten how wonderful Holly was.

"Really?" Her mom leaned against one of the counters of the country cottage-style kitchen she'd recently renovated. Exposed cabinetry, vintage pendant lighting, mahogany wood floors, and an oversized farmhouse-style sink would help the resale value if she ever decided to move.

"Yes, really." She'd always been close with her parents, but especially her mom. Before she'd moved home, they'd talked every other day on the phone. But living nearby was different. "If I ever decide to settle down and have a family, I want them to know you."

And that wouldn't happen if she was living across the country.

Her mom's grin turned sly and it was like looking in a mirror for a moment. "So are you thinking of settling down?"

"Ah, no." Okay, that was a lie, but she didn't want to talk about Maguire. Things were too new and tentative between them. Yes, the chemistry was there and she was certain there could be so much more between them, but they'd only had a week together all those years ago. She wanted to keep this private. At least for a little bit.

"Hmm. Well, I'm ready to head out if you are." Her mom glanced at the slender silver bangle watch on her arm. "I don't want to be late to my appointment." She patted her shoulder-length dark hair. "Gotta cover those grays."

Sam just laughed, but picked up her travel mug and purse from the center island. She'd already planned to shuttle her mom around today since her mom's car was in the shop. With only a few places scheduled for showings, it would be easy enough to drop her mom off and pick her up from the various places she needed. "About how long do you think it will take at the salon?" she asked as she looked in her purse for her keys.

"About two hours, give or take. And once I'm done I might walk down to Nora's for coffee and to check out her new book selection. So if you can't get me right away, don't worry."

"I'll be in the downtown area around then, so it will work perfectly with my schedule. Maybe we can do lunch today too."

"I'd like that." Her mom set the alarm to away mode before they stepped out the front door.

Sam had parked in the driveway out of habit, but realized that she could have used the garage. As her mom locked the front door behind them, Sam stepped off the porch and saw that her back tire was flat. "You've got to be kidding me," she muttered.

"What... Oh."

"It's no big deal." She knew how to change a tire, but she didn't relish the idea of doing it. "I'll probably change my clothes first though." She unlocked her mini SUV with the key fob as they headed to it.

"Did you drive down Candy Cane Lane yesterday? They've had that annoying construction going on for weeks longer than necessary. I bet you got a nail in your tire there." Her mom made an annoyed clucking sound as they reached the back of Sam's BMW.

And that was when Sam saw that both back tires were flat. That was...strange. She pulled her phone out of her purse right as it started ringing. Pleasure infused her at the sight of Maguire's name on the caller ID.

She swiped her finger across the screen. "Hey, I was just thinking of you."

"Oh yeah? In what capacity?" His voice had dropped a few octaves, sounding wickedly sexy and making heat pool between her legs.

She cleared her throat and hoped her mom didn't notice the sudden flush to her cheeks. "Ah, well, I have two flat tires this morning. I was getting ready to head out with my mom and was prepared to change one, but I don't have two spares." And she was pretty sure it would be too dangerous to drive around on two spares anyway. "I'm going to call my insurance company and have them set up a tow service, but—"

"I'll send one of my guys to get it."

"You don't have to do that." Even though she appreciated it, her insurance covered it. And she didn't want to put him out.

He just snorted, as if the discussion was closed. "I've got it. And I checked after you told me her car was in the shop. She's moved to the front of the line and her car will be ready this afternoon."

"Maguire, that was... Thank you."

"I'll pick you guys up in about ten minutes."

"What?"

"I was headed in that direction anyway. And I've got a free day so whatever errands you planned to take her on, I can do while you're getting your tires fixed."

"That's really not necessary. I really appreciate the offer though." There was no way the man had a free day. He ran multiple businesses. He was doing this for her and no other reason. A warm frisson of awareness spiraled through her.

"I'm getting a call from the shop that I've got to take, but I'll see you in a few minutes." He disconnected before she could respond and she was pretty sure he'd been lying about getting another call as well.

Which she couldn't exactly get annoyed at. Not when he was heading over here, ready to shuttle her and her mom around in the middle of his workday. It was ridiculously sweet of him.

"Was that Maguire O'Connor?" Her mom's voice pulled her out of her thoughts as she turned to face her.

"Yes. He's going to send one of his guys to tow my vehicle, and your car will be ready this afternoon." Instead of tomorrow, as was the original schedule.

"That's quite generous of him." Her mom took a sip of her coffee, eyed her carefully over the top of the mug.

Sam cleared her throat. Oh, this was going to be walking a tightrope. "Yes, it is. He's one of my clients," she added, hoping that would pacify her mom. Thankfully their conversation was cut short when a neighbor from across the street waved at her mother and headed over.

Mrs. Rooney called out a hello, in case they hadn't seen her. Which was near to impossible. In her seventies, Mrs. Rooney had been wearing pastel-colored, matching jogging suits as long as Samantha could remember. She was pretty sure that was all the older woman owned. Today she had on a pale blue one and huge plastic hoop earrings with blue and white polka dots.

The woman was nice, but a chatterbox. For once, Sam was glad for the interruption because she did not want to get into a discussion of what Maguire O'Connor was to her.

Especially since she had no idea herself.

"Thank you for taking my mom to the salon—and for moving her car up in your schedule." Samantha gave him one of those heart-stopping smiles as they headed down the sidewalk on Main Street.

Today she had on another dress with cap sleeves—and he only knew what they were called because of his mom and sister—that hugged her long, lean form in all the right places.

Maguire guessed she was about five foot nine, but with her heels she wasn't that much shorter than him. He shrugged, pushing back the urge to take her hand in his. Yes, they'd fooled around yesterday afternoon. More than fooled around. But he still wasn't sure what they were. Tonight when he cooked for her, he planned to get a straight answer. Maybe it was too soon, but while he didn't want to push her, he wanted a clear direction for them. "She was scheduled to be finished early anyway."

"Liar." Grinning, she nudged him with her hip as they reached the door of Nora's Books and Brew.

He opened the door for her and placed his hand at the small of her back as they stepped inside. No matter how hard he tried, he couldn't force himself to not touch her at least a little. Soon he wanted to stake a claim so every guy in town knew she was off-limits. It was soon, but he wanted exclusivity with her. Because he didn't share.

When she leaned into him it fed some part of him he hadn't even realized existed. "I'm getting your drink today," she murmured. "So don't even argue. Save us a table."

"I like this bossy side of you."

"Maybe you'll see more of it tonight." Her voice was low and seductive before she strode off, leaving him wanting so much more.

Looking away from her—so he wouldn't stare at her ass as she headed up to the front counter—he scanned for a table. Two high-tops were available so he snagged one next to the Baker sisters. Eleanor and Macy were friends of his mother and pretty much said anything they felt like. It was as if they had no filter. And age wasn't the reason. They'd been like that for as long as he could remember. If he was being honest, he'd chosen this empty table deliberately because he wanted word to spread that he was with Samantha.

"Morning, ladies," he said as he took a seat next to them.

The rich scent of coffee and the steady hum of voices filled the air.

His soon to be sister-in-law had really turned this place around when she took over.

"Maguire O'Connor. I hear that you're house shopping," Macy said. The sisters looked similar but Macy had dark hair where Eleanor had blonde.

"And that you kicked that old geezer Jeff Crawford to the curb," her sister added. "I'm glad. He's getting lazy in his old age. He either needs to retire or get his head out of his ass and do his job."

He cleared his throat. No way was he talking about the Realtor he'd let go. They were completely right, but he wasn't gossiping about anyone in town. "You ladies looking forward to summer?" That seemed like a safe-enough topic.

Macy rolled her eyes. "We don't want to talk about the weather, young man."

Young man? He bit back a grin, but didn't respond as Samantha joined him, sliding his drink in front of him. It felt wrong to let her pay, but he hadn't wanted to make a big deal over something so small. And he hadn't been kidding—he'd liked that little bossiness to her. He liked everything about her.

She smiled at the sisters. "Hi, ladies. I don't think I ever got to thank you in person, but the donation you made in my father's name was so sweet. It really touched my mom and me."

"He was such a good man. We were both glad to hear you'd moved back to town, for more reasons than one. It'll be nice for your mom to have you back and now we can stop listening to Alison complain that Maguire will never settle down." Macy slid off her stool as her sister did the same.

Samantha's eyes widened as they left. She avoided his gaze as she picked up her cup. "I…don't even know what to say to that."

He hadn't planned to have this conversation until later, and not in a fairly public place. No one around them was paying any attention though. And he didn't really care. "So…what are you looking for? With us?" Because he knew what he wanted.

She seemed to struggle for a moment, but finally spoke. "I want to date you, see where this thing goes."

He didn't like the word date, but he could live with it. Because it was what people did. Well, normal people. He hadn't been on a date since Samantha. "Exclusively."

Her eyes widened a fraction before her lips curved up. "I love that you're not asking."

"Not a question. If I'm dating you, I'm not dating anyone else." *And neither are you* was the silent statement.

"Good. Then we're exclusive." She reached across the table for his hand as if it was the most natural thing in the world. "So...it's not a secret."

"Hell, no." He slid his fingers through hers, tightened them. "I want the whole town to know you're mine."

Her cheeks grew pink even as she straightened. "Me too."

Seeing her like that only reminded him of how sexy she'd looked in that closet yesterday afternoon, her hair tousled and color flushing her skin from the orgasm he'd given her. Tonight couldn't come soon enough. "Not that I mind driving you around, but I have an extra car for you to use today." A Mercedes sedan he'd recently bought at an auction.

"I should tell you that you don't have to, but thank you. I...don't know how you're still single."

"Right back at you." He figured they'd talk more about that tonight. There were some things he didn't want to discuss in a coffee shop.

Her dark eyes flared with heat. "I was waiting for the right guy."

He sucked in a breath at her words because he felt the same way. Even if he hadn't actually been waiting for anyone. He'd been more or less hiding in his work the last three years. Now, he realized, that wasn't such a bad thing. Because if Samantha was what he got after years of celibacy?

Worth it.

"You still want me to cook for you tonight?"

She nodded, taking a sip of her drink. "Definitely. And thank you again for being so understanding about last night."

His eyebrows drew together. Of course he'd be understanding.

Her dad had just died and her mom wanted to spend time with her. How could he not? "How's your mom doing?"

"Really good, I think. Relatively speaking. She's staying really busy with her clubs and her friends but...I think it's hard for her some nights. *Obviously.* Last night we just watched a movie and had popcorn. It was really fun. Not that I'm not sad about bailing on you," she added.

He let out a little laugh. "It's good you're there for her. My mom's made it a point to include June in different committees in the upcoming months." Which he'd thought was wrong until he'd realized *why* his mom had done it. She wanted to keep Sam's mom active too. He hadn't realized that June and his mom were that close, but he shouldn't be surprised. His mom had a ton of friends. "You and your mom want to come over for dinner at my family's Monday night dinner thing?" he asked.

"Wow, yeah, that would be great. I've heard about it from Nora."

"It'll be official, then. Because once you have dinner with my family, you know my mom's going to get ideas." Family dinner was a big thing. Only significant others were invited. The kind of significant others that mattered, as in fiancées or soon to be. It was probably too soon to be thinking like that, but Maguire didn't much care. Samantha was his.

She just lifted a shoulder. "Fine with me."

Her reaction made him pause. "So what's on your agenda for today?"

"Couple showings and running my mom around to various places. It's a pretty slow day. Next week is going to make up for it though, because I have three closings lined up."

"Already?"

"Yeah. I landed more clients than I'd anticipated when moving back. Mostly through word of mouth. And some were in the process of making offers and wanted me to draw up the final contracts."

He knew she was working with a local real estate company but was more freelance than anything. "Have you thought about opening up your own agency?"

After glancing around once, she nodded. "Yeah. It's just a little nerve-racking, I guess."

He could easily see her making a go of it on her own. After inadvertently hiring her, he'd made some calls and heard exactly how driven and sharp she was. And, he grudgingly admitted to himself, if Ethan Thaxter had hired her, she had to be good. "I think you'll do well on your own."

"Thanks."

He tightened his fingers around hers, not quite ready to let them go. When his phone buzzed, indicating a text, he almost ignored it. But he hadn't been entirely truthful earlier. It wasn't a free day for him. He had a lot of shit to do. He'd just decided to prioritize Samantha. He glanced at the screen and frowned when he read the message from one of his guys.

Changing those tires out for your girl. Someone slashed them. Not an accident.

CHAPTER SIX

"I'm not sure what else you want me to do, Maguire." Brad—who was the sheriff and also Maguire's soon-to-be brother-in-law—sounded only mildly exasperated.

Maguire reined in his temper as he steered down Samantha's street. After he'd gotten that text this morning about her tires being slashed he might have gone into slightly obnoxious protective mode. He'd had Brad meet them at his shop and take a report for property damage, but neither Sam nor Brad had been concerned about the tires.

"There's been a rash of petty vandalism the last two weeks and I'm ninety percent sure I know who it is. I've got one of my guys sitting on the little shit's house right now." Definite frustration colored the sheriff's voice now.

Under normal circumstances Brad wouldn't tell Maguire something like that, but they were family and Maguire was being pushy as hell. So he knew that a teenage troublemaker was the suspect behind Samantha's slashed tires. He still wasn't satisfied.

"Yeah, all right." He was just frustrated so he'd called Brad, hoping to get to the bottom of this. "How's the construction coming along?" Brad and his sister had just closed on a new home that included a mother-in-law suite behind the house that they were turning into a commercial kitchen.

"Good. Might ask for your help next weekend. Fallon wants to repaint a few rooms inside the house."

"No problem. I'm sure Jackson and Nolan won't mind either." Then they could knock it out in no time. That was one of the great things about having family nearby. His brothers would always help out if he needed anything, and vice versa.

"I'll let you know for sure what we decide."

"Sounds good—" His blood turned to ice as he pulled into Samantha's driveway. His headlights swept over the hooded figure of a male standing on the edge of the small front balcony of her home. "There's an intruder on Sam's balcony. Get to her place *now*," he snapped before ending the call.

He called Samantha even as he leaned down and reached under his seat. Turning the phone on speaker, he unlocked the container for his SIG as it rang. Out of the corner of his eye he saw the would-be intruder scaling over the balcony. Likely ready to jump and run.

"Hey, I was just thinking about you."

"Where in your house are you right now?" He pulled his weapon out, slid the magazine in. No one was going to hurt Samantha. They'd have to go through him first.

"Ah...my bedroom."

"Get downstairs now and make your way to the front door but don't open it until you hear my voice." He kept his car lights on, shining bright against the front of her house and partially illuminating the balcony—that was now empty.

"Okay." Worry tinged that one word, but she didn't question him, didn't say anything else. But he could hear her moving around.

Slowly, he moved from the vehicle, using the street lights, lights from Sam's house and the smattering of stars above to guide his way. His instinct was to run after whoever had been on Sam's balcony because he didn't want that bastard to get away—but that wasn't happening. For all he knew there was more than one intruder and he'd be leaving her vulnerable.

Un-fucking-likely there was more than one guy, but he wasn't taking a chance with her life. Weapon up, he checked the front of her property and home as he hurried to the front door. He knocked once. "It's me," he said.

Moments later she opened the door, her eyes wide as her gaze landed on his SIG. After stepping inside, he locked the door behind himself then pointed at the door. "Stay here. Don't open the door for anyone except Brad. He's on his way."

She opened her mouth once, then closed it and nodded. Good. He didn't want to waste time explaining now.

Methodically, he swept through her house, checking each window and door to make sure everything was secure. If someone truly wanted to break in they'd just smash a window or kick in a door, but that wasn't what he was looking for. If there was a weakness such as an unlatched window, someone could easily take advantage. First he wanted to check for any sign of a break-in on the chance that someone was hiding in the house, like a partner.

When he was certain her house was clear, he found her downstairs by the door just as someone knocked on it. After looking through the peephole, he opened the door to Brad, who was still in his uniform. The flashing blue lights from his car flickered over the yard and house.

"I saw a man wearing a hoodie on Samantha's balcony when I drove up," he said to Brad, ignoring her gasp of surprise for now. "He scaled down it and was around the side of her house by the time I'd retrieved my weapon." Keeping his SIG pointing downward, he added, "I have a concealed permit for this."

Brad simply nodded, so Maguire continued, even as he tucked his weapon into the back of his pants. He would secure it as soon as he could. But he wasn't leaving Sam. Not for a second.

"I would have gone after him, but I wasn't sure if there was anyone else already inside or nearby and I didn't want to leave her vulnerable." He itched to race outside after the guy but it was far too late for that.

Brad nodded again and held up his radio, giving quick instructions to one of his deputies about the situation and ordering two of his guys to do a sweep of the surrounding neighborhoods.

But it wouldn't do any good. Maguire understood that this was a small town and resources were limited. The department was only as large as it was because of all the tourism Holly saw.

"I'll be back," Brad murmured to the two of them, then focused on Maguire. "I'm going to turn your car lights off."

Maguire nodded and shut the door behind him before facing Samantha. "You okay?"

"I guess." She started to wrap her arms around herself but he pulled her into his arms. Without pause she rested her head against his chest. "So you saw someone on my balcony?"

"Yeah." And he really wished he'd pursued him. But if the guy hadn't been alone he'd have never forgiven himself if something happened to Samantha.

"That's super creepy." She pulled back slightly to look up at him. "I'm really glad you're here."

Yeah, he was too. "Do you have a security system?" He'd seen the keypad by the front door, but that didn't mean it was activated.

"The system is in place, but the security company isn't coming out until next week to add contacts to the windows and activate it."

"You're staying with me tonight." There was no other option after this.

She stepped out of his embrace and looked up at him with raised eyebrows. Wearing a sexy multicolored summer dress that molded to her curves, she placed a hand on one hip. "Can you think of a better way to phrase that, Mr. Bossy?"

He cleared his throat. He was used to taking charge of most situations. It was one of the reasons he ran his own businesses. "It was pretty likely you'd have been staying over anyway." Because they were definitely getting naked tonight. He couldn't wait to peel that dress off her, inch by inch.

"So?"

He bit back a grin, glad she wasn't denying it. "So...will you please pack a bag and stay over at my place tonight?"

The smile she gave him almost knocked him on his ass. "Yes, I will. Thank you for *asking*." She gave a soft snort as she shook her head. "You think...the tire thing has anything to do with tonight? I feel stupid even saying that out loud."

"Honestly, who knows?" But he didn't believe in coincidence.

Sighing, she raked a hand through her long, espresso-colored hair. She'd left it down for their date and must have curled it because it fell around her face in soft, big waves. "I'll go pack a bag. If the sheriff comes back in just tell him I'll be down in a few minutes?"

"Of course." Once she was upstairs and out of earshot, he pulled out his phone and pressed one of his speed dials.

Nolan picked up on the second ring. "Hey, man. Thought you had that date tonight. What's up?"

Maguire didn't waste time in explaining what had happened. "It could be nothing," he said as he wrapped up. "But it could also be the same jackass who flattened her tires. I don't know and Brad hasn't taken a statement yet." Though Maguire planned to ask questions as soon as Samantha was back downstairs. He wanted to know if she had any enemies or if someone had been harassing her through her job. "I have a big favor to ask."

"You want me to stop by her mom's place? Check on her?"

Maguire pushed out a breath, glad his brother was on the same page. Since Samantha's vehicle had been vandalized at her mom's house, he didn't think it would hurt to have someone keep an eye on her mom. "Yeah."

"No problem."

"We'll probably head over there too, but I wanted to make sure her mom had someone over there before we could get there."

"Just text me her address. I'll head out now."

"Thanks. I owe you one."

His brother laughed. "Yeah you do. I'll collect with free labor on my car later."

Rolling his eyes, he hung up right as Brad stepped in the front door.

The sheriff gave him a brief nod. "Where's Samantha?"

"Packing a bag."

"She staying with you?"

"Yeah."

"Good. I was going to suggest it. It's pretty clear that she was home, so if someone was attempting to break into her place knowing she was here..." The sheriff shook his head, his frown deepening. "That's disturbing behavior."

That was exactly how Maguire felt. Even if the vehicle vandalism wasn't related to this, someone had still been either trying to break in or peep on her. Because the balcony led directly to her bedroom and was only accessible through the French doors upstairs. There were easier ways to break into the place, so Maguire figured that the unknown man had wanted to peek on her in her bedroom. It was disturbing and triggered all his protective instincts.

Maguire turned at the sound of Samantha coming down the stairs. Not in her bare feet anymore, she had on sparkly sandals and was carrying a brown and beige overnight bag. At the bottom of the stairs, she set the bag and her purse down.

"Did you find the guy?" Hope laced her words as she looked at Brad.

The sheriff shook his head. "No, but I want to sit down with you and take a statement."

"That's fine, but I want to call my mom first."

"I already called my brother, Nolan. He's headed over there right now to check on her." Maguire glanced at his watch. "He should actually be there soon." Nolan didn't live far and he'd said he'd be heading out almost immediately.

Samantha's expression softened as she moved up to his side and wrapped her arm around him. Facing the sheriff, she said, "I'm ready to answer your questions."

"I can't believe you didn't tell me you had a stalker." Maguire's jaw was as tight as his white-knuckled grip on the steering wheel.

"Maguire." Sam wasn't sure what to say because she was surprised he was so angry about this. After spending half an hour answering the sheriff's questions they'd headed over to her mom's house—where Nolan was already waiting. Maguire's brother had volunteered to stay the night, and even though she'd wanted to stay he'd made the point that if someone was harassing her, it was best to stay with Maguire, not her mom. She felt weird not staying but now she was just frustrated with Maguire. "I wouldn't even call him a stalker."

"A man who made harassing phone calls to your cell phone and office, who showed up at your work and even your home uninvited. A man you had to get a restraining order against? A man who broke into your condo? That's a stalker."

She winced at his harsh tone. "I know. Okay, yes, he was a stalker. But I moved away. Far, far away." It was another reason that moving home had been such an easy decision. She'd left all that grossness of Nelson Smith—aka her stalker in Oregon—behind. Or she thought she had. Actually, she was pretty sure she had. "I haven't even thought of him since I moved." Mainly because the man had an inoperable brain tumor. It was terrible to think, but according to his family—who'd convinced her not to press charges when he'd broken into her condo back in Oregon—he only had months to live.

"Why didn't you press charges against him?" he asked as he pulled up to a stoplight.

"Because I felt bad. The man is *dying*. He was normal before that brain tumor. At least according to his family and his lack of a police record." Nelson Smith was the co-owner of an ice cream shop in the same neighborhood where the corporate office for her former real estate company had been, and he had randomly fixated on her. "I'd interacted with him the last couple years in a completely platonic capacity, so I'm pretty sure they were telling the truth. He didn't just randomly develop a fixation on me after all that time. It was the tumor." She would have felt terrible pressing charges against someone who wasn't in his right mind and was about to die, especially since she'd made the decision to move home by the time Smith had broken into her place. "And we don't even know that it was him tonight."

His fingers loosened slightly as he took another turn. "I know. I just don't like unknowns and I really don't like the thought of you in danger."

"I don't like the thought of that either, but the sheriff is looking into him. Don't get me wrong, I'm scared. But I trust him to do his job."

Maguire rubbed the back of his neck, his arm muscles flexing, capturing all her attention.

She shifted slightly against the leather seat. "You never told me how pretty I am in this dress." Normally she would never say anything like that. She didn't fish for compliments, but it was clear he needed a distraction in a bad way. There was nothing they could do tonight and worrying wasn't going to help anyone. She also didn't want this to spoil the rest of the night for them, not when she'd been looking forward to it so much.

He jolted at her abrupt words and turned to look at her. "You look beautiful."

"It's new. I bought it for our date."

Those ice blue eyes dipped down, taking in all of her before he faced the road again. "I'll try not to rip it later when taking it off you." His voice had dropped, taking on a sexy timbre she felt all the way to her core.

She should tell him that he was being presumptuous, but they both knew he wasn't. Not even a little bit. It was almost guaranteed he'd be taking her dress off later. If he didn't, she'd be taking it off for him.

Reaching out, she took his hand in hers and linked their fingers together. "That's very thoughtful of you," she murmured. "And you'll be happy to know I don't have anything else underneath this dress." She'd never gone completely bare before but had been feeling wild earlier. Well, before the incident with the peeping weirdo on her balcony. She was so glad to be able to go to Maguire's. It was strange to depend on someone, but if anyone could keep her safe it was him.

He shifted once against the seat and she could see the very real effect her words had on him. The thick length of his erection was visible, bringing up so many fun memories with him. She didn't fight the grin spreading across her face. Even with what had happened at her house, she was still excited about tonight, about spending more time alone with Maguire.

"Oh, I'm on the pill," she added, wanting to let him know that up front. Not because she'd had an active sex life. She nearly snorted at the thought. It was the only way to regulate her body.

His fingers tightened on hers but he didn't say anything. He didn't need to. She already knew he was clean from his admission a few days ago. There was nothing stopping them from being intimate with no barrier tonight. Not one single thing.

And she didn't want anything between them. Not now. She wanted to savor every second of her time with Maguire.

CHAPTER SEVEN

Maguire was quiet as Samantha talked to her mom on the phone. He'd just pulled down his street and was counting the seconds until he could get his hands on Sam. He still couldn't believe she'd had a stalker and hadn't told him.

He was likely overreacting but he didn't care. That type of thing was important and would have changed things for him. For one, he wouldn't have let her go off on her own today. And yeah he knew the word "let" would make her crazy, but he didn't care—and he wasn't going to actually say the word out loud to her.

"If you're sure—" A beat passed before she said, "Okay, okay. I'll call you in the morning. But call me if you need anything." Pause. "Love you too." She slipped the phone into her purse as he turned into his driveway. "Well, she's totally fine with Nolan staying over. In fact, she's come up with a list of chores for him to do in the morning."

Maguire grinned, unable to hide a laugh. "Your mom sounds like mine."

"Oh, no doubt. Though she did say something about you coming over this Sunday and helping out too."

"Not a problem."

"Really?"

"Of course. You're mine, Samantha." Maybe it was too soon to admit it like that, but after learning that she had a stalker, he was in pure protective mode.

Her eyes widened slightly, but she didn't respond. Just cleared her throat. He wasn't sure if what he said made her nervous or what.

"I'll help your family out any way I can." He steered into his clean, organized garage and shut the door behind them. He'd paid attention to their surroundings on the way home and taken the really long way in case someone tried to follow them. He was certain no one had.

"Well, thank you. I've hired a few people to start taking care of things for her like lawn care, but it'll be a big help to get some things done around the house."

"I aim to please," he murmured, his gaze falling to her full lips.

"Is that right?" She unsnapped her seatbelt and before he could react, she hiked up her dress and straddled him.

Sucking in a breath, he looked up at her as she grinded against him. Immediately his hands slid up her legs and back around to her... He groaned at the feel of her bare ass. She hadn't been teasing him. The sexy woman had nothing on underneath. "You're killing me."

"Good," she murmured.

He'd felt her before, had made love to her before, but as he slid his hands over all that smooth skin, his brain threatened to short-circuit. He'd planned to cook for her, to take things slowly tonight. She'd just had a scare and he didn't want to take advantage. Clearly that wasn't an issue for her, though.

The dome light flicked off, but he had a light on in the corner of his garage that gave him enough illumination to see exactly what he needed to see—Samantha on top of him.

Keeping her gaze pinned on his, she reached between their bodies and started unbuttoning his long-sleeved shirt. His breathing grew erratic as she released button after button, her eyes filled with a lust he knew matched his own. Once she had it undone fully, he shrugged out of it and tossed it into the back seat.

Then he reached behind her, found the zipper at the top of her dress and slowly unzipped. She shivered as the little straps fell down her arms and the silky material pooled around her waist. He groaned again at the sight of her perfect pink nipples. Even in the dimness, he could see the color and it made him ache. Back in that closet he hadn't gotten to see them again, but he'd thought about them. Fantasized about them.

He leaned forward, sucked on one nipple, earning a surprised moan as she arched into him.

Oh yeah, this was what he'd been missing. He palmed her other breast and gently ran his thumb over the hard bud as he continued teasing her other nipple.

She grinded her body against his, making his cock even harder than it was. Probably a good thing that his pants were between them. Because he'd be inside her right now if they weren't.

He managed to tear his head back so he could look up at her. "Need to go inside now." Otherwise she wasn't making it out of this car without being fully claimed by him.

"No we don't." She reached between their bodies again, running her hand over his erection.

He pulled her to him, crushing his mouth to hers in a savage claiming. He needed this, needed her as much as he needed his next breath. He'd had plenty of fantasies of taking her in his car, and even though it was cramped… Oh yeah, they were doing this. He released the lever on the side of the seat so that it slid back, giving them more room.

"Lift up," he rasped against her mouth. He needed his shoes and pants off right now.

She did as he said and moments later he was naked underneath her, his cock thick and heavy between them. The leather was smooth against his ass and her apples-and-cinnamon scent wrapped around him, making him lightheaded as he arched his hips up to her.

Now she was the one groaning as she settled her body over him. Her dress was bunched up at her waist, the strip of material not covering her breasts or her exposed pussy. Remembering her taste from the other day, how slick she'd been, he cupped her mound as she met his mouth with hers.

Gripping her hip with one hand to hold her in place, he slid a finger inside her with the other. "So tight," he murmured against her lips. "So wet. So mine."

She moaned at his words, her inner walls tightening around his finger. He added another, wanting to torture them both just a little bit before he slid inside her. He preferred being on top, being in control, but having her straddling him like this was all sorts of sexy.

Slowly he withdrew his finger, then slid it back in. She shuddered, her fingers digging into his shoulders as she tried to ride him. But he held her in place with the hand firmly clasped on her hip.

"Don't move." He nibbled along her jaw, dropping little bites and kisses as he made his way to her earlobe. She might be on top but he still had to have some control. He bit down as he withdrew his finger again. "I want you to come around my cock."

"Maguire." She arched again. "Inside me now."

He withdrew his finger completely and positioned his erection at her wet lips. Feeling her slickness, feeling her against him after all this time, he was ready to come right then.

Which definitely wasn't happening.

She was going to come. More than once. Then he would. He lifted his hips as she slid down on him with a yelp, all the muscles in his body pulling taut as her sheath tightened around him.

"I'd forgotten how big you are." Her words did something ridiculous for his ego as she settled on top of him.

And he'd forgotten how damn tight she was. But he couldn't find his voice. Not if his life depended on it. Breathing hard, he kept his gaze locked on hers as he reached between their bodies and rubbed his thumb over her clit.

She jerked against him, her inner walls clenching around him with that one little stroke. He remembered how reactive she'd been to his touch, how getting her off had been his pastime.

"Don't move your hips," he ordered as he removed the hand on her hip. She shifted slightly against him but he nipped her bottom lip. "Be still."

Her chest rose and fell as she nodded. *Good.*

He wanted to touch her everywhere, wanted to stretch her out on his bed and make her scream his name. But feeling her come around his cock—in his car, no less—was just as sweet. He'd had more than one fantasy about taking her in here.

He kept his other hand in place as he strummed her clit in a tight little pattern. Then he leaned forward and sucked one nipple into his mouth.

He could feel her trembling with the need to move, to start riding him and grinding against him. Her body was shaking, her inner walls convulsing as he lashed his tongue against her tight nipple.

When he finally told her to move, he knew she'd be more than ready for release, her body begging for it. His own was begging right now. With each movement of his ass against the smooth seat, each thrust inside her tight body, he was on a razor's edge now.

"Maguire," she moaned out, arching her breast farther into his mouth even as she kept her hips still.

He bit down gently on her nipple as he circled his tongue over the tip, over and over. Her fingers dug into his shoulders. He needed her to come.

"I'm so close," she gasped out. "Just need to move."

His balls were pulled up so damn tight, all his muscles straining as he held himself back. *Barely. Fuck.* He needed more. He needed all of her. "Ride me."

Those two words released her. Like a gunshot at a race releasing the runners, she moaned and started writhing against him.

He increased the pressure on her clit even as he drew his mouth away from her breast and grabbed her head to pull her mouth down to his. His movements were a little rough, his control walking a tightrope, and he didn't care. Because he needed this as much as she did. He could feel it in every tight line of her body.

She ate at his mouth with the same urgency he ate at hers, her hunger a match for his. Oh how he wanted her to come, to feel all that slickness around his dick as he lost himself inside her heat.

She tore her mouth from his, arching her back even in the cramped space as her climax hit, sharp and intense.

He drank her in, unable to stop staring as she continued, rocking against him, her eyes closed and her head tilted back as her orgasm punched through her. Her dark hair fell in waves around her shoulders and breasts, highlighting the tight pebbles of her nipples, the underlying flush of her pale skin.

In that moment, he let go, releasing his own built-up need as his climax crashed through him, slamming out to all his pleasure points. Grabbing her hips, he met her stroke for stroke, all his muscles straining as he thrust into her over and over. It was too much and not enough. He released himself inside her in hard strokes until she collapsed on top of him, burying her face against his neck.

As his breathing evened out he slid his hands down to her ass and cupped her gently, just savoring the feel of her smooth skin. He wanted her dress gone, wanted nothing between them at all so it was pure skin to skin.

"How about we take a shower together and then I feed you?" he murmured into the quiet of his car.

"Mmm, that sounds like the best idea ever." She lifted her head to look at him through heavy-lidded eyes. "That was just as incredible as I remember."

Grinning, he brushed his lips over hers before nipping her bottom lip again. He loved doing that to her. "Better."

"Better," she whispered.

For so long he'd wondered if he'd imagined how good things had been between them, and now he had his answer. Nope. He hadn't. There was no way in hell he could have misremembered this kind of intensity anyway.

Samantha was a one-of-a-kind woman and he wasn't letting her go. If some asshole thought he could mess with her, he was in for a surprise.

Because Maguire would protect her with everything he had. No one was getting past him.

CHAPTER EIGHT

Samantha leaned into Maguire as he wrapped his arms around her from behind. The rich scent of coffee filled his kitchen so she got a double whammy of Maguire's sexy scent and coffee. Two of her favorite things. Unfortunately he was clothed. For that matter, so was she.

He nibbled on her ear, biting down gently and sending a ribbon of awareness pulsing through her. After having sex last night in his car, then in his shower — then in bed again this morning — she was feeling more than a little tender. And it seemed the man was a machine.

Not that she was complaining.

"Let's stay here today," he murmured, the warmth of his breath skating over her skin and sending another shiver through her.

"I wish we could." She really did. But she had work to do: showings, and Thaxter had put in an offer on a place so she needed to make some calls and start that paperwork.

"I don't like you going to work." She could feel the tension ratchet up in him as his grip around her tightened ever so slightly.

Sighing, she turned in his arms and looped her hands around his neck. "We've been over this." And she appreciated his concern, but she couldn't let a potential threat stop her from living her life, working her job — which paid all her bills. She might have done well for herself in Oregon, but living there had been expensive and she wasn't independently wealthy. "I have to work, and I'll be smart. I'm not meeting with any new clients and I'm not even showing that many houses. But the ones I am showing are to current clients — almost all couples. I've got pepper spray and I'll be with people most of the day. Plus, I'll be driving one of your vehicles, which isn't linked to me in any way, so there's an extra layer of protection."

Maguire just gritted his teeth, his stubborn, protective streak shining through. It might be frustrating, but she also adored that he cared about her so much. "We'll see what Brad says when he gets here."

Yes, she supposed they would. The sheriff had texted Maguire half an hour ago and said he was on his way over because he needed to talk to her about something. Which likely wasn't good news if he wanted to do it in person.

As if on cue, Maguire's doorbell rang. He brushed his lips over hers once before heading out of the kitchen. "Will you pour me a mug?" he called over his shoulder.

Smiling to herself, she pulled down three mugs in case the sheriff wanted one too. She and Maguire hadn't been in the kitchen long enough to actually get coffee or breakfast. But he'd pre-set the coffee machine, which made him her hero. Waking up to incredible sex then coming downstairs to a fresh pot of coffee was the best way to start the morning.

As she finished pouring two mugs and pulling out the sugar and cream, Maguire and Brad stepped into the room, the sheriff wearing a full uniform and a grim expression. *Oh, great.* This was not going to be good.

"Coffee?" she asked.

He shook his head. "No, thanks."

"So what did you find out?" She kept her hands busy adding cream and sugar to her coffee as he stepped farther into the room.

"There's no easy way to say this. Nelson Smith has been missing from the care of his family for weeks. His credit cards have been tracked to Holly. He bought a one-way plane ticket to a nearby airport and his card was last used at a local motel. One on the outskirts of town. He's paid up for the next week and a half but hasn't been back to his room in two days. I've got a guy sitting on the place for now and the manager knows to keep me updated."

Ice invaded her veins as she digested his words. Until that

moment she'd assumed that last night and her vehicle being vandalized were two unrelated incidents. At this point she couldn't afford to believe in coincidence, even if the two things were indeed a coincidence. If Smith had come all the way to North Carolina, it wasn't for a good reason. And now he'd fallen off the grid? He had to be in town because of Sam.

Maguire pulled out a seat for her at his kitchen table and she gladly sat. She might not want to let some nut job dictate her decisions, but she was going to have to rethink some of her plans for the day.

"I'll be your bodyguard today," Maguire said.

She blinked, then frowned at his harsh tone.

"Ah, I'm going to give you two some privacy." The sheriff was out of the kitchen in seconds and she heard the soft snick of the front door closing behind him a moment later.

"It only makes sense that I shadow you—unless you decide to stay here," Maguire said, standing directly in front of her, arms crossed over his broad chest. He looked as if he was preparing to go into battle.

"I never said it didn't make sense."

He watched her carefully, his pale eyes missing nothing. "You're pissed off at me."

"Well, annoyed at least. You just say these things without asking me. That's not how relationships work."

His normally kissable lips pulled into a thin line. "I don't have much experience with relationships."

"Much, meaning *any*?" Because back when they'd first hooked up he'd admitted he had zero experience with having a girlfriend. Unless he'd lied—and she didn't think he had—about not being with anyone in the last few years, then his experience was nonexistent.

"Yes." Sighing, he sat at the table instead of hovering, and nodded. "It's my natural inclination to take charge. That's probably not going to change overnight. And I don't want anything to happen to you. I want to make sure you're okay."

"I don't *want* you to change. Especially not in the bedroom."

Definitely not there. She loved how dominating he could be. His lips quirked up slightly as she continued. "I just want you to *ask*. Not say something like the decision is already made. It's not like I'm going to argue with you about having a bodyguard today. I was already thinking of cutting out the completely non-necessary things and passing off any showings to someone else at the agency. But then you just bust in and say that you're coming with me, decision made."

"I should have asked. I'm sorry." He rubbed a hand over the back of his neck, making his forearm flex.

It was hard not to appreciate the hard lines and striations of his muscles when he moved, which were only highlighted by the way his tattoos rippled. And she had to admit she loved that he was so protective of her. She just wanted to make sure they had clear expectations where their relationship was concerned. She'd made a huge mistake once by not talking to him. Never again.

She slid off her chair and moved around the table until she was next to him—where he promptly pulled her into his lap. "It's not like I can be mad at you for wanting to protect me," she said, slipping an arm around the back of his neck as she cuddled up against him. "It's just that I want a partner, not someone who orders me around."

"I want that too. And I'll try to ask first. But fair warning—I'm not going to nail that every time. I'm old and set in my ways."

She snorted at his wry tone. "You're not old."

He lifted a shoulder. "Well, I'm relationship-challenged."

"Me too." She had her parents' relationship as a guideline and they'd pretty much gotten everything right. She'd seen what a partnership looked like and that was what she wanted for herself.

"Somehow I doubt that," he murmured, his gaze falling to her lips.

"Well...you would be wrong. I know we never really talked about our pasts since we were together, other than that comment you made."

For a moment he looked incredibly uncomfortable, but he nodded. It was pretty obvious which comment she was referring to. She'd wanted to ask him about it before, but it had been clear he hadn't meant to admit his celibacy so she'd left it alone.

"Yeah, I was serious about that. In case you were wondering."

"How is that possible? That you haven't been with anyone since…" He was sweet, giving, crazy protective—and off-the-charts sexy. She couldn't forget that. There was no way he would have a shortage of female attention. Which was something she didn't want to think about.

Maguire cleared his throat even as he tightened his grip around her. She snuggled into him, savoring his warm embrace. "When I was discharged I thought it would be a lot easier to transition. Not sure why I ever thought that when all the statistics say otherwise. I needed to get my own head on straight before even thinking about hooking up with anyone—casually or otherwise. So I threw myself into work and it's paid off better than I could have imagined in such a short time. Don't get me wrong, I've gotten plenty of offers from women—"

She pinched his side. "I don't need specifics."

He gave her a wicked grin. "Glad you care. Anyway, no one turned my head enough to make me want to…" He shrugged. "No one until you came back."

"I'm glad."

"I am too. You were worth the wait."

So was he. "Look…not that I think it matters to you, but I haven't been with anyone since you either." At his raised eyebrows, she continued. "For different reasons than you. I tried dating but never got past the first one. Not with anyone. When things ended between you and me it messed with my head. I couldn't believe I'd pegged you so wrong—and I know *now* how wrong I was, but I didn't when I moved to Oregon. I threw myself into work just like you. It was worth it because I grew my clientele quickly and developed a name for myself. Apparently I was waiting for you too."

"It wouldn't have mattered, but I'm not going to lie. I'm glad there was no one else for you either."

He slid his hands through her hair and cupped the back of her head as he brought her mouth to his. His tongue slid past her lips, teasing and claiming in a slow seduction she felt all the way to her toes. She was tempted to straddle him, but didn't want to start something they couldn't finish. Not when they still had someone waiting outside for them and they needed to get on the road.

Groaning, he pulled back. "You shred any good intentions I have."

She grinned at his strained voice. "Right back at you."

Sighing, he leaned his forehead against hers. "So you're going to cut out some of your meetings today?"

"Yeah. I want to stop by and see my mom, maybe take her somewhere else for the day so she's not alone. Then I'll head into the office to draw up some contracts. There are only a couple showings I want to do myself. The others I can pass off for today and get away with it."

"All right. Let me go tell Brad what the plan is."

Reluctantly she slid off his lap. "I'm going to grab my purse and shoes, then."

"Sounds good." He smacked her ass once, surprising her as she stepped away from him.

Warmth infused her cheeks as he gave her a wicked grin. Instead of responding, she hurried out of the room and up the stairs.

She had to get her game face on, and fast. Fear lingered inside her at the thought of Nelson Smith in Holly, waiting to hurt her—or worse, someone she loved. It was hard not to second-guess the decision she'd made to not press charges against him. Now she wished she had. Thankfully, she had Maguire at her side.

Still, that fear only grew when she thought of something happening to him because of her. She'd just found him again. She couldn't lose him.

"Thanks for meeting me a little earlier today," Samantha said to Ethan as they stepped out of the empty commercial building. He'd scooped up a few properties in the last week, and according to him, he was almost done.

"It ended up working better with my schedule, so you did me a favor."

"Well good, then. I've got all the paperwork completed for the Michaelson property and the owner can meet next week to sign. She's out of the country and won't be back until then."

"No problem. I'm going to offer on this one too. Forty thousand lower than what they're asking, though. Cash."

She'd learned not to show her surprise about the cash offers. It seemed he only made purchases in cash.

"I'll draw up the offer and email it to you for review. If you like it, you can electronically sign off on it." It was the same as with the other contracts.

"Works for me. Look, it's not my business, but is everything okay?" He tilted his chin at Maguire's Mustang—where Maguire sat in the driver's seat waiting for her. With the tinted windshield and windows it was almost impossible to see anything other than the shadow of him. "I grabbed coffee at Nora's this morning and heard something about your house getting broken into. Is that why Maguire's with you?"

"My house wasn't actually broken into, but yes, something is going on right now." Something she didn't feel like explaining to anyone. "I'm fully capable of doing my job, but I'll be honest, you're one of the only clients I'm still showing places to." Because she trusted him, and his business was important. "As far as I know I'm not in immediate danger or anything, but…Maguire and I decided it would be best if he drove me around today. The sheriff is aware of what's going on and is happy that Maguire is with me." And that was all she was comfortable divulging.

Ethan nodded, his frown deepening. "Let me know if you need anything."

"I will, thank you. And I'll have that paperwork to you in the next hour and a half."

He paused, as if he wanted to say more, then nodded. "Okay. But seriously, if you need anything or need to let someone else show me places temporarily, you won't lose my business. Your safety is more important."

He really was a good guy. Mary Pierce needed to open her eyes and scoop him up. "Thank you. I'll let you know." She didn't think things would go that far, but she appreciated the offer. She just had to have faith that the sheriff was going to locate Nelson Smith and she'd be able to put this craziness behind her and get on with her life.

As Ethan got into his vehicle, she slid into the passenger seat of Maguire's car and automatically locked her door. Before she'd strapped in he leaned over, cupped her cheeks in both big hands, and claimed her lips with his in a searing, toe-numbing kiss. He completely dominated her, his tongue teasing hers in a breath-stealing mating of their mouths.

It was over all too soon. He pulled back, his pale blue eyes seeming darker as he watched her intently.

She blinked as she tried to regain her bearings. "That was..." She started to say *hot* until it sank in why he'd just kissed her so thoroughly—and in front of another man. "Was that you, like, staking your claim?" Why was that thought so sexy?

"Yep." Absolutely no apologies from him.

She shouldn't like this caveman attitude. She really, really shouldn't. "I...don't even know what to say to that. You know Ethan likely can't even see inside your car anyway. The tint is too dark."

Maguire lifted a shoulder in that casual but ridiculously sexy way of his. "Then I just kissed you because I wanted to. Because I can't keep my mouth off you when you're sitting next to me."

She swallowed hard. That little niggle of worry that this was too good to be true, that *he* was way too good to be true, whispered through her mind. "The feeling is mutual."

Maguire didn't say anything for a long moment. When he glanced away she felt the loss immediately. It was so easy to get caught up in those pale eyes.

As he scanned outside the vehicle, the lines of his body taut, she frowned even as tension rocketed through her. "What is it?" She started to scan their surroundings too, including the strip of stores across the street. All of them were decorated with a Christmas theme. Since Ethan had already pulled away, there weren't any cars close to them along their own parking strip, and the building they'd parked in front of wasn't occupied and hadn't been for a couple months. "Do you see something?"

"No." His sexy voice brought her back to face him. "I just wanted to make sure we didn't have an audience."

Her eyes widened at his seductive tone. He couldn't mean... "Why not?" she whispered even though it was just the two of them.

In response, he reached over and slid his hand up her inner leg. "Lift your hips, pull your dress up to your waist."

Shivers skated across her skin at his words and touch. "Maguire..."

He leaned closer, crowding her space as he watched her intently. "Like I said before, feel free to say my name when you come against my fingers."

Heat rushed through her, creating an ache between her legs she knew he could fulfill. "Right here?" she asked even as she did as he ordered.

His hand crept higher up her inner thigh, sending little pulses of pleasure through her, making her feel even more lightheaded. She couldn't believe he was doing this. That she was letting him. This wasn't her—or maybe it was, and Maguire was the man to bring this side of her out in the open.

No one could possibly see them, and she knew Maguire would keep an eye on their surroundings. It was the only reason she was able to let go of her control as his hand ate up the rest of the distance to her covered mound.

Eyes on hers, he pushed the flimsy material to the side and rubbed a finger over her pulsing clit. She didn't have to look down to know that it was peeking out from her folds, swollen and begging for his touch. If she and Maguire were within five feet of each other, her body was *always* begging for his touch.

Slowly, Maguire slid his finger through her folds until he was cupping her mound. Samantha's wetness slicked his finger as he thrust one into her. Her eyes were dilated, her breathing erratic as she stared at him. He would kiss her in a moment, was powerless to stop himself, but he wanted to watch her like this. To watch her come apart from his touch.

Making her come could easily become an addiction. In his peripheral he kept an eye on their surroundings. This had been her last showing of the day and he'd been patient. Now he had to get her off. So far they were just dating — exclusively — but he wanted to bind her to him, to cement this thing growing between them so that there was no going back for her. He knew she wanted him. That was never a doubt. Their chemistry was off the charts, but he wanted more than sex and dating. He wanted everything from her.

"You're already so wet," he murmured.

Her breath hitched at his words and all she could do was nod. Which was fine with him.

He didn't want words unless it was his name on her lips and she was moaning. Slowly, he pulled his finger out, then slid two back in.

"Ahh." She rolled her hips, letting her head fall back against the seat as he began thrusting in a steady rhythm. He'd learned her body quickly — had never forgotten what she liked from all those years ago.

He barely brushed his thumb against her clit, intentionally just teasing her as he worked her up. "I've thought about this all day. But in my fantasy I bend you over the hood of my car and take you hard and fast from behind."

"Maguire!" she rolled her hips faster, clearly needing release.

He should drag it out, but hell, he wanted to see that exquisite look of pleasure on her face when she came.

Increasing the pressure against her clit with his thumb, he began massaging her in tight little circles even as he thrust faster and faster. His own breathing was uneven, harsh, and over-pronounced in the interior of the car as he watched her with her head back, eyes closed and looking so sexy it made his entire body ache.

He knew no one was near the vehicle and it would be impossible to sneak up on them without him seeing, so he crushed his mouth to hers. She was close and he wanted to taste her, to drink her in as she came.

As soon as his tongue clashed with hers, she clutched onto his shoulders and cried out into his mouth. Her inner walls started convulsing around his fingers as her orgasm slammed into her. The feel of her coming against him had his cock kicking against the zipper of his pants.

Soon enough he'd lose himself inside her again, but for now he savored the feel of her coming against his fingers, of all that wetness that was just for him, proof that she wanted him.

Her orgasm seemed to go on for ages and when she finally opened her dark eyes, hazy with lust, the grin she gave him was enough to knock him on his ass.

She blinked a couple times as she reached up to cup his cheek. Her palm was soft, smooth. "You're bad," she murmured.

"You like it."

"Yeah, I do. And as soon as we get back to your place I'm going to show you how much."

Grinning, he slid his glistening fingers into his mouth, watching with pure delight as her lips parted in shock. "You taste incredible."

Her cheeks went crimson as she pulled her dress back down over her hips. He hadn't thought it possible to render her speechless but it seemed he had as she strapped in and settled back against the seat.

Soon enough he'd have her talking — or crying out his name as he buried his cock inside her.

CHAPTER NINE

Maguire stuck his head out of the attic opening of the ceiling of the garage. "There are a few boxes of Christmas lights marked 'change bulbs.' Should these stay?"

Samantha's mom snorted and shook her head. "No. Haul those down too. They're going in the garbage."

Sam snickered next to her mom. "Dad swore he'd change out the broken bulbs so the rest of the lights would work. That's a decade's worth of lights, I'd bet."

"Longer." Her mom shook her head. "That man had a hoarding streak when it came to stuff like that." For a moment pain etched her expression but just as quickly she shook it off. "I miss him, but I won't miss all this junk."

Sam wrapped an arm around her shoulders. "Want to head back to the guest room?"

Her mom nodded and leaned into her for a moment.

"We're headed back inside. You good up there?" Sam called up to Maguire.

He poked his head out again, a big smile on his face. "Yep. I just found some old Halloween costumes. I don't know if they're yours, but I'm pulling them down too."

"Go ahead and haul all the boxes down," her mom said. "I'll just go through everything at once. It'll be easier that way."

"Yes, ma'am." A smile on his face, he gave a half salute before ducking back out of sight.

"So...you two must be serious," her mom said once they were in the privacy of the guest room. "Because a man—and his brother—

wouldn't be here on a Sunday helping clean out my house unless he was very serious about you."

Sam pulled out a drawer. "It's weird. I never expected this. Not so soon. And okay, not at all, really. And yes, I think he's serious." She knew she was, even as she battled her inner bullshit. If she gave her heart to him completely, then lost him? Hell, she knew it was just a risk she was going to have to take. Because she'd fallen for the man. "We're exclusive." And she felt bad being so happy when her mom had just lost her husband.

But her mom's genuine smile eased some of her guilt. "I'm so happy to hear that. I worried moving back here would be difficult for you. I know what you said about being happy, but I'm your mom. I'm allowed to worry."

"I…thought it might be difficult too. But I really love it here. Even if Maguire and I hadn't started this thing, I'd still be happy." She was glad she'd moved somewhere else for a time, experienced life away from Holly, but coming home felt like the most natural thing in the world.

"Well, Maguire is a nice young man. The whole family is. Though you know Alison will start bothering you about giving her grandchildren soon."

Sam snorted. "We just started dating."

"That won't mean a thing to her. She's got a pool going down at the salon on how long it'll take Maguire to put a ring on your finger."

She shook her head as laughter bubbled out. They were exclusive, yes, but a ring? Okay, the thought freaked her out a little. Because marriage? She'd just gone from moving back home, launching her career here and now she and Maguire were very much together. Not to mention she was dealing with a freaking stalker. She didn't want to think about anything else at this point. "Why am I not surprised?"

"I might have placed a bet." Her mom's expression turned sheepish.

"Yeah?"

"Two months out from now."

She blinked. "That's pretty soon."

Her mom just gave her a knowing look and lifted a shoulder. "All right. I've got a bunch of your dad's old fishing clothes. I'm going to keep a couple shirts out of sentimental value, but the rest... I don't know if I should take them to Goodwill or just toss them."

Even though it hurt that her dad was gone, Sam found herself laughing through an unexpected prick of tears. "That man would wear shirts until they were literally falling off him."

"That's what happens when you grow up with nothing." Her mom's voice was wistful as she hauled a handful of shirts still on the hangers out of the closet.

That was true enough. Sam's dad had grown up poor, a few towns away from Holly. His family had been happy, but farming wasn't lucrative. Not to all farmers, anyway. Even when he'd started his own business and become successful, he still drove his vehicles until they gave out and pinched pennies wherever he could. Sam had learned a lot from him about how to save.

Swiping at another rush of tears, she cleared her throat and pulled open a drawer. It was time to get down to business.

Maguire scanned the street June Murphy lived on before heading back inside the house. Even though they'd been helping out around her house all day, he and his brother Nolan had been vigilant in checking the street at random times. And his other brother Jackson had taken to driving by—as well as the sheriff.

So far no one had seen Nelson Smith, but Maguire sure as hell didn't think the man had left town. According to Brad, most of his stuff was still at the motel. Not knowing where the guy was... It was making him crazy. He wanted to lock Sam down and keep her safe but knew that was impossible.

He understood that she had to work and couldn't let some nut rule her actions and life. But that didn't mean he was going to let her out of his sight. Thankfully, she didn't mind.

"You see anything?" Samantha asked as he stepped into the kitchen where she, her mom and Nolan were all eating sandwiches.

"Nah. We're all clear. I think I'm going to take a load of the boxes up to Goodwill in a bit." He'd already eaten and was antsy to get this stuff done so he could get Sam back to his place. And naked and underneath him.

"I'll take the rest in my truck," Nolan said.

"I don't know how to thank you boys for all you've done today," June said.

Maguire grinned at the term 'boys.' "It was our pleasure. And you can thank us by telling our mom how wonderful we are at dinner tomorrow night." He'd invited Sam and her mom to their Monday night dinner. "Make sure you say it in front of Fallon, really send the message home that we're perfect sons."

Samantha laughed at the same time her mom did, the sound music to his ears.

"I'll make sure to do that."

"I think we'll be ready to head out too, as soon as I load the dishwasher," Sam said, already clearing the empty plates.

Her mom stood to stop her, but Sam shooed her away.

"Mrs. Murphy, you can ride with me. I'll drop you off after we drop everything at the thrift store. Aunt Carly is closer to me than Maguire."

Samantha's mom was staying over at their aunt Carly's tonight. After she found out what was going on, she'd insisted that June stay at least one night. Since Maguire was selfish enough to admit he wanted naked time with Samantha—and her mom would be safer away from Sam, since Sam was the target of an obsessed stalker—he was glad June had declined his offer to stay at his place.

"That sounds good to me. Have you heard anything from the sheriff?" June asked Samantha as she pressed the start button on the dishwasher.

"He texted that he had no news, but just wanted to check in, so...no news yet." She half-smiled but the strain in her expression was clear.

And it made Maguire want to hunt down Nelson Smith and pummel the shit out of the guy.

Less than ten minutes later they'd all left, with Nolan and Sam's mom heading to a thrift store on his side of town, and Maguire and Samantha heading to the Goodwill closer to where he lived.

"I know I've said it, but I really do appreciate all your help today. I think cleaning out the house is part of how my mom's dealing with my dad's death. And you guys helped make a big dent in everything."

"You can show me how grateful you are later." He shot her a sideways glance as he steered into the parking lot of the Goodwill.

She just snorted. "You're a machine."

"Where you're concerned? Oh yeah. Besides, we've got lost time to make up for."

"Fair enough... The sign says to go around back. They're closed." She glanced at her cell phone. "Jeez, I didn't realize how late it was. We really did work you and your brother all day."

"Like I said, I take payments in sexual favors." Grinning, he steered around the side of the building. He'd made more than one drop-off here for his mom when she got in her spring cleaning mode.

"Hmm, not sure I like the sound of that." Her voice was light, teasing.

"Only from a tall, leggy brunette who likes getting off in my car." Her cheeks tinged pink and he had to order his cock back down. Which seemed to be the norm around her.

"That's acceptable, then."

He steered his dad's truck—which he'd borrowed for today's work—right up to the back door. It was a rollup kind, but was down since they were closed. An overhang protected the huge donations bin, basically a steel box with a small swing door for dropping items inside. It would protect anything inside from the weather.

"I'll get all the boxes and bags. Just sit tight."

Samantha gave him a "get real" look and slid out of the passenger seat. "We'll get this done quicker if I help. And I'm ready to get back to your place as fast as possible." The heat in her dark eyes intensified before she shut the door and met him at the back of the truck.

Maguire hefted up the nearest box and headed to the big bin. She was right. The quicker they got out of here, the quicker they'd be naked. He didn't even have to close his eyes to imagine hoisting her up against the wall of his shower, thrusting inside her as —

A jagged awareness sliced through him as he rounded the back of the truck and saw a disheveled man a mere ten feet away from Samantha, a rusty knife in his hand. The guy looked like shit, in clearly days-old, rumpled clothes, dark stubble covering his face, his eyes wild. But Maguire recognized him from the picture the sheriff had shown him.

Nelson Smith.

Maguire was about twenty feet away. Too far, but not so far that he couldn't see the fear etched on Sam's face.

His weapon was in the front of the truck, tucked under the seat. He'd been careful to make sure they weren't followed and there hadn't been anyone back here when he'd parked. Somehow this asshole had found them.

Fuck.

"Please put the knife down." Samantha's voice was surprisingly calm, with only a slight tremor threading through her words. Smith's attention stayed locked on her.

Maguire took a subtle step closer.

"You left me," Smith spat, his knife hand trembling as he waved it wildly around. "I had to find you, to fly all the way across the country."

Maguire took another step, then another, moving at an angle so the man wouldn't realize he was closing in. Smith's attention was mostly on Samantha anyway, giving Maguire a slight advantage. He hated that the man was focused on her, but he'd take advantage of it until he was close enough to take this guy out.

"I just moved back home."

"Without telling me." Another flail of his arm and another step closer to Samantha.

Nope. Maguire forced himself to remain calm, to call on all his training as he crept closer.

"My dad died. I had to move back. Why don't you put the knife down and we'll talk?"

"I tried to show you how much I love you, how much I'll do for you. You're mine!" His voice was high-pitched and unsteady. "I cut your tires, to make you stay and talk to me. But that neighbor bitch got in the way. Then you left again, just like you always do!"

Maguire was close enough to take him out now. He didn't care if he got injured or cut. He needed Samantha safe. Samantha, with her sweetness and big heart, who hadn't wanted to prosecute this guy because of his brain tumor.

Maguire had no compassion where this guy was concerned. Not when he'd terrified the woman he loved, was threatening her with a *knife*.

"Okay let's talk, then." Her voice shook now and Maguire could hear her fear. He couldn't see her expression though because all his focus was on Smith.

"We'll talk when we're alone!" He lunged at her and Maguire pounced.

Amped up on adrenaline, he rushed the tall, reedy man, lifting an arm to deflect the knife. Pain sliced through his forearm as he slammed his body into Smith's.

A crack rent the air as Smith landed on the pavement underneath him. He screamed as his arm snapped under Maguire's force. The knife clattered next to them.

Maguire wanted to lay into the guy, but stayed focused and rolled him over, even as he moaned in pain, his rambling words nonsense. He had no pity for Smith.

"There's a bungee cord in my dad's toolbox. Grab it." Maguire didn't look up as he pressed his knee into Smith's back, kept his wrists secured behind his back. He didn't care that the guy's arm was broken, he was keeping him completely disabled.

He could hear her hurried footsteps as she ran to the truck and then back to him.

Without glancing up at her, he took the cord and began tying Smith. By the time he'd finished, he heard Sam getting off the phone with Brad.

And two minutes later the sound of the sheriff's siren screamed in the distance. They weren't far from the station so it made sense.

"You can get off him." Samantha kicked the knife away as she pressed a hand to his shoulder.

Tense, Maguire looked up at her only because Smith wasn't a threat to anyone anymore. "I'll wait for the sheriff."

She looked as if she wanted to argue, but simply nodded. For that he was grateful. He knew he could move off the guy, but some intrinsic part of him needed to keep Smith down. Completely neutralized and unable to hurt Samantha. Maguire didn't even want the guy to look in her direction again. Though by now he didn't think that was a possibility. Smith was softly crying and muttering under his breath.

Less than a minute later two patrol cars surged around the corner of the building. Only when Brad and one of his deputies jumped from their respective vehicles did Maguire ease off and stand up.

When Brad yanked the guy to his feet with another yelp from Smith, Maguire finally turned to Sam.

"Are you okay?" they both asked at the same time.

On a cry, Samantha rushed at him, throwing her arms around him before either could answer.

He locked his arms around her and rubbed his hand up and down her spine, unwilling to let her go as she buried her face against his chest. "Everything's okay now."

Finally she lifted her head to look at him. "God, Maguire, I thought… You're bleeding!" Her entire body jolted as she stepped back, his blood on her bare arm. "Where are you hurt?" she demanded.

He lifted his left arm. "Just got nicked when I took him down."

"Ambulance is here," Brad said, coming to stand beside them. "We're taking Smith to the hospital to be cared for before we charge him. We'll need to take both your statements, but you're getting patched up too." He handed Maguire a cloth he must have gotten from his car.

"That's not necessary." Maguire lifted his forearm, saw that maybe it was a little deeper than he'd thought. But it wouldn't need stitches. Not even close. About two inches long and shallow enough, it would just require some antiseptic and a bandage and he'd be fine. Maybe steri-strips.

"Oh, it is necessary!" Samantha was shaking now. "You're going to the hospital right the freak now!"

When he realized how upset she was—and of course she was—he nodded and reached for her, wrapped his non-injured arm around her. "We'll head there right now. Can you drive me?" He was fine to drive but figured if he said that, she'd start yelling again.

"Yes. We'll see you at the hospital," Sam told the sheriff, and she wasn't asking.

Holding his bleeding arm to his chest, the cloth secured against it to stanch the bleeding, Maguire let Samantha strap him in. When she jumped into the driver's side, her hands trembling as she took the wheel, he said, "It's hot when you boss me around. Maybe you can boss me around later tonight."

Eyes wide, she glanced at him for a millisecond before turning the engine on. "If you think we're having sex tonight, you're out of your freaking mind."

He just snorted. Oh, they were definitely having sex. A little injury like this wasn't keeping him from the woman he loved. He wanted to tell her right then how he felt but wasn't sure how she'd react. She was stressed and likely feeling out of control. He wouldn't add to her stress by dropping something so huge on her.

Unlike him, she'd never dealt with a situation like this before. Technically he'd never dealt with a knife-wielding stalker, but he had dealt with assholes who wanted to kill him. So he'd wait until later tonight to tell her. Or maybe tomorrow.

But he couldn't wait much longer than that.

Seeing the crazed look in Smith's eyes as he brandished that knife around? He rolled his shoulders once. He could have lost Samantha. Could lose her at any time. Life was too damn short and too precious not to be honest.

She needed to know how he felt. She was it for him, and today had only driven the point home.

CHAPTER TEN

Maguire resisted the urge to get up and check on Samantha—since she was simply in his parents' kitchen with his mom and her mom. After what had happened last night he hadn't been sure she'd want to come to his family's house for dinner, but she'd been insistent. And she'd even worked today, much to his annoyance.

But he understood the need to keep busy. That was the only thing that had kept him sane since getting out of the Marines.

He looked up from his seat at the dining room table as his father squeezed his shoulder once. "You picked a good one, son."

Maguire nodded as he stood, pushing his chair in. Almost everyone had dispersed from the table and were now in various parts of his parents' house, talking and laughing and doing God only knew what. Their family dinner had grown from six to twelve tonight, including Nora's younger sister—who was dating one of Maguire's nephews. "Thanks, Dad. I agree."

At six foot two, his father was burly, with thick, dark hair similar to Maguire's own. Unlike their mom, he was often the quietest one out of everyone. He and Nolan were similar like that. "She the one who broke your heart three years ago?" his dad asked so no one else would hear.

Maguire blinked, surprised his dad knew about that. But hell, his mom had known, so maybe he shouldn't be shocked. "Ah, yeah. But it was all a misunderstanding." Thanks to some woman he barely even remembered and had never touched. Life was such a bitch sometimes.

"Well I'm glad you two worked it out. And no matter what your mom says, don't have kids right away. Enjoy a few years with her first."

"We're just dating." Though he wanted a hell of a lot more than just that. He wanted to move in with her, to put a ring on her finger eventually, and yeah, he did want kids. Not right away though.

"Tell yourself that if you want, but don't lie to me. I see the way you look at her. And if I had to bet, I'd say you'll have a ring on her finger in two months."

"*Have* you made a bet?" His voice was dry.

His dad just laughed. "You know me better than that. But you also know your mom."

"True enough. Thanks. I...I've got plans for us." But first he needed to tell her he loved her. Last night she'd been emotionally drained, so after they'd made their statements down at the station he'd brought her back to her home, where she'd crashed. The adrenaline that had kept her going had fled, leaving her exhausted. Something he understood well.

His dad clapped his shoulder again once before heading out of the room. Nolan and Brad were talking intently at the other end of the dining room table and he wasn't sure exactly where everyone else was. The only person he really wanted to see anyway was Samantha.

Five minutes had passed since he'd last seen her and that was far too many.

In the kitchen he found her with their moms, standing around a cut and already partially eaten apple pie.

He lifted an eyebrow. "Really? I expect this out of my own mother."

Samantha giggled, the sound music to his ears as she put down her mug of what was likely coffee. "We decided to dive into it before taking it out to you vultures."

He pulled her into his arms, muttered a half-ass apology to the others for stealing Sam, and led her out the side door with him onto a deck.

"We're not leaving yet, are we?"

"No. I just want a few minutes alone with you." He tugged on her hand, pulling her along the side of the house until they reached the backyard. It was an oasis of color, thanks to his father's green thumb. Lavender, irises, a bed of black-eyed Susan and fruit trees surrounded a small, man-made pool filled with fish.

"This is incredible," she murmured. "And I thought your front yard was amazing."

"Right?" He led her to a bench that was nestled right next to a triple-layer bird fountain that had bronze peacocks coiled around the base. Taking her hands in his once they were seated, he tried to shake off the nerves humming through him.

He'd almost told her that he loved her this morning, but had been too much of a chickenshit. That was the real reason he'd been holding off. But he needed to say the words, to tell her how he felt. It was time to man up and grab the life he wanted.

"Look...I've never told another woman this. And don't feel like you need to say it back because I know this is soon, but—"

"I love you, Maguire O'Connor." Her voice was steady and the truth in her dark eyes was easy to see.

The band of tension coiled around his chest snapped and he couldn't have stopped the grin that spread across his face even if he'd wanted to. "I love you too, Samantha Murphy. I wanted to tell you last night, but I wanted both of us to have clear heads so you didn't think I was just saying it in the heat of the moment."

Smiling softly, she squeezed his hands gently. "I knew last night too. But my brain was too muddled. And I've never said it to anyone else either."

"You're the only woman I could ever want." That was a fact he knew without a doubt. He'd been wrapped up in her and the memory of her for years. Leaning forward, he claimed her mouth much more gently than he wanted, but they were in his parents' backyard and there were too many windows for nosy people to look through. Including several who had placed bets about what would happen between them.

Later tonight, however, he'd be kissing her the way he wanted, and all over. Claiming her once and for all.

Samantha tilted her head back, letting the jets of water cascade over her. As soon as they'd arrived back at Maguire's place, he'd gotten a work call. Since it had seemed as if he'd be a while, she'd decided to snag a shower.

For the first time in more than a day she could truly relax. Nelson Smith was behind bars and wouldn't be getting bail. He'd crossed the country in an attempt to kill her—or according to him, to "make her his"—so he would spend his last remaining months behind bars. He'd be in a hospital prison setting and he was being transported back to Oregon so he'd be close to his family when he died.

And she was never going to have to worry about him again.

At the sound of the bathroom door creaking open, she smiled to herself.

"I hope you want company." Maguire's deep voice filled the room a second before he slid the frosted glass door open and stepped inside with her.

From beneath the stream of water, she drank in every naked inch of him, right down to his thick, full cock jutting out. Broad and muscular all over, he looked like a linebacker. She itched to reach out and stroke her fingers along the lines of his intricate tattoos, to touch him everywhere and remind herself that he was hers and she was his. Because yesterday could have ended a lot differently. She shuddered at the memory, but shoved those thoughts away.

They moved toward each other at the same time, his mouth crushing down on hers as she went up on tiptoe to meet him.

She moaned into his mouth even as she hoisted herself up, wrapping her legs around him. He had a very familiar look in his pale eyes that said there would be no foreplay. Just hard and fast and she desperately needed that. She needed to be filled by him, to find release, especially after the last twenty-four hours.

She was still reeling that he loved her too. He'd been so adorable, almost hesitant to tell her, so she'd blurted out her own feelings. She'd thought it was too soon, but if he felt the same there was no need to hold back. Not after last night.

Life was way too fragile and she wanted to spend it with Maguire.

His hands slid around her body, gripped her ass hard as he pushed her against one of the tile walls. She loved the feel of his fingers digging into her skin, that little bite of pain.

"In me now," she said against his mouth, though it came out garbled.

In response, he slid his dick against her stomach, not making a move to shift lower. Though she knew he wanted inside her as badly as she wanted him in her.

Her inner walls clenched, empty without him as he palmed one breast.

Teasing her nipple with his thumb, he seemed content to keep her pinned to the slick wall while he turned her on even more.

So she reached between their bodies and grasped his thick length in her hand. She couldn't get a full grip, but she could caress and tease him. Water pummeled against them as she started stroking him and savoring the moans of pleasure he made into her mouth.

She loved that she drove him as crazy as he drove her. It was weird, almost like the gap of the last few years between them didn't exist. Like they'd picked up right where they'd left off. Only they were a little older and, in her case, definitely wiser and more confident. Maybe three years ago hadn't been the right time for them.

Now certainly was. Of that she had no doubt. Because this man was it for her in so many ways.

She nipped at his bottom lip, biting down with more pressure than normal. "In me, Maguire."

Pulling his head back slightly, he looked down at her with pale eyes she could drown in. Oh so slowly, he rolled her already hard nipple between his thumb and forefinger, making her wiggle her hips against him. "No teasing tonight?" he murmured.

"Do you really want to?" She was torn between the need to drag this out or to feel all that thickness filling her right this instant.

He dropped his hand to grab both of her hips and she had her answer. She didn't bother fighting a smile as he readjusted his hips then thrust inside her.

Maguire watched as Samantha arched her back against the wall, her dark hair slicked back, her eyes closing momentarily as he thrust inside her.

He couldn't wait any longer. At least not this first time tonight. His entire body trembled with the need to claim her, take her. To come inside her and mark her in the most primal way there was.

For a moment, he kept her pinned up against the wall, buried deep inside her, and just stared at her. Breathing hard, his heart rate a staccato beat in his chest, he took in every sleek line and curve of the woman he knew was one day going to be his wife.

The thought should have scared him, but instead it filled him with a sense of rightness.

When her eyes opened, her dark gaze captured his, didn't stray. The moment felt impossibly intimate as he started thrusting inside her. In and out, slowly at first.

She clutched onto his shoulders, her hips rolling up and meeting him stroke for stroke. The grip of her legs around him was vise-like, mirroring the feel of her inner walls clenched tight around his cock.

Close to coming already, his balls were pulled up tight as he reached between their bodies and rubbed her clit with his thumb.

She sucked in a breath, her eyes going heavy-lidded as he began massaging the little bundle of nerves over and over in a tight motion he knew would push her over the edge.

It didn't take long until her inner walls started that fluttering rhythm he recognized well, telling him she was close to finding her release.

Leaning down, he didn't stop his frantic pace as he nipped along her jaw, creating a path all the way to her ear. There was a little spot behind her earlobe that seemed to drive her crazy.

He raked his teeth over the spot and she jerked against him right as he felt the rush of her climax and the tightening of her inner walls as her orgasm hit.

He was done holding back. Crying out her name, he thrust harder, the sound of the water and their moans the only thing he could hear as he lost himself inside her. His climax seemed to stretch on for an eternity as he came inside her in long, hard spurts.

When he finally came down from his high and pulled back to look at her, she simply buried her face against his neck.

"You're determined to sex me to death," she murmured, nuzzling against him as she kept her body still wrapped around him.

Her words pulled a surprised laugh from him. "I've had a long dry spell. Making up for lost time."

"I hope I was worth the wait." She looked up at him then and there was no insecurity in her gaze, just a teasing glint.

He pinched her butt. "You know you were."

Her full mouth split into a grin. "What do you say we clean up and then eat some of that pie we took home?"

The way she said "home," as if his place was hers, stirred something deep inside him. He realized that no matter which place he ended up buying, Samantha was his home. As long as she was with him, that was the only thing that mattered.

EPILOGUE

Two months later

"Where are we going?" Samantha asked again.

"Man, you really hate surprises." Maguire glanced at his phone's screen when it buzzed. A text from his sister with two simple words: *Everything's set!*

His sister might drive him crazy sometimes, but she always came through. Heck, his whole family always did.

Very soon he hoped to make their family just a little bit bigger by making things official with Samantha. Turned out his parents had been right. Two months was pretty much his limit. He couldn't go another day without having his ring on Sam's finger. Just no way.

He wanted everyone to know she belonged to him. Even though they already lived together—he'd asked her about a second after telling her that he loved her. Currently they were living at his place while the home they'd bought—that first one he'd looked at—was under construction. They'd decided to hold off moving in until the changes to the kitchen and bathrooms were complete. Luckily she'd loved that home too, though she'd insisted on expanding the master closet. As soon as they were able, however, he was putting his current place up for rent. The mortgage was paid off so it made sense to hold on to it and use it as a source of income for them.

"I wouldn't say I hate surprises, but I certainly don't love them." She crossed her tanned legs, showing off miles of skin thanks to a red and white summer dress.

He just grinned and turned off the main road onto a gravel one that would be easily missed if you didn't know where you were going. His parents owned a little property about an hour away from Holly that was secluded and perfect for what he'd planned.

"You look a little bit like a kid on Christmas," Samantha murmured, narrowing her gaze.

"We're almost there, so you can relax."

She glanced out the side window and saw one thing: trees. Lots and lots of trees.

Anticipation hummed through him the closer they got to the clearing where the house was. He slowed his Mustang as they reached the end of the gravel road and pulled onto the paved driveway leading up to the one-bedroom cabin sitting on a lake. Sunset was a few hours away, and though he could only see a portion of the lake because of the angle, what he could see was a sparkling, smooth pane of blue glass. God, it was gorgeous out here, and it was no wonder this had been his parents' getaway over the years. When they were kids, he and his siblings had never been invited with them when they came here. Only now that they were grown were they allowed to use it.

"This place is adorable. Oh my gosh, did you rent a place for us for the weekend?" Excitement laced her voice as she shifted against her seat to look at him.

"You'll see." He'd asked her to take the weekend off from work for this, but hadn't told her anything else.

They'd both been taking off more and more weekends so they could spend time together, and he'd promoted two of his guys to start taking on more responsibility. It felt good in a way he hadn't quite imagined. For so many years he'd been chained to work, afraid to simply relax. Thankfully he loved what he did, but he loved Samantha more.

He parked in the driveway and hurried around to open her door before she could. Taking her hand, he helped her out and pulled her flush to him before he brushed his lips over hers. "We'll leave everything in the car for now. I want to show you the place."

Slipping her arm around his waist, she nodded and let him lead her to the back of the house. The place was small, maybe a thousand square feet, with a master bedroom, living room, laundry room, kitchen and bathroom. The back portion of the cabin was all windows, so every room had a view of the water.

"This place actually belongs to my parents," he said as they strolled over the grass toward the long dock that stretched out over the lake.

"Seriously?"

"Yep. This was their getaway over the years. Probably how they survived having four kids." As they neared the dock, he grinned when he saw everything was set up just like his sister had said.

Samantha looked up at him curiously as they stepped onto the dock, clearly having seen what was at the end.

A big plaid quilt that had been made by his grandmother was stretched out over the end of the dock. A picnic basket filled with cheeses and fruits — and baked goods from Fallon — and champagne was waiting for them.

"This is the sweetest surprise ever." Samantha squeezed him tightly as they reached the end. "I changed my mind about not liking surprises."

He really hoped she was ready for one more. Before she could sit, he went down on one knee and pulled out the ring box that had been burning a hole in his pocket for the better part of two weeks. Popping it open, he met her gaze. "Marry me?"

Eyes wide, she nodded as she fell to her knees in front of him. "Yes." No hesitation, just her clear, perfect voice giving him that one word.

The only word he wanted to hear. Emotion clogged his throat and he'd barely managed to slide the ring on her finger before she wrapped her arms around him, tackling him to the quilt. "I love you, Maguire O'Connor."

In that instant, he thought his heart might explode. For some reason whenever she used his full name he got hard as a rock. Moving swiftly, he had her pinned on her back underneath him. "I love you right back."

"Is anyone else around?" she whispered, though it was silent except for the nearby birds and squirrels. "I mean, someone had to have set this up."

"Long gone. It's just the two of us." And he planned to take full advantage of their privacy. The woman he loved had just agreed to become his wife.

Her grin was pure, wicked Samantha. "Good.

He crushed his mouth to hers, teasing her lips open as she wrapped her legs around his waist. The champagne and food would have to wait while he made love to his fiancée.

Soon she'd be his wife. Because he wasn't doing a long engagement. Nope. If he had his way, they'd be married by Christmas.

He didn't even care that it would mean his mother would win the betting pool.

Mistletoe Me, Baby

CHAPTER ONE

Nolan knocked on the already open door to Miranda Flores' office at the local community center in Holly. Miranda usually kept the door open, wanting everyone to know they could talk to her at any time.

Phone against her ear, she glanced up and gave him a blinding smile that was a punch to his solar plexus. Which was pretty standard for every time he saw her.

She held up a finger as she continued talking. As she spoke, she was looking at something on her laptop.

Leaning against the doorframe, he crossed his arms over his chest and took the rare opportunity to drink in the sight of her. Her light brown hair was down around her face in soft waves. As she talked she was smiling, which was standard for her. Whenever they talked on the phone, he could hear the smile in her voice. Rolling his shoulders once, his gaze stayed on her mouth, even as he told himself to look away. He'd fantasized about nibbling on her bottom lip too many times. Hell, he wanted to kiss her everywhere, to claim her, to let the whole damn town know she was his.

But that wasn't happening anytime soon.

She'd made it very clear nearly ten months ago when they'd first met that she wasn't looking for any sort of relationship. At the time, she'd just taken her nephew, Mateo, in when her sister had dropped him off and bolted. Her sister had made Miranda his legal guardian. Only recently had Gloria gone into rehab for drug addiction.

As Miranda laughed, there was a little sparkle in her brown eyes. But they weren't just brown. He'd studied them enough to know there were little flecks of amber in them. Every chance he got, he studied the woman. Watching her, being around her, was his own personal addiction. One he didn't plan to give up.

"To what do I owe this pleasure?" Miranda's sweet voice pulled him out of his head.

He blinked once and realized he'd been staring, and that she was off the phone. Clearing his throat, he pushed up from the doorframe as she stood and stepped around the desk. He started to answer when she frowned and closed the distance between them in record time.

Frowning harder, she cupped his cheek. "What happened?"

Nolan wanted to lean into her touch, to savor the feel of her smooth, soft hand on his skin. Today she had on knee-high boots and a red sweater dress that hugged all her curves. "Ah...what?" he wanted to put his own hand over hers to hold her there, but managed restraint. Somehow.

"You have a bruise. Did you get hurt at work?" Concern rolled off her in waves, her distress clear.

Bruise? "Oh, this is nothing. Maguire did this during our last hockey practice."

"Aren't you guys on the same team?"

He snorted. "Yeah. My brother is an equal opportunity bulldozer when he plays."

She stroked her thumb over his bruise and he felt the sensation all the way to his dick. God, this woman had him all twisted up in knots. He'd get hurt more often if it meant she would touch him like this. Feeling her hand on him was *heaven*.

Abruptly she dropped her hand and her cheeks flushed pink, as if she realized how intimate that hold could be construed. "I might exchange words with Maguire later."

He laughed, but it felt strained. Having her touch him like that, whether she meant it intimately or not, affected him. Physically and otherwise. He'd been respecting her boundaries because hell, he *wanted* to be her friend. She was a sweet, sexy woman and in the last year they'd become friends. Best friends, even. Other than his brothers and family, she was the person he wanted to call with any sort of news first. "I'm sure he'll be very scared of you," he murmured.

Narrowing her gaze, she said, "I can be very scary."

"Yeah, scary in the way Mrs. Claus is."

"Are you comparing me to Santa Claus' wife?"

"Nope." Not even a little bit. "Maybe one of his elves, though." A really sexy elf. He could easily visualize the petite and curvy woman dressed up in a dirty 'sexy elf' Halloween costume. Or Christmas. Whatever. The thought of her dressed up in anything remotely dirty—or just flat out naked—was something he shouldn't be contemplating now.

She mock-jabbed him in the side. "Very funny."

Before he could respond, Mateo raced into the room and dropped his backpack on one of the chairs before tackle-hugging her. "School's finally out!"

Miranda wrapped her arms tight around her nephew. Even though the kid was eleven he was already taller than her by an inch. She was only five feet, three inches, but Mateo was tall for his age. "I know." She pulled him to her and kissed his cheek.

"Aunt Miranda," he muttered, stepping back to give Nolan a fist bump.

"Did they let you guys out early today?" Nolan asked.

"It's a half day."

"And I just bet they pumped you all full of sugar." Miranda's voice was dry.

"They did. But I saved you some of the cookies."

"Smart boy." She ruffled his hair, making Mateo turn red, but Nolan knew he liked it.

After the rough upbringing Mateo had been through, he was a completely different boy than the one who had come to live with her back in February. Open, happy and occasionally affectionate.

"When do you leave on your ski trip?" Had to be soon. The church his parents went to sent all the kids on a week-long ski trip when school let out. And selfish bastard that he was, Nolan was hoping to get some alone time with Miranda.

"Tomorrow, but…" Mateo looked at his aunt, his expression hopeful. "I was hoping I could stay the night at Joey's house. Mrs. Sala said —"

"I've already talked to her and it's fine. In fact, I already packed for you. But first you're going to spend an hour with me before I take you over there."

"Can we go to Nora's? Maybe Nolan can come too?" Mateo looked at him, an open smile on his face.

Hell yeah. If Miranda didn't mind, he was in. He took the two of them out at least once a week as it was. And Nora's Books and Brew was owned by his sister-in-law.

Miranda started to nod, when her cell phone rang. "Give me one more second and we're out of here."

Nolan didn't mean to eavesdrop but when he heard her say, "Hey, Ethan," he went on high-alert.

Mateo asked Nolan about one of the upcoming hockey games after the ski trip and he must have answered without sounding like a jackass because Mateo nodded before pulling his cell phone out of his pocket.

As the kid started texting, Nolan heard Miranda say, "See you later tonight. Yep, looking forward to it."

Nolan only knew one Ethan. Ethan Thaxter. A rich jackass — who wasn't actually a jackass at all. But if he was taking Miranda out, Nolan automatically didn't like him. And when the hell had she started dating?

His phone buzzed in his pocket and when he saw the message he sighed. It was work. "I've gotta run, guys," he said as Miranda was hanging up. "But have fun on your ski trip, Mateo. And be careful on the slopes if you've never skied before."

Mateo took him by surprise by giving him a quick hug, but Nolan returned it, patting him on the back. Then he nodded at Miranda. "See you around."

She gave him one of her warm smiles and he tried to return it but wasn't sure if he'd managed. He'd thought that he could handle just being friends with her. But if she started dating, he wasn't sure he could deal with that.

The thought of someone else kissing her, touching her...hell. He should have made his move a long time ago. He'd never been hesitant about anything in his life. Especially not when it came to the opposite sex.

But Miranda was different. Unfortunately, he'd hurt only himself by holding back. If she was dating again maybe it was time to show her that he was the man she'd been looking for.

Nolan slammed his fist into his punching bag for what felt like the hundredth time. Probably was.

Covered in sweat, he should be exhausted. Instead he was amped up and couldn't get thoughts of Miranda on a date with someone out of his head.

This was his own damn fault. If he hadn't been such a coward she wouldn't be out with anyone else. But he'd been dragging his feet for ten months.

Coward.

He slammed his fist into the bag, again and again.

"Whoa, what's got you so revved up?"

He didn't turn at the sound of his brother Jackson's voice. He'd heard the little beep of his alarm system letting him know someone had entered his house a minute earlier. And only his family had a key. "Nothing. Just working up a sweat."

"How long you been in here?"

Realizing his youngest brother wasn't going anywhere, he dropped his gloved-up hands and turned to see Jackson, a beer bottle in hand, leaning against the doorframe.

"Help yourself to my beer," he muttered, stripping the gloves off.

"I always do."

Despite his dark mood, he laughed. Just because he felt like garbage didn't mean he needed to drag anyone else down with him. "What's up?"

"Nothing." Jackson stepped into the basement-turned-gym/

entertainment area and dropped onto one of the couches Nolan had inherited from their parents. "Nora and Sasha are baking at the house and kicked me out."

"They kicked you out?" He went to his mini fridge and grabbed a bottle of water. "That doesn't sound right."

Jackson laughed lightly. It was good to see his brother so relaxed. He'd been with Nora since last Christmas and was now married to her. Nolan had never seen him so happy.

"Maybe not kicked me out of the house, but the kitchen is off limits. Thought I'd come see what you're up to."

"Not working on any projects now?" His brother was a carpenter, and a damn good one. Created unique pieces that sold for a fortune.

"Just finished one up."

And he was bored, Nolan guessed. "Want to get some time on the ice? I've got a key to the community center."

"You sure? We can just chill and watch a game."

Nolan rolled his shoulders once. As a building contractor, he worked hard all day and normally looked forward to down time, but not tonight. He had too much pent-up energy and he needed to not be obsessing about Miranda. He started to answer but his phone rang with her familiar ring tone.

Jackson just gave him a knowing look—because his brother knew exactly how Nolan felt about her. All his brothers did.

He waited until the second ring because…yeah. "Hey."

"Hey, Nolan." Her voice was sweet and melodic. "I hate to bother you but… I'm having an issue with my washing machine. You don't have to look at it tonight or anything but maybe tomorrow—"

"Nah, it's okay. I need to shower first but I can be there in half an hour." He couldn't even play it cool and act as if he wouldn't drop everything for her. Because he would. Every single time. And hell, he wanted to see how her stupid date had gone.

"Really?"

"Of course. See you then." He glanced at his watch. It wasn't even six o'clock. Apparently, her date had sucked. The thought made him smile.

"Going to see your girl?" Grabbing his jacket from the couch, Jackson stood.

"She's not my girl." But she would be. And he wasn't having this conversation.

"Says only you." He took a swig of his beer. "All right, I'm gonna head home. Will I see you Monday?"

"I'll be there." His parents had him and his three siblings — plus significant others — over every Monday for dinner.

"Bring Miranda. I know Mateo is out of town and she'll be missing him."

"How do you know about Mateo?" He headed toward the stairs with his brother, all thoughts on getting a shower then hurrying over to Miranda's. Because apparently, he was a masochist. Didn't matter that he couldn't have her. At least he could spend time with her. And screw it, if she was dating now, he wasn't going to hold back anymore.

Jackson lifted a shoulder. "Nora said something."

Oh, right. Miranda worked part-time at Nora's during any holiday season to supplement her income. Since Holly, North Carolina, a town in the Blue Ridge Mountains, was Christmas all year round, the holiday season tended to be longer here than normal. He'd heard more than once that their little town looked like a Thomas Kincade painting. All the shops had Christmas trees in the windows every single day of the year. And it wasn't strange to see Santa walking down Main Street in July. So in December, Holly kicked up the Christmas spirit to insane proportions. He knew Miranda had been working her ass off the last couple weeks.

Which was why anytime she needed help around the house, he did it for free. Okay, he did it for free because he couldn't actually charge her regardless. He would feel like too much of a dick. But she always cooked for him, which seemed to make her happy. And God knew he loved the excuse to be around her.

At that thought he wondered if she'd cooked for Thaxter. If she had, the date hadn't gone too well if she was home doing laundry already. And that thought shouldn't make him so damn happy. But he was.

"What?" he asked as he and Jackson reached the top of the stairs.

His brother shut the door behind them and strode to the sink where he poured out the rest of his beer. "Just wondering what you're thinking of that's got you smiling like that."

He didn't answer, just tossed his empty bottle into the recycle bin. "Lock up on your way out?" Because he had some place to be. He was starting to wonder if he'd made a mistake in not acting on his attraction to her. It was time to do something about it.

CHAPTER TWO

Miranda's heart skipped a beat when she heard the doorbell. It had to be *him*.

Nolan O'Connor, the man who starred in all her fantasies. With clear blue eyes she could get lost in, and a body that made her weak in the knees, he was walking, talking sex. Not that it was the only reason she was attracted to him. Oh yes, when they'd first met, she'd nearly lost her breath he was so good looking. But after getting to know him — she still couldn't figure out how he was single.

He was always kind to her nephew, helped out at the community center with free labor and coaching, and was quick to help her out if she needed it. Usually when she didn't even ask for it. She'd actually stopped asking him to assist with anything because he wouldn't take any payment. And food didn't count. Tonight she'd made an exception because it was freezing outside and she had four loads of laundry — and really didn't want to lug everything down to the local laundry mat.

Okay that was mostly true. She'd missed getting to talk to Nolan today and needed her 'fix'. Ugh. So pathetic. She loved spending time with him and was glad that they didn't have all the messy complications that a sexual relationship brought. They were just friends. Good friends.

She wanted more, but no way was that happening. Because even if he was interested in her — and clearly he wasn't or a man like him would have made a move by now — she had too much to deal with right now to even think about dating. As Mateo's legal guardian for the foreseeable future, she had too much on her plate.

Taking a deep breath, she pulled the door open and tried to steel herself—as always—to see him. It was a fruitless effort as he still took her breath away. Over six feet tall, his shoulders were broad and his jacket and T-shirt couldn't hide the muscular chest he was hiding. His jet-black hair was cut short, but he'd grown a bit of scruff in the last week—making him even sexier.

"Hey, thank you for coming over. I really appreciate it." She could feel her cheeks flush and cursed her reaction. If he noticed, he'd never let on.

He made a sort of grunting sound and glanced around as he stepped inside, as if looking for someone. Around him, she always felt small, which made sense given his size. She wondered who he was looking for—

"Mateo's gone," she said.

He nodded. "How are you handling it?"

"I'm good." Her voice sounded a little too high pitched even to her own ears. Because she wasn't handling it as well as she'd thought she would.

He just raised his eyebrows as he slid off his jacket and hung it on the coat rack.

"Gah, fine, I'm not okay," she said, shutting the door behind him. "The house is so quiet. I'm happy for him. I really am, I just…miss him. Which is stupid because he's been gone for three hours. And I keep having all these worst-case scenarios running through my head, like what if the bus runs off a cliff or what if he breaks his leg on the slopes or… Now I'm rambling and sound kind of insane." It was like she had diarrhea of the mouth around him.

But Nolan just laughed, his lips kicking up in a sexy half-smile. "No, you sound like a good aunt."

For a moment, she basked in the praise and then felt silly for it. When she'd taken Mateo in she'd felt completely incapable of dealing with an eleven-year-old boy even if she had offered to care for him. Hell, she'd begged her sister because it had been clear Mateo needed someone to look out for him, to make sure he was in school—to *feed* him. Some days she still felt like she was a fraud and barely handling this parent thing. But they were figuring things out one day at a time. Aaaand, she realized she was standing there just staring at Nolan. Okay then. She cleared her throat and took a step toward the hallway. "I made baked ziti if you have time." She really loved cooking for him.

He made an appreciative sound, which warmed her from the inside out. "Sounds good. Let me take a look at your washing machine and then I'll probably demolish half of it."

Once they were in her laundry room, she winced at the sight of water leaking out from under it. She'd shoved a bunch of towels against the bottom and all over the tiled floor but it didn't seem to be helping.

"What were you washing?" he asked, setting his toolbox down on the bench by the door that led to the garage.

"Pillows." With Mateo gone she was washing everything. Not just clothes, but all bed linens, and pretty much anything possible. She felt a little manic with the need to stay busy but with him gone she wanted to get everything clean and ready for Christmas. Which reminded her, she still needed to get a tree.

"Ah."

"What does that mean?"

He just shrugged and seriously, a shrug should not be sexy. But apparently, everything he did was. The simple way he walked and moved was delicious. "When it was washing did it make any sounds?"

"A loud, banging sound. When I came in to check on it, water was everywhere." And she had no idea if it was truly broken or if this was one of those easy fixes Nolan could take care of. Neither of her parents had been handy. If something had needed to be fixed, they'd called someone. But Nolan seemed able to pretty much fix anything. The first time she'd told him she had someone coming over to fix her dishwasher, he'd been mortally offended she hadn't asked him. From then on, she'd started calling him for help—until recently when she'd started to feel as if she was taking advantage.

"I think I know what it is. It might be off balance. Shouldn't take too long to fix. You have any beer?"

"Yep, your favorite kind." She stocked them solely for the times he came by. Leaving him to it, she went to the kitchen and grabbed him one. When she returned to her laundry room she found him bent over the front of the machine.

His plain T-shirt had pulled up, revealing a few inches of his back. His *back*, for the love of God. That little flash of skin shouldn't have any effect on her, but she found herself looking even lower, tracing the lines of his sculpted, unfortunately covered, ass.

She'd never been like this before moving to Holly—and meeting Nolan. It wasn't as if she'd been sexless, but when she was around him it was like her hormones went into overdrive.

"So how was the date?" he asked, still bent over, his question a little muffled.

It took a moment for the actual question to register. "What date?"

"I thought you had one tonight."

Why the heck would he think that? Small towns were so weird sometimes. It was something she was still getting used to since moving here from Florida. "Nope. But I did help Ethan Thaxter pick out some jewelry for Mary Pierce." She and Mary had become instant friends when Miranda had moved to town. "Oh, you can't tell anyone either."

Nolan straightened and turned to look at her, his expression almost...relieved. "Thaxter and Mary are together?"

"Yeah. How do you not know that? That man is over the moon for her." It was so obvious when the two of them were together—and had been even before they'd started dating.

"Huh." He turned back around and started fiddling with...well, whatever.

She had no clue but from past experience, she had no doubt that Nolan knew what he was doing. "You seriously can't tell anyone about the jewelry."

"Well, if he bought jewelry in town, someone's going to tell her. Was it an engagement ring?"

"Oh, yeah. And I'm pretty sure she'll say yes. But he drove us to the next town over," she said, laughing. Something she never would have even thought about doing. "So I think his secret will be safe."

"Good for them."

"Yeah, Mary's a sweetheart." The owner of Pierce Athletics had donated a bunch of sports equipment to the center, which was how she and Miranda had met. Ethan had donated a bunch of money—and met Mary when he'd stopped by to see some of the improvements his money had paid for. "Isn't she related to you?"

"A cousin through marriage—I've got a lot of cousins."

She snorted. His family did seem to be huge. "You need my help with anything?"

"Nah, I'm good."

"All right, I'm going to leave your beer here and go get the salads ready."

"Sounds good."

After one last, lingering look at his oh-so-bitable ass, she hurried out of the room. He was here as a friend. Nothing more.

She'd do well to remember that. Because she was responsible for someone now. No way would Nolan want to get tangled up with her even if he was attracted to her.

Finally finished, Nolan stripped his water-soaked shirt off and tossed it into the dryer. Then he stepped out of the laundry room. He nearly ran into Miranda, whose eyes widened at the sight of his bare chest. "My shirt got wet, but your washing machine is all fixed. I put it in your dryer."

He'd been planning to ask her if she had a shirt he could wear. Not that he relished the thought of her having some guy's shirt at her house. Now, however, seeing the way she was staring at his bare chest, he changed his mind. Instead, he patted his stomach and watched with interest as her breath hitched slightly. "I hope you don't mind if I go shirtless."

She blinked once. "Nope," she muttered before turning away from him and heading back toward the kitchen. It had been impossible to miss the flush of her cheeks before she'd given him her back.

"Thank you for fixing my washing machine." Her cheeks were full-on crimson now as they stepped into the kitchen. When she sort of looked at him, her cheeks were flushed and he realized her gaze was darting around as if she was trying hard not to look down at his chest.

Well that was interesting.

Very interesting. She'd made it so clear that she wasn't looking for a relationship, but she'd also never looked at him like this. Of course, he'd never been half naked around her either. "The ziti smells good."

Cheeks still red she hurried past him toward the oven, more or less avoiding looking at him altogether.

He'd never seen her flustered like this before. Hell, he'd have taken his shirt off a long time ago to get this reaction from her.

"I still can't believe you didn't know about Mary and Ethan." Miranda opened the oven and pulled out the casserole dish.

He couldn't help but stare at her ass as she did. Tearing his gaze from it, he headed for the refrigerator and pulled out an unopened bottle of white wine. "I never know town gossip. Unless my mom tells me." He opened a drawer and found a wine bottle opener.

Laughing, she said, "Your mom is a trip. Did you know she had a bet on how long it would take Nora and Jackson to get together?"

He popped the cork. "She's bet on *all* of her children." Nolan doubted that his mom had one on him, but he never knew when it came to her.

"I can't tell if you're kidding." She set the potholders down on the counter.

"Nope. Definitely not. She had bets on Fallon and Brad and Maguire and Samantha too. She actually started the betting pools at the salon — and I know she won at least one of them."

Miranda blinked once. "Apparently I need to change salons."

Nolan loved his mother, but really didn't want to talk about her anymore. "So are you dating anyone?" He might as well ask the question. He didn't think Miranda was, considering how long they'd been friends and she'd never once mentioned it.

There was a clattering sound and he realized she dropped the serving spoon. She cleared her throat. "No." There was a long pause then, "Are you?" The question came out hesitant and she hadn't turned around to face him yet.

"Hell no." Because the only woman he wanted to date was right in front of him. For so long he'd thought she was unavailable and maybe she was still in that mindset, but he'd seen the way she'd been looking at him tonight. There was definitely interest there. Interest that he hadn't seen before.

Now that he knew she was attracted to him, he couldn't sit back any longer and do nothing.

She mumbled something incomprehensible as she pulled silverware out from one of the drawers.

He wanted to push, but also knew he needed to play this carefully. If he pushed too hard, too fast, he could lose her altogether. And *that*, he wouldn't risk. Her nephew was gone for a week. Nolan planned to use that time to spend with her. "Why don't you guys have a Christmas tree up?" he asked as she started scooping the ziti into bowls.

"I have no good excuse other than we've been so busy. Mateo with school and me with work. And honestly, living in Holly, being surrounded by Christmas every day of the year, it's a little easy to lose track of time."

"I definitely understand that." He'd grown up in Holly, whereas she hadn't.

She'd visited family here when she'd been a kid and had fallen in love with the town. Then when she'd needed a break from her parents she'd packed up and moved here. He was certainly glad that she had. "You want to come with me to pick out a tree?" She set the salad bowls on the table while he retrieved their dinner bowls.

"Sure. You busy tomorrow?"

"It feels strange to say no, but I'm free. I can't remember the last Saturday I had free."

"After we get a tree, how about I cook for you for a change?" he asked. He loved the thought of her at his house, just the two of them.

She blinked, her dark gaze dipping to his bare chest before she glanced away again and pulled out her seat. "Ah, you cook?"

He sat next to her without crowding her space. "Is that doubt I hear in your voice?"

She snorted. "Nora might have mentioned that all the men in the O'Connor family have issues with cooking."

That was just insulting. Even if it was mostly true. But he had a few easy recipes his mother had given him that were impossible to screw up. "I'll just have to prove her wrong."

"All right then. You can cook for me."

"Good." But he planned to give her a lot more than just dinner.

They spent the rest of dinner talking about their week, and how she still had Christmas shopping to do. He did too, usually putting it off until the last minute. But he'd already picked up a few things for her—and he didn't care if it was more than a 'friend' would give.

As he started clearing the table, much to her annoyance, the dryer dinged. Like a flash, she was out of her seat and gone from the kitchen. Moments later she was back, his dry shirt in her hands.

She practically shoved it at him.

He leaned against the countertop, in no hurry to put it on, and enjoying seeing her so off-balance while she struggled to hide her attraction to him. "Should I be offended that you're so eager to see me dressed?"

"Ha ha. You know exactly how good you look. I'm not feeding your ego." She poked him once in his abs. "I just figured you might be cold."

Oh, yeah, she was lying. He grabbed her finger and tugged her closer.

She practically fell against him, her eyes wide as she looked up at him. Her dark eyes completely captivated him. The little flecks of amber seemed even brighter tonight. She swallowed as she looked up at him.

"You think I look good?" he murmured, his gaze dipping to her mouth. How many times had he fantasized about kissing her? Nibbling on her bottom lip, teasing his tongue against hers? He couldn't even count.

She cleared her throat, the sound seeming over-pronounced in the now quiet kitchen. She didn't respond, just stared up at him, shock in her eyes. Her chest rose and fell more rapidly, her breathing as ragged as his as they stared at each other.

She hadn't pulled away. It was time to make his move.

Her phone rang, making her jump and yank her hand from his hold. He gritted his teeth as she turned from him.

"Ah, it's my mom. I need to take this." There was a hint of relief in her voice. Without turning toward him again, she hurried from the room.

And he knew without a doubt she'd taken the damn call to get away from him. Because normally she avoided calls from her parents.

Nothing might have happened between them. Yet. But it was going to very soon. The dynamic had changed between them and he wasn't going to let it go back to the way it had been. He wasn't sure he could.

Even if she tried to retreat from him, he wasn't letting this thing go. He wouldn't let her run away from what they could be.

CHAPTER THREE

Miranda was reeling from what had almost happened in her kitchen as she ducked into the living room. Had... Nolan been about to kiss her? It had sure felt like it.

And she wouldn't have stopped him. No, she'd have kissed him right back. Something told her it would have been heaven. But what good could come of that? They were friends. Somehow, he'd become her closest friend since she'd settled in Holly. If they went down that path and things didn't work out? Nausea filled her as she thought about him not being part of her life. It was unimaginable. And she had a feeling she was going to be Mateo's guardian for a while—something she was happy about.

Gloria was in rehab but her sister had admitted to Miranda that she didn't think she was ready to take on being a parent again. And Nolan didn't want a ready-made family. He was a single, sexy man. And Miranda had baggage.

"Are you listening to a word I've said?" Her mother's voice filled her ear and she shook herself.

Miranda realized she was barely listening and staring out the frosted-over window of her living room. A faint layer of snow covered the yard and bushes. The house's heating system was going strong though, so she couldn't feel the cold. "Ah, yes."

"That's wonderful! Your father and I will be arriving in the morning."

"Wait...what?"

"I swear you have selective listening. I just told you that we'll be in town for a week. We miss you and Mateo and I want to meet that fiancé of yours."

Oh, no. *No, no, no.* She inwardly winced, scrambling for something to convince them not to visit. "Mateo is on his ski trip." Which she'd told her mother about. More than once. But talk about selective listening. Miranda loved her mom. She really did. But there was a reason she lived in another state. Just as there was a reason Gloria had granted Miranda custody of Mateo while she cleaned her life up, rather than grant it to their mother.

"I wish you would have told me!" her mother cried.

"I did tell you." Miranda's voice was dry.

Ignoring Miranda, her mother continued. "That's just as well. If we can make it work with our schedule perhaps we'll extend our stay by another week."

"Another week? How long are you staying?"

"Oh, who knows. We'll just see what happens."

Miranda tried to keep the annoyance out of her voice. Her mother always meant well but she could be a hurricane. Deep down, however, she knew her mother would only stay one week. "I'll make sure the guestroom is ready. But fair warning, I still have work so I won't be able to show you around town until the evenings."

"Oh, that's no problem. I'm sure we can find ways to entertain ourselves. We're really looking forward to meeting your fiancé. When can we expect to see him?"

If it had been possible to go back in time, Miranda would have done just that. Months ago, her mom had been on her case, like always, about being single and how she was wasting her life alone. About how she couldn't use Mateo as an excuse not to date. Miranda loved her life and she loved Mateo. But to her mother, being single was a sin. The worst one there was. Well, look how well being in relationship after relationship had turned out for her sister.

Instantly she felt bad about the snarky thought. But it was true. After Gloria's husband had been killed, she'd gone from man to man—and she'd also never been happy. Her taste in men was atrocious, that being an understatement. But she was trying to clean her life up, and Miranda could respect that.

"He's really busy this time of year, but I'll see what we can work out," she said to her mom. Inwardly she berated herself. She never should have made up a fiancé.

"Well I can't imagine him being too busy to meet his in-laws to be."

Miranda rubbed a hand over her face, closing her eyes. "No of course he won't be too busy to meet you. It just might not be tomorrow."

"That's all right. We're already on the road."

Of course they were. Because her mom made plans without asking other people what theirs were. She made a decision then followed through, anyone else's opinion be damned.

Her mother continued. "We'll be stopping in North Florida soon. I'll text you when we're at the hotel. And I'll let you know in the morning once we've left."

"Sounds good. See you soon."

Once they disconnected, Miranda let out a long sigh. "Great, now I just have to find a fiancé for Christmas."

"Fiancé?" Nolan's deep voice sent a thrill through her even as she cringed.

Oh, crap. He'd heard that? She cleared her throat. "Ah, what?"

He stepped into the living room, his T-shirt unfortunately covering his oh-so-ripped eight pack. Who the hell had an eight pack? "Did you say you have to find a fiancé for Christmas?"

Over the course of the last ten months she'd opened up to him about her family. They weren't horrible, they were simply a lot to take in. And her mother could be manipulative and emotionally draining when she wanted to be. It was a never-ending source of frustration when Miranda had been growing up. Distance had made a big difference in how she handled her mother. And it wasn't as if she could ask her parents to stay at a hotel when they were here. Well, she could but she wasn't going to. Not when she had the space. And even if her mom made her crazy she still didn't want to hurt her mom's feelings.

"I think you misheard me." Even as she said the lie, her cheeks turned red. Dammit, she hated that her emotions were so visible. She was the worst liar.

He lifted an eyebrow as he crossed his arms over his chest. "Seriously? I misheard that?"

Sighing, she tossed her cell phone onto the loveseat and collapsed next to it. "So... I might have told my parents a teeny tiny lie to get them off my back."

He sat across from her on the leather couch. And he definitely looked at home in her living room. Something she wasn't going to think about right now. "You made up a fiancé?"

"Sadly, yes. And yes, I know how pathetic that is. And my mom just called to let me know that she and my dad are on their way here. They'll be here sometime tomorrow afternoon."

He took a moment to digest that information. "Do they know Mateo is away this week?"

"Yes. I've only told her half a dozen times what his schedule looks like but she doesn't listen. Which is neither here nor there. I have an idea. And if you say no I will totally understand." God, this was so embarrassing asking him to do this. "When they get here, I can introduce them to you and tell them that things didn't work out. That we're just friends now. That way no one else has to know about it."

He hesitated for only a moment. "This is kind of insane. But no more insane than my family. I'll do it."

She blinked at him. "Seriously?"

"Of course. What are friends for?"

Friends. *Exactly.* She once again needed to remind herself of that. Whatever that weirdness in the kitchen had been between them, it was over. They were just friends. So why did she feel so crappy about that?

And tomorrow or the day after she would simply break the news to her parents that she was no longer engaged. Sure, her mom would have a whole lot to say about that, but she would just deal with it. Likely Miranda would be too busy with work the next week to worry about it anyway.

"Even if we're going to break things off, we need to come up with a cover story. Like how I proposed and how long we were together. What have you told them about me?" His voice and expression were equally amused.

Gah. At least someone thought this was funny. Okay this was going to be incredibly embarrassing to admit. "Well, I based my fake fiancé on you, but don't read into it! I…might have told her that his name is… Nolan."

A flash of heat flickered in his blue gaze but then was gone a moment later. Maybe she'd imagined it. "Well that saves me from having to use a different name," he said with a laugh. His lips were curved up and his pale eyes practically sparkled.

She narrowed her eyes at him. "I'm glad you think this is so funny."

"It *is* funny. It sounds like something my own sister would have done once upon a time."

"Okay, so… How did you propose? I never got that far in my lies." When her mom asked for specifics she'd dodged answering.

He answered so quickly it took her by surprise. "On a ski lift. I had 'will you marry me' spelled out in the snow and coordinated with the guys running the lift to stop it when we reached the question."

"That's such a cute idea!" And she realized she needed to tone it down. It wasn't as if it had really happened—or would ever happen. "How'd you think of that so quickly?"

He paused. "A friend of mine is planning to do it with his girl."

"Well I'm sure she'll say yes. So…you proposed a couple months ago and that works well with the weather and the slopes. Okay, I think we're good then. In case my mom asks that question, we'll have an answer to it. It probably won't matter since I'll tell her we've broken up, but it's good to have our bases covered." She held back a sigh as she thought about how much this was going to disappoint her mother. Sometimes she felt like her entire life was a giant disappointment to the woman.

He simply nodded and stood, a thoughtful expression on his face. "I'll pick you all up tomorrow night. We can go to Nora's for drinks and do it there."

She stood with him, relieved. "Sounds good. And thank you for this. Seriously. I know it's a giant pain." And embarrassing, but she was keeping all that locked down until he was gone. Then she'd wallow in how pathetic she was.

"It's no big deal."

Well it was to her. She owed him for this, big time.

CHAPTER FOUR

Nolan knocked on Miranda's front door the next evening and tried to temper the adrenaline rushing through him. He kept going back and forth on whether what he was about to do was the right decision.

The one thing he knew, however, was that he wasn't going to say he and Miranda had broken up. Because in no reality would that ever happen. Once they were committed, that was it. She'd thank him for it later. And this way she wouldn't have to deal with her parents all by herself. She'd told him enough about her relationship with her mother that he simply couldn't say they'd ended things and leave her to deal with the aftermath. Because if the stories she'd told him were only half true, he knew she would get grief for the rest of her mom's visit.

And it was no hardship to act the part of Miranda's fiancé. Because he hoped to make that a reality soon enough. It was just a matter of showing her they belonged together.

When the door opened Miranda give him a big smile even if her expression was a bit frantic. Definitely uncommon for her. "Thank you for doing this," she whispered as she dragged him inside. Wearing another one of those sweater dresses that hugged her curves and her sexy knee-high boots, she looked good enough to eat. As always. Just looking at her now made him ache.

Two seconds later her parents stepped into the foyer from the living room. Her mother was petite, just like Miranda. Her hair was darker, and she was older, but still adorable.

Her father was maybe five-feet-eight and gave Nolan a warm

smile as he held out a hand. "You must be Nolan. We've heard so much about you. I'm Oliver."

"Yes, it's so nice to finally meet you. And just in time for Christmas. Though I can't believe Miranda doesn't have a tree up yet," her mother tossed in the last comment and it felt like a subtle dig. "I'm Camila." Miranda's mother held out her hand as well.

Nolan shook hands then threw an arm around Miranda's shoulders, tugging her into his side. He liked the feel of her up against him, soft and warm. "The lack of a tree is my fault. I've been so busy with work that we haven't had a chance to go shopping. But we planned to go today and get everything set up before Mateo gets back."

Miranda looked up at him, her expression slightly confused. Then she looked back at her parents, her expression morphing to an apologetic one. "Listen, you guys —"

Nolan interrupted her before she could tell her parents they weren't together anymore. "I know you've been traveling all day but if you like, I'll take everyone out to dinner. And then we'd love for you to help us pick out a tree."

"Well isn't that a wonderful idea." Miranda's mother smiled broadly up at him. Then she looked at her daughter. "Your father and I will settle in later. If you guys are ready to go now, that works for us."

Her father nodded in agreement.

Miranda tightened her grip around his waist and smiled up at him. It was the fakest smile he'd ever seen. And her eyes sparked with annoyance. "Before we head out, help me in the kitchen with something?"

When they stepped into the kitchen she faced him and set her hands on her hips. With her in that damn dress, all he could think about was slowly peeling it over her head to see exactly what was underneath. He wondered what kind of bra she wore. Would it be sexy lace or would she be more practical? It didn't really matter, anything would be sexy on her.

"What was that all about?" she whispered. "I thought we were going to do this quickly. Not drag things out."

"Change of plans." He reached into his pocket and pulled out a diamond ring.

She stared at him, her mouth slightly open, as he slid it on her left-hand, ring finger.

Before she could respond her mom bustled into the room and smiled as she saw what he was doing. "I wondered why my daughter didn't have a ring. And isn't that just beautiful!"

Nolan didn't miss a beat. "I just picked it up from being sized. It was too big and I didn't want it falling off my angel."

For a moment, Miranda looked up at him as if he'd grown another head, but then she smiled. It was that same almost panicked smile she'd had when she'd opened the door, but her mother didn't seem to notice it.

He put his arm around Miranda's shoulders again. And he loved the way she fit against him. As if she had been made for him. As far as he was concerned, she had been. And vice versa. It was just a matter of showing her that they were meant to be together. It was a risk, doing this. He had a feeling that once they were alone she was going to ream him out. He would deserve it too. But he had no regrets. He'd spent too damn long keeping his feelings to himself. He'd gained a best friend, but he knew they could be more.

If he lost her because of this, it would carve him up. But he couldn't play this coward routine anymore. It wasn't his style. Never had been. And lately he felt as if he was in this waiting pattern. Just waiting for her to find someone else. Or waiting for her to realize he was right in front of her.

It was eating away at him. Because eventually she was going to start dating someone. She was only twenty-five and one of the most beautiful women in Holly. Soon enough, some jackass was going to come sniffing around. And he didn't want to have any regrets where she was concerned, didn't want to look back and think 'what if'. All of his siblings had settled down in the last year and it was a huge reminder that it didn't matter how long he and Miranda had known each other. He knew how she made him feel, how much she meant to him. And he couldn't think of anything better than spending a lifetime with his best friend.

Miranda's mother took her hand and gushed over the ring. "This really is beautiful. You have a good eye," she said to Nolan without looking at him. Then she cupped Miranda's cheeks. "I'm so happy you found someone."

At her mother's words Miranda's smile went from fake to real in an instant. "Thanks, Mom."

"We can drive if you'd like," Miranda's father said as he stepped into the room shrugging into a jacket.

"I've got an extended cab truck. And it's got plenty of room. Since there's snow on the road and you guys are from Florida I don't mind driving," Nolan said.

Everyone murmured their agreement and even though he knew Miranda was annoyed with him, he felt ten feet tall as they headed out of the house. Their engagement might not be real.

Yet.

But the ring was. And by Christmas, he planned to have her locked down. If it had been any other situation he might think it was too soon. But no. They were best friends. They'd been building up to this since the moment they met. Whether she wanted to admit it or not.

Miranda couldn't figure out what Nolan was thinking. Okay, she could admit that she *liked* being able to call him her fiancé. And she loved the way he'd been holding her close ever since they'd left her house. And yes, Christmas tree shopping with him was a lot of fun. Everything they'd always done together was fun. So that wasn't a surprise.

And she could definitely admit that instead of having her mother harass her about letting 'a catch' like Nolan go, all her mom could do was sing Nolan's praises. Plus, icing on the cake, her mom was being incredibly nice to her. Not that her mother was ever directly mean, just…passive-aggressive. And Miranda had gotten used to the attitude. So having her like this now was jarring. Her father, whom she adored, was never any help. He just kept quiet because he liked 'to keep the peace'.

"What about this one?" she asked, pointing at a big Douglas fir. All the trees at the lot were covered by a huge tent so they didn't have to trek through mushed up snow at least. Warmers had been placed around as well and she was glad because her parents weren't used to this cold.

"It's perfect. Like you," Nolan said—loudly enough for anyone near them to hear.

Miranda was torn between wanting to kiss him and punch him. "Laying it on a little thick?" She kept her voice low enough that only he could hear. Her mom and dad were busy chatting about presents so she knew they couldn't overhear them.

In response, Nolan leaned down and brushed his lips over hers as if it was the most natural thing in the world. She felt the caress all the way to her core and a little rush of heat flooded between her legs. Had she fantasized about Nolan? Oh, yeah. But she'd never thought they would actually kiss. Feeling his lips against hers had all her brain cells short circuiting. He was really getting into his role and she was torn between loving it and hating it. Because once this was over, it would hurt when it ended.

He pulled back but only a fraction. "Definitely not," he murmured against her lips. "Because you are perfect."

Okay, what the hell kind of reality had she stepped into? Because this was *not* her life. And she knew he was just acting. She simply couldn't figure out what his endgame was. It wasn't to be cruel, that much she knew without a doubt. They were friends. Maybe he'd just wanted to spare her dealing with her parents in the aftermath of 'their breakup'. And he was going to let her end things so she'd save face in front of them? It was the only logical thing she could think of.

Who knew, and he certainly hadn't allowed them to have a moment of privacy so she could grill him. At least Mateo wasn't in town, so she wouldn't have to lie to him. Not that she would anyway.

She would tell him the truth about all of this. That was one thing she'd promised him when he came to live with her. No lies. Ever. He'd lived with that, and a whole lot worse, when he'd been with his mom.

Miranda didn't think she would have to even go there, however. Because her parents should be gone before he got back. She still couldn't believe her mom had planned a trip without calling her and confirming dates first. Okay, scratch that, she *could* believe it. And deep down she knew that her mom was still hurt and probably a little angry that Gloria had chosen Miranda to be Mateo's guardian. But that wasn't something she wanted to think about right now.

No, she was trying to wrap her head around what was happening with Nolan—and trying to steel herself for when this thing officially 'ended' between them. Even this playacting felt good. Too good.

Nolan gave her another kiss, this time on the top of her head, before heading off to talk to the salesman. As soon as he was gone her mom moved in right next to her, her dark eyes bright with joy.

"I'm so impressed with your fiancé. And I can't wait to start planning the wedding. Have you guys set a date yet? Do you know what kind of venue you want? Will you have attendants?" Her mom was practically jumping up and down.

Oh crap. She hadn't thought of any of that because this was a fake freaking engagement. But she couldn't act as if those things didn't matter because her mom would definitely get suspicious. "Ah, we haven't gotten that far. This is all very new. We'll talk about a date after the holidays."

"Well you better lock that man down and set a date soon. I've seen the way some of the women here have been looking at him. Not that I can blame them. He's *very* attractive." Her mom actually winked at her.

Miranda's eyes widened. She'd never heard her mom talk about any man like that.

Her mom shrugged. "What? I'm not blind."

Okay then. Miranda was definitely in an alternate reality. One she kind of wished was actually her reality.

CHAPTER FIVE

"I really wish you would ask Mateo if he'd come home early." Her mother really wasn't letting this go.

Miranda simply shook her head and glanced around Nora's Books and Brew. After taking the tree back to her house, everyone had decided to get hot chocolate and desserts. And since it was a Saturday night, of course it was busy. Every shop on the cobblestones of Main Street was busy during the entire month of December. It was like walking around inside a holiday snow globe. All the trees downtown were decorated with sparkly twinkle lights. Garlands were wrapped around every Victorian-style street lamp, every shop window had a Christmas tree, snowman, a display of gorgeous ornaments or snow globes. Whatever the display was, it was made crystal clear to anyone who may have doubts, that Holly didn't mess around when it came to Christmas.

"He's been looking forward to this trip for months. All his friends are with him, including his best friend. I'm not taking this away from him." Even though she hated arguing like this in front of Nolan, she couldn't back down about something like this.

"I just miss my grandson."

Miranda softened only a fraction. "He misses you too. And he loves Skyping with you." For all her mother's faults, she was an excellent grandmother. Both of her parents called Mateo at least once a week, usually more. And they always checked in to see if she needed financial help from them. Miranda never took them up on their offer because she never wanted to become indebted to them. That kind of favor would come with a heavy price tag. Since the day had gone so well and her parents would be in town for the next week, she really didn't want to get off on the wrong foot. But she also couldn't pretend as if they hadn't known about Mateo's trip. It was one of the reasons she was standing strong in her decision.

"Look, here come our drinks." Under the table Nolan took her right hand in his.

Earlier she'd been able to keep her engagement ring hidden with her gloves. And when they'd come into the shop and she'd taken them off, she'd kept her hands under the table. A few people she knew had stopped by to say hello and thankfully her parents hadn't brought up her engagement to anyone. She could do this. They could totally get through tonight without anyone finding out about their fake engagement.

Nora smiled brightly as she reached their high-top table, big tray balanced in one hand. Nolan immediately stood so she could set it on the table. He helped her pass the drinks out and when he handed Miranda hers she automatically took it with both hands. The instant she did, she realized her mistake. As she set her steaming mug of hot chocolate down she immediately went to put her left hand under the table again.

But it was too late.

"Oh, my God!" Nora grabbed her hand and stared at the ring, practically squealing in delight. "This is gorgeous! I was wondering when you two would finally stop dancing around each other. This is huge! How have I not heard about this yet?"

Miranda just stared, trying to find her voice as Eleanor and Macy, the Baker twins, women in their sixties who also happened to be two of the biggest gossips in town, turned from their own table a few feet away to stare at her.

"We've kept it on the down low, what with all of your wedding plans," Nolan said. "We didn't want to take away from your and Jackson's big day."

Nora gave Miranda the biggest grin before looking at Nolan. "You guys are just the sweetest. And we wouldn't have cared at all. This definitely calls for a celebration. And all the drinks and desserts are on me tonight."

"We're going to be official sisters-in-law," Nora said, squeezing Miranda's hand in her own.

"Yes, we are." It sounded more like a question and Miranda ordered herself to get it together. Maybe this wasn't as big of a disaster as she thought it was. They could still fix this. She could get Nora alone and explain to her that they needed to keep this a secret for another week. Or just flat out tell her the truth.

All thoughts of keeping it a secret dissipated when Alison O'Connor walked into the shop. Of course, Nolan's mother would walk in right now. Because, why wouldn't she? This day just kept getting better.

Alison immediately headed for their table, smiling warmly at her son. In the last ten months, Miranda had gotten to know the woman and genuinely liked her. She volunteered everywhere and while she could be a little overbearing it was clear that it was always done with love. Plus, she was super organized, and the hugely nerdy part of Miranda loved that about her.

"Nolan," Miranda murmured, not really sure what the heck she was going to say. She wanted to grab his hand and bolt out the front door. Since that wasn't happening, she simply stood and smiled as Alison approached.

He simply slid an arm around Miranda's waist and pulled her close. "Mom, great to see you."

His mother gave them a slightly speculative look, but smiled warmly.

"Alison," Miranda said, trying to smile and hoping it didn't come off as panicked.

She quickly introduced her own parents, who were thrilled to meet Alison. So far no one had said anything about the engagement. And strangely enough, other than that first interested look, Alison didn't seem to think that it was strange that Nolan had his arm around Miranda. Had he told his mom about this? He must have.

"I can't believe I finally know something before you." Nora picked up the tray and tucked it under her arm as she grinned at Nolan's mom.

Alison lifted an eyebrow. Though she was petite with auburn hair, she had the same blue eyes as Nolan. "What do you know before me?"

Nora grabbed Miranda's hand and lifted it up triumphantly.

To Miranda's surprise, Alison just smiled and stepped around the table to kiss both her and Nolan on the cheek. And then she whispered, "Congratulations," in Miranda's ear. "It's about damn time my son put that ring on your finger."

Wait…what?

"I've been waiting for one of my sons to use that ring," she said, turning to Miranda's mom. "It's been in our family for years."

Wait…double what?

"How long are you guys in town for?" Alison asked Miranda's parents.

As her parents and Nolan's mom started talking, Nora hurried away to another table. They weren't exactly alone, but this was the opening Miranda had been waiting for.

"We're going to go to the bookstore side to check on something for Mateo," she said quickly to the others. "We'll be back in a minute."

Neither her parents nor Nolan's mom minded. Not that she really cared. Miranda grabbed Nolan's hand and practically dragged him through the coffee shop to the attached bookstore. It was much quieter in this section, but there were still four people shopping.

"This way," Nolan said, leading her to a door that said 'employees only' on it. Oh, right, he was Nora's brother-in-law.

Miranda felt weird as they stepped into what turned out to be a stock room, but not weird enough to stop.

"This is a disaster," she said as he shut the door behind them.

"Why?"

She couldn't find her voice for a moment but then thumped him on the chest. He looked completely unconcerned about this whole thing. "Everyone will think we're engaged by tomorrow morning. Or more likely in an hour considering how fast gossip travels in this town."

"So?" He lifted a shoulder, looking way too sexy for his own good. "Your parents are in town for the next week and it isn't as if you were going to be able to keep it a secret forever."

"We could have kept it a secret if you'd kept your big mouth shut. I still can't believe you didn't stick to the original plan." She wanted to do something childish, like stomp her foot, but resisted the urge. "You should have let me tell my parents that we just broke up." *Then none of this would have happened.*

"My plan is better." He reached for her, setting his big hands on her hips and pulling her close.

She didn't even think about resisting. "How is this better?"

In response, he leaned down and kissed her. Just…pressed his lips right to hers as if it was the most natural thing in the world.

She thought about pulling back, but her brain decided to stop functioning as Nolan slid his tongue past her lips. She moaned into his mouth. This was stupid, she tried to remind herself. It meant nothing. But…no one was around to see them so this wasn't acting.

And the very real erection she felt against her lower abdomen wasn't fake either. Leaning into him, she slid her hands up his chest and linked her fingers together behind his neck. Even as she tried to come up with reasons why this was going to hurt their friendship, he tightened his grip around her. How many times had she fantasized about this? She didn't think she could count that high. Now it was actually happening.

He was simply holding her, but being in his arms like this had butterflies taking flight inside her. She arched into him, wanting to wrap around him right here in the storeroom. It was as if she wasn't in control of her own body. More than anything she wanted skin to skin contact.

At the sound of a doorknob turning, Miranda jumped back from him. Nolan didn't seem concerned as he stepped forward with the movement of the door. When Nora stepped inside she just snorted at the two of them.

"No having sex back here," she said, matter-of-fact.

Miranda wasn't sure how to respond but Nolan just laughed. "Sorry, we just wanted a couple minutes alone."

"Sorry for outing you guys." Nora pulled down a bag of coffee from one of the shelves without looking at them. "I just saw that ring and freaked."

"It's no problem, we'd planned to tell everyone at Mom and Dad's Monday night dinner," Nolan said easily.

"Oh, that's been moved to tomorrow and your parents have been invited — and accepted." Nora smiled once at them as she reached the door. "And get out of here in the next couple minutes. No hanky panky. If I walk in on another family member going at it back here, I'm going to need therapy."

While Miranda was curious about *that*, she didn't bother asking Nolan about it as the door shut behind Nora.

"What the heck are we doing? You still haven't answered my question. How is this better than my plan?" She held up a hand when he stepped toward her, a hungry gleam in his blue eyes. Oh, no. "No kissing."

"I like kissing you."

Yeah well, she liked kissing him too. But that wasn't the point, and she couldn't think when he put his mouth on her. "Well?"

"Well what?"

"I'm waiting on an answer." She set her hands on her hips as she looked up at him.

Gah, did he look sexy. His dark hair was slightly tousled and he'd let a bit more stubble grow, making him look more hot than scruffy. And those pale eyes had the ability to render her speechless.

He lifted a shoulder, only highlighting how broad they were. Now that she'd seen him without his shirt on, she wondered what he'd feel like on top of her. Okay, she'd wondered that before. But she still wondered what it would be like to run her fingertips over his broad, bare shoulders, his chest and abdomen while he thrust inside her. Since when had she turned into a maniac obsessed with thoughts of sex? Well, sex with Nolan. Because no one else would do.

"There's no point in answering the obvious."

Obvious? What. The. Hell. "Nolan, are you determined to drive me crazy right now?"

His gaze dipped to her mouth. "I could think of a few ways to drive you *very* crazy."

She held up a hand before he'd even taken one step toward her. He had a predator-like gleam in his gaze and she liked it a bit too much. If she didn't stop him soon, they actually might do something in the storeroom that would cause Nora to go to therapy. "There will be no more kissing between us when we're in private. That's one of our new rules. While we're faking this thing for everyone else, we need to keep everything normal in private."

"I'm not following that rule." His jaw tightened ever so slightly.

"What? Why not?"

"Because it's stupid. And I like kissing you." He opened the door and stepped out into the shop. He looked back at her, a completely wicked grin on his face as he held out his hand for her.

Staring at him as if she was seeing him for the first time, she placed her hand in his as she replayed his last words over in her head. *I like kissing you*. Yeah, she liked kissing him too.

Probably too much. They were definitely playing with fire right now. And she was trying to figure out why that mattered when all she wanted was a replay — and more — of that kiss.

CHAPTER SIX

Nolan tried not to smile too big at Miranda's confused expression. He'd definitely thrown her off balance and he was okay with that. It was beyond time for them to take this next step.

As they made their way back through the coffee shop, he saw that just her parents were at the table now. His mom must have left, which was just as well. She hadn't questioned him when he asked for the family ring. He'd been surprised by her silence about it considering she always had something to say about anything. But she'd just given him a knowing look and handed it over.

His phone buzzed in his pocket and though he hated answering when he was out with Miranda and her family, with his job he was always in contact with his crew. In case something went wrong on one of their jobs. There shouldn't be an issue right now but just in case, he glanced at the caller ID. When he saw the name, it wasn't work, but he answered anyway. "Janet?" Janet Ross was a single mother of one of the kids he coached down at the community center. She almost never called him. He motioned to the others that he was going to step outside and take the call.

A blast of cold air hit him as Janet said, "Nolan, I'm sorry to call you on a Saturday night. It's just that I don't know where Trevor is. He didn't come home like he was supposed to this afternoon."

He stepped out of the flow of foot traffic and found a nearby bench. "Do you know who he was hanging out with?"

"Yes. He called me as he was leaving one of his friend's houses. We got into a big fight about college. He hung up on me, something he's never done before. And then he just didn't come home. It's been four hours. I'm starting to get worried. I thought maybe he called you or you might have an idea where he is."

"I might have an idea. Give me twenty minutes and I'll let you know. If I don't find him I think you should call the sheriff."

She let out a watery-sounding laugh. "I've contemplated that a few times in the last couple hours. I'll have my phone glued to me. Please call me if you find him."

Pocketing his phone, he headed back inside. As he pulled his jacket off the back of the chair, he explained what was going on to the others.

"Are you going to the center?" Miranda asked. She knew Trevor as well.

He nodded. "Yes. He has a key because I let him close the gym after some practices if he stays late. It's just a hunch and he might not even be there."

"Do you want me to come with you?"

Before she could answer her mother interjected. "Of course, go with Nolan. Your father and I will be fine. We want to walk around downtown anyway. If you'll be a while we'll just take a taxi back to your place. Otherwise you can pick us up when you're done."

Miranda pulled on her own jacket and gave her parents quick hugs before sliding her hand into his and heading out. Outside she kept her gloved hand in his. He definitely wasn't going to be the one to pull away. And Nolan was pleased that she wasn't either.

It didn't take long to reach his truck. After opening the door for her, he strapped her in, and, taking her off guard, brushed his lips over hers. Gasping slightly, she leaned into it. More than anything he wanted to deepen the kiss, but they didn't have time. He didn't think Trevor was in any real trouble, but he wanted to make sure.

The drive to the community center was familiar and didn't take long. Miranda was mostly silent, only fiddling with the radio stations. She got like that when she was contemplating something and he knew without a doubt that she was thinking about the two of them. And probably wondering if he'd lost his mind. That was okay. He hadn't, and for the first time in ten months a huge weight had been lifted. Because he wasn't living a lie anymore. Miranda meant everything to him and he was tired of hiding it.

"It's hard to imagine Trevor intentionally worrying his mom," Miranda said as he put the truck in park. Bundled up in her ankle length jacket, cap, and green and white scarf—with little Santas on the end—she looked adorable. "He's such a good kid."

"For the most part I agree. But teenagers can be stupid sometimes." He'd certainly had his moments at Trevor's age.

"True."

They got out together and sure enough Trevor's older model truck was in the parking lot near the gym's entrance. Pulling out his keys, Nolan opened one of the side doors. The scent of the gym, basketballs, and other athletic gear was familiar. "I thought he might be in here. But he might be on the ice."

Less than five minutes later they found Trevor skating on the rink, headphones on. When he spotted them, he slid his headphones off and skated toward the boards, skidding to a halt in front of them.

"Mr. O'Connor. Miss Flores. What are you guys doing here?"

"No, what are you doing here this late? I gave you a key so you could lock up when practices went late. Not when you wanted to hide out from your mom."

The kid was seventeen but over six feet tall. He flushed slightly. "She called you?"

"That's not cool to worry your mom like that."

"I didn't mean to worry her. I was just blowing off steam and didn't want to go home. I was going to leave in a little bit, but I guess I lost track of time."

"Well call her right now. Then you and I are talking." There was no room for argument in Nolan's voice.

"Yes, sir."

As he skated off, Miranda let out a low whistle.

"What?"

"Nothing. I've just never heard you sound so authoritative."

"You like it?"

Her cheeks flushed slightly. "I just meant that I've never seen you in 'coach' mode before off the ice."

He leaned a little closer and dropped his voice. "I *know* what you meant. I *asked* if you liked it. Would you like me telling you what to do in the bedroom?" The thought of taking complete control turned him on. Anything to do with her turned him on, however.

She stared up at him, her cheeks going full crimson. Instead of answering she turned away from him and stared out over the ice.

He leaned down so that he was right next to her ear. "I think you like the thought of that a lot."

She tightened her jaw.

"Would you like it if I made you come with just my mouth?"

Gasping, she turned to look at him. Since he was crowding her personal space, only inches separated them. "What has gotten into you?"

"Not a damn thing," he murmured, his gaze falling to her very kissable mouth. He wanted to kiss her, but he didn't want to be the one to initiate this time. No, he wanted her to come to him. Wanted her to crave him so badly she couldn't stay away any longer.

"And I swear to God if you say *you* want to 'get into me' or something to that effect, I'll punch you," she whispered.

An unexpected laugh bubbled up because okay, he'd been thinking something along those lines.

"I can't believe you think any of this is funny."

"I don't." He didn't know another way to tell her that this wasn't a joke to him at all.

At the sound of skates cutting over ice, they both turned. Trevor was skating back across the ice, looking a little embarrassed. "I called my mom. She's pretty pissed but...happier that I'm okay more than anything."

Nolan nodded. "Miranda and I are going to follow you home."

"Coach, you don't have to do that."

"I know, but we're going to. You disappointed me tonight. Your mom works her ass off for you. And she's doing it by herself. You're lucky to have such a good parent."

Trevor rubbed his hand over the back of his neck, looking ashamed. "I know." He reached into his pocket and gave Nolan the key back. "I'm sorry I violated your trust. I know I shouldn't have been here tonight."

Nolan took the key and put it in his pocket. "Come on. Let's get you home."

Once he and Miranda were in the truck alone and following behind Trevor, she surprised him. "Would you like *me* telling *you* what to do in the bedroom?"

"Maybe." Because he did like to be in control. It was part of his makeup. But letting her take over once in a while...yeah, he was on board with that.

"Hmm."

"What does that mean?"

"Just thinking."

Ah, hell. If she'd wanted to mess with his head, that response was guaranteed to do it. And maybe that was the whole point. He knew that he'd thrown her off her game. Maybe she was doing the same thing to him. Turnabout was fair play. And he liked it.

"My parents said they've already grabbed a taxi," Miranda said as Nolan headed down Main Street. Instead of simply dropping Trevor off, they'd stayed and talked to his mother for a while. Miranda really liked Janet Ross and while their situations were different, she could relate to raising a kid alone. She might have only had Mateo for less than a year but it didn't matter. When you were parenting alone it could feel very isolating. Luckily, she'd made friends with a lot of other moms at his school.

"No Uber?"

"No, my mom won't use them."

"Why not?"

"Who knows? She's weird about some stuff." *A lot of stuff.* "She likes what she likes and that's it." There was often no room for compromise with her mom.

He just laughed softly. "They seem to be really happy for you. For us."

"Yes. She likely can't believe I 'landed someone like you'." Miranda nearly snorted, but reined it in.

"I don't understand that."

"My mom is complicated."

Nolan just lifted a shoulder. Right now felt like they were back to normal. Like she wasn't dealing with the man who'd not an hour ago asked if she would like it if he made her come with his mouth. Holy hell, who just blurted that out? No part of their relationship had been sexual before. No innuendos, nothing. Now…it was like something inside him had been unleashed and he had no filter.

Worse, she really liked it. Because yes, she would like it if he made her come with his mouth…or other body parts. Her nipples hardened as she thought about it, a flush of heat sliding through her body and coiling tight right at her core. Something she didn't want to be thinking about right now.

"Why do you think they decided to come up when Mateo wasn't here?" he asked as they pulled up to a stop sign. It didn't seem as if he was heading back to her house by the direction he was going and she was okay with that.

"I… I'm not sure. It could be a power play type of thing. Either she wanted me to pull him out of his trip and somehow 'win' or she wanted to come up here and then when I didn't pull him out, she'll later make a big deal of it to him about how sad she was to miss him. Make me out to be the bad guy."

"Jeez."

"I know. I wonder if it's even a conscious thing she does." Whether it was or not, it was the reason Miranda had moved. Putting physical distance between her and her parents had been the best thing she'd ever done for her mental health. And it was good for Mateo. They were good grandparents but she wasn't going to let that manipulative crap rub off on him.

"No wonder your sister gave you guardianship."

"Yeah."

"Have you heard from her lately?"

"About a week ago." And she'd sounded off. Something Miranda didn't want to dwell on. At first the rehab had seemed to be the best thing in the world for her.

"And?"

She laughed lightly as he made a left turn in the direction of downtown. "And, I don't know. I might be reading into it but she kept talking about this other patient. A male patient. They're apparently 'really great friends'. But I know my sister. And I don't want to be negative but if she's hooking up with a recovering addict…it's not going to end well. She's gotten sober too many times only to go back to using heroin. And *always* with a partner." Her sister's taste in men and self-control were terrible. "And she didn't even want to talk to Mateo. Which was really weird."

"You're a good sister."

"I try. Keeping Mateo isn't a hardship. I thought it would be, but I love that kid so much. If Gloria wanted, I'd keep him until he's old enough to make his own decisions." At first, when she'd agreed to take Mateo, Miranda had been okay with it being temporary, thinking her sister would finally get her shit together and be the mom Gloria always should have been. Now she knew better. It was going to hurt like hell when he left. Miranda just hoped she could convince her sister to move to Holly. Mateo loved it here and was thriving with the stability.

"He's a good kid." There was a lot of warmth in Nolan's voice and she knew he was being sincere. "And he's great at hockey."

She laughed. "Yeah, I think that surprised even him." Mateo had never lived anywhere cold before and had no experience with sports or extracurricular activities—because his mom had never kept him in one school long enough to develop any friends or sign him up for any type of sports. It was a miracle that Mateo was at the right educational level for his age. And that he wasn't full of anger. "Where are we going anyway?"

"Downtown. Figured you'd want to walk around a little before I take you home."

"Sounds good to me. I still need to do some Christmas shopping."

"Me too." Smiling, he reached out and took her hand.

She linked her fingers through his, very conscious of the ring on her finger and that something had shifted between them. To what level she wasn't sure. She just knew that they were more than friends at this point. Any more than that, she wasn't going to dwell on.

Not tonight. And maybe not at all this week. She just wanted to get through her parents' visit. Then she'd figure out what the heck was going on with her and Nolan. Maybe if they had sex, sort of get it out of their system, then they could go back to being friends?

Oh, come on, who was she kidding? If they had sex it would complicate everything. Even if she really, really wondered what he'd be like, she locked that thought up tight. There would be no sex. No kissing. Nothing.

CHAPTER SEVEN

"Stop picking at your dress." At the sound of her mom's voice, Miranda looked up.

She'd ducked into her kitchen to grab a bottle of wine to take to Nolan's parents' house tonight. And okay, maybe she was fussing over her choice of clothing. Which was beyond stupid. But since everyone thought they were engaged, she wanted to look good. All right, that was a lie, she just wanted to look good for Nolan. She'd never put any sort of obsessive thought into her clothing choice as far as he was concerned before. And it felt weird to be worried so much.

Obviously, he wanted her. Unless he was the world's best actor. But there was simply too much weirdness with this whole situation, especially given their fake engagement. "I'm not," she said, unable to hide the defensiveness in her voice. It was always the same when she was around her mom. Even if her mom wasn't being passive-aggressive. Sometimes it was hard to let go of old wounds. She tried, but being around her mom simply brought up too many emotions sometimes. Rolling her shoulders once, she cleared her throat. "Okay, maybe I was. I'm just nervous about tonight."

"Why? I thought you knew his family."

"I do. This is just the first time I'll be seeing them after our engagement was publicly announced." The lie rolled off her tongue so easily. And she wasn't going to analyze why. It wasn't because she liked the thought of being with Nolan. *It wasn't.*

"You have nothing to be nervous about. You look beautiful. They'll be lucky to have you as part of their family."

She finally understood the phrase 'you could have knocked me over with a feather'. Her mom had just given her a compliment, plain and simple. "Thank you."

Her mom started to say something else, when the doorbell rang. "I'll grab it."

Before Miranda could respond, her mom had left the kitchen in a flurry of motion. The woman rarely sat down or stopped moving.

She looked down at herself critically. She had on a plain black sweater dress, a lot of silver jewelry, and knee-high, black boots. It looked good on her, but more importantly she liked the way it made her feel. Sexy, desirable.

And it was new. She'd bought it just for tonight. It had been nearly ten months since she'd splurged on herself and she figured now was the time to do it. She could admit she wanted a reaction from Nolan.

Picking up the bottle of red wine she'd grabbed from the pantry, she set it on the counter next to her purse so she wouldn't forget before following after her mom. Miranda found her parents and Nolan in the foyer talking.

When he glanced over at her, her breath caught in her throat. The way he looked at her was the way a man looked at a woman he wanted to do bad, bad things to. And she was more than willing to let him. She wanted to do a few bad things herself. Because apparently, she'd lost all vestiges of her sanity.

At that thought, she reined herself in. Now wasn't the time to get all hot and bothered. They were about to head to his parents' house.

He handed her a bouquet of brightly colored flowers and she saw he'd brought some for her mom — who was gushing over them. Leaning down, he brushed his lips over Miranda's and she felt it all the way to her toes. It took all her restraint not to lean into it.

"You look beautiful," he said quietly.

Her words caught in her throat for a moment. "Thank you. And thank you for these. I'll go put them in water before we leave." She grabbed her mom's flowers as well and hurried out of the foyer, needing space from him. Which made no sense. What he'd done was incredibly sweet. But she didn't want to get used to this. Even if he was attracted to her, this was just pretend. Nothing about this was *her* reality.

As she started filling up a vase with water, she heard a slight shuffling sound and turned to see Nolan stepping into the kitchen. "What's wrong?" he asked.

"Nothing. What could be wrong?"

His frown deepened. "Don't lie to me." There was a note of command in his voice.

Now was definitely not the time for this conversation. Besides, what was she going to say? *I feel weird that you gave me flowers, don't do it again?* No, she would sound like a crazy person. So she pasted on a smile and nodded toward the wine on the counter. "I have a bottle of red wine to bring tonight. Should we bring anything else?"

"I know you're changing the subject, and I'll let it slide for now. But we're coming back to this conversation." By the firm set of his jaw, she knew he was being serious.

After sweeping a quick gaze over him, she turned away. He was wearing dark jeans, a black sweater—a black and white scarf she'd given him—and a thick pea coat. Nothing about his clothing should be sexy but it seemed he filled out everything to perfection. Now that she'd had a taste of him and seen him without a shirt, she wanted to see all of him. Every single bare inch. Because *that* was smart.

She felt rather than heard him as he moved in behind her. Practically caging her in against the counter and the flowers, he leaned down and gently bit down on her earlobe.

"You're going to tell me what's bothering you later."

"I'm fine." Her voice was raspy, unsteady. Why did he have to push?

"Don't. Lie." He bit down again.

A shudder rolled through her as she slightly pushed back into him. "You don't get to know everything about me," she whispered.

He just made a *hmm* sound and stepped back enough so that she could turn to face him. As always, she had to look up. They stared at each other for a long moment. His pale blue eyes were filled with hunger. For her.

Something she was still trying to wrap her head around. She wasn't sure how long he'd felt this way toward her, but he'd done a good job of hiding it since they'd been friends.

At a faint sound from the doorway she pushed at his chest. He stepped back easily and they turned to find her mother backing out of the kitchen.

"I didn't mean to interrupt you guys," she said quickly.

"It's okay, we should get going anyway," Nolan said. "My mom is excited to have you guys over."

Miranda was quiet as the two of them continued talking. She was glad that Nolan had no problem making conversation with her parents. Because right now she was completely lost in her own thoughts and she wasn't sure if she was capable of carrying on a decent conversation. Not when she wanted to finish what she and Nolan had started, to maybe see if there could be something more between them.

"I always wondered who would get that ring," Fallon said with warmth in her voice. "It looks gorgeous on you!"

Miranda felt herself flushing as she looked down at the engagement ring. She hadn't realized that Nolan had been serious about this being a family ring. Apparently, it had belonged to his grandmother. There was no way he could have gotten it fitted for her though. He couldn't have been serious about that. Except it fit her perfectly.

Sitting at the table with Fallon—Nolan's sister—and Samantha and Nora, women recently married to Nolan's other brothers, she didn't want to talk about her engagement. Lying to such sweet people felt wrong. "So I hear you're driving Brad crazy by not marrying him this year," she said to Fallon.

Rolling her eyes, the pretty redhead leaned back in her chair and picked up her glass of wine. After dinner with everyone in the formal dining room, the four of them had moved into the kitchen to talk. "Just because Samantha and Nora are crazy and need less than a year to plan a wedding, I'm not giving myself that much stress. Besides I want a spring wedding."

"Maguire didn't give me a choice." Samantha shook her head. "That man is ridiculous."

"Too late now," Fallon said. "You're the dummy who married my brother."

"Hey!" Samantha balled up a napkin and threw it at Fallon's head.

Laughing lightly, Miranda picked up her own glass of wine and took a sip. Her parents and Nolan's mom and dad were off looking at a piece of furniture Jackson had made. Nolan, his brothers, and brother-in-law to be, were playing basketball in the driveway like crazy people in the freezing weather. "Is it really true that you shaved the hair off all of their heads?" Miranda asked. Nolan had once told her that Fallon had a mean streak. It was hard to believe looking at the petite, relaxed woman.

"Heck yeah. And let me tell you, they all deserved it. Maguire got his head shaved twice."

"That's not all she's done." Nora's voice was dry as she looked at Miranda. "She also shaved their beards when they were crazy enough to grow them out. She's put itching powder in various clothing and I'm pretty sure she's set some of their clothes on fire."

Miranda laughed again. "Remind me never to piss you off."

"I only do that stuff to my brothers," Fallon said. "And they've done plenty of stuff to me too."

"Like what?" Miranda knew Nora very well since she worked with Nora at the shop part-time. She knew Fallon because of her friendship with Nolan, but there was still a lot she didn't know about his younger sister. And she was just getting to know Samantha. When she and Nolan 'broke up', would she lose friends? Okay, not thinking about that now.

"Well… They used to scare off any guy I wanted to date. And when I started dating Brad, they roughed him up on the ice."

"Oh, please. Brad held his own. And I'm sure you made him feel better after." Nora snickered into her wine as Fallon nodded in agreement.

Sitting here with these women made her wonder how things might have been different if she'd been closer to her sister. There was a six-year age gap between them and while she'd always loved her sister, they'd never been particularly close. She'd always wanted a better relationship with Gloria but by the time Miranda had been old enough, Gloria had lost her husband, been a new mother and gotten addicted to heroin. Her parents had tried to help Gloria but by then it had been too late. Her sister hadn't wanted any help. Miranda shook those thoughts off. She didn't want anything to dampen tonight.

When the side door suddenly swung open, Miranda only had eyes for Nolan. He stepped inside with his two brothers and Brad, the four of them sweaty. And Nolan looked good enough to eat.

He came right for her, placing his hands on either side of the table as he leaned down and kissed her. And this wasn't a simple brushing of his lips over hers. It was deeper and somehow it felt like he was claiming her in front of the others. Which made no sense since his brothers were happily married. But…yeah, that was exactly what he was doing.

When he pulled back he gave her this heated, sexy look she felt straight to her core. "If my sister said anything about me, it's all a lie," he said as he stood and headed for the refrigerator.

"She just confirmed that she shaved your head."

"Oh, that's very true," he said, pulling out bottles of water and setting them on the counter. "But I probably deserved it. I think I'd scared the shit out of some guy who wanted to date her." Stepping toward his sister, he tugged on her ponytail.

Fallon swatted his hand away. "You *did* deserve it. You did that stupid guy thing where you took him to play hockey and roughed him up."

"That's right," Nolan said. "What a wimp."

"I remember that jackass," Maguire chimed in, grabbing one of the water bottles. "I'm surprised he didn't piss his pants."

"Brad's the only one who passed our test," Jackson added, handing a bottle to the sheriff — Fallon's fiancé.

As Miranda watched the camaraderie between all of them,

something shifted inside her. She wanted to be part of Nolan's family. She wanted more than she had with him now. And it was clear he wanted more with her. Not to be engaged of course, because that was insane, but…it wasn't as if he was a ladies' man. No, he was sort of perfect in every way. And they'd been friends since practically the moment she'd moved to Holly. The thought of getting to be part of his family made her ache inside.

Maybe he'd been holding off with her because of her guardianship of Mateo? Nolan had been so vague when she'd tried to talk to him earlier. She needed to demand an answer. Because she couldn't deal with not knowing where they stood. Or where they were headed. It was clear they were more than just friends, but she liked things spelled out. For where she was in her life, she needed to know.

And if Nolan wanted more from her, she did too. He was definitely a man worth fighting for. It was just terrifying to think about what would happen if things didn't work out. He'd become such a huge part of her life. The thought of things going south between them and not working out, carved her up inside.

She hated herself for immediately going negative, but in her experience things didn't work out. She wasn't even sure what he saw in her. She was basically a single mom for however long Mateo lived with her. And the truth was, as far as she was concerned he could stay with her forever. Nolan might like to coach youth hockey, but why would he want a ready-made family?

Shaking those thoughts off, she forced herself into the present as Nolan pulled up a chair next to her. "I would pull you into my lap, but I'm all sweaty," he murmured low enough for her ears only. The others were engaged in a conversation about something Fallon had done to the brothers when they were younger and no one was paying attention to her and Nolan.

Miranda smiled at him because she couldn't think of a response. It was hard enough to remember her own name since things had shifted between them. She felt as if she didn't know anything anymore.

Leaning closer, he said, "Do you want to come over to my place for a while after we take your parents home tonight?"

She should say no. She really, really should. Instead, she found herself nodding. It was only so she could talk to him about what was going on between the two of them. Get some answers. Make everything clear. That was the lie she tried to tell herself anyway. Because she was pretty certain once they were alone at his house they were getting naked together.

CHAPTER EIGHT

"You sure your parents didn't mind us leaving them?" Nolan asked as he steered out of her driveway.

"Do you really care?" Miranda asked on a laugh.

"Will you judge me if I say no?"

"No." She slid her phone out of her jacket pocket when it buzzed. She hadn't talked to Mateo tonight and she missed his voice. *Can't FaceTime tonight, hanging with some girls we met on the slopes.*

She blinked. *Girls?* Wasn't this supposed to be a church retreat? And he was only eleven. How was he meeting girls? No, this couldn't happen yet. She had to call Connie right now.

Kidding! Everyone's tired so we're watching a movie then crashing. I'll call you tomorrow.

She pushed out a sigh of relief. *Okay, love you.*

Love you too.

She quickly shot off a text to her friend Connie and got a positive response that yes, the kids were all in for the night and everyone was watching movies. Connie was one of the chaperones at Mateo and Joey's cabin so Miranda felt a lot better.

"Everything okay?" Nolan asked.

"Yeah. Mateo was just messing with me about meeting with some girls."

Nolan snorted. "I give that a few years yet."

"Me too. Or I hope so. Maybe a decade even. Not that…" She sighed and looked out the window. Sometimes she forgot that he wouldn't be living with her long-term. "I hope I can convince my sister to move here."

"Do you think it's a real possibility?"

"I do." Bright Christmas lights decorating houses and trees all blurred together as he steered out of her neighborhood. She turned back to him. "The first time I brought it up she loved the idea. And I think she wants some distance from Florida." Her sister had lived all over the state, from Key West to Destin, moving from city to city with whatever man she'd been with. Eventually she'd started moving north until she got to Holly — and dropped off Mateo.

"I hope she does," he said quietly.

"So…this is really a family ring?" Miranda asked abruptly. She was getting her answer one way or another.

"It is."

She paused at the quick, honest response. Well then. "It's beautiful." All right, talk about lame. *Just spit it out*, she ordered herself. Demand he give her answers about what he wanted from her. *Exactly* what he wanted. But —

"You're beautiful."

She shifted against the leather seat of his truck, feeling her cheeks — and other areas — heat up at the compliment.

"And you look incredible tonight," he continued. "While we were eating dinner, all I could think about was sliding my hand up your dress and — "

She sucked in a breath. "Don't finish that thought." Was he trying to give her a heart attack? Nolan didn't talk to her like this. They talked about their week and the tidbits of town gossip — usually only she contributed to the gossip since he never knew anything — and what was going on down at the center. Not about sex or anything sex related.

"And bring you to orgasm right there."

She paused, digesting his words as heat flooded through her. "Have you done that to someone before? At your parents' house?" She squished the jealously that bubbled up at the thought because she really wanted an answer.

"Nope. Never even brought a woman home. But I wanted to do it to you." His voice was a low growl, sending more spirals of heat curling through her. "I kept wondering if you were wet thinking about me."

He was all she could think about. "Nolan!"

"And then I started wondering—for about the hundredth time—if you'd be loud when you came. Since I don't want anyone else hearing you climax, I kept my hand to myself."

Miranda shifted again in her seat. There was a note of possessiveness in his voice she liked way too much. All traces of a chill were gone as her body heated up. She'd never been so turned on by simple words before.

"Are you wet now?" he asked quietly.

"Maybe you'll find out later." Oh, who was she kidding? He was definitely going to find out. She wouldn't have agreed to go to his place if she hadn't planned on getting naked with him.

The truck jerked ever so slightly as they came to a stop sign. "Is that right?"

"If you're lucky."

"I'd be very lucky if you let me find out. I'm clean, by the way. I haven't been with anyone since...well before you."

"You haven't slept with anyone since we met?" That was at least ten months ago. That made her way happier than it should have. Because she had definitely wondered. More than a few single moms who picked up their kids at the community center hit on Nolan. He'd always been friendly but never flirty with anyone. But she had wondered.

"No. And I know I shouldn't ask...so I won't." His jaw clenched as he turned down his street. She'd been to his house a couple times before but only briefly.

"I haven't been with anyone either." When she'd moved to Holly, a relationship had been the last thing on her mind. Then her life had changed so drastically that anything sex related hadn't been a blip on her radar. "And I'm clean—and on birth control," she added. She had no idea if sex was really on the menu tonight but she wanted him to know just in case. Of course, she wanted more than sex, but one step at a time.

He made a sort of growling sound but didn't appear to be able to say anymore. Which just made her smile.

Good. He'd gotten under her skin the last two days and she wanted to be under his. As they pulled into his driveway, all sorts of fears and worries bubbled up but she shoved them back down. For now.

Because she had no responsibilities tonight. She needed to take advantage of that. Even if she did get hurt afterward.

When the passenger door opened she realized they'd already pulled into Nolan's garage and of course, he was opening her door. Because that was just the way he was. The perfect gentleman. Something she adored about him — and he was like that with everyone. Not just her.

When he took her hand to help her down, butterflies launched inside her. Something was happening tonight. Something in which some or all of her clothes were coming off. She might be ready for this but she was still nervous. The last guy she'd been with…oh, who cared? No one compared to Nolan.

Which was the crux of her problem. He was totally going to ruin her for other guys. Nolan was the whole package. Sweet, real, and impossibly sexy.

As they stepped into his kitchen she stripped off her jacket while he disabled the alarm. She'd barely even set her purse and jacket on the nearest counter when he had her caged against it, both hands on either side of her.

But he wasn't actually touching her. Just watching her intently. A shiver rolled through her at the hunger in his eyes. Her body instinctively started to arch into him.

"This isn't casual for me, Miranda. I've wanted you since the moment we met."

Her heart rate kicked up a notch at his words. "I want you too." It seemed so obvious now that they were alone at his place, but she wanted to make sure he knew. She'd never wanted anyone with this much intensity.

Slowly, he lifted one of his hands and slid his fingers through her hair before cupping the back of her head. "Not letting you go after this week, either," he murmured, his eyes going all heavy-lidded as he watched her.

His words were everything she wanted to hear. Even if she wasn't sure she could accept them yet. As she looked at him, she knew she could stare into his eyes all day. She wasn't sure if she should respond. She hadn't thought a relationship was on the table for them. She hadn't even thought she had time for one. But single parents dated all the time. Even though Nolan sounded incredibly possessive, she was afraid to read too much into it. She didn't want to let him go either. Because this thing with him had her all twisted up inside. She had responsibilities now. She wanted to ask him if he was really ready to be a parent, at least for the time being — but held back. Because if he didn't answer the way she wanted to hear, she would walk away from tonight.

And she desperately wanted tonight.

"I really want to see you naked soon," she whispered, even as her cheeks heated up to epic proportions. It had been so long since she'd been with anyone and this wasn't just *anyone*, it was Nolan.

He rolled his hips against hers and she let out a gasp at the feel of his thick erection. She loved that his reaction was all for her.

Swallowing hard, she started to lean up on tiptoe. But he crushed his mouth to hers with a hungry intensity she felt all the way to her toes. It was as if he could devour her. Good, because she felt the same. Need surged through her, dancing out to all her nerve endings in one rush of sensation.

She clutched onto his shoulders as he lifted her up onto the counter. She started to wrap her legs around him but he slid his hands up her legs and under her dress, keeping her firmly in place.

She shivered at the feel of his thick, callused fingers sliding over her bare skin. It was impossible not to wonder how it would feel to have one of those thick digits inside her. And she'd definitely wondered more than once — and indulged in multiple fantasies about Nolan.

It was *always* him in her fantasies. Which was the reason she'd used his name when making up a fiancé. Because even if she hadn't wanted to admit it to herself, he was the man she wanted to be with.

When he started nibbling along her jaw, she arched her neck slightly, giving him all the access he wanted. She was desperate to feel his mouth all over her — and to do the same to him.

As he reached her earlobe and bit down, she grasped at the hem of his sweater and tugged upward. It was time to get undressed.

He pulled back only a fraction so he could strip his sweater and T-shirt off. She drank in the sight of his bared abs, sucking in a little breath at the hard lines and striations of his toned body. In her kitchen, she hadn't wanted to stare too hard but now she could look all she wanted. Look *and* touch. The man was incredible, as if he'd been cut right from stone. She knew it was because of his job and all the hockey he played.

"Keep looking at me like that and we're doing this right on the kitchen floor." A growled promise.

More heat rushed between her legs as her nipples tightened against her bra cups. That didn't sound like a bad thing at all. She dragged her gaze to meet his, her heart rate out of control. "Promise?"

Another growl followed before he reached underneath her dress. "Lift up."

Without pause she lifted her hips — and he slid her lacy black panties down her legs and over her boots. Then he slowly unzipped one boot, then the next, before taking them off as well.

His hands were unsteady as he undressed her and she was glad he was feeling this as much as she was. Her breathing was erratic as she watched him, still trying to wrap her head around the fact that Nolan O'Connor was taking off her clothes. With every touch, every item he removed, little tingles erupted all over her body. Her body was practically aching with the need to feel him skin to skin.

They were most definitely about to have sex. She wondered if he would be big all over — and her inner muscles tightened at that thought.

"I want to see more of you." Her words came out breathy, if a little demanding. They were clearly doing this and she was done with patience.

His lips kicked up into a half-smile that was all wicked. "You will. First…" Taking her by surprise, he shoved her dress up to her waist so that she was completely exposed. The feel of the countertop on her bare skin chilled her, but one look from him and warmth spread throughout her like a slow-moving volcano, bathing all her nerve endings. The tingling and aching were out of control now.

He covered her mouth with his in the sweetest, gentlest kiss, his tongue stroking over hers in little flicks that had her crawling out of her skin. He pulled back suddenly, the abruptness of it making her suck in a breath. He couldn't mean to stop now.

"What are you—"

She sucked in a breath when he knelt down—and lifted one of her legs over his shoulder. Oh, hell.

He didn't say a word, just zeroed in on her clit with a single-minded determination.

"Oh…" She jerked against that first erotic kiss, sliding her fingers through his dark hair as his tongue teased against her folds. "Nolan," she moaned out his name at the pleasure he was giving her. The pleasure she'd only fantasized about.

Grabbing her other leg, he settled it over his other shoulder. The position opened her up more to his teasing and she sucked in a breath as he slid his tongue deeper inside her.

Her inner walls tightened, feeling empty, but for now, this was incredible. The man had a hidden wicked side and that mouth… Instinctively she rolled her hips into his kisses. She'd forgotten what this was like, though *this*, with Nolan, was like nothing she'd ever experienced. Everything else paled in comparison.

He placed his hands on her inner thighs when she tried to squeeze them tighter. There was no give to him either. He kept her legs firmly open as he teased her over and over, but was still ignoring her clit.

After that first teasing lick, he'd been avoiding kissing her there, just skating near the sensitive bundle of nerves and it was driving her crazy. Which he no doubt knew.

"Love your taste," he murmured against her slickness, making her jerk again.

How could he talk? Breathing erratically, she dug her fingers into his head as he oh-so-slowly teased his tongue up her folds before finally reaching her clit again. All the muscles in her abdomen were pulled taut at the sensory overload.

"Yes," she rasped out as he flicked his tongue over the little bundle of nerves. "Right there."

He increased his pressure even as he removed one of his hands from her thigh and slid a finger inside her. She clenched around him, wanting so much more. It wouldn't take much to push her over the edge. And she felt as if she was on exactly that, a ledge, ready to plunge into pure pleasure. She was so close.

He groaned against her. "So damn wet." His words were a little muffled but she understood him fine.

Yes, she was wet. Beyond wet. And ready to feel him sliding inside her. *Thrusting.* "Want more than your finger." She didn't care if she sounded as desperate as she felt. She was ready to crawl right out of her skin and all she could think about was coming.

He made a sort of laughing sound against her folds, the vibration adding to her pleasure. "So impatient."

She dug her fingers against him even harder. Yeah, she was impatient. And needy.

To her surprise, he suddenly stood. Before she had a chance to react, he lifted her off the counter so that she had to wrap her legs around him. Then his mouth was on hers, his tongue teasing hers the same way he'd been teasing between her legs moments before.

It was strange and sexy to taste herself on him. She was vaguely aware of them moving through his house as she clung to him. At the sound of a door shutting, she pulled back slightly to see they were in a dimly lit bedroom.

Before she'd processed any of her surroundings, she found herself flat on her back in the middle of his king-sized bed. Exactly where she wanted to be. He quickly divested of his boots and socks, leaving him in just his pants. Which was still too much clothing as far as she was concerned. She wanted to see and touch all of him.

Nolan stared down at Miranda, her dress pushed up to her hips, her slick folds bared to him. He wanted nothing more than to strip fully but he knew if he lost the last barrier between them, he'd be inside her.

Which he wanted more than his next breath. But first she was getting off. He was going to taste her coming against his mouth as she called out his name. He'd been thinking about it for ten months and it was going to become a reality right now.

Taking him by surprise, she pulled her dress fully up over her head so that she was now wearing only a bra. He blinked once and when she reached behind her back, he was on the bed and on her in a second.

"I get to do that." He barely recognized the low tone of his voice. But he felt absolutely possessed with the need to do this. To strip her and claim her.

And that was what this was. She was his. They'd been building up to this for a long damn time. Even if she didn't realize it. There would be no going back to just friends for them after this. Hell, she already had his ring on her finger. And he didn't want it coming off—something he wasn't going to think about now.

She buried her face against his neck, dropping little kisses along his jaw as he reached behind her. He quickly unfastened the sexy scrap of black material covering the breasts he'd been fantasizing about for the better part of ten months. In the summer time, she'd worn little summer dresses that had just fueled his imagination and driven him crazy.

Now…he drew the straps down her arms as he leaned back to look at her. Even with the faint light streaming in from the outside Christmas lights, he couldn't see nearly enough. This was something he'd spent a lot of damn time fantasizing about and he wanted to remember every detail of their first time. So he leaned over and flipped on the lamp on his nightstand.

Her breasts rose and fell with her erratic breaths as he settled back on top of her. "Brown nipples," he murmured, palming one of her mounds. Not too big, not too small. Perfect. Like her.

She arched into his hold, her eyes going heavy-lidded as he

started teasing one nipple. Rolling it between his thumb and forefinger, he watched as it grew to a rock-hard point.

"You're making me crazy," she whispered, sliding her hands around him until she cupped his ass.

Yeah, well, the feeling was mutual. She'd been making him crazy since February. "I'm going to kiss every inch of you later. But first…" Shifting slightly, he slid down the length of her lean body. It was time to finish what he'd started. He couldn't wait to taste her again.

"Nolan—"

He kept his voice pitched low as he said, "That's what I want to hear when you're coming."

She sucked in a sharp breath, making him smile. He'd loved getting reactions out of her the past few days, loved getting her to blush. And now he was going to love making her come.

Gently, he ran a finger along the length of her folds. She was so damn wet. Knowing he was the reason for it had his cock kicking against his pants. Soon enough he'd get to slide inside her, but he was going to enjoy this first.

Instead of using his mouth right away, he rubbed his thumb over her clit. She lifted her hips, gasping slightly. So he increased his pressure and slid a finger inside her.

Her inner muscles clenched around him even as he added another. "So tight."

As her breathing grew more erratic, he pulled his fingers out— then slid them back in. Her inner muscles started clenching around him, tighter and tighter with each thrust.

His dick kicked against his pants again, but too damn bad. For now.

When her hips lifted off the bed he knew she was close. Covering her clit with his mouth, he began stroking with an intense pressure.

"Nolan!" She grasped onto his head as he continued teasing her.

She had to be close. He could feel it in the way her inner walls tightened faster and faster and how her thighs trembled against his head.

He felt the moment her climax hit. She cried out his name again, her fingers clutching onto his head as she writhed underneath him.

When he was certain it was too much for her, he lifted his head, but kept his fingers buried inside her. He felt the aftershocks of her orgasm as her inner walls continued to flutter around him.

Keeping his hand exactly where it was, he moved up the length of her body and felt fucking proud at the half-smile that played across her slightly dazed face. "That was incredible," she murmured, reaching for him.

God, if he could put that look on her face every day she'd never want to walk away from him. Before he could kiss her, she surprised him, by pushing at his shoulder.

"Now it's my turn," she said, sitting up. "On your back."

Oh, hell. He preferred to be on top and in control during sex, but this was hot. And the truth was, he couldn't say no to her. Doing as she ordered, he stretched out onto his back and let her tug his pants and boxer briefs off.

When she climbed on top of him, sliding down until her slick folds ran over the length of his hard cock, he forgot to breathe.

"You're incredible," he murmured, sliding his hands up her hips, over her waist and only stopping when he reached her breasts. Palming them, he shuddered at the feel of them. If he died right now, it would almost be a perfect life. Because first he wanted to experience all of Miranda. Who was he kidding? He wanted to have kids with her, to grow old with her, to do the whole white picket fence thing. This woman was it for him. Something he'd known for a long damn time. And things had finally shifted between them.

Smiling, she slid her hands up over the taut muscles of his stomach and chest. "Right back at you. I can't get enough of touching you."

When she moved up to touch more of him, her body shifted, centering her pussy right over the head of his cock. For a moment, he couldn't breathe—and when she rolled her hips and thrust down onto him, yep, he knew what heaven was.

His balls pulled up tight as she started riding him, her dark hair falling around her breasts as she moved. She was the most beautiful thing he'd ever seen. And for all his dirty talk, right now, he couldn't find his voice.

All he could do was hold onto her hips as she rode him. He strained with the need to hold back, to stay inside her as long as possible.

Her own breathing was shallow, uneven, matching his. Reaching between their bodies, he strummed her clit with his thumb again and she nearly jolted right off him. Hell yeah. The woman was so damn reactive and he planned to learn everything that made her tick, everything that she loved. Bringing her pleasure could easily become his favorite pastime.

Instinct took over—and he had her flat on her back under him in seconds. Next time he'd let her be on top. And there would definitely be a next time.

She wrapped around him as he began thrusting inside her, stroking her fingers all over him. The feel of her hands on him was proving too much for his control. He'd fantasized about this but the reality eclipsed anything his mind had conjured up.

So he teased her clit again, desperately wanting to feel her coming around him before he found his own release.

She dug her fingers into his back as she cried out his name—and started climaxing again. He lost all control at the sensation of her clenching around his cock. It was simply too much.

"Miranda," he cried out as he began coming inside her in hard, long strokes.

In that moment, the world boiled down to the two of them and nothing else. Him, her, and so much pleasure his brain was barely functioning. She completely owned him.

Eventually, as they both returned to reality, he took his time kissing along her jaw, that sweet spot behind her ear and finally he claimed her mouth again. He loved her taste, the way she came, the sweet way she moaned his name. He loved everything about her.

She arched into him, her breasts rubbing against his chest as she plastered herself to him. He never wanted to stop kissing her. Never wanted to let her go.

After tonight, he wasn't walking away.

CHAPTER NINE

Miranda rolled over at the sound of her cell phone ringing... somewhere. She could hear it, but couldn't remember where it had landed. After that first round in his bed, Nolan had gone back for most of her clothes from the kitchen and deposited everything in his room.

"You don't need to get that." Nolan wrapped an arm around her from behind, pressing his naked chest up against her bare back.

For a moment, she pushed up against him, wiggling her ass over his growing erection. What she would give to just stay right here for the rest of the night, but she recognized the ringtone.

Groaning, she said, "It's my mom. I just want to make sure there's not an emergency." She doubted there was, but she had to answer just to be sure.

"It's almost two in the morning," Nolan murmured. But he released her all the same.

The early hour did concern her. By the time she found her phone buried under the dress Nolan had draped on a chair, the ringing had ended. So she called her mom back.

"Miranda?" There was a somber tone in her mom's voice she'd never heard before.

Ice instantly slid through her veins. "Is it Mateo?" In hindsight that was a stupid question because if something had happened to him, she would have been called. Not her mother. But Mateo was always her concern.

"No." There was a long pause, then a rustling sound.

To her surprise, her father came on the line. "Your mom can't talk... It's your sister."

She listened in stunned silence as her father told her that her sister had left the rehab center last night and no one had even known she'd been missing until her body had been discovered in a pay-by-the-hour motel by a cleaning woman. She'd overdosed on heroin. Her partner, the man she'd met at the rehab place, wasn't dead, but he'd overdosed as well and was barely hanging on. The police had found some paperwork in Gloria's duffel bag linking her back to the rehab center—and that was how they'd ended up figuring out who she was.

Eventually Miranda must have said some words to her dad and conveyed that she'd be home as soon as possible. But she didn't remember ending the call.

Now, sitting on the edge of Nolan's bed, Miranda stared at her silent phone as she tried to digest everything her father had just told her.

"Talk to me, sweetheart," Nolan said. Sometime in the last couple minutes he'd draped a blanket around her, but she still felt chilled.

Gloria was dead. Because of the shitty decisions she'd made in life.

Miranda wanted to be surprised, but deep down she'd wondered if her sister would ever get off drugs. Apparently, the habit had been too hard to kick, even with Mateo to motivate her.

Miranda mourned the girl who'd been her older sister, the girl who'd had so much damn promise, the girl who'd gotten straight A's and a scholarship to the University of Miami. That girl wasn't the one who'd killed herself with drugs. No, that girl had turned into a woman who simply couldn't handle life, couldn't handle becoming a mother so young when her husband had been killed in a warzone. The woman Gloria had become wasn't the sister Miranda had grown up with, had looked up to, had one day hoped to actually be friends with. She'd become a shadow of her former self, a woman who put her own needs before her son's. Right up to the end.

Miranda couldn't understand how Gloria could have left rehab when she had a wonderful son waiting for her to get sober. But addiction was a terrible thing. And no amount of logic could get someone clean. Not until they'd hit rock bottom. And Gloria had never gotten to that point. Apparently, life had just been too much to bear.

"My sister overdosed," she rasped out, pulling the blanket tighter around her shoulders. "She left the center with that patient she'd become friends with. That man. I…don't even know his name. My dad said when the police found them, she was dead and the guy is in a coma. They got a bad batch of heroin." Which sounded stupid, because how could heroin be considered good. "It's not just them. About half a dozen other…junkies died too." Her throat tightened as emotions swelled inside her. She wasn't sure how she was going to tell Mateo. He loved his mother—though he'd been honest with Miranda about living with her. He'd been happy to get distance from Gloria. Still, this was his mother and it would break his heart. Tears streamed down her cheeks but she couldn't find the energy to wipe them away.

Nolan made a low sound and pulled her into a hug and she couldn't return it. Instead she buried her face against his chest but her limbs were numb, just refusing to cooperate. After a long moment, she pulled back and let the blanket drop. She had to get dressed and get out of there. There was too much to do and her parents would need her help. They would need her to be strong. "I need you to take me home."

Nodding, he stood. "Okay, let me pack a bag first."

"Why?" she asked as she stood and started gathering her clothing from the floor. She wasn't sure where her panties were, but she slipped her dress on over her head. Her jacket was in the kitchen along with her purse.

"What do you mean why?"

As she sat on the bed to put her boots on, it took her a moment to realize what he meant. It was difficult to even focus on a conversation. "Oh…you don't have to come with me. I'll go with my parents to identify…" She didn't want to finish that sentence. Couldn't.

His frown deepened as he opened his closet door. "I'm going with you. The drive will take a couple hours and none of you need to be operating a vehicle right now." There was no give in his voice.

But she didn't want to hear it. She just wanted to be away from him. She needed to be able to think and deal with her parents without him around. Her sister had died a junkie and...it was embarrassing. Nolan's family was freaking perfect. She didn't want to drag him into this with her. She wanted space to grieve, to be alone. "You're not my fiancé. You're not even my boyfriend. We just had sex. You're a friend doing me a favor. You don't need to come with us to this."

She knew her words were harsh but at the moment she didn't care. All she could think about was her sister lying dead in some crappy motel with a man she'd barely known. Some guy who'd likely made all sorts of promises to Gloria. And her sister, like always, had fallen into that same cycle. After her husband had died Gloria had simply been looking for someone to replace what she'd had.

Miranda simply couldn't understand why her sister had done this to herself. Why she couldn't have kicked her habit. Hell, she'd never understand why Gloria had become addicted in the first place. Part of her could, but the part that loved Mateo could never, ever comprehend choosing drugs over your own child.

"You're grieving right now," he said softly. "And I'm going." Again with the steel in his voice.

Miranda turned away from him and slid her boots on. She wasn't arguing with him now. She would just get dressed, get him to take her home, and then convince him to leave. She did *not* want him coming with her and her parents to identify her sister's body. There was going to be so much to deal with in the next day or two and he didn't need to be there for any of it. He certainly didn't need to see how dysfunctional her family was. He'd see it her way soon enough.

She refused to let him win this argument.

Chapter Ten

Nolan knocked on Miranda's front door, and a few moments later it swung open. He wasn't surprised when she frowned at him. When he'd dropped her off a few hours ago she'd told him to leave. So he had. For a while. But he'd had every intention of coming back. So here he was, ready for her to argue with him, and prepared to stay with her no matter what.

"What are you doing here?" she demanded, eying the box of pastries he held in one hand before giving the tray of cups of coffee an equally confused look.

God, she was barely hanging on. Her eyes were red and she looked so damn lost it carved him up. Nope, he wasn't letting her handle any of this alone. She was his to take care of. If she wanted to take out her anger on him, so be it. He'd gladly be a punching bag for her.

He stepped inside, basically pushing past her and not caring if he was being kind of a jackass. She needed him now even if she couldn't admit it. Her mom appeared in the foyer a moment later, her eyes red and swollen.

"I brought some breakfast and coffee for everyone," he said quietly to her. "And I know you're going to be getting on the road soon. It will be easier for everyone to ride in my truck, and I'll feel safer if none of you were driving right now." It was clear Miranda wanted to argue with him, but her mom teared up and nodded.

"Thank you. With all that ice out on the roads, we were unsure about making the drive." Her voice cracked on the last word. But then she continued. "We need to call Mateo."

Miranda turned then, her expression tightening. "No. It will take time to get... Gloria back to Holly." Miranda swallowed hard then cleared her throat clearly fighting off tears. He wanted to pull her into his arms so badly but her spine was ramrod straight. He knew she was trying to keep it together and he didn't want to be the reason she broke. "And it will be a small service. By the time we get all of that settled, Mateo will be back. He finally has some normalcy in his life. He's having fun. I'm not taking that away from him."

Miranda had told Nolan earlier that they were going to do the service in Holly since all her family was here anyway and Gloria was being cremated, not buried. It would be easier on Mateo to have a simple service here instead of dragging him to Florida.

"But, he needs to know —"

"This is not up for discussion. I love you, Mom. But I am Mateo's guardian now — and apparently forever. This is my decision to make and it's settled. A couple days won't make a difference. Let him enjoy the last couple days of the first damn trip with friends he's ever had." There was a wealth of anger and bitterness in Miranda's words and Nolan knew it was due to years of buried anger. At her sister and probably her mom.

To Nolan's surprise, Miranda's mom simply nodded. "You're right. Of course, you're right. Let me get your dad. We'll be ready to go soon," she added to Nolan.

He simply nodded and headed for the kitchen to set out the coffee and food. The drive to the nearby town was only a few hours away but he wanted everyone fed before they left. It might not seem like it mattered now and they might not be hungry, but it would help everyone get through the day.

"You didn't have to do this." Miranda's voice was accusing as she followed him.

He turned to find her sitting down at her kitchen table, that lost expression firmly in place as she stared at the open box of pastries before her.

"I know. Eat something. You need food before we leave." He set a plate and fork in front of her before returning to grab two more for her parents.

"I don't want you here," she said, even as she cut into the fluffy cinnamon roll.

He could take her words personally but he'd grieved over the loss of too many friends overseas. He understood what she was trying to do. "I know. But I'm here all the same. You're not going through this alone." And that was that. "You're mine to take care of," he added in case there was any confusion.

She made a sort of strangled sound, then focused all her attention on her food. People handled stress in different ways. He understood that. And if she thought she could push him away by being prickly, she'd soon find out how wrong she was.

He wasn't walking away from her, from them. Not now. Not ever.

CHAPTER ELEVEN

Miranda felt as if she was walking around in a cloud. Her head was fuzzy and while she knew she had things to do, she couldn't even think of what they were. After IDing her sister's body, she'd thought that would be that. Turned out the medical examiner still had to release it after the official autopsy. The ME said they should be able to collect her sister tomorrow. She was still trying to come to terms with seeing her sister's body like that. One day she knew she would, but it wouldn't be anytime soon.

Soon she had to…hell, what did she need to do? Miranda closed her eyes and leaned her head back against the headrest in the front passenger seat of Nolan's truck. Her parents were asleep in the back as they returned to Holly. They'd talked about getting hotel rooms there, but the drive wasn't that far and no one had wanted to stay.

"I called one of the local funeral homes and they'll be able to handle the cremation." Nolan's quiet voice seemed overly loud in the truck.

Her eyes snapped open. Staring out at the darkness in front of them, his headlights and the stars above were the only illumination on the quiet, two-lane road. "When did you do that?" she asked, then realized of course, he'd done it when she and her parents had been IDing her sister's body. "Oh, never mind."

"I also called into work for you. You're off for the next week. You'll have your hands full with Mateo and arrangements so don't argue." His voice was calm, steady, just like the man himself.

Man, she was lucky he'd been with them today. She might not have wanted him here initially but none of them were in the right state of mind to be driving and he'd been a rock for all of them. Now she felt bad for pushing him away earlier. "Thank you."

He gave her a sideways look, likely surprised at the words.

She inwardly winced. "I've been kind of a jerk to you all day."

"No, you haven't." Reaching out, he took her hand in his.

Without thinking, she slid her fingers into his. "Well I haven't been nice."

"You're allowed to be however you want, for as long as you want."

Her throat tightened at his words. "Thank you."

"You never have to thank me for taking care of you."

She knew that, but she was going to all the same.

He cleared his throat. "I've also talked to my mom—she and my sisters-in-law have all cooked a bunch of casseroles for you to freeze. This way you won't have to deal with cooking for the next couple weeks and you and Mateo will be able to just be."

She didn't know what to do with that. Any of it. Since moving to Holly she'd learned that baking and cooking was what people did during a crisis. She hadn't expected anything from anyone though. Blinking away tears, she said, "I don't know how I'm going to tell him."

"I'll be with you if you'd like."

She nodded once. Even if she'd tried to push Nolan away earlier, it was clear he wasn't going anywhere—and she was glad. Leaning on him wasn't such a bad thing. She trusted him beyond measure. "Thank you."

He squeezed her hand once. "Get some rest if you can. It'll be another hour."

"I can't sleep."

"I understand that."

"Can I ask you something?"

"Anything."

"I know you lost friends overseas." He'd told her that he'd lost too many. And that even one was too many. She'd never pressed for details, had just listened when he'd talked to her. "How…do you deal with that?"

He was silent for a long moment. "This isn't a flip answer, but the truth is, it's just dealing with it one day at a time. When I got out of the Marines I tried talking to a shrink. It didn't work—but I know it does for other people. It just wasn't for me. But I did keep in touch with some of the guys from my unit. Twice a year we get together and just catch up. I don't know, it just helps dealing with everything. Seeing that some of us made it home and are living normal lives. And I'm not saying you should do anything, but... I don't think it would hurt to look into a family support group for Narcotics Anonymous. Because I don't think you ever dealt with your sister's addiction."

Miranda swallowed hard and glanced over her shoulder. Her parents were still asleep, something she was grateful for. "When did you get to be so wise?"

He snorted softly.

Sighing, she leaned back against the headrest again and closed her eyes. She didn't think she'd be able to sleep but the next time she opened her eyes, Nolan was pulling into her driveway and was talking softly to her parents, who were now awake.

Blinking, she tried to stifle a yawn and failed as he put his truck in park. Before she could move, he'd plucked her purse up and grabbed her house keys. Then, moving with incredible efficiency he was out of his seat and helping her parents out of the back. And in that moment, she realized how frail they both seemed.

Her sister's death was definitely taking a toll on them. For years her mom had been in denial about Gloria's problem. Then when her mom had finally accepted it... Miranda had seen a change. But now, she could only imagine how much her parents were hurting. And she and Mateo were the only family they had left. Hell, her parents and Mateo were *her* only living family.

Sliding from the truck, Miranda shivered as an icy wind rolled over her. She'd been so warm in Nolan's truck, it had been easy to forget how cold it was outside. It seemed so surreal that Gloria was gone. The shock kept blindsiding her.

"I'm going to get some food out for everyone and turn up the heat," she said quietly to Nolan as her parents headed up the front walk.

He nodded and went to grab the bags. She didn't even have to ask him, he just did what needed to be done. Which was incredibly nice.

Inside, she wrapped her arm around her mom's shoulders. "I know you're probably not hungry but I think you guys should eat something." Miranda wasn't hungry either, but was going to eat too. "It'll help you sleep." And they would likely have to return to pick up Gloria's body tomorrow to…deal with everything. Despite the three-hour drive back tonight, Miranda was glad they hadn't stayed in some crappy, bland hotel instead of coming back to her place.

"Okay." Her mom squeezed her once gently before settling in at the table with her dad.

After filling two bowls with leftover ziti, she covered them and put them in the microwave. Then she headed to the guest bedroom to turn on a heated blanket for her parents. They weren't used to the cold and even though she was turning the heat up, she still wanted to make sure they were okay. When she passed by her bedroom she found Nolan inside, his duffel bag on the bench at the foot of her queen-sized bed.

He had a middle drawer open. "My panties are in the top left drawer," she murmured, surprised she even had the energy to joke.

He let out a startled laugh and looked over his shoulder. "I'm finding your pajamas—though I've always fantasized that you sleep naked."

Laughing lightly, she sat on the bench. "Bottom left drawer. Are you planning on staying over?" It was a dumb question since his bag was here but she wanted an answer.

"Yep."

"You're kind of a bulldozer." He'd just pushed his way into today and taken over.

He paused once before pulling out a long-sleeved blue pajama set with little pink hearts all over them. "I know. I could see you were struggling, so I took over. Have I overstepped my bounds?"

"No. I'm not complaining. Not now, anyway. I...thank you, Nolan. Seriously, for everything you've done. You've gone above and beyond what a friend needs to do." They might be more than friends but...she couldn't deal with anything else right now. Not tonight.

Kneeling in front of her, he took her hands in his. "We're more than friends. I love you, Miranda." When she sucked in a sharp breath, he continued. "I don't need you to say anything. But I'm not holding back anymore. So, just so you know, I do. And that's not changing."

For the first time in her life she couldn't find her voice. Absolutely couldn't find it. He seemed fine though since he kissed her forehead then stood, saying something about checking on her parents and... something else. She wasn't sure what.

He loved her? What the hell? How could he tell her that right now? She couldn't deal with that tonight. She couldn't deal with anything. Definitely not declarations of love.

He also murmured something about her taking a shower if she wanted. Since she didn't have the energy to head back to the kitchen and make any sort of small talk, she did just that. And when she stepped back into her bedroom, clean and warm in her pajamas, she was still alone so she slipped into bed and pulled the covers over her.

In the morning, she would have to deal with everything, but for now she was going to try to get some real sleep. And ignore the fact that Nolan had told her he loved her.

Nolan slid into the bed behind Miranda and wrapped his arm around her. She'd passed out quickly and he'd decided not to wake her up even though he thought she should eat. It was only about eleven, and her parents were fast asleep as well. His own mother had dropped off a bunch of casseroles about an hour ago so he put them in Miranda's freezer except for one.

She shifted slightly, turning over in her sleep. When she buried her face against his chest, he realized that she wasn't actually asleep. It heartened him that she reached for him.

"Your parents went to bed about an hour ago," he murmured.

"I felt bad not going back out there, but I didn't have the energy." Her voice was slightly muffled against his chest.

He tightened his grip around her, liking the way she felt against him. If he had his way, they would fall asleep like this every night. But with less clothing. "They understood."

She was silent for a long moment then said, "I feel like I should have seen this coming."

"You can't predict the future." Gently, he rubbed a hand down her spine. She'd changed into the pajamas he'd laid out for her.

"But she'd been so weird on the phone the last time we'd talked. Maybe if I'd said something or reached out to someone at the rehab center, I don't know. I just feel like I should have known."

"No matter what you would have done, she was a grown woman and she made her own decisions."

Miranda sniffled slightly but nodded against his chest. "I know." Another pause. "Mateo should be back by Friday. Do you think I should tell him before?"

"No. You made the right decision. He deserves to enjoy his trip. And there's no way he's going to find out ahead of time. Only my family knows and no one will be posting anything on social media."

"I'm just worried he'll be upset if he finds out I waited to tell him."

"You're protecting him. It's what parents do." When he'd fallen for her, he hadn't realized that Mateo would be a long-term part of her life but he had known it was a possibility. Now she had a lot more to deal with and he wanted to be there every step of the way. For her and Mateo.

"Yeah." She sighed and wrapped her arm and leg around him, shifting even closer.

It was hard to hide his erection but she was clearly choosing to ignore it. Good. Now wasn't the time for sex. But if she was in his arms like this...well, he was going to be hard.

It wasn't long before her breathing evened out and she finally fell asleep. He continued rubbing her back, trying to soothe her the best way he knew how.

It bothered him that she hadn't responded when he'd told her that he loved her, but he'd told her because he'd wanted her to know that no matter what, he wasn't walking away.

CHAPTER TWELVE

One week later

Standing in the parking lot of a small local Catholic church with her parents and Mateo, Miranda hugged her mom, then her dad before stepping back. The service for her sister had been small, but the entire O'Connor family had come. Which, if she thought about it too much, was going to make her burst into tears again. Nolan's entire family had treated her as if she was one of their own and she was human enough to admit that she'd needed the extra support. Right now, Nolan was standing by the back of his truck, talking to one of his brothers and giving her and her family privacy. Most of his family had left by now but he was her and Mateo's ride.

"Are you sure you won't stay through Christmas?" she asked her parents, wrapping her arm around Mateo's shoulders. He'd cried when she'd told him about his mom, but he'd been holding up surprisingly well. But she was waiting for the other shoe to drop, for it to finally set in. Nolan's mom had told Miranda that kids often handled things better than adults, but Miranda wasn't so sure.

Sniffling, her mom nodded and reached out to pat Mateo's cheek once. "We're sure. Your father and I need to process everything at home. And... I think you two need to get back into a routine."

Okay, *that* was unexpectedly insightful. An invisible band of tension around Miranda's chest loosened. Because while she loved her parents, right now she did want to get back into a routine with Mateo. He was dealing with a lot and she wanted to be there for him.

"But I promise to call you every night," she said to Mateo, her eyes filling with tears.

"I love you, Nana," Mateo said quietly, giving her a small smile.

"I love you too." Her mom hugged Mateo before her dad hugged him again. "We left presents under your tree this morning," her mom added as she stepped back.

Her parents had packed up their car this morning before the service. They'd be taking Gloria's ashes as well, which had been fine with Mateo. They'd decided that sometime next year she and Mateo would come down to Florida and they'd spread Gloria's ashes in the ocean.

"Thank you," Miranda said. "Text or call me when you reach a stopping point?"

"We will," her dad said.

Once they were in the car and had pulled out of the parking lot, Miranda turned to Mateo and pulled him into a hug. He was getting so big but right now he felt small and fragile. "I'm so sorry about your mom."

He buried his face against her shoulder, silently crying. "I think… it was always going to happen. Now or later," he said quietly.

Miranda had no idea what to say to that. The kid was *eleven*. "She loved you. I hope you know that."

Pulling back, he nodded and brushed away his tears. "I do know. Can I ask you something?"

"Anything."

"I heard Nana say something to Mrs. O'Connor about you and Nolan…being engaged? And sometimes you wear a ring."

"Ah…" She had on her gloves now but she had indeed been wearing the ring on and off. Mateo had only been home a couple days so she'd been trying to avoid wearing it around him. She hadn't thought he'd notice anyway but she should have known. He'd grown up having to be aware of everything around him. "Well, Nana thinks Nolan and I are engaged."

For the first time since he'd gotten back to Holly, Mateo laughed lightly. "Did you lie to her?"

"Lying is wrong…and yes, I did. There's no excuse for why I did though."

He snorted now. "I can figure out why you lied. And dude, I *know* lying is wrong." He rolled his eyes at that, as if she was ridiculous.

Which made her heart swell. She loved this kid so damn much.

Before she could respond, he continued. "If you guys were engaged, I'd be cool with it. Just so you know."

"Good to know." That was something she'd think about later, not today of all days. She pulled him into another hug and kissed the top of his head.

"You guys hungry?" Nolan asked, stepping up to them.

She hadn't even heard him approach, but she saw Maguire driving off, leaving just the three of them in the parking lot. The branches of the oak trees in the park bordering the lot rustled with the wind. She shivered as the icy breeze blew over them. When she did, Nolan slipped off his wool coat—even though she had on a jacket over her black dress—and slid it around her shoulders. He looked so formal and handsome in his black suit and she wanted to bury her face against his chest.

"I'm actually starving," Mateo said. "Maybe we could get pancakes?"

"And bacon," Miranda added.

"Definitely bacon."

"You two and breakfast foods," Nolan said, shaking his head, a smile tugging at his kissable mouth.

"Breakfast is the best of all the meals." Miranda wrapped an arm around Mateo as they headed to Nolan's truck. She and Mateo ate breakfast for dinner all the time. When he'd come to live with her, he hadn't been used to getting regular meals and he'd been a little obsessed with breakfast foods in general. So she'd started making those types of meals for him. And now they went out for pancakes at least once a week. It was their 'Miranda and Mateo' date as he called it.

"I don't really want to go back to the house after we eat…do you think it would be okay if we went to see a movie or something?" Mateo asked as they all buckled in.

"Yeah, after Nolan drops us off—"

"Do you want to come, Nolan?"

He shot her a sideways glance and nodded. "Yeah, I'd love to."

"Good. I'm gonna see if Joey can come too." Mateo settled in the back and pulled out his cell phone, likely to text with his best friend. Joey and Connie had come to the service too, something Miranda was grateful for. Mateo had needed a friend his own age there.

"You okay with me going?" Nolan murmured.

With the heat blowing and the radio on low she wasn't sure if Mateo could hear, or was even paying attention, but she was surprised by the question. "Of course." Nolan had been a rock the past week. He'd been there for both of them, just taking over stuff without her needing to ask. Taking care of things—like making sure they had enough food at the house—she hadn't even thought of.

She wondered if she'd been leaning on him too much—maybe the reason he'd asked was because he didn't want to go. Or just needed some space? She was worried that after all the time they'd been spending together he was feeling smothered. She wouldn't blame him if he did. He hadn't signed on for all this. And she'd been a mess this past week.

Sighing, she took her gloves off as he pulled out of the parking lot. The sun glinted off the sparkly diamonds and she realized that after today there was no need to pretend anymore.

Nolan had told her he'd loved her once but he hadn't said it again. Granted, neither had she. Saying the words out loud was a little terrifying. At the moment he'd said it, she believed that he'd meant it, but this past week it was almost as if he'd been pulling away. She didn't want him to feel some weird obligation where she was concerned. Now that he'd spent a week with her pretty much nonstop and saw how her life was as a parent, maybe…she shook the thoughts off.

As soon as they were alone she would talk to him. And give him his ring back. It was time for things to go back to normal. Or as normal as they could.

Nolan turned at the sound of soft footsteps as he shut the refrigerator door. It was a little past nine and he wasn't sure if he should leave or not. The past few days he'd been staying at his own place, what with Mateo being back in town and her parents staying in the guest room. While he hated being separated from Miranda, it was just one of those things. Now that her parents were gone...he still wouldn't stay over. At least not until morning. Not with Mateo here.

And Nolan and Miranda hadn't been intimate. Just a few kisses here and there. He hadn't wanted to push her for anything when she'd been dealing with so much.

"Hey, he's asleep," Miranda said, stepping inside.

"You want a glass of wine?"

"Yes, please." She leaned against one of the counters as he pulled down a glass. "Thank you for all you've done, Nolan." When he turned to look at her, he found her looking down at her hand and sliding the engagement ring off her finger.

The sight was a punch to his solar plexus. Turning away, he focused on pouring her a glass—and trying to ignore the tension growing in his shoulders. "You should keep the ring for now," he said, surprised when his voice sounded normal.

"Oh...ah, why?"

"Do you really want to field questions about why we're not together right after your sister just died? People will think..."

"Oh, God. People will think you're horrible if we suddenly break up now. Like, you left me right after her death. I'm sorry, I didn't even think of that."

That was ridiculous because he would never break up with her, but... "I actually didn't think of that. I just meant you're already going to be dealing with a lot of sympathy. Fielding more questions about why we broke up will be a pain in the ass." He handed her the glass of wine, which she took with a smile.

"You're thinking more clearly than me. So... Mateo wants to go to hockey practice tomorrow. I told him yes but wonder if I should. His mom just died." She set her glass on the counter without drinking anything and wrapped her arms around herself.

He wanted to be the one wrapping his arms around her. "You should definitely let him go. She was his mom but...he's had stability since moving here. You're the only stable home he's ever had. Him wanting to get back to practice is normal and healthy." He saw similar situations from the kids who played hockey at the center all the time. Nothing as bad as Mateo, but similar enough.

"He really is holding up well."

Nolan nodded. Mateo might have a breakdown later but it would be normal if he did. And he knew that Miranda would be there for him. The woman was a rock. "Listen, I've got to get up early for work tomorrow and with Mateo back home..."

"Oh, of course. I understand. I didn't mean to keep you so late. Thank you for all you did today. I know Mateo appreciated having you around." She paused and looked as if she might say something more but then stopped.

He wanted to ask if *she* liked having him around but he wasn't a masochist. Well, not completely. Things between them were strained. And he wanted to fix that. Something told him that right now wasn't the right time though. She'd been to her sister's funeral today and had a lot on her plate. He wasn't going to add to it.

"I'm coaching a game tomorrow afternoon. Afterward I was planning to head up to the Holly Christmas Festival. Fallon's going to be there with her food truck and I promised I'd stop by. You guys want to come with me?"

"I'd love to. And I'll go ahead and answer for Mateo because he will too."

"I'll pick you up here?"

"I'll be at the community center catching up on work so we can just head out from there. If that works?"

"Okay." He paused, wanting to kiss her before he left but hell, he wasn't sure where they stood or what they were at this point. And he didn't want to push.

"Great." There was a strained note in her voice and again, he was under the impression she wanted to say more.

But there was no way he was pushing her tonight of all nights. So he gave her a quick kiss on the forehead and let himself out. And cursed his own cowardice the entire drive home.

CHAPTER THIRTEEN

Miranda looked up from her computer as Mateo stepped into her office. She was almost caught up with emails after her week off — and a big chunk of them were sympathy emails. "Hey, how did practice go?" she asked, pushing up from her seat and rounding the desk.

"Good." He picked at the hem of his jersey, looking uncharacteristically nervous. More like the boy who'd come to live with her so many months ago and not the one he'd grown into.

"What's wrong?" She wanted to pull him into her arms but he was standing stiffly near the doorway. "You want to shut the door?" Normally she left it open but he looked as if he wanted privacy.

Nodding, he shut it. Then he took a deep breath and faced her, looking impossibly young in that moment. "I still want to live with you."

"Well... I hope so!" Oh God, she'd assumed he would *want* to. It had never occurred to her he might want to go live with her parents. Her sister's will had given her full guardianship, but Mateo's opinion mattered too.

"Do you...want me to live with you?" he blurted. "I know my mom dumped me on you and it wasn't supposed to be forever so I don't want you to feel—"

She shoved up from where she'd been leaning against the front of the desk, covering the few feet between them in seconds. She set her hands on his shoulders. "Mateo, I love you. And yes, I want you to live with me. And I'm really glad you want to live with me too. You might have been a surprise, but you're a welcome one. I still remember the day you were born—yes, I was in the delivery room with your mom. I fell in love with you right then and I can tell you now, that when your mother dropped you off with me, it was the happiest I've ever been. Because I'd been begging her to do it for years. When I realized how bad things were, I told her that I would take you in with no strings attached. She finally decided to take me up on it." Miranda had never planned to tell him that but figured he needed to know now. "I don't ever want you to think you're a burden. You're not. You're an absolute joy. And I count myself lucky that you're mine now."

He burst into tears and threw himself into her arms. She wasn't sure how long he cried and she didn't care. This boy had been through so much and she hated that for even one second he'd doubted how much she could want him. She rubbed his back as he cried, probably for more than just right now. She had a feeling he was crying for everything he'd lost. A dad he'd never gotten to know, and his mom. And so many other things he'd only ever hinted about.

Eventually he pulled back and wiped his tears away. Some days he looked so much older than eleven but now, he was just a kid.

"I love you, Aunt Miranda. And I just want you to know that... I don't want you to not date because of me." His sniffled, wiping away some stray tears.

"That's not something you need to worry about, okay?"

He nodded. "Can I tell you something?"

"Of course."

"I feel guilty." Pulling back, he sat in one of the cushioned chairs by her desk and looked down at his clasped hands. "I... I'm sad my mom is dead but I still want to do stuff. I want to hang out with my friends. And I feel bad for wanting to have fun when she's gone. Even if she wasn't...the best mom."

She crouched down in front of him. "Oh, honey. That's normal."

His head snapped up. "It is?"

"Yes. And your mom would want you to be happy. She made a lot of bad choices." No need to sugarcoat it. "But she finally made the right one when she left you with me. Because she loved you. And she wanted you to be looked after in the way she simply couldn't."

"I'm glad she left me with you," he whispered.

"Me too." Every day she was happy for it.

He sniffled again but most of the tears were gone now. "Joey asked me to go to the Holly Christmas Festival," he said abruptly in the way that kids seemed to do. "Tonight."

"Okay." She'd probably say yes to anything he wanted right now.

"Well I know you wanted me to go with you and Nolan."

"How about you drive with me and you can meet up with Joey there? I'm claiming one hour of your time, then the rest you can spend with your friends. Deal?"

"Deal." He hugged her again and she gripped him tight.

Miranda might not have planned on taking in Mateo, but she was so glad he was hers now. And now she just needed to work up the courage to straighten things out with Nolan.

Which meant she had to put her heart on the line. If it got broken…well, she wouldn't know what she and Nolan could have if she didn't put herself out there. It was time to stop being a coward and go for what she wanted.

Miranda slipped her hand into Nolan's as they strolled around the outdoor skating rink at the festival. He looked at her with a hint of surprise. Probably because she'd initiated the hand-hold. She inhaled the mix of scents, feeling lighter than she had yesterday. There was a crispness to the air. The snow had stopped falling, leaving the town covered in a beautiful, white blanket. She could smell actual roasting chestnuts, some kind of meat being grilled and of course hot cocoa. Which she wanted some of soon.

"You okay with Mateo being with his friends?" Nolan asked quietly as they stepped around a couple holding hands in the middle of the sidewalk and walking at a snail's pace.

"Yeah. He needs that normalcy. And he asked—pretty sure I'll give him whatever he wants within reason right now."

Nolan just snorted softly.

She felt as if they were in this state of limbo or uncertainty. And she planned to change that tonight. Or at least get some clarification. Even if she got burned.

"Do you want some hot cocoa?" Nolan asked as they neared his sister's food cart.

"You know me too well." Sliding closer to him she savored his warmth. Even with a thick jacket, a scarf and a hat on she was still chilled. As a former Florida girl, she wondered if she'd ever get used to the cold. Not that she was complaining. She loved everything about Holly and having actual seasons.

Dropping her hand, he wrapped his arm around her shoulders and pulled her tight as they moved up in the line. She didn't miss some of the appreciative female glances thrown his way as they waited. And why wouldn't he receive them? The man was sweet and sexy, the whole package. Well as far as she was concerned, he was officially off the market. *For real.*

As they reached the front of the line, Fallon smiled when she saw them. Leaning over the metal countertop, she grinned. "You two are the first I've seen from the family."

It warmed something inside Miranda that Fallon was including her in that.

"Everyone else is here too." Nolan smiled at his sister. "Almost everyone else is ice-skating right now though. You'll probably get a rush of them later."

"Well I'm glad to see my favorite brother."

Nolan rolled his eyes. "Ha ha. I know you say to all of us."

"Yes, but I mean it with you." Fallon winked at Miranda as she said it. "What do you want? Let me guess, hot chocolate."

"I really am predictable," Miranda said. "And yes, definitely hot chocolate."

"Make that two. And some of those cookie things." Nolan made a gesture toward the interior of the food truck.

"I'm going to need more than that dude." Fallon just shook her head.

"I think he probably means the snickerdoodles," Miranda said as she squeezed him closer. She was pretty sure she would never get tired of this man. "He ate the entire last tin of them you made for me."

Nolan glanced down at her. "Ratting me out, really?"

She lifted a shoulder, smiling. "I was pretty sad I didn't get any of them."

"Oh, Nolan. I thought you were the good brother." Fallon shook her head even as Sasha, Nora's sister, stepped up to the counter with two hot chocolates.

"Hey, Miranda!" the younger woman said, sliding the cups toward them.

Sasha, Nora's younger sister, was home for the holiday season and helping out with the food truck while she was in town. Miranda didn't know Sasha well, but what she did know she adored. And she was pretty sure the college-aged girl was dating one of Nolan's cousins. Or someone related to them.

"It's great to see you. I missed seeing you at the family dinner the other night."

"I know. I was out with my boyfriend Christmas shopping. But I hope to see you guys on Christmas. I think we'll be stopping by Mrs. O'Connor's house that night for dinner."

Miranda wasn't sure what her plans were for Christmas. And she suddenly realized Christmas was *tomorrow*. Oh, God. She hadn't gotten a turkey or...anything. Instead of responding directly she just smiled. "I'm surprised you're not working with Nora at the shop this season."

"She's got enough people on staff. Plus, I love working with Fallon."

"I am very lovable," Fallon said, returning with a bag of what was no doubt snickerdoodles.

When Nolan pulled out his wallet she waved his hand away. "This time it's on me. But don't tell anyone else."

Nolan just smiled and set a twenty on the counter. "Keep this as a tip then."

"See, this is why you're my favorite. I'll see you guys later?"

He nodded. "We'll be around for a while."

"What are you doing for Christmas?" Nolan asked as they moved away from the food truck and back toward the sidewalk that encircled the skating rink.

"Ah...can we sit?" She motioned to one of the free benches. A Victorian-style lamppost was next to it, complete with garland and lights.

"Of course."

Once they were settled she turned to look at him, and blurted out the words she'd been holding back all night. "I don't know what Mateo and I are doing for Christmas, but I hope it involves you. And I hope a lot our future involves you. I love you, Nolan. I know what you said before but...things have been strained this past week." When he started to respond, she shook her head. She needed to just get all this out or she never would. "I've been in love with you for a lot longer that I even admitted to myself. You're amazing, something I know I don't tell you enough. You've been the best friend I could ever ask for. You're literally one of the best things about moving to Holly. When I get good news, you're the first person I want to tell. I think about you all the time. Probably more than I'll admit. And I've been denying to myself what you mean to me, what we could *have* together. Because I'm scared. My parents aren't bad people. They did the best they could raising my sister and me. But...you know I've got issues with them. And part of me is scared that if I get married I'll somehow turn into my mother. Which is ridiculous. Especially since you and I are nothing like my parents. Not only that, I've had Mateo to raise and that's clearly not changing. He's part of my life now. So... I guess what I'm saying is, I love you and want to be with you. But if what you said the other night—"

Silencing her, he covered her mouth with his in a somehow gentle, but possessive kiss. Finally, he pulled back, leaving her feeling dazed and breathless.

"I shouldn't have told you I loved you right after you'd lost your sister. But I wanted you to know how I felt so there was no doubt. In hindsight, it was stupid timing. But I love you. And I meant everything I said."

"I love you too. So much." She knew she'd already said it but wanted to make it crystal clear. "So you and I, we are together. Exclusively."

He snorted in that adorable way of his. "That's not even a question."

Smiling, she pulled out a fake bundle of mistletoe and held it over her head. "I brought this along just in case."

"I don't need mistletoe as an excuse to kiss you now." Nolan did that sexy growl thing that sent shivers spiraling through her and leaned forward again.

Normally she wasn't one for PDA but with Nolan, she wanted to stake a public claim. He was hers and she wasn't letting him go.

CHAPTER FOURTEEN

Christmas morning

Miranda opened her front door and dragged Nolan inside. It was barely six o'clock in the morning. "I can't believe you're here."

"I told you I was going to be here at the crack of dawn. I barely slept," he said as he set down a big bag filled with presents. "Especially after that dirty text you sent me."

She gave him a big smile. "I couldn't help it. It's part of your Christmas present."

"I hope the rest of my present is under your clothes." Taking her by surprise, he went down on one knee right in the middle of her foyer.

In her Christmas pajamas covered in candy canes and mistletoe, she stared at him. Before she could ask him what he was doing, he took her left-hand, ring finger—which still had on the engagement ring.

"I know we've been 'engaged', but I want it official. I love you, Miranda. Marry me?"

"Yes." She cupped his cheeks with her hands as he stood. "Yes. Yes." She hadn't wanted to take the ring off last night. Even if they'd both declared their love and agreed to be exclusive, she wanted more. She was glad he did too.

Wrapping her arms around him, she went up on tiptoe as he met her halfway. As their mouths met, she heard a groan from behind them.

"Come on. Not in front of the kid." She turned to find Mateo looking half-asleep, his dark hair sticking out everywhere. "I'm hungry," he said, which was an automatic thing for him.

Stepping back slightly from Nolan, but only so she could slide an arm around his waist, she said, "Merry Christmas to you too, kiddo."

"Oh, right... Merry Christmas guys. I'm still hungry."

"Do you want to do presents or breakfast first?" Nolan asked.

Mateo eyed the big bag on the ground and then glanced in the living room at more presents under the tree. She wasn't surprised when he turned back to them and grinned. "Food. Always food."

"That's the right answer." Miranda pulled Mateo into a hug. She knew that he'd gone without food on far too many occasions because of his mom's addiction. When he'd first moved here, she'd noticed him hoarding food in his bedroom. Sometimes he still did, but it happened far less. "I say we vote and Nolan gets to cook."

"You two are ganging up on me already?"

"You're the one who decided to come over at the crack of dawn."

"Fair enough. Mateo, I proposed to Miranda and she said yes." Nolan was straightforward with Mateo, something Miranda appreciated. And Mateo was pretty much the only person who knew their engagement hadn't been real.

Mateo nodded once. "Good. Will we move in with you, or will you move in here?" he asked as they headed to the kitchen.

Miranda hadn't even thought that far ahead, but she was so glad Mateo said 'we'. After their talk, he seemed secure in his place in her life. Which was good. Because he wasn't going anywhere.

"Ah..." Nolan looked at Miranda as they stepped inside the kitchen. "We hadn't gotten that far in talking. But your place is bigger," Nolan said.

"Let's worry about that later. Because I need coffee." She started making a pot while Nolan started pulling out food.

Mateo sat at the table and started talking about what he wanted to do with Joey over the rest of the Christmas break and how he wanted to try out for baseball when the season started. With her heart full of love, she realized this was the best Christmas she'd ever had.

And it was just the first of many. Because she and Nolan, they were the real deal. She'd never expected to have such a wonderful family like this and she knew she'd be thanking God every day that she did.

EPILOGUE

Three months later

"Like this." Nolan slowly showed Mateo how to tie his black tie. It was a couple weeks before he officially made Miranda his wife, so Nolan, his brothers, and Mateo were all getting their final fittings done.

"Got it." Mateo tightened his tie until it was a perfect fit.

"Oh, look at you two." Nolan's mom came out of freaking *nowhere*, a camera in hand. "Put your arms around each other."

"What are you doing here?" Nolan asked even as Mateo wrapped an arm around his middle. The kid was a lot shorter so Nolan placed his hand over Mateo's shoulder.

"I'm sorry," a familiar female voice said, before Miranda stepped behind the curtain where the private dressing rooms were.

Only he and his brothers and Mateo were back here today. The shop had closed an hour ago, but the owner had kept it open for them so they could all do this together. And this was the only time that worked with everyone's schedules.

"*You* told her we were here today?" he asked accusingly — mostly joking after he smiled for his mother's picture.

"I did. I want your mom to like me." Miranda stepped up to him and Mateo, patting Mateo's cheek gently.

Nolan barked out a laugh at her brutally honest answer. "She does like you."

"I know. But I'm pretty sure I'm beating out all the others for her favorite daughter-in-law."

"Hey! I heard that," Nora said from where she was straightening Jackson's tie.

Miranda snickered. "I meant you to." Then to Mateo, she whispered, "You look so handsome."

"Yeah?" Mateo asked, adjusting his jacket slightly as he straightened, puffing his chest out.

"Oh, yeah. The two most handsome guys I know."

"Did you bring *everyone*?" Nolan asked as the rest of his sisters-in-law stepped behind the curtain.

"Pretty much."

Nolan wrapped his arms around the two of them, pulling them close. He'd never planned on becoming a dad so soon but he loved it. He'd expected to butt heads with Mateo or for the kid to be resentful of him moving in and taking away Miranda's attention. But if anything, Mateo craved his attention too. He was the kindest, most giving kid Nolan had ever met.

Nolan had known that he'd grown up privileged but now that he'd learned what Mateo had been through, Nolan realized just how lucky he'd been. Because not everybody had a family like his.

The one thing he knew for sure, was that he planned to make certain that the rest of Mateo's childhood was everything Mateo deserved. And he definitely planned to make Miranda happy for the rest of their lives.

"I love you guys," he murmured, pulling Mateo close as he kissed Miranda on the top of her head.

"Love you too," they both said almost in unison, even as his mom took another picture of the three of them.

"All right, let me grab my grandson for some more pictures," she said, taking Mateo gently by the arm.

To Nolan's surprise, Mateo had taken to calling her Grandma almost immediately. It was no wonder considering how much his mom spoiled him. And the kid definitely deserved it.

"She's so good with him." Miranda's voice was low enough that only he could hear.

When he looked at her again, he was surprised there were tears glistening in her eyes. Feeling panicked, he cupped her cheeks. "What's wrong?"

Shaking her head, she said, "Nothing. Nothing at all. I'm just so happy. And I know that if anything happens to me that Mateo will be fine because he has you now too. I...can't tell you what a relief that is."

"You're not going anywhere."

"Nope." Blinking away her tears, she wrapped her arms around him. "In just a couple weeks I'm going to be Mrs. O'Connor. You ready for that, big guy?"

"For more than a year." He finally got to claim the woman he loved more than anything. The woman who'd completely stolen his heart with that first smile. Now they'd created something real, a family. She was his happily ever after.

Dear Readers,

Thank you for reading The O'Connor Family Series Collection. I hope you enjoyed it! If you'd like to stay in touch with me and be the first to learn about new releases you can:

• Sign up for my monthly newsletter at: www.katiereus.com
• Find me on Facebook: facebook.com/katiereusauthor
• Follow me on Twitter: twitter.com/katiereus
• Follow me on Instagram: instagram.com/katiereusauthor/

Also, please consider leaving a review at one of your favorite online retailers. It's a great way to help other readers discover new books and I appreciate all reviews.

Happy reading,
Katie

Complete Booklist

THE SERAFINA: SIN CITY SERIES

First Surrender
Sensual Surrender
Sweetest Surrender
Dangerous Surrender

O'CONNOR FAMILY SERIES

Merry Christmas, Baby
Tease Me, Baby
It's Me Again, Baby
Mistletoe Me, Baby

NON-SERIES ROMANTIC SUSPENSE

Running From the Past
Dangerous Secrets
Killer Secrets
Deadly Obsession
Danger in Paradise
His Secret Past
Retribution
Tempting Danger

PARANORMAL ROMANCE

Destined Mate
Protector's Mate
A Jaguar's Kiss
Tempting the Jaguar
Enemy Mine
Heart of the Jaguar

MOON SHIFTER SERIES
Alpha Instinct
Lover's Instinct (novella)
Primal Possession
Mating Instinct
His Untamed Desire (novella)
Avenger's Heat
Hunter Reborn
Protective Instinct (novella)
Dark Protector
A Mate for Christmas

DARKNESS SERIES
Darkness Awakened
Taste of Darkness
Beyond the Darkness
Hunted by Darkness
Into the Darkness
Saved by Darkness
Guardian of Darkness

About the Author

Katie Reus is the *New York Times* and *USA Today* bestselling author of the Red Stone Security series, the Redemption Harbor series and the Deadly Ops series. She fell in love with romance at a young age thanks to books she pilfered from her mom's stash. Years later she loves reading romance almost as much as she loves writing it.

However, she didn't always know she wanted to be a writer. After changing majors many times, she finally graduated summa cum laude with a degree in psychology. Not long after that she discovered a new love. Writing. She now spends her days writing dark paranormal romance and sexy romantic suspense. For more information on Katie find her on twitter @katiereus or visit her on. facebook at: www.facebook.com/katiereusauthor. If you would like to be notified of future releases, please visit her website: www.katiereus.com and join her newsletter.

Made in the USA
Coppell, TX
01 December 2021

66866290R00215